THE
HISTORY
OF
LUMINOUS
MOTION

THE
HISTORY OF
LUMINOUS
MOTION

SCOTT BRADFIELD

 Alfred A. Knopf · New York · 1989

THIS IS A BORZOI BOOK
PUBLISHED BY ALFRED A. KNOPF, INC.

Originally published in Great Britain by Bloomsbury Publishing, Ltd.

Grateful acknowledgment is made to the following for permission to reprint previously published material:

Island Music Ltd.: Excerpt from "Many Rivers to Cross" by Jimmy Cliff. Copyright © 1969 by Island Music Ltd. All rights reserved. Used by permission.

Morley Music Co. and Cahn Music Company: Excerpt from "It's Been a Long, Long Time" by Jule Styne and Sammy Cahn. Copyright 1945 by Morley Music Co. Copyright renewed 1973 by Morley Music Co. and Cahn Music Company. International copyright secured. All rights reserved. Used by permission.

Library of Congress Cataloging-in-Publication Data
Bradfield, Scott.
      The history of luminous motion/Scott Bradfield.—1st ed.
         p.   cm.
      ISBN 0-394-57875-9
      I. Title.
    PR6052.R2515H5 1989
    823'.914—dc19   89–2778
                                                                          CIP

Manufactured in the United States of America
FIRST AMERICAN EDITION

For Felicia

This is the long lulled pause
Before history happens . . .

—TOM PAULIN

MOTION

1

Mom was a world all her own, filled with secret thoughts and motions nobody else could see. With Mom I easily forgot Dad, who became little more than a premonition, a strange weighted tendency rather than a man, as if this was Mom's final retribution, making Dad the future. Mom was always now. Mom was that movement that never ceased. Mom lived in the world with me and nobody else, and every few days or so it seemed she was driving me to more strange new places in our untuned and ominously clattering beige Ford Rambler. It wasn't just motion, either. Mom possessed a certain geographical weight and mass; her motion was itself a place, a voice, a state of repose. No matter where we went we seemed to be where we had been before. We were more than a family, Mom and I. We were a quality of landscape. We were the map's name rather than some encoded or strategic position on it. We were like an MX missile, always moving but always already exactly where we were supposed to be. There were many times when I thought of Mom and me as a sort of weapon.

"Do you love your mother?" one of Mom's men asked me. We were sitting at Sambo's, and I was drinking hot chocolate. Mom had gone to the ladies' room to freshen up.

It seemed to me a spurious question. There was something sedentary and covert about it, like the bad foundation of some prospective home. I had, as always, one of my school texts open in my lap. It was entitled *Our Biological Wonderland: 5th Edition*, and I was contemplating the glossary to Chapter Three. I liked the word "Chemotropism: Movement or growth of an organism, esp. a plant, in response to chemical stimuli." Chemotropic, I thought. Chemotropismal.

"Your mother is a very nice person," the man continued. He didn't like the silence sitting between us there at the table. I myself didn't mind. He smoked an endless succession of Marlboros, which he crushed out in his coffee saucer rather than the Sambo's glass ashtray resting conveniently beside his elbow. Nervously he was always glancing over his shoulder to see if Mom was back yet. I didn't tell him Mom could spend ages in the ladies' room; the ladies' room was one of Mom's special places. No matter where we were living or where we were traveling, Mom found a sort of uniform and patient atmosphere in the ladies' rooms where she went to make herself beautiful. Sometimes, when I accompanied her there like a privileged and confidential adviser, we would sit in front of the mirror for hours while

4

she tried on different lipsticks and eye shadows, mascaras and blushes. Mom found silence in the ladies' room, and in the beauty of her own face. It was like the silence that sat at the tables between me and Mom's men, only by Mom and me it was more appreciated, and thus more profound.

"I love my mom," I said, holding the book open in my lap. Mom's man wasn't looking at me, though. He seemed to be thinking about something. It was as if the silence had actually moved into him too, something he had inherited from the still circulating memory of Mom's skin and Mom's scent. I looked into my book again, and we sat together drinking our coffee and hot chocolate, awaiting that elimination of our secret privacy which Mom carried around with her like a brilliant torch, or a large packet of money. Sometimes I felt as if I were a million years old that summer, and that Mom and I would continue traveling like that forever and ever, always together and never apart. I remember it as the summer of my millionth year, and I suspect I will always remember that summer very well.

Those were nights when we moved quickly, the nights when Mom found her men. Usually I would lie in the backseat of our car and read my faded textbooks, acquired from the moldering dime bargain boxes of surfeited and dusty used-book stores. I would read by means of the diffuse light of streetlamps, or the fluid and Dopplering light of passing automobiles. Sometimes I had to pause in the middle of paragraphs and sentences in order to await this sentient light. In those days I thought light was layered and textured like leaves in a tree. It moved and ruffled through the car. It felt gentle and imminent like snow. Eventually I would fall asleep, the light moving across and around me on some dark anonymous street, and I would hear the car door open and slam and Mom starting the ignition, and then we would be moving again, moving together into the light of cities and stars, Mom pulling her coat over me and whispering, "We'll have our own house someday, baby. Our own bedrooms, kitchen and TV, our own walls and ceilings and doors. We'll have a brand-new station wagon with a nice soft mattress in back so you can lie down and take a nap any time you want. We'll have a big yard and garden. We might even have a second house. In the mountains somewhere."

In the mornings I would awake in different cities, underneath different stars. Only they were the same cities, too, in a way. They were still the same stars.

Mom kept the credit cards in a plastic card file in the glove compartment, even the very old cards that we never used anymore. The file box also contained a few jeweled rings and gold bands which we sold sometimes at central city pawnshops, and a few random business cards with phone numbers and street maps urgently scrawled on their backs. These were the maps of Mom's men, and sometimes I preferred looking at them rather than at my own textbooks. These were names of things, people and places that possessed color, suspense and uniformity, like a globe of the world with textured mountain ranges on it. Lompoc, Burlingame, Half Moon Bay, Buellton, Stockton, Sacramento,

Davis, San Luis Obispo. Real Estate, Plumbing, Fire Theft Auto, 24 Hour Bail, Good Used Cars, Cala Foods and Day-brite Cleaners. Mom's men were accumulations of words, like nails in a piece of wood. When I closed the plastic file again the lid's plastic clamp clacked hollowly. "That's Mom's Domesday Book you've got there," Mom said. "Her Dead Sea Scrolls, her *tabula fabula*. That's Mom's articulate past, borrowed and bought and certainly very blue. If they ever catch up with your old mom, you take that file box and toss it in the river—that is, if you can find a river. Head for the hills, and I'll get back to you in five to ten, though I'm afraid that's just a rough estimate. I've stopped keeping track of the felonies. I think that's the compensation that comes with age—not wisdom. You're allowed to stop keeping track of the felonies." Mom was wearing bright red lipstick, tight faded Levi's and a yellow blouse. She drank from a can of Budweiser braced between her knees. I didn't think Mom was old at all. I thought she was exceptionally young and beautiful.

Outside our dusty car windows lay the flat beating red plains of the San Fernando Valley. Dull gray metal water towers, red-and-white-striped radio transmitters, cows. "Emily Dickinson said she could find the entire universe in her backyard," Mom told me. "This, you see, is our back-yard." Mom gestured at the orange groves and dilapidated, sunstruck fresh-fruit stands and fast-food restaurants aisling us along Highway 101. The freeway asphalt was cracked and pale, littered with refuse and the ruptured shells of over-heated retread tires. Then Mom would light her cigarette with the dashboard lighter. I liked the way the lighter heated there silently for a while like some percolating threat and then, with a broken clinking sound, came suddenly unsprung. Mom's waiting hand would catch it—otherwise it would project itself onto the vinyl seat and add more charred streaks to the ones it had already made. There was even a telltale oval smudge against the inside thigh of Mom's faded Levi's. "Now, keep your eyes out for the Gilroy off-ramp," Mom said. "It's along here somewhere. We'll have a McDonaldburger and then I know this bar where maybe I'll get lucky. Maybe we'll both get lucky." And of course we always did.

2

Because I always identified Mom according to her customary and implicit movement, whenever that movement ceased
or diminished it seemed to me as if Mom's meaning had
lapsed too. It was her wordlessness I recognized first, that
pulse and breath of her steady and unflagging voice. It was
a soundlessness filled with noise, a meaninglessness filled
with words. It was like that intensification of language where
language is itself obliterated, as if someone had typed a
thousand sentences across the same line of gleaming white
bond until nothing remained but a black mottled streak
of carbon.

"This is Pedro," she told me that long ceremonious day
in San Luis Obispo. We had been staying the week at a
TraveLodge on Los Osos Boulevard, thanks to the uncomprehending beneficence of Randall T. Philburn, a ranch supplies salesman Mom had met in a King City Bingo Parlor
the week before. Randall had carried Diner's Club and
American Express. He had shown me a trick with two pieces

of string. The next time I saw him, I was supposed to have memorized the names and chronologies of all our presidents.

"And this, Pedro, this is the only important man in my life," Mom said. "My unillustrious and laconic son, Phillip."

So that was how it began. She told me his name was Pedro, as if all her men had names. Pedro. As if a man's name were something to be uttered and not a bit of embossed plastic to be stored in a grimy beige plastic file box in our Rambler's rattly glove compartment. Pedro. As if I were supposed to remember. As if a man's name was something you said with your mouth so that another's ears might hear.

It was no simpler than that, that first staggering cessation of Mom's body and her voice. Barely an utterance and more than a name. Pedro. And it wasn't even his name, really.

"How you doing, sport?" Pedro asked, teaching me a firm handshake. His real name was Bernie Robertson, and Bernie possessed a round florid face (particularly after his second or third Budweiser), a hardware store in Shell Beach, a slight paunch, and a two-bedroom house in the Lakewood district of San Luis Obispo, where I was allowed the dubious privacy of my own room. It was only a week after our first, formal introduction that Bernie helped us transfer our few things from the TraveLodge into his home where Pedro's real, unvoiced name was everywhere. It was on the mail and on the automobile registration and on the towels and on the hearth rug, it was on the mortgage and the deed. It was even burned into a crosscut oak placard which hung from Pedro's front porch: THE ROBERTSONS. It was a name which, unless we were very careful, might very soon attach itself to both Mom and me.

"My house is your house," Pedro liked to say, sitting on the sofa with his arm around Mom, his can of Bud balanced on his right knee. Pedro's house contained stuffed Victorian love seats, knickknack shelves, porcelain statues of Restoration ladies and gentlemen engaged in rondels and courtly kisses, untried issues of *Reader's Digest* and *The Saturday Evening Post*, lace doilies and even antimacassars. Mom lay with Pedro on one sofa, her head in his lap, his arm across her breast. I sat alone on the love seat with my textbook. It was entitled *Science and Our World Around Us*, and contained a color photograph of *E. coli*. Most human beings and animals contained this bacterium in their intestines, the photo caption said, and though generally benign, it could cause infant diarrhea and food poisoning. Mom and Pedro seemed very happy and warm there in front of the fire. The television was on, generating its soft noise. One slice of dry pizza remained in the oily cardboard container beside the blazing brick fireplace where Heidi, Pedro's smug and disaffected gray cat, paused occasionally in its rounds to lick at it. Sometimes I just read the dictionary. Auto-da-fé, autodidact, autoecious, autogamy, autoimmune. Words in a dictionary have a rhythm to them, a dry easy meaning I can assemble in my head like songs, or caress like pieces of sculpted wood. Autoecious, I thought. Autogamy. Autoimmune.

"Is there anything you'd like to watch, Phillip?" Mom might ask. "Pedro and I just watched a program *we* wanted to watch."

I disregarded Mom's offer, drifting in the currents of words and pictures issuing from the privacy of my own books. The television remained tuned to whatever mundane channel Pedro and Mom had selected. With the conclusion of that sad summer, I was casually enrolled in school.

Needless to say, my first experience of public education was at once harrowing and nondescript. There was something nightmarish about the actual absence of terror in that place, which always struck me as a sort of systematic exercise in vaguely hollow and uneventful routine. There were other boys and girls there of my own age who I was encouraged to get to know. When I didn't speak at the daily Show and Tell, my reticence was attributed to shyness and not intimate revulsion. Stories and fairy tales were read out loud to us, and we read to ourselves tedious true-life stories from the flimsy plastic pamphlets of the SRA Reading Program. (I was assigned to the intermediate level Red, due to my own deliberate stumbling over consonantal clusters and mixed vowels. I was determined none of these strangers would know me.) We were there for seven or eight hours each day. Games, talk, asinine books, endless recesses, stupid unsatisfiable pets in cages lined with their own urine and sawdust, colored paper and paste and scissors which we were told to hold *in* to our bodies when we passed them back to our Art Supplies Monitor. (Every one of us was designated by some such atrocious insignum, like cabinet officials in

12

some tawdry, self-important South American nation. I, for example, was Chalk Board Clearance Superviser.) It was interminable day after day of vacuous and unremitting childhood, unrelieved by any useful information whatsoever. The world had closed itself around me, and threatened to teach me only what it wanted me to know.

"Your mom's a real special woman, one first-class lovely lady," Pedro liked to assure me. Every afternoon we were usually alone together for an hour or so after school, because Mom had taken a part-time job at the local Lucky Food Store, boxing groceries. "You're a very fortunate young man to have a mother who loves you so much." He was never really looking at me when he spoke, but rather pulling the pop tops off beer cans, fiddling with the TV's horizontal and vertical controls, or building something useful in the backyard. He didn't really speak so much as erupt with aphorisms. "Everybody needs to settle down someday," he might say, or, "Sometimes a woman needs somebody who can take care of her, too. Even mothers need a little love and support sometimes." Then he would clamp something to the steel vise, or shave the spine of some unvarnished plywood door. On sunny days we hauled his tools and machinery out to the splintering pine workbench in the yard, and in those dull equivocal months of Mom's immobility the days seemed relentlessly sunny. I would stand and watch from a distance—not for self-protection, but simply because I didn't want to get too involved. Pedro loved to build things out there: a trellis, picnic table and chairs, cement patio, brick fireplace. If there were world enough and time I'm sure Pedro would have built airport runways out there, enormous ivory mausoleums, pyramids and skyscrapers and spaceships and planets. With the hacksaw which I always watched him replace so carefully in his oiled and immaculate toolbox. With the pliers. With the sharp steel file. With the ball peen hammer. With all those solid and patently useful tools he kept filed in the large glimmering steel toolbox and stored underneath the same bed in which he and Mom slept together each night. It seemed the appropriate place to keep them, I thought. They massed underneath there like weather; you could feel the pressure of them in other rooms and houses. With these tools Pedro had built things in Mom's mind too, working late at night while she slept. There was a literal or figurative truth in that image for me, and, during those horribly persistent days of domesticity, I didn't care which was more correct. The literal or the figurative.

Mom began doing strange things after we moved into Pedro's house. She whistled sometimes, or sewed curtains. She darned socks. She even embroidered. I remember sitting beside her on the sofa and watching her hands fumble with the lacy cloth and a sharp, gleaming needle. That needle was the only part of the entire process which seemed to make any sense to me. The needle was abrupt and binding. It carried with it its own sharp logic. Then one day the new curtains were hung in the living room, and Mom put her hands on her hips and smiled. I suppose I was expected to smile too, but I didn't smile. I looked at the thin curtains, though. They seemed to me just perfect for Pedro's thin house.

"Are you happy?" she would ask me during our private talks late at night, for Pedro always went to bed and awoke early.

"I guess."

"Are you making friends at school?"

"I guess."

"Do they ever invite you to their houses? Do they have nice families who make you feel welcome?"

"Sometimes," I said, on very shaky ground now. I didn't know what Mom expected from me. "Sometimes, you know, well. We don't go anywhere. We just sort of sit around, you know."

"Do they have nice yards and gardens?"

"Some of them, I guess."

"Do they have nice rooms filled with nice toys?"

"Sure, some of them."

Mom smiled brightly, but without looking at me. She was crushing out her Marlboro and gazing off into the bright rooms and gardens of my imaginary friends.

"It's better for you this way," she said. "You deserve a normal upbringing, some firm and certifiable life. It's the only time life is certifiable, baby. When you're a child. When you grow up it doesn't make any sense, whatever way you look at it. Would you like to bring one of your new friends home for dinner some night?"

"I don't think so."

"Do you like your new home? Do you like Pedro?"

I thought for a moment. I felt a hot, blazing fire swelling up in my heart, my face, my vision. My throat constricted. I felt suddenly dizzy and blurred. Hoarsely I answered, "He's a nice man, I guess."

"You're right, baby," Mom said. "He is a very nice man."

One unforgivable day Mom even took me to Penney's for what she referred to as my "school clothes," and for one wild catastrophic moment pulled me to a halt beside the racks of Cub Scout uniforms and supplies. Compasses and safety knives and handkerchief rings and merit badges and handbooks and tents. Finally she bought me white wool socks, cotton underwear and a map of the solar system, which she posted on the wall of my room in order to provide what she called a "vigorous bit of brain food," just as proud moms everywhere hang glittering mobiles above the cribs of their dully gazing babies. I always kept expecting things would get better. Instead they just got worse and worse.

There was talk of a birthday party in November, and throughout that entire summer I paced and worried in a monstrous imminence of cakes, candles, other children in foil hats, door prizes and gifts with bright wrapping and scissor-scored, frilly ribbons. We would play party games at this "birthday party." Mom would award little prizes, and be careful no one child was overlooked. I would close my eyes and make wishes. I would greet all my beribboned friends at the front door with an ingratiating look on my face. Ultimately, while Pedro cheerily drank his beers and reacquired his customary flushed smile, I would be ceremoniously required to open presents. New shirts, model planes, transistor radios, "young adult" books, record albums, perhaps even my own portable record or cassette player. Board games, desk lamps, magazine subscriptions, boats and T-shirts and socks. Things and more things, accumulating in my lap, pulling the weight down out of my abdomen, pulling both Mom and me closer to the hard ground, deeper into the intractable earth. Nothing but weight and gravity and mass, immovable mass. And that look of motionlessness in Mom's once beautiful eyes. "For your next birthday, we'll have a party in the park," she would tell me, just as I thought the ordeal was over, still wiping the slightly hysterical tears from my eyes. "You can invite even more friends. You'll receive even more presents."

At this I would awake with a sudden start in my sweaty bed, entangled in my twisted blankets, surrounded by the concrete moonlight, enveloped by the whirling dust. The solar map confronted me then like a graceless benediction, filled with cartoon colors and impossibly tidy convergences. Moons and planets and suns, imprisoned by gravity and centrifuge and chemical weight. Perihelion and apogee. Jupiter and Mars. I would have gladly disappeared into any of them. I would have boiled on Mercury, exploded with my own freezing expanding breath on Pluto. I felt all the movement coming to a stop inside me, like the gestating atmospheres of nascent planets. Someday Jupiter would be like that, a ball of impacted dirt, senseless rigid cities, malign children assembled around some ominous birthday cake with their noisemakers and party hats. I was growing more solid and permanent every day. Perhaps people would even start calling me by a nickname. Buster, or Chipper, or Mac. I could easily imagine Pedro learning to call me Mac. I could even see the word as it was thickly articulated by his fleshy lips, as if he were extruding a soft rubber ball on the tip of his plump pink tongue. How you doing, Mac? How about we go out to a ball game, Mac?

I couldn't return to sleep. I tossed and turned. Before I suffered a real birthday party I would kill myself; I vowed they would all repent their relentless cruelties, and with a certain relish I selfishly imagined my own obituary and funeral. The day would be rainy and dark as they lowered my forlorn, tiny casket into the deep, sculpted earth. Mom would cry and cry, but there would be nobody to hold her like I could hold her. Mom would know then. She would know the horror and loneliness she had subjected me to. Pedro would stand firmly beside her, but there was nothing he could do to stop her crying. Convulsing, weeping, begging me to come back. Uranus, Neptune, Pluto, Planet X. As I diminished in Mom's universe, she could only stand helplessly by and watch me go. If I couldn't live in Mom's universe, then I would teach her. I would find a universe of my own. Those were nights when I actually and sincerely hated my mom. I may never forgive myself for it, but I really hated her then.

————

On rare occasions their bedroom door was locked at night, but usually they left it wide open, encouraging, I guess, some idyllic familial confidence and integrity. On nights I couldn't sleep I might go in there and look at them embraced by their bleached and complicit white sheets. Mom always slept on her right side, near the verge of their king-sized Stayrest mattress. Pedro grunted and snuffled in his sleep like a pig. His belly looked even bigger when he lay on his back, his mouth open, his splotchy face expressionlessly stupid. When I looked at Pedro sleeping I felt something vegetable and hard growing inside me. It whispered with tangled roots and burrs and weaving, fibrous fingers. It moved only at night. It was trying to tell me something about myself nobody had ever told me before. It reached through everything. It was almost here.

3

It was just a phase she was going through, I had convinced myself. Like menstruation or bad luck. Whenever Mom became maudlin and self-involved, I would just lay my head in her lap, wrap my arms around her and listen patiently, without offering her a word of reproach. "You deserve a better life than I ever gave you," Mom might whisper, holding an icy drink beside my ear, gazing aimlessly at her own reflection in the warped vanity mirror. "You deserve a home, baby. You deserve people you can count on, a place you can come to." I wouldn't say anything to Mom at these times. To say anything would only validate Mom's delusory self-recriminations. I was always certain we would start moving again at any moment. Mom was just resting; Mom was just recharging her batteries. Soon, without any fanfare, Mom would be Mom again.

So there I was, immured within Pedro's musty sanctum, my own fault, really. I had never read the signs correctly; I had not anticipated every swerve and convolution of our ragged map. Whenever Mom doubted herself, I should have engaged her doubt in conversation. I should have allowed that doubt to become real, and thus something we could change and modify like any real thing. I should have reminded her of her own words. "Assurance is that evasion by means of which cultures exist. The world we seek to grab hold of often grabs hold of us." But I didn't. I believed ultimately that the world was filled with firm and self-evident truths, like those in the Declaration of Independence, and like all people of true vision, both Mom and I would always share these truths, we would always know where they were located. Thus confidently I had allowed my mom to drift away and grow lost in endless dialogues between herself and her own reflection, believing as I did that the world's firmness would always lead her back home to me. So now I deserved it, wasting my days in that insipid school, drifting aimlessly among the rusting climb-schemes of the playground, engaged by my own subjective and watery dejection. I was beginning to feel not only despondent but unreal. The world was growing filled with sharp things, things that banged and brushed against me, things that crowded and pressed me. I, meanwhile, was growing more and more immaterial.

"Phillip," my teacher would ask, "would you like to be the next one to read out loud?"

"I guess so."

"Do you want to learn how to hold a hacksaw?" Pedro's

hand held my shoulder with genuine concern, a concern that threatened to make my shoulder in some way his. "Do you want to learn how to solder metal?"

"I guess so."

"Do you want to help me with dinner?" Mom asked. "Or do you want to go outside and play with your friends?"

They were embroiling me in these unanswered and impossible questions, questions without answers, only compromises.

"Is there anything you'd like at the store?"

"Do you know what you want to be when you grow up?"

"Can you tell us the capital of Delaware? South Dakota? Spain?"

"Who's your favorite movie star? What's your favorite book or television program?"

Blizzards of questions. Questions that infested the air like battering moths, knocking against things, dying alone in blistering glass lampshades among blazing heat and their own aborted larvae.

Perhaps they couldn't control me, but they could limit my ability to control myself. Perhaps my teachers couldn't transform me into some gibbering Audio Visual Monitor, content with my colored paper and chalky paste. Perhaps Pedro couldn't indoctrinate me with metric drills, high-speed power lathes and hammers. Perhaps Mom, seeking to evade her own tragic and naive compromise with the world of Pedro, could envelop me in draperies and new cotton underwear and the radiant warmth of my own portable TV.

My secret internal motion, however, couldn't be so easily disavowed. At least that was the mythology I tried to weave around myself like a protective blanket or deliberate dream. They would have to disavow my breath first, my heart, the quality of my voice. Some nights Mom would lie in bed with me to help me sleep, and I would remain stiffly and brazenly awake in her cool arms. I couldn't hear her breathe anymore. While she spoke, I pretended not to listen. While I dreamed, she pretended not to know.

"If it makes you feel any better, baby, I'm not doing all this for you. I wouldn't condescend like that. And it's hard to explain what I'm trying to find here myself, but I do think I've found it. Pedro is a very kind, unimaginative man who never bothers me when I don't want to be bothered. He promises me security, baby, and the deepest sort of privacy too." As she stroked my damp brow I felt the entire universe contract around me. Mom's lies were involved in some vaster scheme of lying. There were vaster deceptions being organized in the universe than Mom's passionless bed with Pedro. "But if you ever want to talk about anything, you know you can tell me, baby. It may not change things, but it might make you feel better. Just talking about things helps sometimes. And then sometimes it doesn't help at all."

But of course I couldn't say anything. That would only betray myself to the mindless airy abstractions of Mom's lustrous deception. I could display only my thin affected drowsiness, pretending as if I too were warm and secure in Pedro's ambivalent home. I guess that's what I hated Mom for most, my own timid and recalcitrant dissimulation. I felt

23

like some burglar or criminal forced to flee the world rather than rush, as Mom and I once had, fiercely into its expanding and elliptical heart. The only freedom they allowed me was to dissemble and resist, to disguise that brisk and fundamental pulse of myself from this false world's pulselessness.

They couldn't get inside me, you see, but they could so alter and confuse my world that I might actually forget how to get back inside myself. It was like Wittgenstein's allegory of the matchboxes. Even though I knew and preserved that special and untransgressed secret of myself from the world's systematic fiddling, ensconced in its immutable privacy the secret itself ceased to breathe and turn. It became an artifact, like something buried in the stale air and glass cases of some shoddy museum, one filled with estranged and obdurate guards in blue suits and official-looking hats that didn't quite fit. I wasn't Mom's baby anymore. I wasn't the rider of Mom's ceaseless motion. I was just another kid in school. I was just a child awaiting his "formative years," coddled with warm blankets and bland, nutritious meals of Wonderbread, peanut butter and grape jelly. I was just a matchbox. I was just a thin matchbox in which some broken object could be heard rattling back and forth. It might be a penny. It might be a plastic green soldier. It might be fragments of a splintery pencil, or a pebble, or a rusty nail, or some scrabbling insect. Or it might be just nothing. It might be nothing worth having at all.

———

My diet, education and serenity were strictly regulated and monitored from now on. I was to go to good movies, read good books, eat nutritious meals, defecate and sleep at prescribed hours. I received a haircut at the barber's every two weeks. I received inoculations for polio, tetanus, smallpox, diphtheria. I suffered a visit to the dentist, where a cruel hygienist scraped the hard crusty plaque from my teeth with sharp steel instruments. "You're very lucky not to have any cavities," she told me, and I could only think, There, I told you. I never needed you to begin with, as I spat blood into the white bowl's blue, cascading water. I received stacks and stacks of new clothes, though my drawers were already filled with freshly pressed and laundered shirts and slacks. My old friendly Levi's and sweatshirts vanished while my closet blossomed with toys in boxes, colorful books and sports equipment, flashing electronic games and educational video cassettes. "You know, I was thinking," Pedro said one day, refolding his paper and placing it in his lap, pulling off his sparkling bifocals with a flourish. He gazed blankly at the ornamental knickknack shelf he had installed just that evening. "You know what Phillip needs? Phillip needs a dog. A nice little puppy he can raise and take care of. It will teach him a little responsibility. It will be his good friend whenever he feels dejected and alone. If he keeps it well brushed and groomed, he can even let it sleep at the foot of his bed. I don't know why we didn't think of that earlier," Pedro said cryptically. "A dog."

And then, wordlessly suffering on the carpet with my

schoolbooks, raptly gazing at the heatlessly flickering television, I could only listen as Mom concurred with an earnestness which made me sick to my stomach. I felt deep intestinal kicks and grinding. Heat lifted in my heart, my chest. The blood rushed to my head and I felt dizzy and slightly nauseous, as if I were ascending into the high air on some sudden spaceship. We will go to the pound on Tuesday, Mom said. No, Wednesday, because Tuesday I work. We'll get a license. And Pedro, honey, you can build a little doghouse in the yard. We'll make a little mattress inside with old rags and things. When it's potty trained, we'll even talk about letting it sleep at the foot of Phillip's bed. We can buy books about training dogs, dog grooming and health care, dog dogness and doggish dogs. Bland little puppies which you hold in your arms like presents. They all have big floppy ears, big soulful eyes. They always love you, no matter what. No matter how you feel about yourself, dogs think you're the greatest. No matter how harsh and insincere the world is, dogs aren't. Dogs love you even when you kick them, even when you don't feed them. Dogs love you even when your hands clench their throats. Dogs love love love you even when they can't breathe, even when their tiny soulful eyes grow more bloodshot and confused with actual terror, even when they give that final, galvanic little kick and their breath stops. When they grow rigid. When their eyes turn glassy and reflective. When you bury them in the garden with a tiny wooden cross and pray for God to forgive them all their sins.

4

With all my polluted and forlorn heart I prayed Mom would shamelessly murder me just like that, the same way I would surely murder any conceivable puppy with which they might seek to burden and restrain me. Kill me and let it be over with, I prayed each night in my feverish bed. Kill me with your own hands so I know it's you. Like the puppy, I will still love you; I will never stop loving you. Like the puppy I will trust you always and forever, right up to the very end.

I felt weaker every day, more listless, distracted and pale. Mom, though, never seemed to notice. Vulnerable and more diffident, smaller and smaller, I was drifting further and further away from her like some eccentric planet. "Culture has a valid purpose," Mom said, seated on the verge of my bed with her cool hand in my lap, abstractly gazing out the window at the red apocalyptic sunset, distantly contemplating the intricacies of her own subversion. "It's not like culture's out to get us. It's not like we have anything to fear from culture but ourselves." Sometimes, as I stared at her,

27

her voice seemed to grow dimmer and more diffuse. I was beginning to realize that Mom had not succumbed to the world's lies, but rather to the sudden swerve and convolution of her own extraordinary mind. "Culture's just a scheme of rules and regulations we've all quite happily agreed to. It's not like all the clichés, baby. Like we submit. Like we're oppressed or imprisoned or enchained. Culture's got our best interests at heart. Culture's just the walls of a house. It's that house I always told you we lived in, only I didn't realize that house was culture before." Mom was wearing a slightly ragged and pulpy white nightgown which had belonged to Pedro's deceased wife, Marjoree. Mom was gaining a little weight; her beautiful face had grown slightly pale and flaccid. The palms of her hands felt cold and dry. "Freedom is a place inside your own mind," she said. And now we were in different galaxies, Mom and I, spinning among remote civilizations and suns. "Culture's just a set of rules that makes life comfortable. That give us time for the freedom we can only live inside ourselves."

Mom said I was suffering growing pains. Pedro was the one who began bringing home the doctors. My temperature was taken, my blood and pulse. My malaise was misdiagnosed as influenza, trauma, shock, diabetes and once even leukemia. I never bothered to get out of bed anymore. Letters were written to and from my school; a tutor occasionally arrived and sat beside my bed, as cold and indifferent as Mom with his mundane assignments and texts. I spent all day watching TV. The morning news. A few hours of game shows in which the world's insipid and luxury-starved eagerly competed for new washing machines, trash compactors and automobiles. Perhaps a soap opera or two and then, finally, the talk shows. Mike Douglas was my favorite, but there were days when Merv Griffin was my favorite too. I liked the talk shows because they featured a revolving panel of guests who had just flown in from limited engagements in Tahoe, Reno and New York. They all had many stories to tell, most of them amusing and comfortably inconsequential. They knew that language was a sort of padding or excess. It was uttered with practiced enthusiasm. You could talk and talk and talk on TV and never have to say anything. I lay in my bed and never said anything either.

Where Mom had once lived her life in the world she now lived her world in the mind. It was a secret world filled with dark speculations and sober intricacy. Vast and comprehensive theories were worked out down there, enthralled by senseless reason. Complicated chiaroscuros of reflection like magnificent Venetian tapestries. Extensive logarithms of interpretation like sculpted white clouds. Mom's secret self sat there in its immaculate kingdom, merely dreaming of other kingdoms like mine. "We've started your college fund," Mom said, enthroned on the edge of my bed, her cool hand petting my sweaty brow. "Pretty soon we'll start looking into a few of the better prep schools. When Pedro retires in a few years we'll look for a larger house. You can travel in the summer. You will always have a home to come to, always a little money in the bank. Then you'll be free to be anybody you want to be. You can go to medical school. You can be a rock star. You can be a stage actor or a vice-president. You can shoot drugs or hire hookers. You can become homosexual or a hired assassin. It's your life, baby, and you live it anyway you choose. I'll always love you, no matter what. Just always remember—you need to play the game if you want to break the rules, and even if you play by all the rules, deep in your brain you'll always be playing your own game. You are immaculate. You endure for numberless centuries. You persevere in a world of pure gravity and sound. You are like light, baby. You are like a sea of air. You are history, and make all of history something else."

I could hardly sleep at all anymore, tossing and twisting among my feverish sheets, hearing Mom's steady breath in the bedroom adjoining mine, Pedro's own antiphonal and staggered snores. When I did sleep I dreamed I was awake. I dreamed Mom was sitting on my bed. I dreamed Pedro was building and hammering in the backyard. I dreamed the teachers and other schoolchildren were telling me I had done a very good job. I was easy to get along with, they all liked me better now that I tried, now that I made some effort to be fun to be with. A spectral puppy licked my face. The ghosts of my delirious life assembled around me even in the dark, compensatory and half-lit world of my dreams.

Pedro built me a sturdy lap tray so I could eat my meals in bed. He built me a bookshelf and a large wooden toy chest, and subsequently filled them with board games, jigsaw puzzles, woodburning and constructor and Lego sets, sacks of green faceless plastic army men, a variety of baseball mitts and a solid, unscratched hardball, seamed and dense. My room was filling up with more and more weight and mass. I could feel the foundations of our ranch-style open-plan house beginning to creak and kneel—I and my room full of things poised to abrupt through the floor, through the earth's crust and mantle, rejoining that infinite and unseen history of strange misshapen creatures with rattling carapaces and stunned, minuscule brains. I was nothing but pure weight now, hard matter. I couldn't move; some nights I couldn't even breathe. "You stay in bed all your life if you want to," Mom said, after the bespectacled psychiatrist suggested I go away for a few months. He was a member of the advisory board to a "special" ranch where children like me conventionally responded well to treatment. This hypothetical summer camp was filled with ponies and swimming pools and campfires; young boys and girls of my own age slept in tents there, sang campfire songs and traveled down rivers on rafts. But Mom wouldn't let them take me; Mom told them I would be all right. That was my mom. Even while she was destroying me, she would take care nobody else destroyed me. "There's nothing wrong with a few months of uninterrupted reflection," she told me that night. "As long as we're happy. As long as we're all happy in our house together, there's no reason why we should be in any rush to go anywhere."

5

I knew where they kept the Seconal. On the top shelf of the master bathroom's medicine cabinet in an amber child-proof bottle. You had to depress and crank the lid of the bottle with the heel of your hand. Then you held it there, a sweet unconscious turning in oval gelatin capsules. Sometimes I might take one, letting the capsule dissolve on my tongue, tasting the grainy barbiturate seeping through, bitter and full of life. Then I would replace the pills in their container and step quietly back through Mom and Pedro's room. Mom lay on her side, facing me, her eyes glassy and volitionless, watching me without deliberation, permitting me at least my secret life. I saw myself reflected in her eyes, and the moonlight where we converged. "I'm going to do it, Mom," I whispered. "I don't want to make you unhappy, but I think about it every night."

Mom didn't say anything. Perhaps, absently, her right hand might gently stroke her left shoulder. Her dark eyes might turn and follow me to the door.

"I know you'll let me," I told her. "I just want you to know. I don't want to hurt you, but I can't stand to let myself be hurt any more, either. If it was between you and me, Mom, you'd make the same decision. You'd always choose to hurt me rather than hurt yourself." And then I crept silently back to my room, tracking a spoor of glowing red ash across the carpet of Pedro's dreadful house, dreaming my inviolate dreams of motion again. In my dreams I was moving, with or without Mom, across lawns and galaxies, streets and stars, suburbs and unraveling solar winds. The Seconal was my ticket out, and I was going to use it.

Mom was working late that night due to a last-minute change in her schedule.

"Hey, sport." Pedro was watching a Dodgers and Giants game on TV and drinking his customary Budweiser. "Out of bed tonight, I see. Good game here, if you want to watch it."

Mike Marshall had just fouled a hard sinking fastball off his right foot.

"Now Marshall's walking away from the plate and *boy* does that smart," Vin Scully, the announcer, said.

"Used to play a little pro ball myself." Pedro was digging into his ear with the little finger of his right hand. After he was finished he shook his head slightly, as if he heard something rattle inside. "Some double-A ball in the Texas League. That was back in sixty-two."

It was funny, because suddenly I didn't even hate Pedro anymore. In fact, as I sat and talked with him that night,

33

the world of menace I once associated with Pedro's name seemed to withdraw a little. Grow lighter and more gaseous, its molecules quicker and more excited. Pedro. I was suddenly convinced of the fact that Pedro *was* a very nice man, and that conviction filled me with an impossible sadness.

"That's where I got my nickname, you see." Pedro's glazed eyes dimly apprehended Marshall on first, Guerrero on second. Atlee Hammaker was pitching for the Giants. I really liked that name. Atlee Hammaker. "I never said a lot when I was a kid, and everybody thought, because I had really black hair back then, that I was Mexican. I really did look Mexican. I looked about as Mexican as you could expect a Mexican to look." Pedro ran one hand through his gray and thinning hair. Hammaker struck out Bill Russell on four pitches. "Damn," Pedro muttered. "Damn it, Billyboy."

"Sometimes you just have to make the effort," Pedro consoled me later. The game had gone into extra innings, tied 2-2, and Pedro had turned the volume down by means of his remote control. He was on his sixth or seventh Budweiser, and I was preparing to fetch him another from the fridge. "I mean, it's not like I ever had these big *ambitions*, you know, to run a *hardware* store, for chrissake. I mean, opening a hardware store wasn't something that, you know, woke me up excited every morning. Like I'd wake up thinking, *Hey*, I own a *hardware* store! *Hey*, I'm on my way to work in my very own *hardware* store! Hell, no. It wasn't like that at all, kiddo. I mean, running a hardware store was just a lot of hard work every day, believe you me. There were plenty of days when I just wanted to lie in bed too. No lie. I would have loved to just lie in bed and watch TV and listen to ball games on the radio. But back then, you see, I couldn't afford to hire any help, and if *I* had stayed in bed all day, just who do you think would have run that hardware store? Who do you think would have paid my mortgage so I *could* lie in bed all day? Nelson Rockefeller? Think again, kiddo. Howard Hughes—my good old buddy Howard? Well, I doubt it. I can't say for sure, but somehow I doubt my old buddy Howard *Hughes* would've come round to help pay off *my* mortgage."

He opened another beer, and I warmed some canned chili on the stove. Pedro ate most of it, sponging up the red chili sauce with slices of his doughy Wonderbread. "This is a hard fast world we live in, kiddo—and I'm telling you this as a friend, now. All this teary-eyed feeling sorry for yourself *childhood* crap just doesn't work—doesn't work for long, anyway. I can promise you that. I mean, your mom wants you to have this *idyllic* childhood and all. She thinks this is Camelot or something, your childhood. Well, I want you to know, kiddo. I looked up 'idyllic' in the dictionary and I wouldn't hold my breath. I wouldn't lie in bed all day just waiting for some idyllic childhood to come along."

I know, I wanted to tell him. You're right. Love often requires sacrifices which simply aren't worth it.

"So maybe you've had a few hard knocks. So maybe you've lived a sort of fly-by-night existence and all. That's just the breaks, kiddo," Pedro said, and for once I listened. For once I wanted us to hear each other. "That's just life.

And believe you me, we sure live it a damn sight better than we do lying in bed all day feeling sorry for ourselves. I think that's the truth, kiddo, and . . ." He gave a tremendous yawn. "Jesus." He blinked his eyes. His crumpled Budweiser cans lay toppled around him on the table, sofa and floor like crude chess pieces. "Boy. I guess I'm really bushed." Pedro pushed himself to his feet, slouched, pot-bellied and creased by the rough sofa cushions. "You take care of yourself, kiddo," Pedro told me, and shuffled in his wrinkled suede slippers toward the master bedroom. "I think I'm going to hit the hay." And then I heard him groaning into the squeaky bed, drifting into his slow aimless dreams of the soft red barbiturate haze that filled him like warm air fills a balloon. Meanwhile the ruptured gelatin Seconal capsules lay scattered on a sheet of Kleenex on the desk in my room.

I finished my diet soda and went in to see how he was doing. He looked very warm and peaceful, his face flushed and puffy, his vital bodily signs sailing along gently and intrepidly and slow. All the long steel kitchen knives were unsharpened and dully glimmering in the kitchen cabinets. There was no heavy cord or rope anywhere to be found, and though I suspected there might be some in the basement, it was dark down there, cold and damp, and I wasn't wearing any shoes. Then, like weather, I felt it first, just the heavy simplicity of it, a faint steel resonance underneath Pedro's bed. For a while I stood there and appreciated that strange, almost tactile presence. It was very solid. It was very useful and perfectly designed. Clearly it would do the job.

After a while I pulled Pedro's toolbox out from under the bed where it waited for me like history. I lifted its impossibly heavy weight onto the foot of the mattress. The toolbox contained hammers, screwdrivers, ratchets, Allen wrenches, hacksaws and spare, gleaming new replacement hacksaw blades. I knew that Pedro wanted a world as secure as the things he constructed in the backyard, a world with perfectly articulated joints and level, sanded surfaces. I knew that Pedro deserved a world like the worlds he built out there, like the worlds he built inside himself and Mom. "Death is the hard song, Pedro," I told him. "We only sing it once, and none of us ever gets it exactly right."

Even as I inaugurated my secret ceremonies of redemption that night, I knew something vaster and more important than myself was responsible for all my actions. Me, Mom, Pedro, and Mom's vast world were all just fragments of a process that would soon consume us all. I didn't want to give in to that mindless process, you see. I wanted to leave something behind, like the pyramids in Egypt, or the heads on Mount Rushmore. I wanted to build something formidable and good for all of us, but especially for Pedro. All that long night as I feverishly worked, what I wanted to do more than anything was build something for Pedro that would last forever.

LIGHT

6

I thought when Mom saw what I had done to Pedro she might stop loving me, but from that night forward I think she may have started loving me even more. When she emerged expressionless from the master bedroom I was sitting on the living room sofa, gently stroking my wet clean hair with a brown towel, still stippled and muggy after my long mournful bath. She didn't pause or speak to me. She just began packing our few belongings into pillowcases, and after a while I dressed and helped her carry everything out to the garage where our old Rambler had sat gathering dust and ticking these many months, sluggish and thick with its own unstirred oils and rusty water. It started up on Mom's first try. Then she held down the accelerator for a while and we sat there sleepily in the dark garage, staring out at the brighter and more opaque darkness beyond the roar of our Rambler's V-8. We were lifting off. In a moment, we would be hurtling through space. Mom released the emergency brake and the V-8 subsided to a rough, hesitant idle.

Then we glided down the long cement driveway while Pedro lay asleep in his calm and remorseless home, dreaming
his dreams of barbiturates, beer and the soft biting blades of
tools and things. God, I was filled with light that night.
I was filled with Mom's voice and the very light of her.
We were moving again. We would never die. We would
travel together forever in the world of inexplicit light,
Mom and I.

"The history of motion is that luminous progress men
and women make in the world alone," Mom said. "We're
moving into sudden history now, baby. That life men lead
and women disavow, that sure and certain sense that nothing is wrong, that life does not beat or pause, that the
universe expands relentlessly. You can feel the source of all
the world's light in your beating heart, in the map of your
blood, in the vast range and pace of your brain. That's the
light, baby. You don't need any other. Just that light beating
forever inside of you." We were turning onto the freeway,
which was filled with other, hurtling headlights, enormous
menacing trucks and buses. "We are like astronauts, we are
like wheeling planes and spaceships. We are like swaying
birds with soft stroking wings like oars. We beat against the
heavy air, and carry our silent and regenerate light with us
wherever we go."

It was nice Mom telling me that, that the light was mine
too. But I knew the light was Mom's and nobody else's. For
months I had seen nothing but my own interior and subjective darkness, and now, against the glare of Mom's resumed
motion, I could see the entire world again. No, all the light

we gathered was Mom's light, Mom's progress into places I could only dream about. I was just a passenger, and like all passengers, fundamentally unconcerned with landscape and plot, enveloped only by the simple movement of it all, the cumulate graph of those coherent points where we ate, slept, went to the bathroom, and awaited movement again. We could live together forever and ever, again and again, life after life. Mom didn't have to lie anymore. She didn't have to run or hide, she didn't have to journey further away from me in order to remain with me as she did, deeper into her dreams of me and further away from my untrained arms. I didn't know it then, but I was soon to learn I couldn't follow Mom everywhere.

These days I was intent on immortality, because I knew Mom's only hope of redemption lay in time itself, some expansion and unfocusing of time that would swallow Mom and all her imaginings into one formless shape and sound, not a place so much as a force or dispersion of force, an abstract location that bound and contextualized things, like gravity or sound. "Low-cholesterol diets, Mom," I told her, browsing through a college nursing text entitled *Health and Our World: 32nd Edition.* "Then there's the DNA, those complex looping signals beeping in our blood and our lymph. Death's a program, Mom. Like eating, sleeping, sex and hate. Our bodies generate death like fluids, waste, carbon dioxide, anticoagulants, marrow. DNA's the beeping clock, unraveling time in our bodies like smoke from your cigarettes. It's the tiniest force; it responds with information, not blood; it circulates raw and genetically contrived data, not life exactly. The heart—we'll leave that to the regular scientists. There's some oils in fish that cleanse the body of fatty tissue and keep the rich blood pumping. But down into the DNA is where I'll go, Mom. When I grow up I'll have a laboratory. I'll invent a lot of stupid consumer junk so I make lots of money. Then I'll sink everything I've got into the DNA. I'll climb down into its bristling helical nets like a spelunker. I'll dig out every secret, and then they'll be our secrets, Mom, and we'll live forever. We'll have a house overlooking the beach, and my laboratory in the basement. And we'll live together without anyone bothering us for thousands and thousands of years."

Most of the time Mom just drove without looking at me, wearing her tortoiseshell sunglasses and a floppy straw hat. She was listening, somewhere deep in her brain, but she was watching other roads now besides 101, other routes besides the one on a map. "This is King City," she might say. "I think we've been to King City." Mom's face was very pale without makeup, but very beautiful as well. "Let's try it anyway," and pulled onto the next off-ramp. Soon we were winding down into a Burger King, a Wendy's, a Motel 6, a King's Bowl Bar and Grill. I always insisted on a salad bar in these days of Mom's growing disaffection. I urged her to eat plenty of raw vegetables and fresh fish. We would pull into the parking lot and she would turn to me. "It's got to be better than San Luis, doesn't it? It's got to be better than that hellhole." Then she gave the fleshy thigh of my arm a little squeeze and smiled. Only she wasn't looking at me in a way. She was looking at me, but she wasn't looking at me at the same time.

Rather than disappearing into neon bars with her strange, generally unmanicured men, Mom took longer and longer looks at herself in the vanity mirrors of our motel rooms, drinking her Seagram's and 7UP, her Scotch and Tab. She would wear her laciest lingerie and just sit there alone. Perhaps she would paint her face with very bright makeup, or contrast her pale cheeks with soft blushes and eye shadows, leaning forward, one elbow against one dimpled knee, one brilliantly manicured hand splayed gently against the top of the dresser, her other hand producing various vials and Maybelline from her handbag, which bristled with crumpled Kleenex, tattered road maps, plastic cutlery, and the various salt, ketchup, and NutraSweet packets she had lifted from fast-food restaurants. Her breasts were fully outlined against the sheer fabric of her lingerie; her long, slightly pudgy thighs (of which she was curiously ashamed, and over which she generally wore pants or thick cotton "middie" skirts); her legs glistening with dark nylons. Sometimes, as she watched herself applying makeup, she might take a few long slow breaths. I could feel her breath warm in the air around me; I could taste its warmth against my skin and face. Sometimes her nipples grew more prominent and stiff. She would remove her left hand from the table and place it against the inside of her left thigh. Lying on my side of the bed I watched her, and my body filled with strange, smoky sensations. She wasn't looking at me. She wasn't looking at me. But I was looking at her.

I began to feel a little out of breath, resting the open textbook against my thin, almost concave chest. Mom was a bird, a cloud, a car. Mom was something that breathed like me, that felt warm like me, that could move her legs like mine. She wasn't looking at me, but I was looking at her. Her face emblazoned with cosmetics, her body firm and distant and unbelievably warm. I was becoming her only man. No other men ever came around. I was watching Mom and, after a while, out of the corner of her eye, Mom began watching me, her hand which held the lip gloss hovering against the edge of the dresser, her cool gaze turned in my direction now, as if she saw me and she didn't see me, and I felt my entire body burning and pulsing with the light, the light, all the night's darkness which was now suddenly turning into light, and all the sleepiness pulling at my face and filling my eyes with heat and softness and a sort of blurred and amorous detachment, and then I was falling asleep, and my body gave a sudden little kick. And as I slept I dreamed of Pedro. I dreamed of Pedro dreaming of me. Because Pedro and I understood one another perfectly now. We both loved Mom. And now we were all that was left of that strange and delusory world of Mom's numinous men.

Many of our surviving Visa and MasterCard cards were beginning to reach and overreach their expiration dates, and Mom and I soon grew stingier with our fund of invisible credit. We began pulling "runners" at restaurants, coffee shops and motels. While Mom flirted in the office with mechanics and gasoline attendants, I would jimmy open the cash box out on the service island with a screwdriver and pull out the large bills from underneath the steel change tray. We lifted food from grocery stores and clothes from clothing stores. We took magazines, beer and cigarettes from 7-Elevens, Stop 'N' Shops, Liquor Barns and Walgreen's drugstores. One afternoon at the Van Nuys Motel 6 I was returning to our room after playing one of my slow games with a sharp stick and a dead, forlorn blackbird, and found Mom carrying the color portable television from our motel room downstairs to our car. We sold it that night to a pair of diminutive and portly Mexicans—very pleasant and smiling men, as I recall—for twenty-five dollars in the parking lot of Serra Bowl in Encino. "Value's generated by the world, not consciousness," Mom said that night as we drove south to La Jolla. "The trick is to take the world and its values and generate better worlds inside. You've got a choice, baby, and it's the only choice you've got. Either remake the world, or allow the world to remake you. Did that sign say 101? Look for my glasses—there, on the dash. And keep an eye out for Highway 101."

We were driving, always driving, and always it was night. Outside our hurtling car the darkness simmered with radio waves and the swirling, hot Santa Anas. Everything converged out there, even the heartbeats of other stars and galaxies. Pulsars, quasars, fissioning novas and supernovas, the radar of airplanes and control towers, the diminishing cries of hidden and crepuscular birds. I couldn't look out into that eternal night—those inconstant oceans of static engulfing our AM radio every few miles or so—without thinking the question. The question surfaced like some underwater creature. It was learning to oxygenate. It was crawling from the sea's boiling muck.

"Whatever happened to Dad?" I asked Mom, against my will. I couldn't help myself. The question was like force, blood pressure, chemistry or light. "Where is Dad now? Is he still alive? At night, like this, when the night is just like this, does Dad ever think about us? Is Dad a person in the world, Mom? Or does he just lie in his bed and dream? And if so, Mom, are we his dream, or is he ours?"

But Mom had already grown very quiet. It was almost as if the question were not mine at all, but rather part of some thin formless lapse within the continuity of Mom's diminishing world. She never said anything for hours at a time. I began to realize my mom was going very far away. I merely traveled, but Mom journeyed.

7

Then one day I awoke puffy and unbathed in the backseat of our car and Mom told me. The hot sunlight was filling the cracked vinyl upholstery, the warped, discolored dashboard and dirty windows. Mom was leaning inside and pushing my shoulder. "I've done it," Mom said. "I've rented us our own house." So finally, after years and years without memory, Mom inaugurated time for us again. We had our own house now, and nobody lived in it but us.

"I think I can say I've learned a lot of important things in the past few months or so," Mom told me that night. "About myself, and you, and our world, and our future. And about the sort of unrealistic expectations people can have about one another. Everything's going to be a lot different, this time," Mom promised. "I think I've learned to be a little more realistic about things. I've learned there are some things we simply can't expect from one another."

Every few minutes she took her glass into the kitchen and hacked at the bag of ice we had purchased that evening from the neighborhood liquor store. The ice rested in the rusty and chipped Formica sink, thawing and reshaping itself. Then Mom returned to the living room with her ice-filled glass and poured more Seagram's and 7UP.

"I don't care, Mom," I said, compelled by my own confessions too. "I just want you to know that I'm not mad at Pedro anymore. I think I may have been very selfish and confused lately, and I don't mind if you want Pedro to come live with us again. I know I can't keep you all to myself, because my love for you can't be a selfish love if it's to be honest and true. I know now I have to let you live your own world, because that's what I love about you. That world you are apart from me. I think I'm beginning to learn a lot about myself as an individual, Mom. And if Pedro comes to live with us again, I promise I'll be nice to him this time. I promise I won't do anything I shouldn't do."

Mom sipped her drink in the cold room, the candles flickering around us, impaling the mouths of Mountain Dew and Coke bottles streaked with ruddy wax. Mom just looked away. It was as if she didn't hear me. It was as if she were listening to Pedro dream, the man whose name she taught me once to say and then taught herself never to say again. I wondered if in Pedro's dreams there were visions of Pedro dreaming, like the way angled mirrors reflect one another infinitely in department-store dressing rooms. In Pedro's dreams there was Mom, me, and a dark gathering shape underneath the floors of our new house. The dark shape said, "The family environment is a very important place for growing children. A stable family unit environment determines whether a young child will grow up feeling assured and self-confident, or simply undisciplined, slothful and insecure." Whenever we heard that voice coming, Pedro always shot me a glance of warning. Pedro and I both knew Dad would be with us again very soon.

"Sometimes it's hard to tell the difference between your conception of the world and the world's conception of you," Mom said, swirling thin ice in her glass. We slept on the shag carpet on the rolled-up blankets and quilts we had lifted the previous evening from the Best Western Motel in Van Nuys. "It's very easy to fool yourself," Mom said. "The harder you think about things, the more confused you get." She was lying on her back and gazing at our white, water-stained ceiling. Her hands were resting very quietly on her breathing stomach. "When I was just a little girl I would sit on the living room couch for hours sometimes, just trying to figure out the simplest things. I couldn't even move. My mind grew fuzzy and dim. I felt as if my skull was inflating with chemical pressure or anesthetic. It grew dark outside. My mother returned home from work. She fixed me dinner, but I wouldn't eat. I just sat there alone until I could feel this sort of moving black cloud slowly engulf me. Inside the black cloud, I couldn't think about anything. I couldn't even remember what I had been trying to figure out. Sometimes I couldn't remember my own name, or the address where I lived. Sometimes I couldn't even be sure if my mother was really my mother at all." Stealthily, the gas heater gave a tiny kick in the kitchen. Outside, the city was filled with bright, airy noise, whisper-

ing against the thin walls of our house like something cor-
poreal, filled with hissing and irreducible life.

"Go to sleep, Mom," I told her, and placed my hand on
both of hers. "Get some rest and we'll talk about it in the
morning."

"Sometimes, lately, I've started feeling like that again,"
Mom said. "I see this cloud of blackness moving in around
me. I start to forget things. I can't even tell if I'm dreaming
or not."

Outside in the bright night, the full moon gazed over
everything, gravid with implications which, at my still tender
age, I could suspect but not yet comprehend.

"Your father took me away from all that," Mom said
distantly, "and that's why I'll always be very grateful to him.
I'll always be very grateful to your father, Phillip, but that
doesn't mean I want him back."

Mom always said we would buy furniture someday, but we
never did. Instead we purchased a Hitachi color television,
VHS recorder and remote control with one of our few
remaining credit cards on which time, like the vital current
of some living creature, was gradually running out. We purchased a pair of springless Sta-Easy mattresses from a ridic-
ulously exorbitant Salvation Army thrift store and placed
one in each of our musty, isolate bedrooms. We purchased
an audiocassette recorder and various new tapes from Tower
Records in Van Nuys, and a small unvarnished desk with a
built-in bookshelf for my room, one on which I assembled
my various stained and pulpy textbooks, a new notepad,

pink rubber eraser, plastic ruler, pencil sharpener and pencil case. These were my tools now, and like Pedro I kept them all in their proper place. There was something submarine about them, even anxious. Mom had recently determined I would be a writer someday.

"Take words and make them useful," she told me. "Drain them of all the crappy meanings they *used* to mean, and make them mean something useful instead." I assigned myself to my room for exactly two hours every morning, where I studied my books and wrote my clean words. With my elbows propped against my splintery desk, I plunged into books and histories and explicable mysteries like some hungry and lucratively sponsored wilderness explorer. I made vast new areas of knowledge cultivable and known. I descended to the ocean floor and encountered bloated, symmetrical creatures with pumping white hearts and translucent skin. Collapsed blue civilizations lived down there, fissured and antiseptic, craggy with barnacles and blistering rust. I reached into the heart of the earth, the sky, the moon. I colonized language, mathematics, schemes of chemical order and atomic weight. I studied the manufacture of automobiles, microcircuitry, Kleenex and planets. I memorized the gross national products of nations and hemispheres, the populations of cities and states and principalities, the achievements of presidents, tyrants and kings. I was trying to learn what I suspected Mom had learned already: that there were journeys we all make alone that take us far away from one another.

Every morning I awoke alone in our cold house and padded softly into the kitchen, where I prepared myself Pop Tarts, hot chocolate and perhaps a small bowl of cold cereal. Then I would turn on all the stove's gas jets to break the kitchen's chill, and sit at the wooden breakfast nook perusing last evening's *Herald* (I disdained the *Times* for political reasons). I might listen to a little local all-chat radio for a while, and then fix myself a small pot of coffee and return to my study, always attentive as I passed Mom's silent room, where she remained discreetly asleep or self-absorbed until around midafternoon. Then I read alone in my room until at least noon, spilling the strange energetic words into my head. Geology, psychology, ancient history, applied linguistics, German, modern philosophy, South American etymology, Central American politics, Fourier, Rousseau, Marx—a vast boil and suck of words and languages. I recall very little of what I learned then; the ideas didn't really cling. Rather they seemed to seep into my skin and belly and condition rather than fill me. It was as if I were just modifying the shape of my hunger rather than appeasing it. The only knowledge that really mattered to me then mattered because it was linked somewhere in my feverish imagination with the emerging shape of Dad. I remember quantum physics because I felt that Dad, like the movement of planets, was not a fact of data so much as a quality of interpretation. I remember European revolutionary governments of the eighteenth century because their subversion of "Father" had never eliminated so much as merely redesigned his very real presence. I remember Hegel because I always imagined that the thisness which was Mom and I was always transforming itself into the thatness which would be life with Dad. Dad was the thatness towards which all our complicit motion yearned. It was in February that he called for the first time.

Is this Phillip? he asked when I answered. I had never answered a phone before to the sound of my own name.

"Who's this?" I asked, but I didn't really need to ask. There was only one other person in the world who knew my name.

This is your dad, he said. This is your dad who misses you both very, very much.

I hung up, and he didn't ring back. At least not that same night.

Later when I went to bed I tried to distinguish the different schemes of light that infiltrated my room. There was the lunar and the electrical, the stellar and the reflected. There was the light of ghosts, and the light of living things. That night Pedro spoke to me for the first time since he began dreaming of those hard lightless objects which filled his somber toolbox.

"I forgive you what you did to me, but I'll never forgive you what you did to your mom. I'll never forgive you what you did to yourself."

"But what about the light, Pedro?" I asked him. "What sort of light do you see now? Does the light that fills you make you feel warm, or safe, or sad?" But Pedro's voice had grown silent again. He had said all he wanted to say. It was as if, while he dreamed, someone was keeping watch over him. Dreaming was a prison of some kind in which you were never really alone even for a minute, in which you were responsible to a legion of regulations, timetables and personnel. I couldn't understand why Pedro said he could never forgive me. It had to be a code or a cipher of some kind. If he told me the truth about his new life, he might get himself in serious trouble with the people who gauged and monitored that life. I would have to ask him about it later. For now, effortlessly, I could only sleep.

8

Dad called the next morning around ten thirty.

It's been five years, he said. You guys are a hard act to follow, but not so hard to trace. I may not always know where to find you, but I always know where you've been. In fact you've left a trail which you might say is at least a mile wide. Hearing my detective agency's progress reports on your travels is more fun than watching television, and there are some pretty good programs on television these days, or so I've heard. I was worried when I learned you'd stopped again. I was worried when I learned you'd had the phone connected in your mom's name. The electricity and the gas.

Dad wasn't a voice at all, not even on the phone. Dad's voice surfaced in my life that day like something vaster and more comprehensible than speech, like language itself. I tried to convince him he must have a wrong number, but Dad wasn't buying.

Your mom's had a lot of tough breaks in her life, Dad

continued. (I couldn't imagine what Dad looked like, but I could distantly envision his large body out in some nonde-script backyard wielding a long green garden hose. He sprayed the grass and flowers, the easily contented trees and saplings. Then he filled a large plastic bucket with soapy water and went out front to wash the car.) Your mom is a very good woman who doesn't always do very good things. She's not really what I'd call an appropriate role model for a young boy. I think what I'm trying to say, Phillip, is that it may be time for you to come back home and live with your dad again. We'll fix up your old room. We'll get you enrolled back at school. Your mom's welcome to come back home as well, Phillip. I still love your mom, no matter what she's done. And so far as I know, she's done some pretty bad things. There was that poor fellow, Bernie Somebody-orother, in San Luis Obispo. And then, a year or so earlier, that architect in Simi Valley.

I felt a cold breeze moving into my legs, my buttocks, my stomach. It reached into my chest.

"What architect?" I asked. Other worlds were opening themselves to my inspection when I was seven years old—not just the worlds in books, not just the worlds in words. "What architect in Simi Valley? Did he have a red beard?" I asked, not remembering so much as describing him to myself, as if I were the one making the world real with my voice. "Did he have a deep basso profundo singing voice? Did he drive a brand-new green BMW?"

———

Dad called every afternoon and told me things Mom had done. Felonies, assaults, mild flurries of misdemeanors and unacknowledged traffic citations, suspected manslaughters in Burlingame, San Jose, even Whittier. Mom was becoming even more glorious, transubstantial and unreal. She was moving further away from me and into the realm of raw, undifferentiated nature. Mom was a bat, a wolf, a bear, a tiger. Sometimes, as I grew to love her even more, I began to imagine she was luring me into the nests and secret networks of her own convoluted self. Alone in my bed at night, I heard myself talking like her, my mind working like hers. "The irregularities of the world's body correspond with the map of our own brains, baby," I said in my dark room, entangled by my dark and muddled blankets. Gently my hands stroked my stomach, my thighs, the stray black hairs beginning to emerge on my breathing chest. "We travel across the world and into the ways representation works. Trees aren't trees, roads aren't roads, moms aren't even moms. The history of motion is that luminous progress men and women make in the world alone." Sometimes I couldn't even remember which words were mine and which words Mom's. Whose voice was it, whose tongue and whose lips? Where did my flesh of words end and Mom's words of flesh begin? Was this Mom's face and stomach and beating heart, or was this mine? Was I becoming her, some mere reproduction of Mom, or had she so totally and unselfishly invested herself inside me that she no longer really existed at all? I tried to tell myself that I was still me and that Mom was still my mom, but never with any conviction. I am myself, I whispered again and again in the dark. I live my own life. I imagine my own worlds. That's what I kept telling myself.

"Mom's been arrested for soliciting," I told Pedro one night. "That means Mom slept with men and they paid her. She didn't just take money from men, she engaged in business relations. That means they took something from her too." Pedro was dreamily envisioning a new redwood knick-knack shelf with Y joints and notched shelves. He was twiddling his thumbs in his lap just like a little boy. "Mom has been committing crimes I didn't even know about. She has stolen real cash and valuable cars. She even sold hard drugs once. She put two men in a hospital, and at least one in a morgue. Mom has been committing these secret acts without my help, because she's got a terrible temper and she can't help herself. What's more, Pedro, Mom can be cured. Her condition is something that can be altered by the proper medication, regulated by trained doctors and commercial, cost-effective therapy. Mom has a very bad temper, Dad says. Mom has a very bad temper, and I've never even seen it." I was feeling very hot and flushed. Something gave in my stomach, like a loose floorboard. I started to cry. "Mom's someone I don't even know at all, Pedro. That's why I'm growing up so wild. That's why I'm doing things I really shouldn't do. Perhaps that's even why I did the things I did to you, Pedro. But I can't remember. I can't even remember what I did to you anymore." I tried to stop, but I couldn't stop crying. The atmosphere of my small room turned moist and clinging. I felt as if I were crying in the womb of some hibernal animal.

"If you're gonna play hardball, you're gonna get hurt," Pedro said wisely, drifting away into the mist. "We're all grown-ups in this game, kiddo. We've all got to live the lives we've got to live."

Pedro's easy aphorisms disguised a real truth. There were still some very important things Pedro wasn't telling.

SOUND

AND

GRAVITY

9

Oddly enough, it was during this period of Mom's increasingly alcoholic estrangement that I began to experience anything like that "normal childhood" one usually encounters only in books. I grew inured, if not accustomed, to the patent bliss of domesticity. I developed a system of routine chores and scheduled ambitions, marking each day on the calendar as I doled out payments to our landlord and utility franchises, milkman and insurance broker. I took two paper routes. I studied every morning and, every evening, fixed both Mom and myself a perfectly edible meal. Two or three afternoons each week I would go out to what I referred to as my "job" in order to earn money with which to put bread on the table.

As a paperboy, I was kept informed of my client's vacations, and so, on routine afternoons, I would break into carefully preselected homes and take jewelry, portable televisions, cordless phones, microwaves, along with many other alluring household appliances, and transport them downtown on the bus, where I sold them at one of the various pawnshops frequented by gaunt men with loose socks who stood about exposing swollen veins in their necks and foreheads, or glowered at me from behind massy and varnished oak countertops as they inspected my merchandise and contemplated ludicrous sums.

"Ten dollars," they said, eyeing me suspiciously, not concerned with where I got it so much as how little I would take. "It isn't worth my trouble. It isn't worth my time."

"Make it fifteen, then," I replied, chewing my impassive bubble gum. "Maybe it's worth a little of your trouble. Maybe it's worth a little of your precious time."

I even acquired during these days a friend. Rodney was twelve years old, and lived in the corner house with his mother, a rather fragmented and conspicuous woman named Ethel. Rodney was the perfect friend for me, really, and introduced me to a world far more disorderly, I imagined, than my own. Rodney was submissive without obedience, patient without serenity. He had a Stingray bicycle, a rather brutal attitude toward his unfortunate mother (which, I must admit, caused me some uneasy admiration for him, as an aborigine might admire the miracle of a cigarette lighter or a beeping digital watch) and a top-floor bedroom filled with marvelous and very dispensable things.

"Why don't you take this shirt," he might tell me. "These are some pants I grew out of. You never change your clothes, guy. You never wash your hair."

Usually I wasn't listening. I was far too preoccupied with

the room's many bright objects to feel at all self-conscious about my appearance. There were board games: Stratego, Pollyanna, Monopoly, The Game of Life, Battleship and Risk. We constructed monstrous machines with red and white Lego blocks, Erector sets and plastic, prepackaged model kits. Mostly, though, I was thoroughly taken with Rodney's chemistry set, a somewhat corroded metal cabinet box which, unfolded, displayed tidy bottles of strange substances with unfamiliar smells, tastes and textures in them. Some of them, like tannic acid, were labeled with urgent red crosses and warned of deadly dangers which should be investigated only "in the company of adults." The set contained beakers and flasks and test tubes and even a small chemical fire with metal clasps and braces. "This is life's sudden start," I said, the first time I saw it. "This is chemistry." I purchased a loose-leaf notebook and began keeping track of the various chemical mixtures I contrived. Sulphuric acid and nitrous oxide and carbon, zinc and pure rubbing alcohol and long-grain white rice. Then, under what I considered "controlled laboratory conditions," I exposed small animals to them. Bugs, butterflies, lizards and frogs. Sometimes the small animals betrayed no reactions at all. Sometimes, a few hours or a few days later, they died. "Science isn't reason, Rodney," I told him. "Science is pure chance and sudden luck. It's magic, in a way. Chemistry is that unstable and perfectly coordinated music of the fundamental that lives in our skin and our shoes. This is where life achieved its sudden flash, and where time itself will someday rediscover its own timeless regeneration." I contributed tannic acid to the beaker labeled POETIC TROPE #117, thiamine spirit and, from Rodney's mother's kitchen cabinet, vinegar, baking soda, and just a touch of oregano. A thin sudsy foam gathered around the beaker's rim. "We'll seek secrets in the random," I told Rodney. "We'll discover truth in chance's sudden dances."

Rodney, leaning against the table and gazing into the brownish fluid, displayed only that marvelous and half-lidded unconcern for which I always envied him. He wasn't after anything, my friend Rodney. He sincerely didn't care if he lived forever or not.

"What about a booger?" Rodney asked. "What about if we put a booger in it?" Without looking at me, he tapped the beaker's rim with the nail of one of his clean, well-manicured fingers, as if trying to startle into existence whatever soft chemical reactions lay down there in the hidden world of chemistry.

The homes Rodney and I systematically violated that spring were very wary places, hollow, haunted and impercipient, like very old lovers or dying trees. Because I was smallest I always entered first, through basement windows, up trellises into high bedrooms or, more usually, through the opaque and slender windows of bathrooms which had been left open to air out the muggy shower smells. Then I would come around to the front door where Rodney would snap his gum at me with his weary and somewhat affected nonchalance and help me peruse the belongings of these soft and dimly dreaming houses.

"What a bunch of crap," Rodney said. "What are we going to do with all this crap?"

Rodney was an idealist, and refused to be corrupted by mere matter. If I was a sort of exemplary enlightenment scientist, Rodney was a romantic poet, airy and uncompromised. "Crap crap crap crap crap," Rodney said as I loaded pearls and sparkling brooches into my green plastic Hefty bag, watches and piggy banks, digital clocks and compact discs. "They'll never even notice it's gone. They're probably at the shopping plaza right now, buying more crap." He shook his head wearily, and poured himself a stiff drink from the liquor cabinet. If he found a pack of cigarettes on a bedroom bureau or kitchen counter he would chain-smoke casually, filling these transgressed homes with the roiling, misty odor of Marlboros and Kools. I had great hopes for Rodney in those days. I believed then, as I believe now, he was destined for far greater achievements than myself.

"Good riddance," he always said, slamming shut the garage or front door as we walked down the suburban streets with our loot. We wore the purported innocence of childhood wrapped around us like menacing cloaks and fog in some old movie. Only Rodney and I knew what we hid inside those cloaks. Only Rodney and I knew the secrets of the movies we lived inside, the movies other people only watched on TV.

The History of Luminous Motion

These were the days of my exile, a time of dense silence, strange houses and broken basement windows. They contained locks that could be uncranked with tire irons, or cats that purred and rubbed themselves against you. Sometimes the dogs barked, but if you approached them in a certain way they would bow submissively and allow you to scratch their foreheads. Sometimes we fed the pets while we gathered up the belongings of their masters, and they curled up purring and dreaming on the living room carpets where we would activate the TV for them, for Rodney and I also felt more at home with the sound of the television around us. Game shows filled with jeering buzzers and brand-new cars. Morning chat shows which interviewed interchangeable circus clowns and members of the board of supervisors. Inexhaustible diurnal melodramas in which beautiful men and women lived and loved, hated and died. Then there was only the resinous darkness moving into the houses when we left them. Sometimes we transported our new stuff home in stray shopping carts; sometimes, brazenly, we parked these indemnified carts outside a McDonald's or Burger King while we paused inside for a well-deserved cup of coffee, a sweet roll or fries. I always knew in those days that this was not the world I really belonged to; it was not my mom's world, which both Mom and I had lost, but a world of other moms and dads I would never comprehend. A stony vast plateau without any landmarks or colors on it. A pale cloudless sky in which nothing moved, nothing sounded. You could walk and walk for miles in this world without

70

ever seeing anybody, except of course at night when you were asleep and dreaming about the dense silence, strange houses and broken basement windows. Locks uncranked with tire irons, purring cats and submissive, basement-anxious dogs. Exile was a dream of a return to something you couldn't remember. It took you back to a place you'd never been.

"I think we should burn the dump," Rodney said sometimes, languorously reviewing a *TV Guide* on the living room sofa while I did all the hard work, disengaging the VHS from the Panasonic, stuffing my coat pockets full with quarters from a tin cookie jar in the kitchen. "I think we should see if shit burns." Rodney never seemed the invader of these broken homes, but rather their more legitimate occupant, as if his invisible royal blood admitted him to secret kinships and demesnes. Sometimes I felt rather awkward, looting the silver and jewelry before Rodney's calm and disaffected gaze. It was as if Rodney was allowing my trespass and at any moment, if I made one wrong move or discourteous gesture, such license would be summarily revoked. His expression always seemed remotely curious whenever he looked at me, or at the items in my hands, as if he retained some unflagging interest even though many thousands of years ago he had given up the possibility of ever being surprised again. "There's a good movie on Channel Four we can watch at my house," he said. "It's got Ginger Rogers in it. I think Ginger Rogers is a great piece of ass, don't you?"

All these houses seemed like one house, just as all the

71

silence of my strained exile seemed like one continent, one forlorn place without a name. I could hear my mom in these houses, I could see her dazed looks as she sat drinking alone in her room, waiting while Dad gathered somewhere in the world like moisture, like thick clouds, like heavy black currents. My sense of exile was my inheritance from Mom; it might somehow, without my even understanding why, constitute my one real gift to Dad, to whom I still owed the ominous debt of conception. I was off in the world alone now. I was investigating strange rooms, basements and gardens. I was trundling off with my pillowcases and Hefty bags filled with merchandise like some sort of diabolical and inverted Santa Claus. All of the houses were part of one house. All of the houses in the world were part of that one house by which Mom and I were divided as well as embraced. "Growing up" began to signify one thing only to my feverish imagination. Mom and I could live in worlds without each other in them.

I never understood Rodney, but I was always a bit awe-struck, if only because of the incomprehensible life he lived with his own mother. Ethel had a generous pension from the Marine Corps subsequent to her husband's death at Tet, very gray hair, and bad circulation in her legs. Usually she sat all day and embroidered in a big stuffed chair, her feet propped by cushions and a macramé footstool; when she walked she walked with the aid of an aluminum cane. Whenever we came in the front door with our new stuff she would put down her knitting and watch while we stored it all in the large hall closet alongside the departed Mr. Johansen's crisply dry-cleaned military uniform, unused golf clubs, and loose photographs in a chipped Macy's gift box (I was forever examining the contents of other people's closets). After we were finished, Ethel offered us food and refreshments. "There's tuna salad, Roddy. In case you and your friend are hungry. There are some Snickers bars in the freezer, just the way you like them. Only have some tuna salad first. Have some good canned soup—there's mushroom and tomato. Then, if you and your little friend want, I could fix us all a Manhattan."

Rodney said, "Mmmm." He went into the kitchen and began banging cupboard and refrigerator doors. I stood noncommittally in the hall, watching Ethel in her chair. Ethel was reading one of her old "collector's" editions of *The Amazing Spider Man,* and the plastic envelope lay across her knees like some official procedure. "There's Sara Lee pound cake, and even a couple of Twinkies hidden away. And of course I could fix you both that Manhattan. Would you like a Manhattan, Phillip?" She started to lay her comic on the coffee table and reach for her cane.

"Do me a favor, Ethel," Rodney said. He had suddenly appeared beside me, one foot on the stairs. He held a pair of tuna salad sandwiches on a white plate, and a large bag of Nacho Cheese Flavored Doritos under one arm. "Just sit down, read your comics, and shut the fuck up."

I couldn't look at Ethel. I couldn't look at Rodney. I felt a deep painful turning in my body. My face was filling up with heat. I was walking through a stunned silence, my feet on the stairs, Rodney already at the top. I was still trembling. Everything was a blur. I could hardly see where I was going.

"Don't tell me to shut up," Ethel said, quite simply and unemphatically at first. It was as if she were telling us where the mayonnaise was. "Don't tell your mother to shut up. Rodney. Rodney, come back here."

Breathing a long sigh, Rodney gestured me into his room. He handed me the plate of sandwiches. Then he shut his bedroom door firmly and locked the flimsy knob.

Ethel's voice was growing louder now. "Don't tell your mother to shut up, Rodney. Rodney! Don't you dare tell *me* to shut up! Rodney! You come down here! Rodney! Why don't *you* shut up, Rodney! Why don't *you* shut up, then! *Rodney! You* come down here! *You* shut up, Rodney! *You* shut up!"

Rodney pulled a pair of Cokes from underneath his bed and ripped them free of the stiff plastic spine. "It's like living in a madhouse," he said, not even looking at me. I felt complicit in a frame of violence I couldn't understand. I just sat there hoping his mom wouldn't remember what I looked like. I just hoped Rodney's mom wouldn't remember my name.

"Sometimes I think she's the biggest asshole in the entire universe," Rodney said, pulled the television closer on its wobbly castored frame and switched it on. You could hear the charge of it before you saw the light abrupt to its screen. Suddenly we were in any house, every house; suddenly we were drifting again through the space of my exile. We watched cartoons, movies, detective and western programs while I listened to the outside hallway for the steps of wounded Ethel on the thin carpet as she moved, slowly and eventually, to her own empty bedroom down the hall, awaiting the moment when I could escape this house and my own complicity in Ethel's systematic humiliation by Rodney, the most remarkably powerful person I have ever known in my entire life.

10

I celebrated my birthday in secret that year, on a day I firmly refuse to commemorate or even mention. There was something firm and round about the new age which filled my body like a very old song, or smoke from a cigarette. Usually I didn't return home until one or two a.m., since Rodney and I regularly stayed up drinking Ethel's whiskey or smoking Rodney's grass. My feet staggered and slipped against the knotty carpet as I let myself in the front door. My tongue felt thick and swollen. I staggered down the dark hall, already sensing the thick silence behind Mom's steadfast door. "Mom," I said, leaning against her door, uncertain of the floor's balance. "Mom, it's me. It's your son. Mom. It's Phillip." I heard my own whispered words deep in my throat and chest, resonating like bones. I could hear her taking her breath as my hand gently grasped the loose aluminum doorknob. The knob ticked in its frame when I turned it. Its resistance was at once strange and comforting, like the taste of a new tooth. Mom's door was always locked. She never let me in anymore.

"Mom." I tried to sound firm now. I tried to sound sober and mature. "There's money on the kitchen cabinet. There's still some Colonel Sanders in the fridge. It's cold, Mom. Just the way you like. And coleslaw. Have a banana. Bananas are filled with potassium." Motes and air whirled in Mom's dark room, rustling and indifferent. This was the sound Mom lived. The long slow pause in her heart where she gathered language and waited for history to resume again.

"Thank you, Phillip," she said, as obliquely as she might acknowledge some porter in a hotel. "Thank you very much."

"I'm in my room, Mom. I'm in my room if you need me." I felt the pulse of alcohol in my blood as if the entire house were contracting gently around me. Then I heard the unmistakable gurgle of liquor being poured into Mom's smudged glass.

"You're a very good boy, Phillip. Don't worry about me. I'm fine. I'll be all right. You just make certain you're going to be all right, too." There was a rustle of newspapers. I could feel the darkness assembling in Mom's room, like clouds and gulls around some alien shoreline. For months I thought I was the one who had eliminated the buzzing opposition of Mom's men, but now I knew it was that gathering darkness. It was descending in the elevator from its high luxury office building. It was accepting the keys to its

Triumph from the black attendant. It was flying off across freeways and cities. It loved us. It loved Mom and it loved me. It loved both of us very, very much.

I didn't think of Ethel as a surrogate so much as a compensation. She could never take my mom's place, but she could make that place seem less cold and drafty. Some days I arrived deliberately early at Rodney's house, when I knew he was still in school, and drank generous Manhattans with Ethel while melodramas played at us from her blurry black and white television (the good color television, of course, was in Rodney's room). Eagerly she told me all the lost, distracted secrets of her prodigal son. "Rodney is actually a very affectionate young boy. Like you, Phillip, he is patient and attentive. He's a good listener. He's considerate and well-mannered—when he wants to be, that is. He always helps me with the housework if my legs are sore. Sometimes he saves money from his allowance and buys me little presents. If he's rude, it's just because he likes to show off in front of his friends. Young men, as you know, are a little embarrassed to show affection to their mothers, particularly when their friends are looking."

I wanted to ask her why, but was afraid such a hard awkward question might give me away. I might suddenly divulge the secret life I lived in strange houses, the secret life my mom had begun living behind the bolted door of her minimally furnished room.

"Would you like another Manhattan?" Ethel asked.

She showed me her empty glass and I took it.

"I'll get these," I said, and returned to the kitchen for the Jack Daniel's. Ethel had taught me how to mix a number of competent drinks, a feat in which I admit I took some pride. I returned and sat on the sofa beside the morning's smeary newspaper and watched the fabulous television. Ethel was absently handling her embroidery frame and gazing out the window at the harsh, smoggy sunlight, the palm trees faded and unraveled like some overexposed snapshot, the uniform houses and pavements and flashing cars. "People don't always intend to make other people feel bad, Ethel," I told her, though I was never sure she was listening. "Sometimes people just forget other people are even around. I know it sounds strange, but people work that way, I swear. Sometimes they don't know what they're doing. Sometimes they don't even know you're there at all." I was grasping at straws. Whenever I found myself trying to excuse Rodney's disgraceful behavior I became tangled and caught in my own inflexible words. Ethel, meanwhile, gazed out the window. "Maybe people just don't know where they are sometimes," I said, afraid to stop talking because then the judgment would come. In the long pause my talk would have to mean something. "Maybe people just talk without remembering who it is they're actually talking to. Maybe you just shouldn't think about it, Ethel. Maybe you should join a health spa, or find a hobby that interests you. Do you hear me, Ethel? Would you like another drink? Ethel? Are you listening?"

Before too long I was taking lunch with Ethel every afternoon around one o'clock. The casual scheme of my domesticity was growing more fulfilled and content. My paper
route, breakfast, morning study sessions (I was currently
investigating Plato, biophysics and Freud), afternoons with
Rodney burgling strange homes, television, evening meals
and bed. And every afternoon before I left the house I would
leave Mom's lunch wrapped in plastic and deposited outside
her bedroom door. Ethel was instructing me in the art of
fine sandwich building. Tuna and chicken salad, avocado
and sprouts, bacon, lettuce and tomato, roast beef, pastrami
and turkey with cottage cheese, peanut butter and banana.
Whenever Ethel sliced the sandwiches in their rich brown
bread the divided segments always looked impossibly tidy
and controlled on their clean white plates. "Sometimes at
night," Ethel said, humming and staring out the back window while she washed her hands at the sink, "sometimes at
night Rodney's father calls me from a long way away. He
says he would like to move back in here. He says he misses
my cooking." Ethel's voice trailed off aimlessly, like late
night drivers descending off-ramps in search of a quick, in-
expensive meal. "I tell him I wouldn't mind, if it was just
up to me." Drying her hands on a thin patterned towel,
Ethel was gazing over my shoulder. Her eyes looked so
intent, I often turned to see what she was seeing. I suspected
a grown man had appeared behind me, perhaps a taller and
more mature version of myself, Ethel's more substantial
companion which my thin body merely represented. " 'But

it's not just up to me, Harold,' I try to tell him." Ethel was sculpting soft white flower petals from the bodies of scoured radishes with a small sharp paring knife. " 'We have to do what's best for Rodney. We have to do what's best for our son, who has been raised under very trying and unfortunate circumstances, as I think you well know. It's easy, being a father, to think you can just show up when you feel like it. But children need someone they can count on, Harold. And as much as I may want you back, I just don't think Rodney could ever count on you again. You'd only disappoint him.' "

Ethel never disturbed or embarrassed me. I knew she had her own secret life to live, just as all mothers live fair portions of their lives down there in dark secure rooms and hidden gardens filled with strange plants and trees. I was simply grateful for the time Ethel spent with me here on the outside while I learned to prepare bases for soups and gravy, toss Caesar and fruit salads, cook purées and stews. I fricasseed, baked, boiled and roasted. I cleaned chicken and fish, basted lamb and pork, pressed my hungry hands into the thick dough of breads and cakes and cookies and pastry. I loved Ethel's warm kitchen and the heady smell of bread baking while I waited for Rodney to return home from school and transgress with me those other, colder kitchens, where I was picking up handy appliances, kitchen pots, pans and utensils and reassembling them in the hard irrefutable kitchen of Mom's silent and discriminating house. I wanted to build Mom a strong home that would always be there for her and provide her anything she might ever

need. I was beginning to realize I would have to leave someday. I still loved Mom more than ever, but I was learning
life carries us places, like rivers and winds carry things, often
against our own will.

Rodney may have been only twelve years old, but he had
big ambitions. "I need real estate," Rodney often said after
his second or third drink. With our merchandise gathered
around us in the living room like a family at Christmas, we
were lingering overlong in a particularly commodious four-
bedroom Spanish-style home in the foothills of Sherman
Oaks. Outside the streets were filled with dry, amber lawns
and stark, shedding palm trees. Every once in a while a
bright bluebird flashed. "I need tax incentives, money market liquid asset accounts, diversified stock portfolios, trea-
sury bills, low-interest tax deductible loans, property, houses,
income property, cars, trucks, buses, planes. I don't need
this. I don't need this crap," he said, making his customary
gesture at the huddling portable televisions, radios, jewelry
and microwave and, still in its original Sears packing case,
an adjustable three-temperature electric blanket which I in-
tended to leave that night, like a meal or some religious
devotion, outside my mom's bedroom door. "I don't need
a bunch of crap just weighing me down. I need negotiable
capital. I need security and a firm financial investment base.
I need money, property and women. I'm talking gash, now.
I'm talking poontang. I'm talking scuzz. I'm talking countless good-looking, insatiable young women with big tits."
Aimlessly Rodney's left hand began stroking the inner thigh

of his Levi's. Then, abruptly, he leaned forward and reached for the margarita mix in the blender's thick Pyrex bowl. "I need money and sex and more sex. I been thinking about it every day lately, Phil. I gotta get laid, man. I really gotta get laid."

Then, contemplating his refreshed glass for a moment, Rodney slumped back against the sofa. Meanwhile, I tried to appear as calm and unaffected as a prayer. I was practicing with a cigarette, sucking the thick smoke into my mouth every few seconds and then expelling it, pushing it out with my tongue and cheeks. Phooh, I said, as quietly as I could, because it wasn't a sound Rodney or Mom ever made when they smoked. Phooh. A very ugly miniature terrier lay asleep dribbling in my lap. Gently I lifted it onto the sofa's side. "Don't talk about it," I told him. "Don't talk about what you want too much. You'll lose the edge."

"I need to fuck women." Rodney's voice was growing subdued, distant, ritual and dark. "I need to fuck fuck fuck until I can't fuck anymore."

"It's all a dream, Rodney. If you talk about it too much, you wake up. Then there's just the bright sun. Then there's just your cold bed."

Suddenly Rodney sat up straight and placed his margarita on the table. He cautioned me with his left hand and gazed off intently at the far wall, as if listening with his eyes, poised like a diver.

I heard the footsteps too. Keys being shaken. Then a sack of something banging against the porch while keys rattled more distinctly. Implicitly feminine sounds.

83

"If you keep dreaming, you can have it all, Rodney. If you keep dreaming you can even be a grown-up. You can even fall in love."

"Fuck love," Rodney said.

We were grabbing the most compact and obvious loot, then slipping down the back stairs and out the rear garage door, through the yard and backyard gate while upstairs that stupid terrier was yelping and throwing itself up and down in the air as its master incautiously opened the front door.

"Fuck love, man," Rodney said later at Burrito King. "Fuck family. Fuck people and things. I want the real *stuff*, man. I want currency, I want sex. Give me the *stuff* and save all the bullshit. I've had it up to here with all the bullshit, Phillip. I'm tired of rotting away in Ethel's lousy household. It's time I started living my own life. I'm telling you, guy. Life is something you do. Bullshit is just something you've got."

Currency and sex were forces in our lives now, like smoky, violet surges of electricity and light. Sex and currency, currency and sex. The hum and the pop, chirring and turning, beating like electricity. We could drive cars with that force radiating deep inside us. We could activate industrial machinery. We could generate enough massive interior energy to drive cities, planets and suns.

I didn't feel the same sudden push inside my flesh that Rodney felt, but rather a sort of anxious intellectual charge. The energy whirled aimlessly inside my mind, where I nightly replayed that sudden film I had viewed with Mom only a few months before on a hotel-room closed-circuit television, *Sexually Altered States*. Sexually altered, sexually altered altered states, states of sexually altered states, altered states of sexually altered states. Sometimes the images sped and raced in my mind, and I imagined myself taking a seat in my own subjective cinema. I imagined the curtains sweeping open and the light dimming. I imagined the credits, and then the first exuberant breathless cinematic fuck. I tried to contain all the events within the frame of a plot. I tried to imagine the interstitial scenes, the dinners and champagne, the slow dances and undress, often growing so involved in them that I never got around to thinking through to the serious action again, the way the karate master is supposed to think through boards and blocks of concrete. I thought it was the anticipation which made sex real, but now I know it was merely my explicit faith in that imagination which unreeled around me in my childhood like the spokes of a milky galaxy. I was beginning to learn that the imaginative act was more important in my life than action itself. Action merely articulated you with an exterior and superficial network of facts, data and information which superimposed itself across the real world of my imagination like a restraint, or a clinging, oily film. I wanted the dream of sex, the energy and heat of it. Had I been able to articulate the problem for Rodney, I'm certain he would have preferred the dreams too.

11

"I've never considered myself beautiful," Beatrice said, listlessly running her hands through her tangled blond hair. Beatrice was twelve years old and attended Rodney's sixth-grade class at Junípero Serra Grammar School. "But I don't think beauty's the only thing men are looking for, if you know what I mean." Her look let us know she didn't expect there was any chance we would ever know what she meant. She tugged at her slightly soiled dress and crossed her legs. After a second of demure hesitation, she accepted Rodney's cigarette. Then Beatrice lit it with a Ronco from her purse, which she snapped shut with a practiced flourish. "Beauty's just what a woman seems. Plenty of women can be made beautiful. Look at *Vogue*, for instance. Look at *Cosmo*. That's not all men are looking for, you know. I *know* that's what they say men are supposed to be looking for, but that's just a male myth. That's just capitalism. That's just the psychological domination manifest in all competitive class struggle.

Basically, you see, I think men are a lot more capable and intelligent than that. I think men want a woman they're attracted to, sure—I'm no spiritual idealist or anything. I don't subscribe to bogus Christian dualism—all that repressive male ideology we've inherited from the Greeks. But there's a natural woman men are looking for underneath all the Clairol and Maybelline. There's a raw—oh, I don't know, call it sexuality, or passion, or molecular urgency—that marks a woman out from the pack. It's in her eyes, in her smell, in the way she combs her hair." Delicately, Beatrice jiggled in her seat, tugging her skirt straight underneath her.

We were all sitting at the Formica booth in Winchell's, feeling that warm arousal of steam from our fresh coffees. I held my Styrofoam cup between my hands. I was trying to keep my eyes expressionlessly focused on Beatrice. I was certain any expression on my part would be a sort of self-betrayal. Better to give her nothing about me she could analyze or remember, nothing she could keep for years and years, like nail clippings or stray buttons with which she could cast intricate social spells. I just wanted to watch Beatrice, her lips so hastily smudged with the chocolate rainbow donut, her pink skin and knotty, unwashed hair. Beatrice lived in a trailer park with her father. The trailer park, located in Encino, was called Trailer Town, and Beatrice's one-bedroom trailer was a 1959 Spartan Luxuryliner with polished wood interior and fully operable stove and central heating.

"I think that's what I'll always have to offer my men,"

Beatrice said, and took the first brave sip of our scalding coffee. Rodney and I had ordered it black because Beatrice had. She put it down with a little emphasis.

"It's like television, movies, books, even record albums. *This* is what beauty is. *This* is how you're supposed to look. *This* is a girl's *normal* height, how much makeup to wear, how big your tits should be"—I felt Rodney give a little jump beside me—"and all that long morose unforgiving catalog of what women are *supposed* to be, how women are *supposed* to feel. Beauty is the culture industry's attempt to make each of us a commodity. The culture industry, guys, is vast and incredibly articulate. It knows exactly what it wants to say all the time. It wants to make each of us the same on the outside, while letting us pretend we're somehow marvelously special on the inside. The culture industry hasn't invented 'beauty' in order to control how we look, but how we *are*, and that's the scary part. How we think. How we *be*. I guess you guys should know right away I'm a Marxist. I support the Sandinistas, and the leftist guerrilla forces in Chad. I'm not a vulgar Marxist or anything—I mean, I don't pick my nose in public (that's supposed to be a little joke)—no, I guess you'd have to call me a post-structural Marxist. I give credit to Althusser, but I'm not an acolyte of *anybody's*. Anyway"—with another little flourish of her black purse—"if you'll excuse me, I've got to find a ladies' room." Beatrice glanced over her shoulder, then pointed. One tiny cuticle of her index finger was perceptibly tagged with chocolate. "That's it there, I think."

When she was gone, both Rodney and I took long, contemplative sips of our hot, bitter coffee. Around us the scrubbed linoleum still smelled strongly of ammonia and disinfectant, and every once in a while the matronly woman behind the counter, wearing a black hairnet and plastic gloves, gave us a rather dirty look, as if she expected us at any moment to run off with something. Coolness drifted through me. I was very high in the air, drifting among birds and planes. It was incredibly quiet in the high air. There were no words in sight, not even fragments of words. Eventually, without looking up, I leaned toward Rodney.

"What's she talking about?" I asked.

Rodney didn't say anything right away. I heard the flash of a match which he dropped into the black ashtray. "I don't know," he said after a while, watching the bright match flare, beat and extinguish with a tiny puff. "But I think it may be another load of crap."

We would take Beatrice to my house in the afternoons when we weren't scavenging other houses, but she never put out. She always said she was going to put out, but she never really did. Though my interest in the outcome was philosophical rather than immediate, I would watch the slow struggles Rodney waged with Beatrice on the poor, makeshift couch in my living room with perfect equanimity. They would kiss for hours, penetrating into the roots of one another's mouths, breathing deep into one another's lungs and hearts, shifting and turning very slowly, Rodney's leg between Beatrice's, his arm around her waist. Sometimes I would watch them for a while, but then I would watch the television instead. "The Rockford Files," perhaps, which I adored, or "Barnaby Jones," which I could at least endure. "Mmm," Rodney might say, though Beatrice herself always remained chastely, even demurely silent. "Mmm, baby." It didn't sound quite right to me, but perhaps, I thought, Rodney was still practicing. Perhaps love wasn't something you felt, but rather something you learned. Then, abruptly, Rodney's hand would stray too far and, before either of us knew it, "it" would be abruptly over.

"It's just not right," Beatrice said, sitting up and running her hand through her stringy hair. One leg was folded underneath her, and a hard, reasonless and abstract gaze made her eyes seem very cold and distant. "I guess I'm not in the right mood or something."

"What do you mean it's not *right.*" Rodney was running his hands anxiously through his own unsprung hair. He resembled a broker during a crash, his shirt rumpled and undone, his eyes slightly wild and bloodshot. "What's *right* like? How am I supposed to know the *right* time? How'm I supposed to know what the *right* mood's like?"

Sometimes she petted and tried to console him, and sometimes they would even start kissing again, their thin lips bumping again and again at one another. Then their bodies would do that slow horizontal dance again, and I would watch just for that movement, that steady and directionless rhythm of their bodies on the sofa. Bits of foam rubber were spilling from underneath the tangled bedspread like sawdust from a lathe. My interest was merely clinical.

I knew it was the vital dance. I knew it was something very serious and inexplicable for Rodney and that, with luck, it would someday be the same for me as well. But for now the irresolvable dialectic of that motion was what fascinated me. I wanted them to be like that forever, like a glittery mobile or a perpetual object of performance art. I wanted them moving there together on my sofa until I forgot about them, until I accepted that movement of theirs as calmly as I accepted the walls and ceiling of my house, as firmly as I accepted my mom's secret and brooding presence in the silent back bedroom. Motion not as a way of living, or as a dance of bodies, but as a sort of universal presumption. Bodies moved, cars moved, planes moved in the sky. Rocks and trees and garbage cans and concrete cinder blocks moved. The earth moved and the stars moved. There was the spiral movement of entire galaxies, and the fundamental movement of atoms and quarks and merely theoretical matter. Everything was moving everywhere all the time, because nobody was anywhere they wanted to be in the first place. Time, when you considered the elemental, even archetypal fact of motion itself, was just a formality, a record, a graph. Movement was life, and when you moved your body into the body of a woman you initiated other movements, other lives. Cells moved, proteins and enzymes moved together, particles of minerals and plasma moved in the blood. I didn't care whether Rodney consummated his obsession with Beatrice or not, because I had come to realize that motion itself was destiny enough. Its consummation would only inaugurate a moment of dulled, sleepy disavowal. You could pretend motion had stopped for a little while. Then you would lie down and sleep until your dreams woke you.

"You know what America is, don't you, guys?" Beatrice asked us one day, examining herself in her compact, plucking at one damp, tangled eyelash. "It's a big black hole that sucks everything in. You know who founded America, don't you? People who could pretend they were anybody they wanted to be, because that's what America is. Anything you want it to be."

"America's the frontier that's never conquered," I said, reaching to turn the television volume down. I swiveled around on the rug to face her, feeling something slip in my stomach, my groin, a feeling as if I had swallowed something very cold and heavy. "America's motion, America's always somewhere else. If we can't go other places, we can be those other places instead. My mom always said that's why we're Californians—because we don't need to be here. We can always be anywhere else in the universe besides California, and still be here too. America's the dialectic. It's what Hegel talks about in *The Phenomenology of Mind.* The dialectic."

Somewhere deep in my house I could hear Mom silently nodding her head. She wasn't approving, though. She was just nodding her head.

Rodney let out an exasperated sigh, and reached for his Dos Equis. "Jesus Christ. Just what I need." He took a long pull from the beer and quickly lit a Tareyton. He looked dispassionately from me to Beatrice, from Beatrice to me.

His face was puffy and creased with worried lines. "Fucking stereo," he said.

I felt very good sitting there, watching Rodney and Beatrice on the couch. Rodney looked at his cigarette. Beatrice, out of the corner of her eye, looked at Rodney.

Life had grown very substantial and real for me while my mom lay quietly in her room. I had everything now. A family, a house, a lucrative job, good times and faithful friends. I had the sweet clutter of books in my room. I had cigarettes, good whiskey, excellent home-cooked meals, a reputable broker, new shoes, the privacy of my own mind, healthy sexual curiosity and, somewhere in the world, Dad, who would always take me back if things got too rough. I felt settled, but not conventional. I was learning how to live my own life and yet still love Mom too, the lesson I knew Mom had always meant for me to learn. Mom was very real and immanent all the time. She was a vast incontrovertible force, extensive like gravity or sound. She was like God, she was like air. And she was always in perfect control, especially when she wasn't in any control at all.

12

"Is your mom seeing anyone?" Dad asked me, over and over again. "You know you can tell me. You know you can tell me if she's seeing someone." His voice grew somewhat webbed and anxious. There was something sudden about Dad's voice when he considered Mom's possible infidelity. He reminded me of Rodney, exasperated by Beatrice's muggy sex. He was always very quick to change the subject. "Is she all right?" he asked. "Is she eating properly? Do you have enough school clothes and spending money? Should I wire you some? Should I stop calling? Should I let you go on pretending I don't exist at all?" Dad's voice strained against the force of our lives, divided from us by a thin, translucent bubble. The bubble's skin transmitted Dad's voice and texture, but not his body, not his acting presence. "Does she ever ask about me, or wonder how I am? Do you think some nights she misses me, or says my name out loud?"

"She's not seeing anyone right now, Dad," I said. "She's working very hard, and likes her job very much. She's trying to work out a lot of things right now, and just needs to be left alone for a while. She asks about you all the time, and I tell her that you've been asking about her. She wants you to know she still misses you, but that she needs this time to think about nobody but herself. She needs to live as if nobody else in the world exists except her. She needs to be left alone awhile longer, Dad. She needs to know we love her enough to trust her to be by herself.''

Dad's voice was growing more tinny and desperate as Mom's voice, sinking into the silence of her own room, grew more inaudible and self-assured. Sometimes static swirled and seethed on Dad's telephone line like foam on a seashore, leaving behind broken bits of shell and rock and bone. "I think it's time you both came home," Dad said one night. "I think I've been patient long enough. I think it's about time you both learned a little something about responsibility. I'm talking about things like right and moral duty. I don't mean I believe in God, but I do believe in responsibility. And so will you someday, sport. So will you someday.''

"What does your dad do?" Beatrice asked one night after I hung up and returned to the living room. The distant, stellar noise of the telephone continued to wheel around me like lights in a planetarium. "Is your dad in business? I always imagined your dad a big, successful businessman, Phillip. It's in your blood, I can tell. You'll be a businessman too, I'm sure. When you grow up."

Dad was still there in the house with us. He was more

idea than thing, more impression than voice. Dad wasn't life. Dad was history.

"It's nothing to be ashamed of—business. Business convenes secret and ghostly ceremonies in the world. Ceremonies which the world needs, or else the world wouldn't have them." Beatrice was gazing abstractedly at the living room wall, turning one long tangled coil of oily hair behind her ear. "It's as real as rocks, as organic as trees." It was almost eleven o'clock and Rodney had gone into my bedroom to sleep. Beatrice held a half-finished glass of Nestlé's Quik in her lap, its rim whorled with milky deposits and fingerprints like the etched fossils of intricate trilobites. "Business always works, even when nature doesn't. When plants stop photosynthesizing, business will manufacture its own atmosphere. When other moons and planets crash into our seas and wreck the world, business will mine and redistribute them. Business is the world's real nature, Phillip. We are all fleeing nature and using what it has taught us about business to make our world vaster and more perfect."

Beatrice had breasts—little breasts, granted, but breasts nonetheless. When I lifted up her mascara-smudged Lacoste T-shirt and reached underneath to touch one, it was as warm as I expected. I brushed it gently with the palm of my untrained hand and then, softly and with clinical care, palpated it the same way a doctor might examine for cysts. I could feel the clusters of glands like tiny grapes all joined up to the nipple's tuberous root. The surface skin was soft. I could smell Beatrice's slightly unwashed odor, like the smell Mom's laundry used to make when soaking in some motel sink. Holding Beatrice's breast in my hand made me feel a sort of cool and intellectual redemption. I don't mean I wanted to be a baby again; I didn't want to be nurtured by this breast. I wanted only to regain a sort of molecular integrity. I wanted to crawl back into the cellular warmth of my own body, not some woman's womb. I wanted to grow so small I could see protons and electrons bristling in my tiny night sky like showers of meteors and cosmic dust. I did not want to procreate that first time I touched a girl's breast, I wanted to uncreate. I wanted to penetrate life in search of the unliving. I wanted to exonerate the fundamental and fragmentary lifelessness of things. Without a second thought, I leaned forward on my tiptoes and kissed my Beatrice on the lips, which were still slightly smudged with Nestlé's Quik. Her lips didn't move a muscle. I don't believe either of us felt a thing.

"You can't hide your desire for me," I said.

Beatrice snapped her gum.

"Our two bodies are meant to be one," I said. "You know it's true. You knew it was true when we first met."

I stepped back, removing my hand from her. I expected I would touch a girl's breast again someday, and remembered the cocoon I once discovered on the branch of a rosebush. I had broken off the branch and placed the cocoon inside a glass jar, the lid of which I punctured with a sharp knife to allow air so the cocoon could breathe. I included branches of other trees and bushes, leaves, stones and dirt for both scenery and a sense of environmental continuity. The cocoon just hung there, day after day, motionless, cobwebby and dry as a bone. Then one day I decided it must be thirsty, and poured in a generous helping of Coca-Cola through the punctured aluminum lid. A few days later the cocoon withered and collapsed on the branch like overripe fruit. Then, one night, when I was asleep, a few green drops oozed out.

I took Beatrice's hand. It was, as always, grimy and smudged. It left a soft glimmering residue wherever it touched.

"I think it's time you met my mom," I told her. Then I took her down the long dark hallway to Mom's silent room.

"Hello, Mom. It's me. It's Phillip. You remember me. Your son."

The darkness seethed behind the door. Dead planets moved there. Somehow comprehensible alien languages whispered and transformed themselves into things. Light wrapped textures around itself, like young children in their parents' clothing.

"I know I said I'd leave you alone for a while, Mom. I'm not trying to hurt you, or break any promises. Dad called and I only told him what I knew you wanted him to hear. There's a fresh salad in the Tupperware bowl on the bottom shelf of the fridge. There's a frozen lasagne you can heat up in the microwave. Now, Beatrice and I will go back into the living room and leave you alone, and if you want to go fix yourself something to eat you can. I promise we won't get in your way, I just wanted you to meet my friend Beatrice. I'm in love with Beatrice, Mom, but it's a completely different type of love from the way I love you. I just wanted you to know."

I could feel Beatrice's body standing beside me in the dark hall. Tonight her body was the only warmth in our house.

"It's love without passion, Mom. I don't feel any passion for Beatrice, just love. She might as well be a rock, or a landmark, or a memory, or a curious bug as far as physical passion's concerned. She might as well be chemistry or math. Anyway, Mom. This is Beatrice."

I gave Beatrice's wrist a little squeeze.

"Hello, Mrs. Davis," Beatrice said after a while.

Beatrice's calm voice resounded in our still house like a summons.

"Now, Mom, we'll leave you alone."

Both Beatrice and I thought we could hear Mom breathing in her bed as we returned back down the dark hall to the living room sofa again.

That night while Beatrice and I slept huddled together on the living room couch I awoke and heard movements in the kitchen. The weak filmy light from the streets filtered through our dusty venetian blinds, thinning and thickening like pages being turned back and forth in a book. I heard a single glass fall and break. I heard rummaging in the ice-maker. I wondered if Mom was feeling OK, and thought I should start leaving vitamins out for her. I heard the coffee grinder, and waxy cardboard being torn from the frozen lasagne. Dishes and silverware began to clatter, the refrigerator door opened twice. Then the initiating chime of the microwave, and I did not hear so much as feel that long slow charge of heatless energy building, a kind of cosmic affinity being conceded deep down there among our secondhand kitchen appliances. The coffee was percolating on the countertop, the aluminum lid rattling. The microwave chimed again and buzzed, and a firm quick hand clicked it off. I could smell the antiseptic prepackaged smell of it, the thawed meat and cheese steaming. Beatrice, asleep against my thin pale chest, stirred; she muttered something. One of her bare legs slowly wrapped itself around mine and she began faintly snoring. I heard the footsteps in the kitchen going back and forth, and boiling coffee being poured into a ceramic mug.

"I think it's time you came out again," I whispered, watching the door to the kitchen which adjoined the living room. "I'm getting worried about you. I don't know how much more neglect I can promise. I miss you, Dad misses you. We all miss you, even the vast world. I'm sure it will all get better. I'm sure if you come out and try to face things, things will get better again on their own."

The noises stilled in the kitchen. There was a slow breathing hush filling up the flashing lacquered walls. There was thinking going on in there. A very strong and willful mind at work. Then, succinctly, a long sipping of coffee.

Beatrice, in her sleep, gently kissed my shoulder.

The footsteps swung through the kitchen again and then, in the doorway, I saw a tall shadow which only slowly, holding the coffee in one hand and the lasagne on a plate in the other, emerged into the dim mothy light of the living room windows.

"What you think you're doing?" Rodney asked, wincing against the bitter coffee. He gestured with the cup at Beatrice. "That's my woman you got there." His face was puffy and his hair stuck out like Larry's on "The Three Stooges." He stood there for a few moments, not looking at Beatrice and me so much as through us. Then he sat down on the floor and began to eat his lasagne. His fork ticked dully again and again against the cheesy plate.

"Sometimes I don't know," Rodney said, wiping his brow with the back of his greasy hand. "Sometimes I don't know if I was born mean, or if the world just made me that way." He lay the dish and fork on the floor with a deliberate clatter. He looked at the musty, glowing venetian blinds. Outside the phototropic streetlamps were beginning to dim; the power lines and parked metal cars began to buzz slightly and deeply on the empty street, filling up with the sun's early warmth.

"I think Dan Duryea said that," Rodney said. His sleepy eyes remained trained upon the cracked venetian blinds. "I really get a kick out of that goddamn Dan Duryea."

13

The following evening we finally decided to take Mom's car out for an exploratory little spin. The engine started rough, but it started, and I let it warm up in the strange and generally unglimpsed garage of Mom's house where everything, even the shadows, seemed inverted and unreal.

"We got wheels!" Rodney declared, jiggling in the front passenger seat and thrumming Beatrice's thighs with a paradiddle, a flam-paradiddle, then a spotty double roll. "Phillip's got us wheels, man! Let's *roll!* Let's do like they do on TV and let's *roll!*" It was the only time I ever saw Rodney excited about anything. Rodney even offered to give me five, but my mind was too intent on the various pedals and knobs and levers before me. They were all familiar, but they were all unfamiliar too. They articulated me with that world of adults which was accessible in every way except the mind's. When I touched them, I was touching some ineffable something of adults which made adults different. It was not the things themselves, but some mysterious identity behind the things. Signals, ashtray, wipers, defrost, tone and volume, fan, air, seat belt, dash. I eased the accelerator down and up, the engine expanding in the damp garage with a choppy roar and then diminishing again like passing private airplanes. I practiced engaging the clutch and killed the engine three or four times. Each time the car started with a throatier, smoother voice. It was the voice of mechanical discretion. It was the voice of the whirring conspiratorial notions of engaged mechanical parts.

So that was the winter I learned to drive, propped up by two volumes of the Yellow Pages, and always at night. It was a dry, brittle winter in the San Fernando Valley, and the only snow around was painted on the shopfront windows of barbershops and Exxon stations. Santa Claus, flanked by bikinied elves, sweated in his bright red underdrawers as he lugged his gifts past high palm trees and a bright yellow sun. The streets were filled with young girls and boys standing about, leaning against their bicycles and eating ice creams and candies and bright orangish Slurpees they had just purchased from 7-Eleven. The air was heavy still with the always rich jacarandas, as if winter never came.

Some nights it rained, and we drove our car through long ripping puddles in the flat streets of the poorly irrigated basin, around Valley College, down Van Nuys and up into the Burbank Hills into Glendale, Pasadena, Whittier. When it rained the entire San Fernando Valley flooded with the bright rainwater and the reflected lights of other cars. I liked to downshift at stoplights and then, in neutral, coast through when no cops were watching and jerk quickly into second again, sometimes feeling that sudden loss of gravity when the tires spun and the smoke and water steamed together and wrapped us up in a world very invisible, yet also very real. The windows of the houses all betrayed bright Christmas trees with silver tinsel, red bulbous ornaments and inconstant strings of flashing lights. Enormous plastic Santas, reindeer and manger scenes stood out on the front yards like migrant workers, and whenever we turned on the radio they were playing Christmas carols. "Jingle Bell Rock." "A California Christmas." "O Come All Ye Faithful." "O Little Town of Bethlehem." O Christmas, I thought. O Mom, O Dad. O History and Motion, O Motion and Light.

"Turn off that crap," Rodney said, still happily thrumming his hands—against his own thighs now. Another of the bitter silences had interrupted his necking with Beatrice, who sat between us in the front seat now, one hand surreptitiously on my knee. She was sucking a LifeSaver. "It's still fucking November," Rodney said. "I haven't even digested my Thanksgiving fucking turkey yet."

"Do you believe in Christ?" Beatrice asked, gently disengaging Rodney's hand from her shoulder.

"You mean like Christ, the son of God?" I had just lit my Tareyton, and was reinserting Mom's lighter into the dash.

Beatrice, her eyes somewhat dazed by the glimmering streets, nodded.

"You mean like the bread and fishes?" I asked. "You

104

mean like the Star of Bethlehem, and the three wise men, and dying for all our sins?'' I was starting to get a little excited. "Christ wore a halo on his head, even when he was a baby. He slept one night with the carpenter. He gave speeches on a mountaintop and collected apostles like trading stamps. One day they nailed his hands to a cross. Then, a few days later, he lived again. Which always made me wonder why God let him die in the first place. Because it was a symbol, that's my guess. God never cares about human beings. God, like any halfway decent politician, only cares about symbolic language.''

"I dig the story about the bread and fishes," Rodney said. "We're talking luncheon meat for forty thousand. We're talking pimento, and coleslaw, and fried chicken. We're not talking your average lousy tuna salad. If my stupid mom had been there, she'd have been asking why they didn't serve any fucking tuna salad.''

"I think Christ is an idea we came up with because we needed it," Beatrice said. I glanced at her in the rearview mirror. Her eyes were still closed.

"I think we might as well believe in Christ as believe in anything," Beatrice said. "I mean, Christ makes just about as much sense as anything else I can think of."

"Like Success," Rodney said.

"Or Self," I said.

"Or Family," Beatrice said. "Or Woman. Love. Disease. Heartbreak. Death. God. Goals. Reification. Fried food. High fiber optics. Disinvestment. Cancer. AIDS. Genes, skin, tissue, soul." Beatrice's face and neck were covered with so many of Rodney's red, splotchy hickeys she resembled a victim of the Great Plague. "They're all ideas we need. The question shouldn't be whether they're real or not, or whether we believe they're real. I mean, I can't tell you how impossibly *mundane* that all is, all these ridiculous endless arguments about what's reality and all. They're such imbecile restraints upon our thinking. Empiricism isn't a way of thinking; empiricism is a way of being. Of being a dickhead, anyway. Do we *believe* we need the idea, that's what interests me. Do we *believe* we need Christ, Phillip? Or do we believe we have any good reasons for *not* believing?"

"Don't forget childhood," I said. "Childhood's one thing don't forget."

"I believe we got to stop at a service station so I can drop a log," Rodney said. "I mean, I'd really *love* to continue this highly intellectual conversation and all, but first I think—I mean, I *believe*—I *believe* I've got to chop me some wood. I *believe* I've got to cut me one mighty humongous loaf."

Whenever I returned home Mom left traces of herself around the house just so I would know she was all right. It was like a secret Morse of displaced objects, punctuated by unvoiced sighs and iconic, invisible gestures. An unwashed glass on the kitchen countertop. A bottle of Seagram's discarded in the trash basket under the sink. Sometimes she would leave a pillowcase stuffed with dirty linen outside her door for me to wash. Sometimes there might even be a little note attached to it. Usually it said:

Dear Phillip,

I love you.

Love, Mom

And of course I always left Mom a note in return:

Dear Mom,

I love you too.

Love, Phillip.

"You can't grow up thinking life's like your mom lives it, Phillip. I think that's the important thing. I think that's the real reason I want you back home with me. I'm not trying to say it might not seem fun, especially to a young boy. But what seems fun isn't always right, and I think you know what I'm saying. What's right isn't always fun. I'm talking of course about all those corny, old-fashioned values your mom used to ridicule me for trying to hold on to. Things like honor, commitment, duty, and yes, even good old-fashioned family loyalty. Hell, I'm not trying to sound like some sentimental old fool or anything. It's just that the love you feel for your lawful wife and child happens to be a lot more 'fun' in its very difficult, thankless way than any free

107

ride in your mom's car. I think you know what I'm saying, Phillip. If I'm not too far wrong about my own son, I think I can say you've got a good idea what your old dad's talking about."

Often after Dad hung up my head continued ringing with his voice. His voice was something I carried with me now, just as I'm sure Dad carried my baby picture in his wallet. "What if everyone behaved like you and your mom. What if the police, or the firemen, or the president just did whatever they damned felt like it, whenever they damn felt like it." That Christmas Rodney and I would park Mom's Rambler in the driveways of the homes we looted. We not only took resalable commodities now, we took the heavier and more flamboyant presents from under strange Christmas trees. We took many of the brighter trees themselves, and lined them up, already decorated, in the living room of my mom's house. "What kind of life would that be like, Phillip, where people completely forgot the responsibilities they had towards other people? I think it would be a pretty frightening world, don't you? What if there was a fire and the firemen were all off having a good time with their friends?" We took festive wreaths and strings of popcorn and hand-painted porcelain angels and music boxes in the shapes of coned trees or leering Santas or elves in workshops. "What if Russia invaded and our president was traipsing off somewhere and hadn't even left a forwarding address? What do you think those Russians would do? I think I can tell you what they'd do, Phillip. They'd walk all over us. They'd walk all over this great land of ours." We found a dog tied to a building support post in the basement of one house, ringed by its own puddled urine and moldering, cocoon-like feces, its skin scraped and chafed under its collar, its leash entangled by its tattered smelly blanket. "They'd start putting people into concentration camps. They'd ruin our industries and entire free market system. The government would tell everybody what everything costs, and exactly how much they could buy. Nobody'd have one ounce of individuality left anymore. Nobody'd ever remember, after a few years or so, how wonderful things had been, and what a terrible mess we made of our great country."

We unleashed the dog and carried it down to our car. It was a dachshund, and we named it Contrite, because it always looked very apologetic about everything. Contrite slept in Rodney's lap all the way home. Sometimes I couldn't hear anything during the day except Dad's voice. Sometimes, though, if I tried hard enough, I could hear Rodney's.

"You know what Christmas means? It means if I love you, I'm going to buy you a whole load of crap. The more I love you, the bigger the load gets. Sometimes, if you can afford it, you can get your loved one literally tons of crap, and then they're really loved. Love love love. It's a terrific idea. Low overhead. Unbelievable mark-up value. I think love is one thing that will always sell really well. Ho ho ho. Merry Christmas." Rodney was rolling a loose joint on his knee. He twisted the ends and then held it up for my inspection. "Ho ho ho. *Merry* Christmas. Buy some more crap. Come on, line up and buy yourselves a whole lot more crap. Here's something nice. Bought any crap quite like *this* crap recently? Crap crap crap. Ho ho ho. Like that mechanical Santa Claus in the Montgomery Ward's window display. Ho ho ho. Merry Christmas, everybody. Have yourselves all one fucking hell of a *merry* little Christmas, all you poor stupid saps. Line up and get taken, that's what I say, that's what Santa says. We take MasterCard cards and Visa cards. Come on, losers. Line up on this side. Get your money taken on that side." Contrite lay asleep in Rodney's blanketed lap. The car smelled faintly of Contrite's urine, which had a tendency to dribble meekly out whenever he wagged his tail with particular enthusiam.

"Could you do me a favor, Rodney?" I said. I was looking past him in the rearview mirror. Then, at the next streetlight, the police car behind us turned left. "Could you lighten up just a bit? I mean, it is Christmas and all. Just do me a favor and lighten up a little *tiny* little bit, OK?"

MASS

14

Then one afternoon after New Year's Rodney and I were transporting a Panasonic color portable television upstairs to my living room when we discovered Dad sitting very obvious and awkward on the sofa's warped foam rubber. He was wearing a very nice navy-blue Brooks Brothers three-piece suit. He was wearing polished cordovan shoes. He was wearing a white knit tie. "Merry Christmas," Dad said. His golden cuff links gleamed. "Do you remember me? Do you remember who I am?"

Rodney and I very slowly set the Panasonic down upon a pair of wooden crates which were filled with soft drinks looted from the home of some Pepsi executive. I suffered a few moments of light-headed, almost giddy disorientation. Everything about my living room seemed either too large or too small. I didn't know what to say. For a few moments I thought I had staggered stupidly into the wrong home.

"I know I said I'd leave you both alone," Dad said, "but I wanted to bring your presents. It is Christmas, after all."

By way of explanation, Dad gestured at his alligator-skin briefcase with silver clasps. The briefcase was open on the plastic coffee table, revealing festive packages wrapped with bright foil paper, ribbons and blossoming bows. "I even brought a few things for your mom."

"I think I better go," Rodney said. He took the smoldering cigarette out of his mouth and cupped it in his hand. The smoke uncurled secretly through his fingers.

"I'll call you," I said, and then suddenly found myself alone in the house with Dad.

Dad had very distinguished graying blond hair. He had large, ruddy and perfectly manicured hands. His white teeth flashed like spotlights on a movie set. He was a very handsome man, I decided. Even handsome enough for Mom.

We ignored the silence together for a while. The silence inhabited the room like a third presence, or a block of raw marble, implicit with its own hidden Aristotelian form. We smiled at one another. Dad looked at me, then at the Panasonic on the Pepsi crates, still smiling, as if trying to distinguish our relative value.

"That's a nice TV," Dad said after a while.

"Yes, it is," I replied, thinking, This is history. Today I grow up. "It's a Panasonic."

I couldn't just dispatch Dad off without dinner and a few seasonal drinks, especially not after the gifts. A portable CD and cassette player with extendable stereo speakers. Def Leppard. Simply Red. Bryan Adams. Rossini's *Guglielmo Tell* and Strauss's *Der Rosenkavalier*. "Even when you were

114

little," Dad said, "you always loved opera." There were dictionaries and desk lamps and an electronic typewriter. There were shirts and sweaters and underwear and socks. There was five hundred dollars cash, and two five-hundred-dollar money orders, one in Mom's name and one in mine. There was a fully assembled Stingray bicycle, a pair of walkie-talkies, a crystal radio set, a deluxe Sony Walkman and two ten-pack boxes of Maxell XLII-S 90-minute blank cassette tapes. "You can tape directly from the CD onto the blank tapes," Dad said. "You'd be surprised. It sure sounds a lot better than those prepackaged tapes you buy at the record store." For Mom there was a string of white pearls, and one red rose tidily enveloped by clear cellophane. "I'll trust you to make sure she gets them," Dad said. "I haven't any intention of bothering your mother if she doesn't want to be bothered. I'll be gone bright and early tomorrow morning. You won't even hear me leave. Here—save these receipts. If anything doesn't fit or doesn't work or you just plain don't want it, make sure you take it back and get a full refund." While Dad spoke he gazed off down the hall towards Mom's room. He knew exactly where it was, and that Mom was in it. "I know how she gets. I know there's no sense trying to make your mom change her mind about anything."

I fixed almond and broccoli Stroganoff. "It's got broccoli and carrots and cauliflower in it," I told Dad. "It's got rice and chick-peas and zucchini. It's got paprika and pota-toes and seaweed. It's vegan, so if you want a little cheese on yours, I'll melt some mozzarella in the microwave. I've

been getting more and more into vegan food lately, Dad."
I wondered if he was impressed, and passed him the orange
juice. I served the Stroganoff on our house's only two
chipped white plates, allowing Dad the fork while I used
one of our plastic spoons. There was a large hot fire cracking
in the fireplace, and the living room was still littered with
bright crumpled Christmas paper, ribbons, frilly bows and
cardboard packaging.

"Isn't this nice," Dad said. He had taken off his jacket
and unbuttoned three buttons of his vest. He had rolled up
the sleeves of his starched white shirt, displaying the deep
tan of his hairy arms. His teeth flashed, either cavityless or
immaculately capped. "You've turned into quite a respectable little cook, Phillip. I used to be a bit of a cook myself.
Back when we were all together, and you were still a baby.
Every evening when I got home from work, I used to cook
meals for you and your mom."

We drank Manhattans beside the fireplace. Once all the
gift wrapping was consumed, Dad walked down to the corner 7-Eleven for a pair of Presto Logs. After my third drink
or so, I loosened up enough to request one of Dad's Marlboros, and even smoked it in his presence. "It's OK to have
a cigarette every now and then," Dad said, examining the
dim ember of his own. "But when you start smoking like
me—two or three packs a day—then you better think hard
about quitting. Otherwise, there's nothing wrong with doing
anything, so long as it's in moderation."

———

I couldn't let Dad drive home alone that night. His face was flushed, and there was a remote, insipid smile on his face as he contemplated the fire. I offered him the troughed sofa, the pillow from my bed, and my new sleeping bag. "I'm really glad we did this, sport," Dad said. He had taken off his shirt and loosened the belt of his trousers. He was still holding the empty glass in his hand. "I know it's been a strange situation for a young fellow your age, but I want you to know I'm proud of the way you've handled everything. You're a strong, bright young man, just as I always knew you'd be. Your mom's very lucky to have someone like you who understands and loves her as much as you do. I never expected everything to work out perfect for us, in fact I always sort of expected things wouldn't work out at all. But I'm glad we can spend this sort of time together and just be friends, you know? I'm hoping that whatever happens to all of us, you and I'll always have that."

I don't remember what time we finally went to bed, but my dreams that night were thick with visions of carnival and violence. Strange misshapen men with guns tramped through dry, brushy forests; drunken women danced wildly on tabletops, eventually tearing off all their clothes while crowds of voices roared inarticulately around them like an ocean; alien creatures descended the black night sky in tremendous spaceships, filled with terrible viruses and gigantic, ciliated bacteria which throbbed and pulsed in deep chambers, energizing the ships like fuel. A beautiful white-haired man in flowing white robes emerged from the spaceship and offered me something from one of his soft pink hands. I was on my knees before him. His other hand stroked my brow. Politely, even demurely, I refused; his hand offered again. I refused again, and hard multiple arms grasped me from behind and handed me up to him, bound and helpless on a gold and silver tray. The church below was filled with thousands and thousands of people. At that moment, as I was ritually dismembered before the adoring cries of thousands of dark shapeless figures (the event was being televised, I knew, for modular black cameras weaved the air around me on the platform, attached to long intricate metal cables and winches), I awoke and heard Dad outside in the hallway prying at the lock to Mom's bedroom door. I got up from my bed. I walked to my door and opened it.

"It's very simple, really," Dad said, not even looking up at me in the dark hallway. "You just have to fiddle this little doohickey inside. It's vertical when locked. You've got to fiddle it around until it's horizontal." Dad was sitting cross-legged on the hall floor, wearing only his finely woven and partially unzipped navy-blue trousers and a white Hanes T-shirt. He had an icy, fresh Manhattan in his lap. "Your mom used to do this to me all the time. She was always locking me out when she was upset, but she wanted me to come in and comfort her. It was like a little game we played." He held an untwisted paperclip in one hand, and peered into a tiny round hole of the rattly aluminum doorknob. "These stupid doorknobs are designed to be picked. You used to accidentally lock yourself in rooms all the time when you were little." Dad inserted the paperclip, fiddled around a bit. I couldn't hear another single sound in the entire world. "I'll never forget how scared you used to get. By the time I'd get the door open you'd be hysterical. You'd just be standing there, clenching your tiny red hands, the tears pouring down your little T-shirt."

"Mom," I said, as gently as I could. "Mom, it's Dad. He's coming in."

At that moment the tinny doorknob clicked, and Dad turned it. Dad was still sitting cross-legged on the floor with his Manhattan, and I was standing looking over his shoulder, when the door of Mom's bedroom finally opened.

15

"She's beautiful," Dad said.

"I don't think she's awake."

"Her eyes are open."

"Sometimes her eyes are open but she's not awake."

"Has she been eating properly?"

"I do my best."

"What about vitamin and mineral supplements?"

"I started leaving them out for her, but I don't know if she's been taking them or not."

"What about her cigarettes?"

"I think she's stopped. She's still drinking, though."

"That'll have to stop too. We'll want her eating more fresh fruits and vegetables, more salads. Hot soups and plenty of juices and mineral water. Mainly she just needs a little more exercise, some sun, a few less worries. She'll have to see a good doctor, perhaps a nutritionist."

"I think she's better off staying at home."

"I'll find doctors who make house calls."

"Mom needs her own space, Dad."

"Everybody needs their own space, son. But sometimes their space isn't just their own. Sometimes their personal space infringes on the personal space of other people. That's just a way of saying we all have responsibilities, son. I think I've told you this before, haven't I? We all have very important responsibilities to people other than ourselves." Dad was cautiously approaching Mom like some aborigine trying to console an electric light bulb.

"Dad. I don't think I understand."

Finally, gently, Dad sat on the edge of Mom's bed. The springs emitted a tiny, querulous creak. He wasn't looking at me either. He was looking at the empty bottles of Jack Daniel's and Wild Turkey piled in the corner beside some tattered, outdated issues of *TV Guide*. The neglected vitamins lay heaped on the untidy bureau. Dad's hand gently stroked Mom's stomach underneath the blankets. Mom's face was flushed and serene, like the face of a Madonna. She really was just as beautiful as ever, I thought.

"What I'm trying to say, son, is that very soon you're not going to be alone anymore. You're going to have a little brother, or maybe even a little sister, to take care of. Your mother's going to have a baby."

For a few moments, nothing moved in the entire universe.

"Just look at your mom's smile and you'll know," Dad said. "Just look at her. Your mother always did have a very beautiful smile."

––––––

Understandably, I greeted Dad's arrival with rather mixed emotions, to say the least. Because he was my dad I loved him, but because Mom was his wife that meant he loved her too. There were enough men in Mom's life already, I thought, preparing breakfast for four now instead of two. Dad's lap-top IBM computer was equipped with a modem, which he was usually plugging into the telephone line about the same time I began frying bacon and eggs. Dad sat very erect and deadly serious at the new dining room table he had bought us while strange graphs and data flashed on the amber screen. The lap-top made beeping sounds every once in a while. "What's the dividend yield on that?" Dad asked the phone, when his computer wasn't on it. "Why can't we convert into unit trusts? Sure, sure, but I can't make a living on theories, Harry. I can put credit in the bank. I can invest future expectations. But I can't buy a meal with theories. I can't even buy a good song." Sometimes Dad just sat there and listened. He always wore cleanly laundered and pressed striped shirts and pure wool slacks. His face was always closely shaven. He wore a mild, somewhat suggestive cologne. "All right," he told the phone. He punched buttons on his lap-top, reengaged telephone and modem. "You can start transmitting now." Additional figures and charts emerged on the bright screen. Sometimes Dad paused for a while, watching the cool articulate data emerging from his humming monitor.

Dad communicated all over the world with stock investment analysis coordinators, banking management consultants, corporate holdings portfolio advisers, industrial efficiency maintenance engineers, agents and brokers and realtors and accountants and bankers. While I set our table and prepared our generous meals, while Mom lay in her bed growing my young, immaculate and ethereal sibling in her womb, Dad spoke words not with other people, but with the entire system of language itself. Dad didn't speak things, he spoke systems. Just as systems, I was equally sure, spoke him.

"One of these days we'll have to get you started managing your own money," Dad told me one day, drinking Dos Equis and reading the Dow figures as they unreeled from his ink-jet Epson printer.

"I've got a little money put aside already," I said. I was pouring green soap powder into the soap dispenser of our new Whirlpool dishwasher. I closed the lid, cranked it shut, and engaged the first rinse cycle. "You know, in case of emergencies." The spraying water sounded like static on the radio.

I brought Dad the latest Sears money market statement. I brought him the Dividend Reinvestment figures for my 200 shares of San Diego Gas and Electric. I brought him the joint savings account Rodney and I held at Bank of America. I brought him the savings deposit key. The savings deposit box contained a number of gold and silver coins, some small diversified holdings in various California utility companies, and Mom's diamond wedding band.

Dad examined the various documents for a while. Figures were flashing on the screen of his lap-top, but he wasn't watching them. Every once in a while he whistled a tiny, indefinite melody, not with his lips but with the tip of his tongue against the hard edge of his palate. Ever since I could remember, I always wanted to whistle like that.

When Dad finally looked up at me, his eyes held that reflectionless, distracted expression they usually held whenever he spoke about Mom. He gestured with the various papers in his hand. "This isn't too bad," he said after a while.

"When's he leaving?" Rodney asked. "I thought you said he was leaving yesterday."

Dad was in the shower. I had detached the phone from the lap-top, which had emitted a treacherous little beep.

"That's what he told me."

"Why don't you tell him to leave?"

"I can't just do that. He's my dad."

"Your mom doesn't want him around, does she? What's your mom think about all this?"

"I don't know," I said. "I don't know what Mom thinks about anymore."

In fact, Mom seemed a lot more peaceful and happy now that Dad was back to take care of us again. Because Mom refused to take the lithium Dad's doctor prescribed, every afternoon around four o'clock a private nurse named Syd arrived and gave her an injection. Mom didn't resist with anything but her eyes. "Now be a good girl," Syd said, and officiously posted me from the room. When I returned later, Mom was holding a tiny ball of cotton against the inside of her arm.

"It's OK," Mom told me afterwards. Her right arm was growing more and more tracked with tiny scabs. "It didn't hurt at all."

I brought Mom cool pitchers of water, fresh apples and citrus fruits, carrots and hummus sandwiches. Her stomach seemed very taut and smooth when I touched it, like the expanded tube of a tire.

Every morning Dad worked on the dining room table with his lap-top and made phone calls. In the afternoons he took trips into Westwood, Hollywood, Burbank, and often returned long after I was asleep. Mom, meanwhile, lay in her bed, awaited her daily injections and grew more placid and content. This was the only movement left us now, the movement in Mom's stomach. Sometimes she let me place my ear against that smooth and ageless skin. I felt its tiny kick at the world outside. Kick. Kick again. I liked to place my lips against Mom's stomach and speak to it. "When you come out here, don't expect any free ride," I said. "I think I'm gradually working through a lot of the anxieties and insecurities your arrival may bring. By the time you get here, I hope I'll be able to treat you with love and respect for your own individuality. I hope I won't burden you with a lot of silly resentment you won't even understand."

Kick, it said. Kick kick.

"That other noise you hear is just the TV," I said. "Those aren't real gunshots, but just fake gunshots on TV. Sometimes you'll see men fall over dead on TV, but they're not really dead. They're just pretending they're dead. That's the way TV works. People get paid to act like they're people in real life. But they're not, really. They're just actors. On the news, sometimes, you'll see real dead people. I'll have to explain that part to you all over again when you come out. That stuff about dead people on TV always confused me when I was little."

I didn't want any child of Mom's to be confused about anything. Even though Mom had retreated into her formal silence, I wanted our baby to enjoy all the warm immanent attention I had enjoyed, to find itself enveloped in that same constant and imperturbable voice with which Mom had once enveloped me. "In a minute, you'll hear the vacuum cleaner," I told it. "I use the vacuum for cleaning the rug. The suction sucks all the dirt and grime and lint from the floor through this long rubbery hose, and then puts it into this big blue paper sack. Every once in a while, you have to put a new vacuum sack in it. Now that I've finished cleaning, I'm going to be leaving you and Mom for a little while so I can cook us all a good dinner. A pot roast. I roast it in the hot oven. I serve it with vegetables and gravy. That's what you'll be tasting later when it arrives through Mom's umbilical cord. Pot roast and gravy." I never left until after the baby had given me some response. A kick, perhaps, or a hormonal grumble. Then I patted Mom's warm stomach as a sort of telegraphic farewell. I wanted the baby to know I wasn't just talking at it. I was talking with it.

―――――

Mass

I rarely saw Mom and Dad together during the day, but often at night I would awake to the sound of Mom screaming. She wasn't screaming words, she was just screaming. This was another world that emerged in our dark house at night, the screaming of Mom's voice. It was even comforting in a way, formalized by the grammar of our household, by the deep structure of our seemingly eternal and regenerate family. Mom's scream was just a word, like Mom herself, Dad, Dad's lap-top and car, the garage, Mom's TV, and the tiny rough scabs sprinkling Mom's arm like crushed white grains of salt. Covert in my room, I awaited Mom's screams each night like a kiss on the forehead or a glass of warm milk. She'd start screaming for what seemed like hours and hours some nights, as if with her screams she were trying to inflate some enormous circus balloon. One night I went to my bedroom door and peeked across the hall into Mom's room. All the lights were on. The TV was blaring. Mom's face was twisted and angry, flushed and mottled with tears. She gestured wildly with the jeweled compact Dad had brought her from Westwood two days before. She screamed and threw it, and I heard things breaking. She was wearing the white hospital robe Syd made her wear. The robe hung open, revealing her quaking breasts and pale concave chest. And Dad in the doorway too, turning to look at me. He was still wearing his three-piece suit. The buttons of his vest, however, were all undone, and his hair seemed slightly mussed. "Go back to bed, Phillip." Dad's voice was the sternest word. Dad's voice was the world's first word. "Everything's all right. Your mom and I are just talking about something." Then I closed my door again and lay in my cold bed listening to her screaming until Dad finally gave her one of her injections, a sedative prescribed by one of Dad's "specialists," and then presumably they went back to bed together and fell asleep.

16

Suddenly I began to feel different and talk different, as if a different person entirely were developing from my thin body. Dad's arrival really had begun to teach me things about personal responsibility. Every morning I padded softly into Mom's bedroom where I found only the impression of Dad's body in the mattress and pillow beside her. She didn't even look like Mom anymore, but more and more like one of those crepuscular figures who emerged from Mom's dark bed in my most feverish nightmares of Mom. Her mouth hung open, revealing gold crowns and silver cavities. This was Mom's skull, that deep interior world into which Mom could retreat whenever she wanted, and where I could never follow. Mom snored deep in her throat. Her eyes were lashed with milky sleep. "Mom," I said, pushing her shoulder. Her entire body shook with the force of my hand. "Mom, it's me."

The drained hypodermics with their needles snapped off lay in the wicker basket, bedded by bloody Kleenex and balls of cotton. I could hear Dad in the living room, his fingers clacking against the dull cushioned keys of his lap-top. Every once in a while the lap-top beeped or the phone rang. Dad's dark, muffled and sinewy voice would some-times turn underneath Mom's bed like a buried stream or a shifting geological plate.

"Before your dad came I thought everything was starting to work out," Mom said. She slurred a lot. With a Kleenex I wiped bits of saliva from the corners of her mouth. "Before your dad came I was beginning not to be afraid anymore. The spell of my own blood actually made sense to me. Sometimes I even looked forward to having the darkness take me places. It took me down luminous rivers on large rotting rafts and barges. I saw strange birds flying overhead, and the eyes of other creatures emerging from the mucky water. I traveled down the river where twisted houses sat on shores filled with dark men who wouldn't come outside. The dark men were inside whispering about me. They held heavy spears and weapons by their side while their addled women cooked large pots of gristly meat and hung their washing out to dry. The men wore loincloths and streaks of paint on their arms and faces. A few mangy dogs lay around outside the circle of men, contemplating the dim fire. One of the dark men was my father."

Mom sat there and stared into space. She clasped the half-pint bottle of Seagram's against her breast. The bottle was almost empty. Every few nights or so I would go down to our local Liquor Mart, purchase some milk and beef jerky and request cardboard boxes from the bespectacled elderly clerk. While he was out of the store I stuffed bottles of gin and whiskey under my blue Derby jacket. Later, while Dad was away on business, I smuggled them into Mom's room. The bottles, I hoped, would keep Mom company when I couldn't.

"That's not your dreams, Mom," I said. "That's Conrad. That's *Apocalypse Now*. Don't you remember? We saw *Apocalypse Now* at the Sunset Drive-In in San Luis Obispo last summer. At the end, Martin Sheen kills a bull with his ax."

"My father was always a very gentle man with my mother," Mom said. "He had big soft hands. Sometimes he placed one of his hands on my knee when he drove me places in the car. He drove me to doctors mostly. We used to sit together in the waiting rooms and read slick magazines. I always liked *Vogue* best. My father, however, preferred *Popular Mechanics*. Sometimes it seemed like we were sitting in those waiting rooms for days and days, and all the time my father's hand was on my knee. It looked like some sort of animal. I was never really sure if I liked my father's hand there on my knee or not."

"It's OK to be a little confused," Beatrice told me one night on the phone. "It's even all right to be a little afraid. Give your emotions some credit, Phillip. Stop trying to be in *control* of everything all the time."

"I'm not afraid or confused," I said. "I'm not trying to *control* anybody. It's just that I feel there are a lot of decisions being left up to me, and frankly, Beatrice, I don't know if I'm up to them. I love my mom, but I love my dad too."

"You love the idea of your dad, Phillip. You don't love *him*. You love what you want your dad to be. What you want to make him."

"I don't want my dad to be anything, Beatrice. He's just there. I didn't ask him to come."

"Yes you did. You asked him to come."

"No I didn't. He just came, Beatrice. I swear. I didn't have anything to do with it."

"You're afraid it'll all turn out exactly the way you want it to. You never loved your mom, Phillip. You only loved the idea of your dad."

"I love my mom," I said.

"You never loved her, Phillip. You're a man. You're weapons, notions, deeds. You're technology. Your mom's the earth. She's the woods. Your mom's the rain and the wind. Your mom's nature. Your mom's what men's words wreck. Your mom's abundance, but men are cold and hungry. Your mom's life, while men aren't even death, they're just nothing. They're just the cold gray void death presumes to be. Men are the end of space and the beginning of metal."

"I never hear from Rodney anymore," I said. Beatrice's words swirled in my head. I felt dizzy and weightless, like a space-walking astronaut. I leaned against the wall and tried to find assurance in my house's body and mass. I considered tying myself down to something—the kitchen cabinet, or the dining room table. I might float off the face of the planet otherwise, and then I'd never have any idea where I was. A dull ache began to throb in my head. "I call and leave messages, but Ethel says he's out with his friends. She says he'll call me soon. He's just going through a stage, she says. It's just a stage he's going through."

"Rodney's feeling a little hurt, Phillip. I don't think you should have done that to his dog."

I wasn't sure I knew what Beatrice meant. Dogs guarded houses. Sometimes they crawled into your lap and slept there until their owners returned home. My mom had once considered buying me a dog.

"Rodney used to be my best friend," I said after a while. "Rodney and I used to do everything together."

I was only a child. How was I to know what was real and what wasn't? I slept in my clothes—a habit learned during the years of Mom's motion—and often late at night while Mom screamed in the other room I would get out of bed and go to my bedroom door. I had no reason to believe sound was real or even important. While Mom screamed I might also hear the sound of Dad's firm and reasonable voice. "Now, Margaret, you'll wake Phillip." "Especially in your condition." "No you don't. You don't really want to." "I love you, Margaret. I think you know that. Because somewhere in your heart you love me too."

I would sneak down the hall, down the back stairs and into the backyard, where tall weeds towered over me, amber and dead. Morose spiders spun glistening webs in the moonlight, and the high power lines sizzled in the starless sky like

Dad's voice. The power lines were filled with the voices of the world's other dads, calling their sons on the telephone. The world's other dads were real too. They were real people who dealt with real things in a real world. Sometimes they found bits and pieces of the world which were not real, and then they had to make them so, or dispense with them altogether. Things were never as real as they could be for the world's dads. Someday everything in the entire universe would be real, and the world's dads would finally prevail. When that day arrived, civilization and not nature would be rampant. When that day arrived, you could talk to everybody in the universe on the telephone.

"Hello, son."

"Hello, Dad."

"We'll go to the ball game. We'll go to the beach. On the Fourth of July we'll watch the fireworks. Then you and Judy and I'll go to see Judy's parents. You'll like Judy's parents' house. How's your mom? Is there anything you'd like to talk about? Did you finish your science project? Did you get your report card? Is your mom still seeing What's-his-name? Is your mom alone right now? Are you sure? What *is* his name, anyway? I thought I heard a voice. What *is* she doing? What television show? I didn't think that was on tonight. Oh, just in summer, huh? You're sure? You can tell me if she's not alone, son. You know that, don't you? Your mom has other friends now who may even sleep with her from time to time, and that's perfectly natural, OK? There's nothing wrong with that at all. But don't worry. Don't worry one little bit. You don't have to tell me anything if you don't want to. No, of course I don't think that. But just the same. Did she want to talk to me? Are you sure? Do you want to check? Just in case. I'll wait. If she's busy, I'll understand. If she's got company, don't bother her. I'll understand, I really will. I was thinking the weekend after next we'd all drive out to Marineland. Of course Judy'll come too. You like Judy, don't you? I thought so. And she likes you, too. In fact, Judy likes you very much, son. I think sometimes Judy likes you as much as if you were her own son."

I could even hear Mom screaming out here in the overgrown backyard, standing in that strange inverted darkness I found comforting after Dad came to live with us. In Los Angeles the night simmered with its own logic and ceremony. I heard the buzzing earth, the whispering light, the conspiracies of mere matter. Our yard was filled with the ruins of a fallen cement birdbath and weed-sprung brick barbecue. Collapsed trellises, moldering rosebeds, strange, twisted bushes and syllableless insects. I could step into the high weeds and actually feel the language out there, like a human body, like Dad's firm words. Broken cinder blocks, decomposing garbage, the corpse of a sad, tiny sparrow chewed and discarded by some spiteful tomcat. Forgotten civilizations I had read about in books. Mu, Atlantis, Greece, Egypt, Crete, Babylon. Perfect calendars and ritual sacrifice. People torn apart by dark machines. Virgins devoured by sharp blades. The hard inedible fruits of the weeds with hard bright colors. If I owned a telescope and lived on a high mountaintop I could see the stars. Not the stars on a wall map but the stars themselves. Stars exploded and collapsed. They turned and spun. If other people lived in the universe they might be looking at my sun now and contemplating me while I contemplated them. They might be creatures composed of gas or foam or rock or fire. They might live forever. They might love their moms. They might travel across landscapes filled with strange sounds, plants, birds and clouds. They might eat time or fart philosophical propositions. They might live language or speak matter. They may never have heard a single note of music in their entire lives. They might possess the advanced technology required for journeying from sun to sun, but then they might be too lazy and self-involved to bother. Some nights I stood there in the darkness and cried for my lost mom. I was finally beginning to realize that just because I hated Dad didn't mean I didn't love him too. Dad was a house. Mom was just infinite space which Dad's house isolated and defined. Mom was the sadness I couldn't express. She didn't stand a chance. To be perfectly fair, Mom hadn't stood a chance from the very beginning.

17

I began taking less care of myself. I rarely showered or brushed my teeth, and soon grew inured to my own sweet, soury smell. My teeth and gums felt coated with a thin, gritty film. I kept many of the Jack Daniel's bottles I originally pilfered for Mom in my own room now, and dark, amiable boys at the neighborhood bowling alley sold me marijuana, hashish and belladonna. I spent a lot of time alone in my room, listening to Pink Floyd on my headphones. Dylan, Van Morrison, Strauss and Rossini, Handel and Bach. Stoned I felt diffuse and more real. I ate packaged sandwiches, cookies and mints. I watched late-night television. I was growing more solid and real alone in my room while the rich saccharine smoke shaped itself in the air. Men, monsters, sailboats, planets, forests and rivers. Nobody needed me, and I needed nobody either. When I inhaled again from the joint I felt the harsh air filling my abdomen. My blood grew heavy, tranquil and slow, my eyes bloodshot and watery. Sometimes I touched my face, just to see if I was grinning or not. My face felt tight and strained. Every so often I caught myself squinting.

The Jack Daniel's and 7UP always tasted sweet and strong. I could taste it and then, after rolling it on my tongue, swallow and inhale it at the same time. I could feel it going down my throat and esophagus. I could feel it trickling through the twitchy pyloric into the stomach's mus-cled mouth. The icy drink still felt cool and fresh. Alcohol was pure, like snow. It felt and even tasted like snow, or so I imagined, since snow was one of the many things I had never seen. Sometimes I imagined flaky white snow falling in my stomach. Sometimes I just lay flat on my back on my bed and tilted the icy glass to my lips, leaning it against my doubled chin. Cigarettes tasted better and harsher when you were stoned. I grew filled with a sense of intense well-being. I was not a child, but rather a very wise old man. I had made billions on the stock market, and endowed many large museums and worthwhile institutions. Younger men like Dad were envious of my boats, luxury resorts, gambling casinos, tame striped tigers and insatiable women. My women were of every conceivable nationality and shape. Some of them had enormous breasts, which I fondled one at a time. I made love day in and day out with an impossible assortment of attentive and beautiful women. When I imag-ined these impossible orgies I placed my hand between my legs. Sometimes it felt hard, but it also felt remote and slightly detached, like a heavy steel pipe or a dictionary. I might start laughing without any reason. I would reach for my Jack Daniel's or my Bud. As I laughed, tears rolled down my face.

"Phillip. Are you all right in there?" Dad's voice roamed outside in the corridor, testing doorknobs and latches, brushing the loose leaves of wallpaper.

"Fine!" I said, and started laughing again.

"What's that smell, Phillip? What's that you're smoking in there?"

The doorknob rattled flimsily. I could hear the tiny lock brace and clack. "Phillip? Why's your door locked?"

"I'm in bed, I'm trying to go to sleep."

Dad's voice waited. Dad's voice was a thing, immobile and immense. Dad's voice lived in the corridor and made lots of money. Sometimes I imagined myself searching through the corridor and uncovering the vast sums of cash Dad's voice had hidden out there. I invested it in Alcoa. My dividends would be nearly eleven percent.

"I don't want you smoking in bed, Phillip. Now put out whatever sort of cigarette you're smoking and go to sleep. I don't want to have to come in there."

"I don't want you to have to come in here either, Dad," I said, and started laughing again. The tears soaked my T-shirt. "I'm putting it out. It's just a cigarette, and I'm putting it out." I was laughing at the impressive mahogany bureau Dad had bought for my room. I had pulled the bureau up and braced it against the flimsy aluminum doorknob. The bureau was exactly like Dad's voice. It was as if the bureau held my door in place on one side, and Dad's voice held it in place on the other.

Dad's voice stayed where it was. It seemed to be trying to confirm something. It was very hard and resolute.

"I love you," Dad said. "And your mother loves you, too. She said kiss you good night."

And then I heard the familiar footsteps, and the door of the master bedroom brushing shut against the shag carpet. I heard the deep breathing house. I heard the distant ticking thermostat. I heard the beetles in the yard, and the electricity hissing in the streets. I heard the stars and the moon. I took another hit off my joint. The tiny pinprick ember flared, seeds popped. A fragment of paper ignited and flashed and its ember drifted up into the air and vanished.

Within minutes, Mom had begun screaming again.

I never wanted to be loved when I was eight years old. I wanted to be crushed by soft massive arms. I wanted to be lifted into some towering embrace. I wanted to be hugged so tight I couldn't breathe. I wanted to be hugged until my eyes watered and my lungs collapsed and my heart popped. I was often awake all night, pacing through the halls and yard of my house, pausing sometimes at the door of my parents' bedroom. After the screaming stopped you couldn't hear anything. My parents' bedroom was perfectly quiet at these times, hollow and hard, as if it had been drained of atmosphere, like some unmanned spacecraft sent off aimlessly into outer space.

"Sometimes I'm not even thinking," I tried to explain to Beatrice one day. "Sometimes I just pace, as if momentum alone compels me. It's like I'm not going anywhere. Just into the living room, the kitchen, down the stairs to the basement, through the icy stone garage, remembering how Mom looks at me sometimes. Her face is flushed and ruddy. She has this insipid smile on her face. Whatever's growing inside her has become wary and suspicious, as if it knows I'm outside waiting. Perhaps it has simply grown stunned by Mom's screaming. 'Everything's going to be OK,' I try to comfort it. 'Once you're outside, you'll have your own crib. We'll put you in my room where it's quiet. You'll eat well. You'll see the sun. You'll reach out your flabby hands and grab my face. You'll wear tiny clothes. We'll hang a bright, intricate mobile over your crib, and it will glitter, so you can watch it at night when everybody else is asleep. You'll stare at the bright mobile and contemplate ideas like motion, light, repetition, difference. These are the best ideas you'll ever have.' ''

"Why don't you try taking a Valium?" Beatrice was sitting with me on the garage stairs. The front garage door was hanging wide open. Outside the hot sun flashed across everything: white pavements, white stucco houses, gleaming white windows. Beatrice was twisting the ends of her shirt around one index finger. "If your mom hasn't got any, I can get some from my old man. My old man loves Valium."

"I want things to be different for her," I said. I was staring at the bright sunlight and the wide empty streets beyond my garage door. Inside here the light seemed to radiate from the beamed walls and ceiling, the waxed tarpaper, the cold Rambler. "I want her to be happy. She's a lot smarter than I was at that age. She knows what's out

141

here because I've been telling her. When she's born, she'll find out I've been lying about how much fun it is and she'll hate me."

"Why do you think it'll be a girl?"

"Because I know."

"It'll be a boy, Phillip. Your mother will have about a million sons."

"I want everything figured out before she gets here. I want everything to be perfect for her."

"We all like to think we'll grow up," Beatrice said. "History's the one dream we all try and dream together."

"I don't want to grow up."

"You already have."

"I want to grow down. I want to bury myself in the hard earth. I want to root myself there like a dead tree. I want to entangle myself in the earth's heart so nobody can ever pull me out."

"You'll buy a condo in the Valley. You'll meet a beautiful young woman who drives a silver RX-7. You'll get married. You'll buy a house. You'll have babies."

"No," I said firmly.

"You'll take up gardening, skiing, stamp collecting. Your dad will take you on in the firm. You'll have color televisions in every room of your own house, and video recorders which function by remote control. You'll have second thoughts. You'll wonder what you're missing. Your wife will develop a very distant expression. Her expression will be exploring other continents, even while she's sitting right next to you. She'll start sleeping with other men. You won't even

142

mind that much. Sometimes she'll look very sad. You'll teach your children to be independent, and shower them with presents. You'll tell your children you want them to have all the things you never had."

"You don't know what you're talking about. You don't know me at all."

"You'll buy a sports car, to make yourself feel young again."

"There's things about me I've never told."

"We all never tell things. And we all never tell the same things. They aren't secrets, Phillip. They're conditions. As much as we may all hate to admit it, I'm afraid we all live the same worlds inside."

I awoke every morning with a terrific hangover, parched and aching. Usually I smoked a little grass and took some Tylenol, just to get me started. I watched daytime television in my room. There were game shows which would last forever. They seemed to take up infinite space with their glittering prizes. Each prize bore a cardboard placard describing its retail value. Usually this value was hyperinflated, but always impressive. Sometimes, unconsciously, I tried to add these sums together in my head: $679, $2,807, $99, $3,499. Often the prize was a brand-new car or a world cruise. I imagined myself winning these prizes and taking these cruises. The cruise ships were filled with other boys and girls my own age. There were sundecks and swimming pools, shuffleboard tableaux and billiard tables. We played Ping-Pong and pinball. The girls all wore bikinis. Even though they were only eight or nine years old, they all had very large breasts. I drank Jack Daniel's and Wild Turkey, Stolichnaya and Kamchatka, Southern Comfort and Jim Beam, Gallo and tawny port, Coors and Bud.

"Rodney," I said. I was leaning into my bedroom closet, as far away from Mom and Dad's room as I could get with my telephone receiver. "I need to talk to you. I can't figure this out alone. I need to see you."

"I'm kinda busy."

"Just for a half hour. Maybe I could come over there."

"I said I'm busy."

"But, Rodney—" I was prepared to protest, to cry and shout and hammer and beg. Then I heard Dad's footsteps. They paused outside my door. Then his hand, very faintly, rapped.

"Are you asleep in there? Phillip?"

"I gotta go, Rodney," I said. And then I hung up.

1 8

"Phillip?"

"What?"

"Are you in there?"

"Of course I'm in here."

"Don't talk back to me, son. I just wanted to see if you were all right."

"I'm all right."

"Do you want anything?"

"I don't want anything."

"Did you fix yourself any dinner?"

"I fixed my dinner."

Dad went silent for a moment. His voice seemed to be gauging things like mass, humidity and weight. "Your mom and I were worried about you."

I refused to dignify such duplicity with a response, and wondered if there was life on other planets. Perhaps it was only microscopic and stupid. Perhaps it wasn't even self-conscious.

"You're spending a lot of time in there alone, Phillip. What do you do in there all day?"

I poured more Jim Beam into my ceramic mug. The ceramic mug said SON, and was part of a family set Dad had purchased at the mall a weekend before. "I read," I said. I reached under my bed for my Marlboro carton. "I'm trying to get some reading done."

"All right, son." Dad stood quietly out there for a moment, like some primitive landmark, or guards outside a condemned prisoner's cell. "I'll leave you alone."

Dad's footsteps beat loudly in the hall. I heard dishes clattering in the kitchen. The television started up in the living room. It was as if my house were inhabited by disembodied sound. Then, after a while, Dad's footsteps returned down the hall. Very softly this time. Then his pocket screwdriver began investigating the lock of my bedroom door. Tick tick. The doorknob rattled slightly. Tick. Tick tick. A flashlight skittered underneath the door a few times.

The locking mechanism on my side of the door was fastened with heavy black electrician's tape. My bureau was braced against it. On the bureau in a small brown bag was the new bolt lock I had purchased at Walgreen's just that morning. I would install it later that night, after Dad was firmly asleep.

The books on my shelves stared down at me like statues or awards, mementos of some former life. They seemed very cold to me now. Books were just the raw matter of education. They were stuff, like coal or minerals. They could be accumulated, quantified and known. I was no longer concerned with the known, but with the process of knowing itself: pure motion, which did not render things known or visible. It did not transport you to any fixed location on a map. It was into the very function of the self that I journeyed now, and like Mom I could only journey there alone. Misery enveloped me with soft black robes. They were warm and clinging. They held me in place so I wouldn't get lost. Misery was my map, my boundary. It held me in place in this world of constant motion.

Whenever Mom started screaming again, I knew that inside she felt warm and safe like me. Sometimes I could hear other voices in there, hidden in that moist miserable world of my own private suffering, the voices of other people Mom and I might have been.

"I'm not a monster," Dad said in my hallway after the lock stopped rattling. "It's not like I don't have feelings too, son. I know I'm the outsider. I know it's going to be hard for you to get used to having me around. I'm not trying to rush things. When I first arrived and everything seemed to be going along so well, I knew this had to happen eventually. You had to start making a lot of heavy psychological adjustments. I just want you to understand I'm doing the best I can, under the circumstances. I'm trying to do what's best for everyone. So I'm not saying you should feel any different. I'm not saying you shouldn't go right on hating me, if that's how you sincerely feel. I would never violate your privacy like that. I'm just saying try to respect my position here as well. Things aren't any easier for me than they are for you or your mother right now." Times like this I thought Dad was a lot like Jerry Lewis on the annual Jerry Lewis Telethon for Muscular Dystrophy. Like Jerry, Dad seemed prepared to go to the most grotesque and inhuman lengths simply to prove his own humanity.

For the first time in my life I was utterly alone. I examined the desultory, overinflated images of naked women in men's magazines. I bought a harmonica which I liked to hold in my hand and imagine myself playing. Sometimes I danced alone in my room, listening to Bruce Springsteen or Joe Cocker on my Sony Walkman. I preferred Jim Beam, but I cultivated a taste for gin as well. I drank and danced until I grew dizzy and surfeited with a thick, swollen stomach, and collapsed on my unsheeted mattress, beating my feet in the air, watching the room swirl around. When it started swirling I knew I might throw up at any moment. That's what the plastic-lined trash bin was for. I lay very still and tried to make the room stop moving. It required an act of intense concentration. It was as if this swirling room was itself a mockery of movement, pulling up through my stomach while the alcohol moved through my blood, lifted into my brain and skull and sinuses. I wanted more to drink and tried to sit up. I knocked over bottles and ashtrays. The gray ashes spilled across my clothes and sheets. There were beer cans everywhere. Everything reeked of gin and cigarettes. The floor of my room looked like the high school parking lot. The world seemed to be growing darker and more desperate. "I don't know where I'm trying to go,

Mom," I whispered, as if she could hear me. "Maybe I'm already there and I don't even know it."

Whenever I was this drunk I couldn't sleep, though that didn't stop me from dreaming. The alcohol seemed to drive my blood and adrenaline as if I were a car, and I experienced strange visions of my progress through the world of light. I proceeded through dense green bushes and foliage. Insects chittered and flashed in the air around me, glancing off my face, biting my arms and neck. I was wearing a large khaki explorer's hat. Native drums beat in the air, and the tortured cries of captive white slave women. I was moving towards a secret road. The road was white and powdery, like the beach of some pristine sea. It extended in two directions. It might take me anywhere. It might take me nowhere at all. The roaring of an airplane filled the blue sky, the beating of helicopters. Everything was blowing around me, even the road's white dust. The plane was descending to take me away, but I didn't want to go.

I would sit up on my bed and reach for the cigarettes, sometimes pulling the glass ashtray or half-empty bottle of Beefeater's onto the floor. I grew obsessed with the idea that dreams were trying to communicate something very real to me, perhaps even the secret advice and admonitions of Mom herself. Dreams were life's base or undergrowth. They were the rich earth from which real life blossomed. The white road, native drums, women crying. The arrival of planes and helicopters, and then the sudden disavowal of everything, the whirling of dust and drums and sky. In the world, perhaps, my progress had been halted indefinitely. But I could still move in my dreams, and in my own feverish and desperate recollections of them. I was learning what Mom had been trying to teach me all along. When I could no longer live in the world, I could live the world alone in my heart.

"I think it's about time you started thinking about somebody other than yourself," Pedro said. "You're not the only person in this world who's lost somebody he loved." Pedro's face was out of focus. I couldn't tell whether it was because of the things Pedro had seen or I had seen that made his face so indefinite like that. "Just think about your dad for a minute. Just think about me, even. Try thinking for one minute about how *I* must feel." Pedro was drifting away. We were all drifting away.

"There's only one thing I've learned in my entire life, Pedro," I told him, though Pedro didn't exist as a body anymore. Pedro existed in the country of my imagination like deep buried formations of rock and basalt. Vast geothermal plates shifted and moved down there. The heat was intense and unremitting. "And I'll tell you, Pedro. I'll tell you what that one thing is." I had spilled Jim Beam down the front of my shirt. I took another long drink from my glass. "I don't care who lost what. I don't care who's gone without love. I don't care about money, or people, or countries, or politics. I only care about me now, Pedro, because now I'm like Mom. Because now I'm never thinking about anybody except myself."

———

Like Mom I journeyed now into my own artificial country—a country much like California, I thought. This country had fields and trees. It was divided into counties, towns
and cities. Several languages had developed over the centuries which, like the landscape itself, were often broken, dis-
continuous and unreal. There were, however, no other
people to be found anywhere. No other people lived and
worked here. No other people dreamed of other countries
like my own. Nothing moved here at all, in fact. Not even
the wind, or the intricately sculpted and often sentient
clouds.

If I were to meet that other woman here, that special
person in my life without a name now, she could not speak
to me. She might not even recognize me. In this privileged
country my imagination had translated everything, even
sensations and appearances, into solid matter, things, atmosphere, nature, earth. That other woman might try to
read to me from books I remembered from my childhood.
Big red and green books with pictures of bears, zebras and
pelicans in them. That other woman might try to speak to
me, feed me, smell me, touch me, but she couldn't do anything about it. She had lost all pretensions to form and
become only a force, a dream of falling. She could only run
through her accustomed routine—combing and petting my
hair, stroking my warm stomach, clipping my toenails—
while I drank my gin and tonics and contemplated the walls
of my country. My country had fissures and cracks, exposed
plaster and wiring. The doorknobs didn't always correctly

articulate with their locks. The windows were often painted shut, their curtains torn and dingy. Dishes were chipped, and glasses were filled with spongy cobwebs. None of the silverware matched. If you stood on a chair and gazed into the highest cabinets of my country you could just see, in its very furthest, dingiest corner, something tiny which didn't move. It was gray and shapeless. It possessed no smell or texture. If you looked at it too long, it wasn't even there at all.

I no longer wanted to live forever. I wanted only to burn intensely in the sun and extinguish, seedless and unforlorn like some unpopped pinecone. I began taking foolhardy walks at night into the worst parts of town, where strange dark men and women stood in doorways which were often plastered over by promotions for rock concerts and record albums. If I possessed no home, then logically my only home lay everywhere. The streets were filled with refuse. Garbage cans were overturned, and the wild dogs did not approach you. The dogs always looked at you over their shoulder as they paced anxiously away. They seemed to be calling you. Perhaps they were just hoping you would call out to them. They suffered terrible skin rashes and limped, like many of the strange men and women who stood loitering in doorways, or pushed large shopping carts about. These parts of the city were like some postnuclear landscape. These broken people had survived the extinction of an entire civilization. There was something admirable about them, about their rashes and strange growths and misshapen features.

They drank very cheap wine out of paper bags. Sometimes I stood and watched, and they offered me some. I always refused. It was not because I was afraid of contamination. It was because I was afraid I might contaminate them.

"How you doing, Johnny? How you doing, baby?" The sexless old woman had a faint gray beard and a pale face. "You coming home tonight? I'll fix your bed. You come home tonight and I'll fix your bed." Her fingernails were dirty and untrimmed. She held in her hands a gruesomely stained and tattered paperback copy of *The Hite Report on Female Sexuality.*

"Johnny's dead," I told her. "Johnny died last night in the hospital of tuberculosis. He asked why you weren't there. He asked why you weren't even there to say good-bye."

Sometimes I would walk all night, through unmapped and remote parts of the city which might have been only dreams. I remember long dark alleys filled with yowling cats. I remember men dressed as women, and women dressed as men. I remember bodies asleep or dead, and when I touched them with my foot they didn't stir or respond in any way. Every few blocks or so I might find a well-lit liquor store open where I could purchase cigarettes from an indifferent clerk who watched X-rated movies on his videotape machine. I remember horrible-looking men who called out to me when I passed. Sometimes they might start to follow. Their bodies seemed to have collapsed inside their matted gray clothes. Sometimes they emitted terrible, half-human sounds, and I would run away. I don't remember what was real and what wasn't real during those long restless walks I took far away from my home. I only remember myself moving deeper into the buried countries of my imagination, where one found one's way purely by instinct. I could never be sure where I might arrive next. By now, of course, I had said good-bye to California altogether.

"It's not a plot or anything, Phillip," Beatrice told me. "You're not history. You're not what things happen to. You're just a little kid, Phillip, who's got a number of severe personal problems right now. I've never suggested this sort of thing before, but maybe you should see a counselor. Perhaps you should seek professional help."

"Fuck you," I said. This was the rage I loved. I could drink and rage like this for hours, if only someone was there to help me. "Fuck you, Beatrice. I know what I'm fucking doing. I don't need any fucking body. I don't need you or Rodney. I don't need *any* fucking body to tell *me* what I should be doing."

I wasn't even listening for the click of the extension. Silence emerged suddenly from the telephone line like an official sanction. It was the world of electricity. It was the world of pure force.

"Fuck you, Beatrice," I said. "Just fuck, fuck you."

Eventually of course even Beatrice stopped returning my calls, and at night I nervously explored my neighborhood and the dark, abandoned playground of the local elementary school I had never attended. On this grass, and among these swings and monkey bars, children my own age played every day at appointed times. They ate their lunches on these splintering wooden benches, underneath these deliberately shady (and somewhat smog-tarnished) elms and sycamores. They took their schoolbooks home and, after they had completed their homework, they were permitted to watch TV, or invite friends over. In class they constructed synonym wheels with colored paper, scissors, paste and a dictionary. They banged wooden blocks together. They presented staged dramas about ecology, history and tooth decay in the echoing, cathedral-like auditorium. Tanbark and blacktop, hopscotch and four-square diagrams, softball diamonds and backstops, volleyball chains whispering against tarnished steel poles. At night, encircled by the sloped hills and hedges and the higher streetlamps, the shadows were gigantic here. For me childhood seemed like a sort of ghost town. It was ancient history. Its remnants hung about like some forlorn and noble calculus, Stonehenge or the pyramids.

It was as if I didn't even exist anymore. I didn't have a home. I didn't have friends. I didn't even have a mom. I just had the shadow of him, him in my house, him with the key to my car, him with the checking account now, and my mutual funds, and my T-bill account, and my government bonds and silver certificates. The emerging shadow of him with the MG, the beeping calendar watch, the Filofax, the Ralph Lauren cologne.

It was hot out here, even at night. The smog and city lights of the San Fernando Valley extended into the sky, absorbing stars, galaxies, even notions about the way worlds worked. It didn't even feel like loss anymore. It didn't feel like dispossession or grief.

"I can't go back there," I said out loud. "But I can't go anywhere else."

On the suburban streets and avenues surrounding the schoolground car doors slammed shut. Entire families were coming home together from movies, pizza parlors, bowling alleys. The doors of houses and garages opened and closed as well. Lights went on and off. A dog began to bark.

"Hush, Luke!" someone demanded.

"You can mope and feel sorry for yourself all you want," Pedro said, obscured by the bristling darkness. "But I don't think that's going to change anything, do you? I think it's time you started taking responsibility for yourself, and stopped blaming everything that happens to you on everybody else."

"I don't hate him," I said.

"But you want him out of the way."

"I understand how he feels. I know he just wants to help."

"But look what he's done to your mom."

"He transferred most of my stocks into money market accounts at just the right time. He saved me almost a thousand dollars."

"You can't even control your drinking anymore. You can't control when you drink, or how much."

"I'm just like him. Beatrice is right. Dad and I are exactly the same man. I'm like a homunculus, Pedro. It's like Dad's the body, and I'm the DNA. That's the unit measurement of life. That's where all the most complex, unconscious decisions are made. They're made every day when we're not looking down inside the DNA."

"He's taken the keys to your car. He's locked your car in the garage."

"He's a very successful businessman."

"He won't let you touch your own money."

All of the sky's stars were invisible tonight. The sky was only a haze of city lights. And this bristling noise—the noise of high crisscrossing power lines and tall streetlights.

"I don't know what to do, Pedro."

"You know what to do."

"I'm completely confused. I can't think straight anymore."

"You know what to do."

I turned. The schoolground seemed to be glowing. It wasn't like night so much as like night on some high-tech movie set. Invisible machines operated everywhere. Hidden technicians monitored, taped, replayed and edited. Truth could be collapsed and disarranged. Life was not fact, but montage. I might even be an actor playing somebody else's role. My mind might be the stage upon which some cultural drama played.

"You tell me, Pedro." I couldn't see him anywhere. "You tell me what to do."

The entire universe took a long deep breath. I was part of that universe. These planets, these stars. This was my real home.

157

"Kill him," Pedro said. "Kill him. Kill him tonight in your mother's bed, just like Hamlet. Kill him at breakfast— I'll show you how. You can run him down in your car. You can poison or cut him. You can strangle him in his sleep. But kill him. Kill him anyway you can. Kill him now, Phillip. Kill him now. Kill him now."

CHEMISTRY

19

"Good morning, Phillip."

Dad was wearing a three-piece pinstriped navy-blue Brooks Brothers suit. He was wearing leather Rockport shoes, a white knit tie, matching 24-carat monogrammed cuff links and tie pin. Everything looked really good on him. My father, I had to admit yet again, was a very handsome man. He looked much younger, in fact, than I felt. He took up his folded cloth napkin and sat down. Each morning I would begin setting the breakfast table as soon as I heard Dad's shower start up in the master bathroom.

"Decided to join us back in the real world again, huh, son?" Dad poured ringing Cheerios into his blue ceramic bowl. "I'm glad."

Cheerios are a happy cereal, I thought. I hadn't slept all night, and was sipping my fourth cup of black coffee. Cheery Ohs. Cheerios.

Dad opened the massive *Times* and deftly disengaged the Business section. I was gazing dully at the muted yellow standing lamp in the dining room. My mind was keen with adrenaline, but my body sagged.

"Gold's up," Dad said behind his paper.

"I've been thinking, Dad. I've been thinking a lot about us lately. You know. You, me, Mom."

Dad's paper minutely rustled. The rest of the *Times* lay massive on the table like a fish tank. The front page said things about the Middle East, unemployment, presidents, Taiwan. Someone had survived an attempted assassination. Someone else had just been born.

"I'm not proud of the way I've been behaving," I said. I was still staring at the yellow lamp. My body seemed to be shifting. Or perhaps it was the house that was shifting under me. "It's not like I'm trying to be selfish. I know things haven't been easy for you either, Dad. What with Mom pregnant and all, and me just sitting in my room feeling sorry for myself. I haven't been helping much around the house. I haven't been keeping up the yard." My first and only substantial memory of Dad was much like this. We had been divided from one another by the thin fabric of Mom's stomach. He had said things to me in his deep voice. The words had reverberated in my warm, amniotic placenta like chimes in an iron bell. "I'm going to try and make it up to you," I said. Now my words reverberated, now my words filled things. The Formica table, the plastic chairs, the dishes in the cupboard, the bills on the microwave. "I think it might make things better for all of us."

With a flourish, Dad shook the leaves of his newspaper back into conformity and refolded them. Dad's face was flushed and slightly sunburnt. I was beginning to suspect a sunlamp in Dad's office. He was smiling. He, too, thought things would soon get better for all of us. He suggested a movie that afternoon; he would take off early from work. Or a baseball game. The Los Angeles Dodgers, as I understood, were our home team.

Yes, handsome. Very youthful.

I told him I'd think about it—I had many errands to run that day. Maybe tomorrow—or better yet, next week. Sometime that afternoon there were a few things I needed to pick up at the hardware store. Dad loaned me his Visa Gold card.

We were both still smiling very energetically at one another when Dad left for work.

The body, I have often thought, is like a promise. You keep things in it. Those things are covert, immediate, yours. There is something lustrous about them. They emit energy, like radium or appliances. They can be replaced, repaired or simply discarded. The promise of the body is very firm and intact. It's the only promise we can count on, and we can't really count on it very much.

"We'll need this," Pedro said. We were touring the hard aisles of Ace Hardware and Plumbing Supplies. I was pushing the Ace Hardware shopping cart, on which one eccentric wheel wobbled and spun contradictorily. "We'll need this, and this, and this and this. We'll need one of these. And we'll need one of these." Finally we decided on a large steel toolbox with trays which extruded when you opened the toolbox lid. I was very impressed with Pedro's knowledge of tools. He knew which had the sharpest blades and points. He knew which ones were built to last.

"My, my," the checkout lady said. The checkout lady had very gray hair. She wore an official red Ace Hardware apron and name tag. The name tag said her name was Doris. "You look like you're going to start your own little business." She held herself with such ardent restraint I knew she could barely prevent herself from patting my "tousled" head. She took Dad's Visa Gold card.

"Did your father tell you you could use this?" Doris asked, still beaming her flawed white dentures.

I offered to show her my ID.

"No, no. That's fine." Doris ran the card through the gutter of an electric scanner. "You're a very industrious young boy," she said. "How old are you, dear?"

"I was eight years old last November," I said. Then I carried the toolbox back up the street to my house.

The tools fitted snugly into their appropriate compartments. The lid of the toolbox closed securely. It was like a body with its tidy organs hidden inside by warm, glistening envelopes of tissue.

"Where'd you go, Pedro?" I asked.

"You didn't need me around. You had your dad's credit card. You had all you needed. You didn't need me."

Only after I urged him repeatedly did Pedro show me how to fit the gleaming hacksaw blade into the firm steel handle. Outside it was very hot and sunny. Outside, the sun-dazed birds in the trees didn't make a sound. Later I stored the pregnant toolbox in my closet under a heap of new clothes Dad had been buying me over recent months. When I closed the door, I could still detect the gravity of it there. It seemed charged with its own imminence. It cooked there, like the dashboard lighter in the days of Mom's luminous motion.

"If Dad's body was a house, Mom, what kind of house would it be?"

"It would be a very big, safe, well-built house with stone walls and turreted balconies. It would be made from the best materials. It would be perfectly designed to benefit the needs of its specific occupants."

"Would it have heavy doors?"

"The heaviest."

"Would there be alarms? What sort of alarms, Mom? Sonic or wire? Would they be hooked up to some private agency, or to one of those shrill fire bells? Would there be dogs, Mom? Would private guards check the place out whenever people were away?"

"Sonic," Mom said. "Everything in this house will be very clean and compact. There won't be any wires or cords to entangle or confuse you. Everything will be in its proper place."

"Will I have my own room?"

"We'll all have our own rooms. Our own bathrooms and baths. We'll have private brick fireplaces and balconies. We'll have well-equipped bars and portable color televisions in every room hooked up to satellite-dish reception antennas."

The History of Luminous Motion

"Will there be a yard?"

"A vast green expanse of it. You won't even be able to see let alone comprehend its gate. There'll just be a distant green vanishing point. You'll think you're losing your sight. You'll feel like you're living on your own little planet, a planet with abrupt horizons and green earth. Your eyes will strain and water if you try to take in too much of it at once."

"Is it in the country?"

"It's in the city and the country. That's how big it is."

"At night can you see the stars?"

"You can see the white buzzing band of the Milky Way. Every star in the sky shining at once. It won't seem like light, but matter. It will weigh against you like mass. It will shine like gold. You'll be lying on the green grass at night and you'll try to reach out for it. You'll try to touch it. Your hand will ache, just thinking about it."

"I can enter Dad's house any time I want."

"Of course you can. It'll be your house too. You'll have your own key."

"I'll have keys to all the rooms."

"Except the most secret ones."

"But even then, I can peer in the windows. I'll be allowed in the secret rooms when I'm older."

"When the time comes, you can discuss that with your father."

"I only want to go into rooms Dad's already been in himself."

"You'll have to be careful."

"I'll find thick complex networks of lymph and artery and tissue there. Fatty deposits, moist and cellular, like the eggs of fish or amphibians. The hard moist marrow filled with yellow matter. Renal ducts and spongy scoops of liver. The hard muscled heart. The body's stringy muscles knitting ribs and shoulders and stomach. Bones articulated with tendons, cartilage, gristle. Bones articulated with other bones."

"That's something that's all none of my business," Mom said. She was staring at the television screen. Neon cash amounts flashed on an enormous multicolored board. The faces of celebrities beamed and flushed. One hugely happy and obese female contestant began to cry, surrounded by gigantic photographs of all the wonderful, exotic places she would soon be visiting. "That's all something you'll have to discuss with your father."

I felt the cold strobing black atoms humming around me in the darkness as I swayed back into my room through the swirling hallway. It was just Mom and me again. Mom in her room with the baby growing inside her like a secret, like the secret promise of bodies, and me in my room across the hall with Pedro, spinning our thin schemes of savagery and mutilation, trying to push Dad into the future again where he belonged, into the future's deep dark earth where the black atoms hummed and spun like elementary planets. Mom and I had grown so far apart we could understand one another again. Ours was a cellular complicity. Even when we lived in different countries and spoke untranslatable languages we still knew each other. Mom knew what

I had to do, and approved with a covert dense resignation. It was an approval that made Mom's body hard and perfect and safe.

"That's a Conready steel file," Pedro said, showing me how to hold it. "Feel that weight. There's a lifetime guarantee on that sucker. You want to know how many steel tool manufacturers offer a lifetime guarantee on their merchandise? I'll tell you. Not too damn many, that's how many. Not too damn many at all."

I was suffering giddy delusions of grandeur. I considered writing the local newspapers and confessing to them all my plans. Then later I would send them photographs of what I had done to Dad while they stood helplessly by, pretending their authority over world events. I felt like an astronaut who had just returned from deep space and the exploration of rich worlds inhabited by aboriginal cultures and convoluted blue cities into which random asteroids often crashed. My mind and knowledge were astrally privileged; I had returned to live in a world of tiny, ineffectual ants. Just as the baby was assembling itself in Mom, I now felt Mom assembling herself in me. Everywhere I went I went with Mom's implicit consent. Everything I did I did at Mom's unspoken command. I felt incalculably brave. I felt invulnerably correct. I felt like science or politics. I had broken the cipher of eternal language; I was learning new words about the real universe, and with this eternal language I would live forever. Words were what mattered, not bodies, not things breathing, vulnerable and vile. Life was a hard word, or a sentence filled with hard words. The process of living was not a problem of biology but of grammar. One simply needed to know how to arrange oneself within the proper sentence. One simply needed to comprehend not one's substance or actuality, but rather one's relationship with the world's other hard objects. One night I was filled with such weightless soaring arrogance I even called Beatrice and confessed everything.

"You can't fool me, Phillip. Don't call me up at home just to hand me this line of nonsense." I heard the pronounced puff of Beatrice's lips against her filtered cigarette. She exhaled the smoke with a long theatrical sigh. "You love your dad. You'd never do anything to hurt him, and you know it."

"I hate him." I was finishing the last of Dad's Wild Turkey, garnished with a splash of crushed ice. "It's all going to work just perfect. I know exactly what I'm doing, because I've done it all before."

"You *can't* hate him, Phillip. He's your *dad.*"

"I've got it all worked out. I know exactly what I'm going to do."

"You're going to kill him," Pedro whispered, somewhere in the dark.

"Isn't that just like a man," Beatrice said. "To say he knows what he's going to do when he hasn't got any idea what he wants or even who he is to begin with. Who the hell are you, Phillip? That's the question I'd like answered. Not what stupid things you're going to *do.*"

"Kill him," Pedro said. "Kill him, kill him, kill him."

"I hate him," I said.

169

"*You* hate *him*, Phillip? That's just what I mean, isn't it? Man's myth of intentionality. *I* do things to *you*. Predication. Subject and object. The dream of perfect cosmic grammar. Well, dream on, kid. Dream on till you're old and gray. Because you're old already, Phillip. You're already older than your own dad. If you want to know the truth, I think I like your dad better. At least he *tries* to make things work without bullying everyone all the time, like you or Rodney. In fact, Phillip, I think I like your dad a whole lot more than I'm beginning to like you."

The black atoms swarmed and rushed around me again and again. They were my private, internal atmosphere. They would take me back into the darkness with them again very soon. "Fine," I said. "I don't really care what you think, anyhow."

"Let me put it to you this way, Phillip. *You* don't matter. Neither does your dad. We're all nothing but heat, motion, gravity, sound, history, light—that's all that matters, Phillip. Just force and stress, time and matter. Start thinking about those things. Get outside your feeble, crowded little brain for once in your life and try looking at the big picture, will you? You guys all like to think you're such hotshots, you're all in such control of everything. Well, you're not. You're nothing but a bunch of dicks, that's all you are. Us women, on the other hand, we're what you call heterogeneous. That means we're everywhere, everybody at once. We're both good and bad, right and wrong. We're the great resolvers of conflict, Phillip. We're like octopuses—because we'll swallow *anything*. Even men. Even battling and forlorn men like you and your dad. You guys try so hard to be subjects, characters, things, you forget us women are the whole story. We embrace you all. What you really want to destroy is women, that story of yourself you can't control. Women are what you really hate, Phillip, not that poor dumb jerk of a dad you've got. I've been reading a lot lately, Phillip, since we broke up. French feminists, existential Marxists. I'm teaching myself French so I can read Sartre's *Dialectic of Pure Reason*—much of which has been improperly translated, from what I understand. You should learn to speak French too, Phillip. Then we could talk French to each other over the phone."

"I'm sorry I called," I said. I could hear something clacking wetly in Beatrice's always lugubrious mouth. I could even hear its faint reverberation against Beatrice's crooked teeth. Hard candy, I thought. Perhaps a Tootsie Pop.

"Do you miss me?" Beatrice asked after a while. "Have you missed me since I haven't been around?"

There was more to the universe than light, gravity, mass, history, motion and sound. That's where she was wrong. I was in the universe, too. Me and Pedro.

"Sometimes, I guess," I said. "I guess sometimes I miss you a little bit."

We would have to move quickly—finally Pedro and I agreed on one thing. Dad had begun talking about returning Mom and me to our true home.

"As you know," Dad said to me one night over dinner, "I haven't wanted to rush things up till now. I didn't see any hurry. But now I don't see any need to waste any more time around here, either." Dad indicated the thin dismal living room, made even more sad and depleted by the bright new furniture and drapes Dad had installed since his arrival. "I don't think I'm just speaking for myself here, but let's face it. It's pretty depressing, wouldn't you say? It seems to be getting on everybody's nerves."

"It's just a house," Mom said. "It was just the first thing I could find when I needed one."

Mom was seated across the table from Dad. She was wearing a broad-waisted cotton summer dress. She gazed emptily at the curtained window behind Dad as she chewed her Chinese noodles. Mom had only lately, at Dad's polite insistence, begun taking meals with us.

"Our real home's still waiting for us," Dad said. "There'll be a nursery for the baby. There'll be room for a live-in nurse to help your mom out. And you, sport. You."

Dad offered me the rest of the cashew chicken, which I perfunctorily declined. I had suddenly lost my appetite.

Dad forked the remainder onto his own plate. "You'll be going back to school. You'll have a nice room, and a proper library to study in. You know I bought the Britannica School Edition for you since you left? I put it up in your room already, along with a few other things. A word processor, your own video machine, some classic movies on cassette. I think you should start filling in some of the gaps in your education—I'm talking popular culture, here. The entertainment industry. That's the business I've always expected might attract you someday. Film, television. Cable's opening up

172

a lot of new ideas in marketing. The production end, that's what you'd be good at. Technical equipment, where the real money is." Dad poured himself the rest of the lapsang sou-chong. He gazed into the tepid brown water, as if he were reading the arrangement of leaves at the bottom of his cup. I wondered if they said anything interesting. "I think it's time we got on with our lives," he concluded. "I think it's high time we all stopped messing around."

2 0

"Hi, Ethel. How you doing?"

"Phillip. Phillip. Oh, isn't this nice. Isn't this nice to see you. *Phillip.*"

Ethel's voice sounded and recoiled at the same time, stepping her lightly backward into her immaculate living room. Even as she called my name she seemed to evade me. I stood on the sunny porch and she in the shadowy doorway. The contrast made her appear at once firm and unfocused, as if every particle of her was being diffused by some foggy outdoor film screen. She looked like an apparition, like one of my recent dreams of Ethel.

"Is Rodney home?" I said. "Do you think I could see him?"

As she was letting me into the hall Rodney's voice abrupted warily from the top of the stairs. "Who is it? Ethel? Is it someone for me or what?"

"I think it's good you've come over to make up," Ethel whispered. Quickly she began handing me whatever was

174

available on the dining room table. A plate of crescent-sliced, crustless sandwiches. A bag of Cheetos. A couple of cold Buds. "It doesn't matter who starts an argument, now, does it?" she said, winking. "It just matters who's man enough to make up. If you're friends with somebody, then sometimes you've just got to swallow a little of your pride, don't you, Phillip? It's good to have you back, dear. I think he's missed you. I think maybe we've both missed you."

I really wasn't up for Ethel right now. Every gesture she made suggested she and I shared some secret agreement which either excluded or diminished Rodney. I wanted to tell her that she didn't matter. That the friendship Rodney and I shared not only superseded her, but was actually none of her business.

I carried all the stuff up to Rodney's room, balancing it against my stomach. I knocked lightly with my knee.

"Conviction's all we lack," I said. "That determination not simply to be ourselves, but to be *anybody*. We should carry our conviction like a hammer. It doesn't matter what we build. It only matters that we *act*. It only matters *that we build.*" I was soaring now. I was thipping across the lane dividers in Mom's luminous car again. I saw Buellton. I saw Fresno. I saw Salinas. I felt Mom's voice rising in me strong and intrepid for the first time in months. I would never die. Mom would never leave me. "We're like armies of men, political nations, the corporate arrangements of cells, tissues and bodies. We're not children, Rodney. We're the world. We're greater than the world, because we can make it be anything we want it to be—no matter who tells us other-

wise. We're all that matters, Rodney. All that matters are
our strategic situations, and the tactical *stuff* we use in order
to get where we want to go, in order to take what we want
to have. Where we are, what we get, how we get it—*that's*
all that really matters. We act together, Rodney, just like
always. You and I. It's not like we have any choice. It doesn't
matter if you like it, or if I like it, or even if we like each
other. It just *is*, Rodney. You and I just *are*. We're stuck
with each other. We're friends for life.''

Rodney had hardly touched his tidy fragment of sandwich. He examined it distantly now where it rested on his
jiggling knee like a trained hamster.

"I liked that damn dog, Phillip. You knew that, too. It
wasn't like you had any right. It wasn't like it was your dog
or anything."

I could hardly recognize Rodney. A blue pentangle had
been tattooed around the frame of his left eye. His hair had
been shaved back to reveal a high, shiny forehead; it was
tonsured and dyed a streaky, phosphorescent green. His
room was filled with books on voodoo, black arts and magic.
A cone of sandalwood incense burned on a tiny brass de-
votional tableau decorated with the bodies of naked, writh-
ing women with serpentine hair and pointed breasts. From
his left pierced ear dangled a silver earring intricately carved
with the skull of a leering baboon. The floors and furniture
were littered with various lurid paperbacks with bright red
colors depicting flames, apocalypse, demons and witches and
complicated demonic symbols. The books were entitled
things like *Hell Town U.S.A.*, *Cry the Children*, *The Book of*

Satanic Myth and Lore, UFO Sightings Unveiled, and *Sydney Omar's Guide to Astrology: Taurus.* "I'm glad you've finally developed an interest in reading," I said after a while. "It always helps to find a subject that interests you."

"I guess I've just been bored," Rodney admitted later, while I was searching through his closet and rearranging the piles of moldering laundry I found there. "Bored bored bored. Jesus Rice Krispies I've been *fucking* bored. Getting up, eating Ethel's lousy goddamn breakfast, going to school. And the teacher's droning on about this and that and the other thing. I try to tell the teacher, you know. I don't give a fuck about geometry or English. Like I'm probably going to drive a truck or something when I get out of school. Join the army or something simple. I'm sure in the *army* they're all going to be wondering what an acute angle is. I'm sure I'll make lots of friends driving my truck because I can diagram some lousy goddamn sentence. And then after school I'm free, right? What's that mean? I go down to the bowling alley or the shopping mall with my friends. We scope the girls, smoke a little doobidge, maybe a tab of acid every now and then. But that's not really living, is it? I mean, if that's living, then excuse me right now. I'll go out and put a bullet in the old brainpan. But if that's *not* all there is, right, well, maybe there's something I could do a little less radical, like, you know. I don't mind life or anything—I'm perfectly willing to give it a try. So what the hell, I figured. I'm sick of school, drugs, this goddamn oppressive house of Ethel's and all. Maybe it's time I experimented a little more with my life, took a few more chances. So that's when I decided to become a warlock. To master the satanic arts of black magic. Devil worshiping, for you laymen. I want to learn to master what they call the black arts."

I moved aside cardboard boxes filled with Marvel and DC Comics, dismembered football and hockey uniforms, baseballs and baseball gloves. Then, behind some crumpled *Playboy* magazines, I found it.

"It's all relative," Rodney said. "Black magic's no 'better' or 'worse' than white magic. It's not like one's 'good' and the other's 'evil.' It all just depends on what side you're rooting for. In other words, it's all relative. Black magic can go places white magic can't, that's all. Satan's not any more evil or good than God, he's just trying to move in on God's territory, like General Motors or Chanel. Everyone faces competition—that's what makes the strong stronger. That's why civilization gets better and better instead of just falling apart. I say use what you've got in this world, because nobody else is going to give you anything *they've* got. Use what you've got, or else the other fucker's going to use what *he's* got on *you*, and I'm not kidding. I think you hear me, Phillip. I think you know where I'm coming from."

A Judas Priest album was playing full blast on Rodney's stereo. I couldn't make out the lyrics very clearly. It seemed as if they were screaming, *Retribution, retribution, retribution, retribution* . . .

"Could you turn that down?" I asked, unlatching the slightly oxidized steel clamps and unfolding the chemistry set atop Rodney's rolltop desk. I pushed some of Rodney's soiled paperback books out of my way. Aleister Crowley's *The Book of the Law*. John Knox's *Satan's Women: A Guide to the Pentagram*. A couple of James Herbert and Stephen King novels. L. Ron Hubbard's *Dianetics: The Modern Science of Mental Health*.

"I've even managed to explain this all to Ethel so even *she* understands where I'm coming from," Rodney said. "And Ethel, as we all know, is a stupid cunt."

"Now," I said, "how about a little more light?"

2 1

I couldn't just go and kill Dad, say with a gun or a knife or a bomb. He couldn't be obliterated, like propositions or houses. He was far too vast and remote to be assailed by small hands and arms such as mine. No, if I wanted Dad out of the way, then I had to deploy Dad's strength against himself. I could not conquer, Dad could only succumb. I could not be the agent of Dad's death, only its engineer.

While I tapped a few intricate crystals of sodium into a beaker, I suggested Rodney turn on his cassette player.

I would have to insinuate the diffuse, inorganic world of chemistry into Dad's body while Dad wasn't looking. Rodney put on the Grateful Dead, and I began furiously assembling compounds with which, over succeeding days and weeks, I regularly began dosing Dad's coffee, cookies, roasts and steaks. Dad always said he and I should go more places together, so I proposed we go everywhere, everywhere at once. We were going to journey into the real scheme of life, Dad and I, into life's basic and molecular stuff. The assemblies of atoms and molecules, that systematic world of electrons which orbited and contextualized mere physics. Appearances, behaviors, properties, symbols and formulae, enumeration and analysis, polymers, fuels, oxides and energy. I was going to return Dad to that world where he truly belonged, that fundamental world of basic particles which breathed underneath our realer world of mere events. Meanwhile, in Rodney's room, the stereo played:

Many rivers to cross,
And I can't seem to find
My way over.

Soon Dad was suffering colonic spasms, flatulence, rashes, dizziness, occasional vomiting, boils, sore throats, hemorrhoids, blurred vision and acne. "I don't know, sport," Dad said, one hand resting covertly on his stomach. Mom was still patiently chewing her prawn salad. "I don't know if I feel like dessert or not." I had been experimenting with sodium compounds that night. Sodium sulphate in Dad's mushroom soup. Sodium thiosulphate in Dad's tandoori shrimp.

"Don't worry about it, Dad," I said. "I'll do the washing up. You get yourself some rest."

Mom, impressively large now, sat resolutely at her place, eating everything in sight. Once the salad and entrée had vanished, Mom commenced tearing into the sourdough french bread and margarine.

"I think something's bothering your father," Mom said,

after Dad had gone into the living room to lie down. Mom was crunching french bread in her mouth, scraping crumbs from the corners of her mouth with one long fingernail. She was staring off into her private country where our baby was lifting itself onto its hind legs and uttering its first hesitant vocables. "Your father hasn't been sleeping well," Mom said. "Sometimes he wakes the baby. Sometimes he's so restless I can't sleep, I can't even relax." Mom made soothing motions against her stomach. "I may begin asking him to sleep on the living room sofa." Mom was wiping the doughy center of the bread at her plate until the plate was white and dry like a bone. Then she put the soft, moistened bread into her mouth, a patient, animal expression on her face, complacent but alert.

"I guess you can say I started taking a serious interest in Satan about six months ago," Rodney said, while I heated random substances in a beaker over a thinly glowing can of Sterno. "But that doesn't mean Satan hadn't been in my thoughts long before, or that I wasn't in some important way already under his influence even when I was very small, even before I was old enough to talk or read. I think I always knew about Satan, but it was only unconscious knowledge, if you know what I mean. There's lots of knowledge that's important in this world, and you don't necessarily have to be able to explain it for it to be valuable to you personally. I've learned a lot of really strange things about myself and the universe around me, Phillip, especially since I've been contemplating the powers of darkness and all. In

182

fact, I've even traveled back to visit my prenatal existence with the benefit of this really interesting book." Rodney showed me L. Ron Hubbard's *Dianetics: The Modern Science of Mental Health*. "Because of this interesting journey into my past, I've learned that the very first face I ever knew was Satan's face. I saw him while I was growing in Ethel's womb. I know it's kind of a disgusting thought just thinking Ethel *has* a womb and all, but there you have it. Satan singled me out even when I was just a batch of simmering molecules. I guess that's why I've always been a rather unpleasant sort of person. It's not like I ever *wanted* to be such a pain in the ass—I just couldn't help myself. It was sort of like my destiny, in a way. What's really great about this scientology stuff I've been reading—this idea that we have all these infinite previous existences and all—is that it doesn't *matter*. I mean, it doesn't really matter at all who I am *now*, that I may be a devil worshiper or even worse. Because I might have been a bunch of really *nice* people in my previous incarnations. Priests and ministers, even. Kings and queens, paupers and dogs. I might have been Sir Francis Drake in a former life. I might even have been Willie Mays."

"Willie Mays isn't dead," I said.

"Yet," Rodney reminded me.

As I tapped chemicals into beakers, flasks and test tubes, as I scraped pungent growths from the surfaces of petri dishes and damp Wonderbread, Rodney often chattered animatedly like this, filling his own room with strange new notions and imaginings. There was something fecund about Rodney now, vigorous and irrepressible. Rodney lived and thought and ate and dreamed. He was a different Rodney from the one I had known before, and I must admit that now I liked him a lot better. He seemed more involved in life. He didn't just wait for things to happen to him.

One afternoon when I arrived at his room Rodney had erected the collapsible card table and covered it with a somber damask tablecloth. At the center of the tablecloth a white candle burned auspiciously on a white plate. A few of Rodney's books—*Demonology and the Occult* and *Making the Spiritual World Work for YOU*—lay haphazardly about on the floor. Three chairs were situated around the table, and Beatrice sat in one of them.

"Hello, Phillip."

I turned to Rodney. "What's she doing here?" I asked.

"The spirit world is a very feminine place," Rodney said, motioning me to sit down. "It's filled with all sorts of feminine forces or something. We need her to help us reach into the feminine half of the void. Now, does anybody want a Coke before I turn off the lights?"

Beatrice did. Then the room went dark and we all joined hands around the table.

"All right," Rodney said. "I guess we can get started." He shifted in his seat a few times. A large poster of Aerosmith gazed down meaningfully from Rodney's wall. The luminous dial of Rodney's private phone seemed to hum faintly, and Rodney cleared his throat. "So I guess, you know, we're all gathered here to talk to the spirit world. So I guess we should sit real quiet for a moment, and just listen."

184

The luminous dial hummed, the large poster gazed. I could still smell the odor of marijuana and cigarettes which Beatrice and Rodney must have shared before my arrival.

"So," Rodney said, clearing his throat and fidgeting impatiently in his rattling folding chair, "I guess this is sort of the part where we have to get in touch with the cosmic vibrations and all. We're very spiritual people here, waiting to meet some interesting people out there in the spirit world. I mean, if anybody out there's listening, we're looking for a sort of guide, some sort of friendly spirit who's still tied to the material world in some way, but basically who's dead already."

I heard a throat lozenge clicking about in Beatrice's mouth. Her hand gave mine a slight, conciliatory squeeze, but she wasn't looking at me.

"So we'll just wait here," Rodney said after a few moments. "We won't say a word or disturb any of you. We just want to sort of know what you're all thinking, and if any of our former loved ones are out there, and if there's anything we can do for you down here on earth. That sort of thing. You know, like maybe we'll scratch your back, you'll scratch ours. Then if later like maybe *we* need anything from *you*, you know. Well, I think you get the picture. Now, I don't want to be hassling you and everything, so I'm going to shut up for a while, and just get in tune with your vibrations. OK? So none of us are going to say anything for a while. I really mean it this time."

I don't know how long we sat there, but it seemed like hours. Eventually the noisy lozenge dissolved in Beatrice's mouth—like one of her erotic promises, I thought—and when I peeked covertly out of the corner of my eye I saw she had fallen asleep. She sat slumped forward slightly in her chair, her tiny pink tongue extruding from her too-thin lips, like the tongue of some sleeping terrier. I wondered if Beatrice dreamed of her long abandonment of me, and if she dreamed it without remorse. Rodney, on the other hand, sat unreflectively alert in his chair, his wrists braced against the flimsy table. His face didn't flinch, nor his expression waver. I had never seen Rodney so firmly involved in anything before. As my half-open eyes peered into the dark corner of Rodney's room, I thought I saw something beginning to cohere. It was red, and hot, and tiny, like a tiny glowing red eye, a canny wolfish red eye. There was a thin ribbon of steam rising from it. Then I detected the odor of sandalwood, and recognized the cone of burning incense in a delicate brass tray on Rodney's bureau. I wondered then if it mattered, whether a vision had to make itself real in order to achieve spiritual validity, or whether the world's mundane objects could be significant too, like St. Augustine's rotting fruit.

To prevent my mind from drifting, I tried to concentrate on the spirit world and the slow, bitter ghosts of the dead and unborn I expected to find there. My active mind, however, kept returning to Beatrice's damp, muggy palm I held so carefully in my left hand. This warmth had once comforted and consoled me, like heat or light. There was a special spiritual electricity here which I had considered then private and inexpressible, but which I now considered diffuse, conglomerate and altogether human, like Southern California Edison or the Department of Water and Power. This warmth could sleep and live without me, without even thinking of me. It could be my warmth, but then someday it could be somebody else's warmth too. Somebody else's hand might hold it, somebody else might kiss it with their lips. It could go away from me and live in its own house. Warmth was a sort of spiritual force too, I realized then. Ghosts often exist even in the bodies of people we love.

Rodney began to hum. A low, Gregorian, extensive sort of hum which expanded in the room like warm air or rumors. Until now I had been squinting, but as my eyes began to relax I closed them. The darkness under my eyelids was slightly phosphorescent. With my eyes closed and my mind alert, the world made a lot more sense. Warmth, light, motion, mass, gravity, weight, space and sound. These were all around me, but sometimes I could not see or sense them because the world got in my way, sometimes even the thickness and delirium of my own body. Rodney hummed, and Beatrice's soft hand nestled in mine like some submarine creature, convoluted and brainless, a mass of uncomprehending nerve and muscle. I could travel away through worlds of weight and sound, but only with this sleeping hand to guide me back again. The world of sensation was very dim, and Rodney's humming voice trembled everywhere like loose wallpaper. Dark shapes turned around me, and I descended through notched cavernous chambers of impacted weight and mass. Sound resided everywhere, but mass resided only in strategic places, places where it waited to influence human events. Light always resided somewhere other than where it was. I traveled without body or form. I was just an envelope of heat and sensation, diffused by the radiant warmth of other hands and bodies. You couldn't make out faces or landscapes down here. You could only detect the irreducible heart of things, things like light, and motion, and weight, and mass, and sound.

"Hey!"

Someone shook my shoulder. I opened my eyes.

"Hey, did you feel anything? I think I started to feel something."

All the lights were on. Rodney stood over me, a freshly lit cigarette smoldering in his hand. He had taken off his T-shirt to reveal the green tattoo of a dragon uncurling around his pale navel. Rodney's chest was smooth, muscled and hairless.

"Didn't you feel something there at the end? Not a voice, exactly. It was like we were slipping, like we were getting through somewhere."

Beatrice sat on the edge of Rodney's bed, her legs primly crossed, turning the pages of *Biker's World Magazine* and snapping her gum.

"I don't know," I said. Rodney's room seemed very smoky and unfamiliar. I reached for one of Rodney's cigarettes from the card table. "I can't really say yet."

"You'll see," Rodney said. "We'll do it tomorrow. We'll keep doing it until we get it right." Rodney went and sat on the bed next to Beatrice. He put one arm around her. "How you doing, baby?"

I placed my hands in the pockets of my Levi's jacket. Concealed there were the chemicals I had wrapped in baggy sandwich bags. I couldn't even remember what they were anymore. Just chemicals, I thought.

I asked Beatrice if she wanted me to walk her home.

"That's OK, Phillip." She didn't take her eyes off the turning pages in her magazine. "I think I'll stay here with Rodney a little longer."

Rodney didn't look at me either. His arm remained awkwardly draped around Beatrice's neck. Rodney and Beatrice posed there like lovers grown bored of both themselves and friendly cameras. They had moved out of the world of motion where I once adored to watch them kiss and pet. They had entered the realm of family photographs now, but it was not my family. It wasn't even really my camera.

I let myself out the front door without encountering Ethel. The light was still on in her room, however, yellow and very bright, and I could see it from across the street, where I stood for almost an hour, wondering how cold she was in there and whether she was listening, as I always suspected, for every movement Rodney made, for every sound and every breath her cautious silence might elicit. The light in Ethel's room was hard, like space, not airy at all. I stood on the street corner near a flickering, buzzing lamppost. The light was already out in Rodney's room, and I figured they must know I was out here. It seemed to me implicit in our relationship, that I would be standing on a street corner watching the dark window of Rodney's room while Ethel's light burned cold and useless alongside it.

After a while, Ethel's light went out too, and, abandoned even by the abstract movement of contrasts, I returned again to my real home.

Dad was lying on the living room sofa with the television on. Johnny Carson was saying, "I don't know about you, Doc, but I'll be damned if I'll spend the night with Ed in a urinal, mirrored ceilings or not!" Dad chuckled feebly. One hand was propped behind his head, the other pressed against his stomach. An open blue glass bottle of Maalox stood beside Dad on the mahogany coffee table. As I stepped slowly into the room, my reflection crossed the Panasonic's dusty screen.

Dad cocked his head to see me. Then he looked back at the television. "Hi, son. I didn't hear you come in." Dad took a swig from his Maalox and replaced it on the coffee table, which showed a few faint white rings where Dad had placed the bottle before. "I think I'll sleep in here again tonight," Dad said. "I've been restless lately. I don't want to wake your mom or the baby."

"Do you want a blanket?"

"Sure, maybe before you go to bed. How were your friends?"

"OK, I guess."

"You should bring them by sometime. I'd like to meet them."

I was staring at the television. "I'm sure they'd like to meet you too," I said emptily, without any enthusiasm. Johnny was talking about Ed's drinking. Johnny didn't want to say Ed drank a lot but. Johnny'd been out with Ed a few times, and wow-a-wow-a-wowa.

"How's your stomach?" I asked Dad.

"I don't know. I think it may be getting a little better."

I fixed Dad strong black coffee laced with tannic acid, brought him a blanket and a pillow from our well-stocked linen closet (stocked, incidentally, by an invisible maid who always arrived and departed before I was out of bed in the morning). Then I went down the hall into Mom's room, where Mom was watching Johnny Carson too.

Mom was radiant, propped up by a brown corduroy backrest. On a handsome tray beside her bed was an ice chest, bottles of Perrier, orange juice and a small untouched bell glass of rosy port.

"Hi, Mom," I said.

I could see the flickering television reflected in Mom's eyes. Mom's protuberant stomach underneath the taut, tucked blanket was filled with movement, just like Dad's. Mom's movement, though, was the movement of life. Molecules assembled, deploying minerals, proteins and enzymes. Routine circulatory, digestive and pulmonary processes began to beat inside the still gelid mass of it. You could already begin to see the tiny eyes. You could already begin to hear the tiny mind learning to click, click.

"Dad's sleeping on the couch tonight," I said, crawling onto the bed beside her, touching her blanketed stomach. "So he won't wake you or the baby."

"That's nice, dear."

"I want you to know I'm taking full responsibility for

everything that happens from now on." I had taken Mom's fair freckled hand between my hands. The skin was soft and faintly translucent, knitted with fine blue veins. "I'm not going to go drifting off again when things get too confusing or complicated. I know I went pretty far into myself for a while there, but I've come out the other side, now. I think I've grown up, Mom. That means I can be a lot more help to you from now on."

Mom transferred the glass of icy Perrier to her right hand. Her left hand touched my wrist. For the first time since Dad's arrival, Mom was wearing her expensive wedding ring and engagement band which used to lie neglected in the bottom of her big black purse among crumpled gum wrappers and Kleenex. "I'm sure you will be, baby. I'm sure you'll be a lot of help to me and your father. You always meant well. I never thought for one minute you didn't mean well."

I fell asleep that night in Mom's bed, with the warmth of her hand on my wrist. This was the vital current. Beatrice's hand, mine, and now Mom's. It was like genealogy, race, intertribal culture, migrating birds, evolution. The warmth traveled from one person to another; it changed people and people changed it. It grew warmer, it grew colder. Sometimes it grew warmer again. Soon Dad would be a part of it too, I thought, pulling the smoky dreams into my body and face. Soon Dad would be the warmth I shared with other people and there was nothing, really, nothing he could do about it.

2 2

"The occult is that relative half-world into which we journey to make our own world more real," Beatrice said, while Rodney and I squirted Hansen's airplane glue into our Kleenex. I kept my eye on Rodney. "I don't think the occult dimension is necessarily more invalid than our own, or more valid either. It's just that big black gap of things we don't know. I think we should learn to accept the things we don't know on their own terms, without wondering things like, you know. Whether we're *really* talking to our departed great-grandmother or not. Or whether it's the devil out there, or demons or goblins. We have to accept life's gaps and lapses as well as its hard promises. I think that's your problem, Phillip. I think you need answers to everything. I think something's not real to you unless you can use it exactly the way you want."

Rodney pinched shut his left nostril and applied the wadded Kleenex to his right. Then he inhaled a long whistling rough breath and the Kleenex popped. I followed his example, though perhaps with less ardor.

"I mean, if you guys could just see yourselves," Beatrice said, overturning her book on her knee. The book was Nietzsche's *The Genealogy of Morals*. "Shoving crap up your nose so you can feel less real. Trying to move into the half-lit world of the doped, the dreaming and insane. Now, if you guys were just trying to experience it, I might have a bit more sympathy for you. If you were just charting maps, trying to move to the edges of the experiential precipice, so to speak, then I'd just say you were kids stretching your wings. It would just be part of growing up—and a *good* part, as far as I'm concerned. But you guys don't think that way. You want to move into the unreal so you can turn it into property. You want to build houses there, motels and swimming pools, convenience stores and parking lots. You want to find escape, pleasure, pain, spirits, things. Things you can use, just like you use those chemicals, Phillip. You don't care about chemistry. You don't care about abstract knowledge—no matter what you say. You're just using those chemicals to kill your dad. And that's what this whole occult thing is all about, too. So you and Rodney can take control of everything, because that's how you see life. Use or be used. That's so goddamn male, Phillip. That's so goddamn hopelessly . . . oh, I don't know. So goddamn *penile* of you. It makes me just want to throw up. You notice I'm talking to you, Phillip, and not to Rodney. That's because I always expected more from you. It's not like Rodney's ever listened to a word of sense in his entire life—certainly not if it would do him one bit of good. But I always expected more from you, Phillip. I thought you and I shared a certain unexpressed sympathy about the unknown world. I thought you loved it as much as I did. But you're no better than Custer. You're no better than the goddamn Mormons. You just want to make the unknown profitable. I guess I've been really disappointed in you lately, Phillip. I guess I've really been disappointed in you ever since your dad came."

A hot burning sensation lifted high into my skull. It was not unpleasant, and quickly diminished to a soft convincing whisper. I rested the wadded Kleenex on my knee. I felt very good and relaxed. It was not as if I was under the influence of anything at all. It was a sensation just like breathing or drinking cool water. A thin fog entered Rodney's room. I heard Rodney taking another long sniff, and when I looked at him again he was withdrawing the Kleenex from his nose. Fragments of the pink tissue were attached to the rim of each nostril like confetti.

"Pretty heavy, huh?" Rodney's voice was nasal and rough. He leaned back on his bed, adjusting pillows, then crossed his arms and looked at me, grinning remotely like a forgotten relative at some tedious family get-together. "Do you dig this stuff, dude, or what?"

Beatrice was wrong. I did not feel more distant from the world so much as more firmly rooted in it. I was caught among its tangled whispering earth and dense folds, like a sparrow in a blanket. Small animals hypnotize themselves when trapped by some urgent predator. It's not so painful then, life's last moment.

"Just keep pouring more fuel on the fire," Beatrice said, as if she were reading my mind, or I were reading hers. "Keep acquiring more property. Keep buying more nice pretty things and stuffing your bodies with more burgers and cheesecakes and candy bars and bonbons. And don't stop just because you don't want any more, or even because you don't need any more. Because you always want more. You always need more."

I sniffed. Rodney sat across the table from me. His expression was remote and diffuse. He sniffed.

"She never shuts up, does she?" he said. "All day and all night. Yap yap yap. Even in bed when you're doing it to her, she talks right through it. She doesn't shut up for one minute." Rodney sniffed, and ran the back of his hand across his nose. His eyes were red and bleary. "It can get pretty frustrating sometimes."

We all joined hands around the table again, Beatrice with her armed and petulant silence, more ominous even than her most dire predictions. Rodney and I shared our gazes with the flickering candle flame.

"Now, I've been reading up a little more on this stuff," Rodney said.

I sniffed (or was it Rodney who sniffed?).

"Now what I should've done first is gone off and purified myself, by drinking pure water and meditating," Rodney said. "But since we didn't do it last time, I figured we might as well skip it this time, too."

"You'll both end up in reform school," Beatrice said. "You think you're a couple of real rebels or something. But when I look at you all I see are a couple of little kids."

Rodney sniffed noisily. After a moment, I sniffed too, but more succinctly, as if to dissociate myself from Rodney.

"Now," Rodney said, switching off the light and taking our hands, "let's get down to business."

Over succeeding days and weeks the three of us settled into our new routine with a sort of grateful complacency. It was like the days of our burglaries, only more patient and informal. I would spend the day at home watching TV with Mom on the big bed, while Dad was either at work or sleeping fitfully on the living room sofa. If Dad was home, I would hear him go into the bathroom every twenty minutes or so, then the flush of the toilet. Mom and I watched the game shows and soap operas together, and sometimes I tried to explain the rationale of these programs to Mom's baby.

"The woman's voice you're hearing now," I said, "is the voice of Victoria Morgan, the youngest and very spoiled daughter of Joshua Saner Morgan, the richest man in Creek Valley. Victoria is used to getting her own way, and she'll get it no matter who tries to oppose her. She's not really the mother figure in all this. She's sort of the evil-twin type, though she doesn't look at all like her sister, Felicia Morgan, who's actually a very nice person. Felicia's daughter, Jeremy, is the illegitimate daughter of the police inspector, David Rampart. I think of her as the sort of heroine of the show, because she's really pretty—almost as pretty as Mom—and she's always trying to help her friends get out of trouble, like when they tried to frame Tad Stevens for murder that time. When you get out, we'll probably watch "Heartbeat County General" every afternoon, so eventually you'll catch on to all the names and faces, though you don't really need to know all the characters and plots that well to enjoy the show. Also, I better warn you. People are always extra serious about how they feel on this show. They're either *really* happy, or *really* sad, or *really* having a good time. It can really get on your nerves after a while. It's something you just have to get used to, I guess."

Late in the afternoons I would tuck Mom into bed after she had fallen into one of her dozes, then slip down the back stairs to avoid Dad on the living room sofa, and arrive at Rodney's around four o'clock. Ethel would present me a small snack. We would exchange some light banter about weather and current events. If I waited long enough, she would inevitably try to engage me in conversation about Rodney.

"Is there anything bothering Rodney that you know about?" she might ask, while I munched my carrot sticks, or contemplated my hot black coffee. "Is there anything Rodney's not telling me?"

I tried to remain as noncommittal as possible, but confronted by Ethel's strained and withering sadness I could not help but offer her tiny gifts.

"I think it's just school," I might say. "He's having trouble adjusting." Or: "I think it's just his age, Ethel. You know he's practically a teenager and all. Everybody starts acting a little weird when they go through puberty, or so I've heard."

"I don't know where he goes at nights," Ethel said. "People call on the phone for him. Sometimes they're grown men. I don't trust their voices. They have very dark, rough voices. They want Roddy to meet them places. Some nights, Roddy doesn't come back at all from these meetings. Sometimes he's gone for days at a time, and won't tell me a word about where he's been. He won't even call to tell me when he'll be back."

"He's just practicing a little independence, Ethel, that's all. It's perfectly normal for kids his age. Especially for young men."

"When he's in his room alone at night I hear him talking to himself out loud, saying the strangest things."

"He's just exercising his imagination. Rodney," I assured Ethel, as if it were some sort of cherished compensation, "has a very active imagination, as you well know."

"Sometimes I get very worried, Phillip. I can't sleep at night. I start thinking, well . . . I start thinking terrible things about Roddy. I'm embarrassed to admit it. But I start thinking maybe he's not turning into a very nice person. I can't help myself. I know it's a horrible thing to say . . ." Ethel turned and looked away. Tears formed in her eyes. Her voice grew rough and swollen. "I just don't know sometimes." One tear ran down her cheek.

"It's OK, Ethel. I understand." I reached across the table and took her hand. "I really do understand, Ethel. Don't cry. Sometimes we hate the people we love. Freud said that. It's perfectly normal. Whatever you think, for God's sake don't think there's anything wrong with you, because there isn't anything wrong. There really isn't."

"I don't mean hate." Ethel took her hand away. She had abruptly stopped crying. Her voice had returned to normal. She gazed off at chrome fixtures on the stove, her hands nestled together in her lap like lovers. "I mean I start having these terrible thoughts. Roddy's a *good* boy, and I know that. I really do. But sometimes I think, well, he may have gotten in with the wrong crowd. I don't mean you, Phillip, or Beatrice. I mean the sort of crowd he hangs around with when you're not around. Like the boys at the bowling alley, or the boys who hang around at Shakey's Pizza. Then there's those strange boys I always see outside on the street at night. There's usually just one of them. I can see him from my bedroom window. Sometimes he's staring up at me, like he knows I'm watching. They frighten me, Phillip. I'm so worried about Roddy I can't sleep or go to the bathroom I'm so worried. I think it's happened. You know, Phillip, I think Roddy may be doing it. He may be experimenting, you know. With drugs, marijuana. Or maybe even worse."

"Ethel, look at me." My voice was very firm and direct. I leaned earnestly across the table, pushing aside a depleted wooden bowl of corn chip fragments. "Ethel, look me in the eye." Her hands began to fidget as her eyes rested on mine. The hearts of her eyes were fractured and simian. Her hands began pinching at one another, like quarrelsome crabs. "Rodney has a cigarette every once in a while. Maybe a beer or a drink. But he's not crazy, Ethel. He's got his feet planted firmly on the ground, and you *know* that. I'm Rodney's best friend, and *I* know that. OK, so he likes to wear some offbeat clothes—but that's Rodney. He's a trend-setter, he's his own man. I'm telling you—all the kids at school look up to Rodney. They're always imitating him. If Rodney's going to keep one step ahead of the pack, he's got to go for the more outrageous sorts of styles, you know? But, Ethel, now listen to me carefully now. Don't ever, *ever* think *that* about him again. It's just plain wrong, that's what it is. It doesn't do you any good. It doesn't do Rodney any good. Just trust him, and trust me. Rodney's a good kid, Ethel, and you know that. He's good inside—he's good inside *here*"—I thumped my chest affirmatively with my fist— "in here where it matters. He's going to turn into the sort of man you're going to be very proud of one day, Ethel. I promise you."

I got up from the table, took the bowl to the sink and rinsed it in cold water.

"You're right, Phillip. You're right. I shouldn't doubt him. You're right, Phillip. Oh, you're so, so right." Her eyes were filling with tears and admiration for me, even longing. Our conversations always ended this way, with her palpable desire for me filling her eyes with tears. She wanted to keep me here, I could tell. She wanted to keep me here forever, her adoring and adored second child. She wanted to lift me up and hold me in her arms as tightly as any lover. I couldn't stand it—I finally understood how Rodney felt. I had to get away from here. I had to get far, far away. I had to get as far away as I possibly could from Ethel's oppressive arms.

LIFE

23

After our little meals Ethel would grant me a few of her Ziploc sandwich bags and I would go upstairs where Rodney was listening to Judas Priest or vintage Alice Cooper on his ghettoblaster. Removing his chemistry set from the closet I would check my pocket notebook and mix new, untried combinations which I then wrapped in the plastic bags and hid in my inside jacket pocket. Then Rodney and I would smoke a little marijuana or a fragment of hash, just to put ourselves in the mood. If we were feeling particularly uneasy or discomposed, Rodney would get the airplane glue out from under his bed. By this time Beatrice had arrived, presenting us with baleful forecasts of our adult years when we would certainly turn out to be just like our fathers, oppressing women with our corporations and pocket calculators, adding to the world's heartless mountains of wealth, credit-wealth, consumer goods and other mere things and numbers. "You're all the same," Beatrice complained, reluctantly taking our hands at the dilapidated card table, which was chipped, water-stained, and tracked in places by globular wax. "You just want to be the center of attention all the time. Me me me. That's all you care about." I was already feeling tremulous and thin from the grass and the glue. My eyes felt slightly sore and fuzzy. But I felt lucid as well, lucid inside my own mind, where hard crystal shapes emerged, and spirits gathered firmness, gravity and substance. These were real things in here, not just ideas or shadows. When I closed my eyes everything suddenly made more sense. Then Rodney would begin to hum.

On a Wednesday, separately and silently in Rodney's dark room, we all experienced our first real encounter with the purer world of spirit.

I was feeling particularly heady and diffuse with marijuana and glue, sitting on my seat like a swami floating on a carpet. Lights, candle, smoky incense, cabala, grimoires, totem and taboo. "I think we've been patient long enough," Rodney said. His entire tone and demeanor had changed. He was wearing a Nazi insignia framed by a pentagram on a leather thong around his neck. The knuckles of his right hand displayed his new tattoo, a bright caduceus with rippling scaly skin. His hair was shaved in a mohawk and dyed an almost fluorescent orange. "We're not looking for handouts, you know. It's not like we're asking for favors or anything. We just thought, like, we're young, and we're going to be around on this earth for quite a while, and we're willing to do literally *anything* you want, and all you've got to do is just *speak* to us for about five seconds and let us know you're interested. But do you guys have the time? I mean, do you guys even make the measliest little effort? I don't think you seem to appreciate all the time and energy my friends and I have been wasting here."

Beatrice took her hand from mine momentarily and yawned, holding her tiny hand to her smudged moist mouth, her eyes closed while she stretched. She looked like a small white kitten when she yawned. Whenever Beatrice yawned it reminded me of how much I once loved her.

"So anyway," Rodney concluded, "let's get this relationship going, and stop beating around the bush. We're here, you're there and it's about time somebody made the first move. You guys are more experienced in all this than we are—we're looking for a little mature guidance in the matter. So let's *go*. Give us a *sign*, for chrissakes. We're starting to look pretty stupid, if you want to know the truth. Holding hands and waiting for you to take your sweet time and all. Look, you want sacrifices, blood rituals? You want our *souls*, for chrissakes? I'm not doing nothing with mine—it's *yours*. You hear me? Come and take *all* our souls—all except Beatrice's, of course, because she's such a perfect angel, as everybody knows in the entire universe by now since she's probably told them herself personally. Phillip and I, on the other hand, don't give a fuck. We're yours. But if there's something you want us to do, then you've got to tell us. OK? Are we getting through to you guys? Now, we're going to be quiet again for a while, but that doesn't mean we're like suckers or something. That doesn't mean we're going to sit here forever. I'm sorry to be sounding so impatient and all, but I'm starting to feel a little used, if you want to know the goddamn truth. So look, whenever you're ready, you just let us know, OK? We'll sit here nice and quiet, and you take your time and think about it. Then, if you want, you contact *us*, OK?''

So we sat in the darkness, and Rodney hummed, and Beatrice fell asleep, snoring slightly. It seemed a night like all the others, chemicals in my pocket, this strange house of Rodney's around me, Ethel downstairs with her doubts and unsteady aluminum cane, while back at home Dad was being steadily dissolved by the universe of rushing darkness and Mom watched color TV. Again I descended through the earth's dark layers into a subterranean world where strange prehistoric skeletons etched the dense basalt walls; broken human bones and teeth lay strewn about like discarded toys in a cannibals' kindergarten. I was expecting to find the dead down here, spirits with scores to settle, or even vast shapeless things without thoughts, things that just shifted and turned. Perhaps it wasn't the afterlife at all. Perhaps it was the pre-life. Or perhaps it was just nothing and nowhere, where beings just lay around waiting for things that never happened. Non-life, anti-life. Proto-death, death in life. I was moving through a convoluted passage which seemed only dimly familiar. Death. I'd never encountered it before, not even in my imagination. Death was in these passages I had until now blithely elided in both my texts and my dreams. Death was something permanent. Death never moved. I began to feel an ominous presence in the darkness around me. Dead. Voiceless. Pitiless. Lucid. Hard. Death was matter, death was pure mass. Death might even

208

be better, I was beginning to suspect. Death was real, while life by contrast seemed little more than a presumption, something broken which rattled and would not last. I was moving into the lightless heart of something I had never seen. It was filled with shapes and presences, but you could not see or touch them. Instead they seemed to elicit a sort of buried radar from my skull and sinuses and teeth. The world of death was very simple. There was no more thinking or being thought down here. There was no more fear or suffering or hate. Ever since I could remember I had been trying to discover my own Way in life, that journey I would make in the world alone. Perhaps I had been looking in the wrong place all along. Perhaps this was my true path down here. Something cold passed by me. Everything was growing misty and damp as I waded into the mud which grew deeper and marshier. It grasped my ankles, calves, thighs. It made sucking sounds against my skin. I realized I wasn't wearing any clothes. I felt very cold all of a sudden, as if all the cold shapes passing me in the cavern were now gathering around, pressing closer against me, untextured and weightless and dull.

"It's all the same slow dream," Mom's voice said out loud, loud and real in this underworld like the voice of the Mom who, I understood only now, was dead forever. "You, me, Dad, our home back in Bel Air. It's a beautiful big house that's waiting for us, baby. It has a pool and a big yard."

"This is the history of motion," I said. "You and me, Mom. The history of motion."

"There's nothing for you down here, Phillip."

"I want to stay."

"You wouldn't like it. You'd catch cold. I wouldn't always be around, and you'd be frightened. You'd wonder where I was. After a while, you'd start to resent me."

"I resent you now."

"You've spent too much of your life alone, baby. That's my fault. I never helped you become properly acclimated to the world. There's a real world in which we all have to live together. That means we have to make concessions for the benefit of other people. That means we simply can't have everything exactly the way we want it all the time. This life you're living inside yourself is just a dream. A dream of you, me, and your father which doesn't work. Or maybe it works too well."

"I've decided I'm going to do it." I could not disguise the lift of triumph in my voice. "Rodney's going to help. Rodney and I are going to do it together."

"Then do it, baby. At least you'll be functioning. At least you'll be making some sort of impression out there, instead of just down here in your own mind. Live in the world, baby. That's all I ever meant for you to learn, and you never did. It's my fault. I can't blame you. It's my fault entirely."

"Is Pedro down here?" I asked. I had felt another cold shape approach me. I was filled with either fear or hatred. Something burned in me, some impalpable fuel. "Is that Pedro with you?"

"Of course not, baby. Pedro's upstairs with you. Pedro's out there in the real world with you."

"Pedro?" Tears were forming in my eyes, cold, freezing. "Pedro? Is that you? Pedro? Are you out there? This is me. This is Phillip."

"If you're going to do it," Mom's voice said, "then you better do it now. Stop beating around the bush, baby. If you're going to kill your father, then kill him tonight. Kill him tonight and get on with your life."

It was Pedro out there, but Mom was hiding him from me. It was Pedro. His multitudinous arms came up around me, icy and damp and formless and thick. It was Pedro. Pedro was dead and waiting for me. For me. Pedro was waiting for me.

"Why don't you go kill everybody while you're at it? But start with the men. Kill all the men, you guys. Then get back to me in a few thousand years or so. We might have something going then. We might be on our way towards some practical solution to things."

"If you're not going to help, Beatrice, just put a lid on it, OK?" Rodney was selecting a cord of rope from a cabinet drawer. We were standing in Rodney's basement in the cold fluid light of a naked overhead bulb. I was on my knees going through my steel toolbox. The lid of the case was open, displaying cold gleaming tools in red steel compartments.

"I'll tell you what. *I'll* even help." Beatrice was sitting atop Ethel's Maytag dryer. She had lit a cigarette, and was gesturing it with dramatic disregard just like Greta Garbo. "We'll buy us some machine guns, some Uzis, and some

211

army issue bazookas. Then we'll go down to the shopping mall and start blowing everybody's goddamn head off. OK? That'll teach them. That'll teach them all a good lesson or two, won't it? I can hardly wait. I really can't wait another minute."

"Do we need these?"

Rodney showed me a rusty pair of gardening clippers.

I thought for a moment. "Sure," I said. "Why not."

"Look, we'll get us some hand grenades. We'll start lobbing these big hand grenades into B. Dalton's and the May Co. We'll blow the fuckers to kingdom come—that's what we'll do. We'll be just like Dirty Harry. We'll be just like John Wayne. Sure, some innocent lives may be lost, but there's nothing we can do about *that*. If you're going to fight evil, ma'am, then sometimes you just gotta be a little evil yourself. We'll detonate the goddamn mall, that's what we'll do. Save ourselves the trouble of going in there. Then we can move on to the Ford dealership. Cost Plus. The Warehouse. City Hall. We'll teach all those liberal phonies what real suffering's all about, won't we, guys? Sure, they can all *talk* about peace and love and brotherhood, but when it comes right down to getting things done, well, that's where *we'll* move in. Whistling our national anthem and spraying bloody death wherever we go, because we're *realists*. We want peace too, but we don't have any liberal bullshit illusions about how it's gotta be achieved. War's hell, but sometimes it's just goddamn necessary if peace is to be preserved. I'll meet you guys in the car. I'm going to go take a long piss in the alley." Beatrice flicked her cigarette and it arced across the dim garage, crashing against Ethel's Toyota Corolla in a shower of sparks. "Bring beer. Afterwards we'll go down to the whorehouse and get ourselves properly laid." Beatrice stared at my toolbox with a sort of weird inanition.

Rodney stacked a long extension cord beside the toolbox, in case the rope was not enough. We stood there for a moment thinking, looking at the gray steel box.

"Next stop, the Middle East," Beatrice said. Her voice was clipped and mechanical. "Peace through strength. Wealth through poverty. Love through death. Once we've taught those Palestinians a lesson they'll never forget, we'll build this humongous K Mart. Then we'll move on to take care of those fucking Chinese. We won't even try to set up any sort of provisional government there or anything. We'll just kill all the fucking Chinese. God, how I hate them. God how I hate those goddamn Chinese."

Rodney's hands rested on his hips. His expression seemed momentarily to approve of our preparations. Then, as if approval in any form was for Rodney a sort of lapse, he scowled bitterly. He reached to his shirt pocket for his cigarettes, offered me one, and shrugged in Beatrice's general direction.

"She thinks this is all some sort of game," he said. "She thinks this is all just some big har-de-har laugh or something."

"I know," I said. It was time for us to leave. "But in her own way, I think she's trying to understand, Rodney. We've got to give her credit for that much." Then I knelt and cranked shut the toolbox's strong steel clasps.

24

"We've unleashed strange forces in the world tonight," Rodney said. "That's what confuses her. In fact, that's what I think women in general don't ever seem to understand. Not that these forces exist. But that we can use them. They aren't just ideas. They accomplish things. They go places."

We were laboring down the ill-lit rubbishy streets off Van Nuys Boulevard, Rodney carrying the toolbox and I the cords of rope, electrical extension cords and a few random saws and hammers. The night air was thick with smog, palpable and rough. Like the smog itself, the darkness did not radiate so much as settle over everything.

"That's the illusion women prefer. That everything can be reduced to talk. I'm warning you, Phillip, I got this one figured. Women are really great and everything. I'm not saying otherwise. But they've got their own sort of truth and it has a way of confusing things sometimes. Men do things. They get things done. That's what men do. Women, on the other hand, talk about things. Why they weren't done quite right. How you might want to go about doing it better *next* time. Which things to do first, and which things last, and which things after that. Talk talk talk. I mean, like Beatrice and all her Communist bullshit. She wants to feed the world, right? But I don't see her feeding anybody. I mean, when's the last time you ever saw Beatrice feeding anybody? I'm talking even a sandwich or something. Never, that's the last time. But when's the last time you heard her *talking* about feeding everybody? She's got a million ideas as far as talk's concerned. If talk was wheat, Beatrice and her Communist sympathizers could feed the whole world. But talk ain't wheat. It's nothing like it." Rodney's pace and expression were gripped by sudden purpose, as if he and I were hurrying to impart some crucial theorem to Rodney's bemused colleagues back at the lab.

"These forces we've unleashed tonight aren't new things, Phillip," Rodney explained earnestly, shifting the toolbox into his left hand, swinging the entire weight and balance of his body along with it. "These forces have been around forever and ever, since the beginning of time, in fact. They've been around since before mankind, even since before the dinosaurs. They were roaming around the universe before the Earth was anything more than a bunch of cosmic debris. They knew what they wanted the world to be, and so they made it that way. They didn't talk about it; they *did* something. They got things done."

Needless to say I was elated, higher than a kite, breezing through the muggy breezeless night. In the wide sun-bleached and pitted streets we walked past dilapidated au-

tomobiles, fading lawns and houses, thinning and recalcitrant trees and foliage. Mimosa, jacaranda, fig, palm,
eucalyptus, dry and spotty bamboo. The air was pungent
with gasoline, smog, and the fishy smells of cooking which,
along with brief bursts of salsa music and Julio Iglesias, filtered from the expressionless facades of Latin households.
Inside those houses people glanced out fitfully from behind
cracked venetian blinds. Timid small children with big eyes
hid behind their parents' legs, waiting for their mothers to
drive them to the laundromat, supermarket and home again
in broken automobiles. At supper they ate with vaguely
surreptitious expressions, their ears alert for any sound in
the street, awaiting that penultimate knock on their door.
These were families who were always waiting to be sent
away, and as a result you never really saw them. These were
the citizens of my secret community I most cherished and
admired. They, like me, lived their secret lives in public
places.

I was going home and taking Rodney with me this time,
and that made a difference. My dreams weren't secrets anymore, but rather part of a common purpose, a scheme of
shared knowledge. Rodney and I were going home together
to see my dad.

Rodney was right—we had unleashed strange forces tonight. Severe black things that had moved up from the
caverns of the dead. Every once in a while I felt them bus-
tling invisibly past me in the street, obloid and featureless,
like faintly disembodied laundry hampers. You could hear
tires careening on Sepulveda Boulevard almost a mile away.

Everything in the world seemed to be aligning itself with these invisible forces, assembling like military units or pieces in an intricate, vast puzzle.

"I don't think evil's such a bad thing, really," Rodney said. "I think it's just something we've got to get used to. It's certainly been around a lot longer than we have. It'll certainly be here long after we're gone. During our séance tonight I heard it speaking to me, Phillip. It said, Get on with it. Live your life. Make things happen. If you listen to Beatrice, you'll never go anywhere, you'll never do anything. For some reason, when I heard that voice, I wasn't really excited or anything. I felt sort of bored, really, like everything had already been figured out. It wasn't something I really enjoyed, just something I simply had to get over with. Frankly, that's what it was like the first time I went to bed with Beatrice. It was like I had to get this over with. I really couldn't get into it that much, once we'd started and I was getting the hang of it. It was like mowing the lawn, or putting away groceries. I guess it's because I'm evil, Phillip. Ethel told me that once when she was really angry. Even a teacher once—even a teacher told me once I was evil. That I'm no good, a bad seed, a black sheep. Evil is just mechanical activity, Phillip. That's what I think, anyway. There's no thought behind it at all. It just goes on and on and on. They say the universe started from a tiny ball of matter, no bigger than this toolbox. I always thought the universe would be a lot more various than that, but now I see it's just the same stuff, stretched out all over space and eternity, filling everything."

We had arrived outside my house. I felt the rushing, formless shapes hurrying faster around me in every direction. There was no wind, no sound. In the living room window, the light was on. The colorless heat of the television glowed steadily.

"I guess you can probably tell I've never really been that big a fan of women's lib," Rodney said. "I say let women stay at home and talk all they want to. Men are the ones that get things done." He wasn't looking at me. He was looking at the toolbox, which he rested against his knee. The ropes and cords were wrapped around my neck like the bandoliers of some South American revolutionary. Rodney was right. I felt bored, inanimate, sleepy. Quietly I opened the garage door, and we carried all our materials up the basement staircase. Mom would be asleep by now. If we hurried, we could be finished by morning.

2 5

Dad hardly stirred on the sofa when Rodney and I entered the living room. I closed the back door and turned the dead bolt. Both the radio and television were on. On the radio Rosemary Clooney was singing:

> *So kiss me once, then kiss me twice,*
> *Then kiss me once again,*
> *It's been a long long time . . .*

Dad lay contentedly asleep, one arm across his chest, his head tilted to one side. The bottles of Maalox stood empty on the coffee table. Dad seemed posed and forlorn, like an expired romantic youth in some pre-Raphaelite painting. On the television Tom Snyder was discussing the secret lives of "sexual deviants" with a transvestite. "Though of course if you look at it from their perspective, I guess," Tom said, "it's probably the rest of us presumably *normal* people who seem like the *deviants*. I mean, we all do our own thing, right, and then when somebody doesn't like us they say that we're a deviant. But for want of a better term, and since such people are often linked in our minds with the term deviant, I guess I'll rudely refer to our next guest as just that, and hope they can understand and bear with me for just a little while . . ." Tom Snyder chain-smoked and gestured vigorously at the camera with both hands. The close-up of Tom's head framed by his easy chair made it appear as if he were in the living room with us. The transvestite's back was to the camera, and his voice was being distorted by the sound engineer. "It's like waking up every day knowing somebody will find out," the transvestite said. "Somebody very close to you. Somebody who loves you, and believes she knows you, and yet she doesn't really know you at all."

> *You'll never know how many dreams*
>   *I dreamed about you.*
> *Or just how empty they all seemed without you*
> *So kiss me once, then kiss me twice*
> *Then kiss me once again,*
> *It's been a long, long time . . .*

"Should we wake him up?" Rodney asked.

Dad's lap-top, his briefcase, his stacks of printout and papers were on the dining room table. Some coffee in a mug splotched with scummy cream. A moldering and half-eaten French-style donut on a sheet of corrugated white paper towel.

"It's up to you," Rodney said. "He's under a spell I cast back at my house. I like to call it the Spell of the Sleeping Man. When men sleep, their souls travel around the world, trying to shape themselves into other things. I've had your dad's spirit held incommunicado. He won't wake up again until I let him."

I switched off the radio. "I want to check in on my mom," I said, and led Rodney down the hall. Mom's bedroom door was open, and Mom was sitting up in bed. Her face was brilliant with bright cosmetics and white, grainy talcum. Her hair was bundled up in a black net cap. The light from the television flickered across her face, like radar scanning the moon. She looked a little like Bette Davis in *Whatever Happened to Baby Jane.*

My hand rested on the cold doorknob. I wanted to pull it shut before Rodney saw her. But Rodney was already standing there beside me. It was important to me not to appear ashamed. Now that Rodney saw her, I wanted him to be able to take his time.

"Jesus," Rodney said after a minute. I was starting to tremble, awaiting Rodney's judgment concerning the truest, most secret part of me. "For some reason I thought your mom was good-looking."

"She used to be," I said. "She used to be really good-looking. She's started letting herself go lately. I think it's because Dad came back. Or maybe because of the baby."

221

Outside Mom's bedroom window a searchlight flashed through the alley. Out of the city's general white noise emerged the hard beating sound of a helicopter in the air. The searchlight flashed again.

"Does she just watch TV all day?"

"No." I shrugged. "She talks to me sometimes. Sometimes she talks to Dad."

"What sort of programs does she watch?"

"Old movies, usually. Game shows and soaps. That sort of thing."

"It doesn't like give you the creeps to have her sitting there all the time with that look on her face? I think it would me. I think it would really give me the creeps."

"Long ago Mom and I came to a sort of understanding," I said, and realized suddenly it was not the sort of understanding one could easily explain to a third party.

On the television the transvestite was saying, "It was nice just to meet people who understood how I felt, and didn't make me feel like some sort of weirdo or something. It was nice to know I wasn't alone, and that what I was doing was perfectly normal to a lot of perfectly normal people like myself. Many of these people had prominent careers in business, advertising and even television broadcasting."

Rodney struck a match and took a long hit off a joint. He took two more quick hits, just to get the ember flaring. Then he handed it to me, speaking deep in his chest while he held his breath.

"She's knocked up, isn't she?"

I looked at the bright ember. A hard green seed blackened and spilled onto the rug. I stepped on it.

"I know," I said. "She's really knocked up."

Then I pulled shut Mom's bedroom door.

We bound Dad on the sofa with the clothesline and electrical extension cords and gagged him with a pair of his own white monogrammed handkerchiefs. Dad didn't move or make a sound or open his eyes. His face was flushed and pouting, like the face of a small child who has just awakened in the lap of its parent at some endless holiday party. There was something very warm and innocent about Dad now—if I still believed in innocence, that is. Occasionally, when his head lolled to one side, he might momentarily snore or kick. Dad was definitely very far away. Perhaps Rodney really had managed to arrange his spiritual kidnap. I had a pretty good idea what we had to do now.

I was high on the marijuana and my first few sips of a Budweiser I had found in the refrigerator. Rodney was drinking Jack Daniel's on ice, crushed glittering rattly ice from the freezer's automatic icemaker. "It's not what we do that matters," Rodney said, opening the toolbox on the floor. "It's our frame of mind when we do it. This isn't another person, Phillip. The person inside your dad's already dead. This is just a body filled with energy. This is a body filled with energy that we can join ourselves with and use to make ourselves stronger. We can shape, funnel and redirect it places. We can use it to our own purposes."

Rodney handed me one of the sharper tools. "All right, Phillip? Do you understand? How do you feel? You ready to go?"

The tool felt very firm, like the edge of a desk, or the fender of an automobile. The weight was reassuring, in a way. But there was something in its dull edges that disturbed me for a reason I couldn't quite articulate. "I don't know," I said. I waited for a moment. Already I felt his presence in the room, as if a large window had opened to admit a soft cold wind. He deserved to be here, I thought. It was perfectly fair. I turned and looked over Rodney's shoulder. Pedro was sitting at the dining room table beside a stack of Dad's business papers. "Do it," he said. "Do it, do it, do it."

I looked at Rodney again just as Rodney turned to look over his shoulder. After a moment, he looked at me. He didn't look like he trusted me very much.

"I feel good," I said quickly. I didn't want him to see Pedro for the same reason I didn't want him to see Mom. It seemed to me a sort of personal violation. "I think I feel all right."

I leaned over Dad with the sharp tool in my hand.

"This has nothing to do with your dad at all," Pedro said very loudly. "I don't have a single bad word to say about him. It's your mom we're thinking about now, Phillip. I think it's about time you stopped worrying so much about your own damn self and started paying a little attention to *her* feelings. You shouldn't have done what you did to me, Phillip. I was good for your mom and you knew it. You only loved your dad because you knew he wasn't any good for her at all. Your dad didn't threaten you. Maybe he could destroy your mom, but he couldn't destroy your mom's love for you. That was all you cared about, Phillip. Your mom's love. You don't care what happens to other people. You just care about maintaining those private temperatures inside yourself."

My hands were shaking as I handed the tool back to Rodney and he handed me another, like a surgeon and his faithful, highly qualified nurse in a long intricate operating theater while young students observed from a high balcony. I felt Rodney's hand grasp my shoulder.

"You all right?"

"I'm all right." I took the next few tools without examining them. I felt hot and dizzy. Magnified and eccentric, the motes swirled around me in the dim light of the television. The television volume was turned down low, and someone was whispering something about Islamic Fundamentalism. I applied the tools, one at a time, to Dad's flushed, warm skin. Gently, at first. My skull throbbed with a low dull ache which seemed to intensify with every move I made. It was a sharp, shooting pain at times, into my sinuses and eyeballs.

"You know what you did, Phillip," Pedro was saying, without bitterness and without remorse. "You did it, and now you have to know you did it. You have to know you did it, Phillip. Otherwise it doesn't mean anything. Otherwise it's like it never happened. Then I'd hate you, Phillip. Then I'd never forgive you."

My knees buckled slightly as the blood rushed to my feverish head. Pain expanded in my skull like the skin of a balloon. I handed the tool back to Rodney. I touched Dad's hot flushed skin with my trembling fingers. There was a large blue vein under his neck.

"He's still breathing," I said. "He's still got a pulse."

"Of course he does. You haven't *done* anything to him yet."

"I haven't?" The room was turning slowly around me. "I haven't done *anything?*"

I heard the tool clatter into the steel box. Then Rodney said disgustedly, "I thought you said you knew how to do this."

"He does," Pedro said.

"I do," I said, stepping away from the ambient warmth of Dad's trussed body. "I do, I really do." I was gesturing with both my hands, trying to make the room stop moving. I heard something kick. Weight was pouring from the mouth of the Budweiser can into the thick pile carpet at my feet. "I just need a drink, that's all. I think I'm coming down with something." I brushed my forehead with the back of my hand. "I think I may be coming down with a fever. I may be coming down with a cold or something." Tears were forming in my eyes, and I wiped them against my shoulder. I was backing out of the living room. I didn't look at Pedro as I passed him. Suddenly I was in the bright latex kitchen. All the lights were on. One of us had left the refrigerator door open, and the engine was humming, generating its icy mist. One of the eggs in the egg rack was cracked and exuded a yellow, inflating gel.

"Hey, Phillip! We gonna get this over with or what?"

I wanted Rodney to go away, but I knew he wouldn't, he wouldn't go away. I grasped the open door of the refrigerator and braced myself against it. The cold air rushed over me, like water in a bath. I needed this. I reached for a liter bottle of 7UP and took it to the beige-tiled kitchen counter. As I was reaching a glass down from the cupboards, I saw Dad's note on the counter beside the matching flour, rice and sugar bins. An empty pharmaceutical vial rested atop Dad's letter like a paperweight. The letter was printed on Dad's Epson printer, like junk mail advertising some new MasterCard Card Bonus Club Service. The empty vial said, "Phenobarbitone 50 mg. Take one in evening to sleep." Inside the vial was a thin white powder, like the powder you find at the bottom of an extinguished loaf of Wonderbread. I picked up Dad's letter. Dear Son, it said,

I hope this is something you'll understand better than your mother, who has a lot of other things on her mind right now. I just think that perhaps things will be much better for both of you when I'm gone. Please do not feel guilty about this even a little bit, since it is a decision I have made without you knowing it or having anything to do with it. I think this is the only way to provide a quick resolution for everybody, since I am certain I am *suffering from some irreversible stomach cancer or maybe even something worse, since I can't sleep at all and my stomach feels terrible all the time and there are worse symptoms I won't really go into right now. Just remember that whatever happens wherever in your life, that your parents really did the very best they could to make you happy, it's just sometimes they couldn't stop themselves from being selfish, stupid or confused. All parents fail their children and we all have to get used to that, I guess. You'll have children of your own someday and maybe then you'll understand. I'm counting on you to take good care of your mother after I'm gone. I know you can do it since you did very well without me before I came to make both your lives so miserable. Everything is in very good shape with my lawyer, whose business card you will find attached, and whom I have carefully informed as to your mother's condition so he will keep a good eye on her from now on. There is $5,000 cash in my wallet.*

Love,

Dad

I put the letter down on the counter. Immediately it began absorbing a semicircle of 7UP, causing many of the words to expand into nervy blue blotches. My hands were trembling, and I felt a slow descending warmth in my stomach.

I felt insecure and dizzy. Rationality had abandoned me like a boat or a train. I wanted to grasp hold of something, but I couldn't find anything firm enough. I heard the letter crumbling in my fist, the thin computer paper like something you'd wrap around steaks at the butcher's. I was hot with sudden steaming rage. Dad thought he was going to leave me. He was going to abandon me and Mom and the baby. He didn't care what happened to us, or what sort of place we might end up. He wouldn't even take us with him. Suddenly I recalled a solitary moment from my childhood. I was standing on the front lawn, watching Dad's car pull out of the driveway. I was holding something in my hand— a toy truck, or a plastic soldier, or perhaps a partially macerated baseball card. It was an offering, but he wouldn't take it. He was climbing into his big automobile and slamming shut the door. He was pulling out of the driveway, looking over his other shoulder, not even seeing me. Then I was watching the taillights of his car fading in the gray dusk. I called his name but he didn't turn around. I started to run after him. The streets were boundless, punctuated by simple trees and hedges. His car was pulling further away, he didn't see me. I was running further into the darkness. I didn't know where I was, or where Dad was. From that day forward, Dad stopped being Dad altogether. From that day forward, Dad became somebody else entirely.

"Hey, Phillip! This is your party, guy. We're still waiting in here. Bring me a little more Jack Daniel's—and while you're at it see if you've got anything munchable, you know? Pretzels, or sardines or something."

I returned to the living room with Ry Krisp, beer nuts, Hershey's chocolate kisses and a renewed sense of purpose. Dad thought he could go places without me. Dad thought he was a man and I was just a boy. Dad thought he was special, and I was nothing. I reached into the toolbox and took something which looked interesting. Then I stood again over Dad's unconscious and fleeting body, like a surgeon conducting life's most sacred rites.

"There you go," Rodney said. He was flicking beer nuts into his mouth with one hand; his left arm embraced his can of 7UP, into which he had poured prodigious whiskey. "Now we're getting somewhere. Ease up—we're in no hurry, right?"

Rodney's hand took my arm firmly. Just as firmly, I shook it away.

"Be careful, there. Hold on, you want me to go get some towels or something? Phillip? Are you even listening to me or what?"

I wanted to be good. Feverishly, as I worked, I knew I wanted to be good and to enter the kingdom of Heaven. "I used to pray," I said out loud, to nobody in particular. "I remember when I was little, I used to pray every night."

"What's that?" Pouring more whiskey into his soda can, Rodney dripped some onto Dad's white shirt sleeve. Then, after a moment, "Are you sure you don't want me to hold something for you?"

Again I shrugged him away. "I used to pray on my hands and knees, and imagined a Heaven filled with white lacy clouds. Many pleasant men and women came out to greet me as I entered through these tall, alabaster white gates. There was a young girl there about my own age. I thought she was really beautiful, and we became close friends. One night she let me kiss her, and another night I saved her from the hordes of Satan's evil minions. I imagined all this while I prayed. I prayed to be good and pure. I wanted to remain a child forever."

"I never prayed to be good," Rodney said, reflectively sipping. "I only prayed for three things in my entire life. Money. Women. And power. And when you get right down to it, I'm not in such a hurry about the women and the money. Power's the main thing, Phillip. Power's the only thing worth really praying for."

"I wanted to do good deeds. I wanted to help cripples and old women who nobody loved. I wanted to save puppies from the pound, and teach broken birds how to fly and be free again."

"What are you doing with that—"

"I wanted there to be absolutely no pain and suffering in the entire world. Sometimes I wonder why I wanted that. I can't understand the dreams I dreamed then. What did they matter? What did pain and suffering have to do with me? They had nothing to do with me. They were things in the world, they were things different from me. I'm not really in the world at all, Rodney, am I? I'm really not, am I?" I was hot with dizziness and my own blood. With the back of my hand I wiped the sweat gathering on my forehead. I needed to lie down for a minute. I needed a glass of ice-cold water. But I couldn't relax just yet. I wasn't finished.

231

And then I heard the sudden crack of Mom's overpainted door opening down the hall. It all seemed perfectly natural—the world right now, events and circumstances. Then Mom's slow, balancing footsteps, her large stomach preceding her into the mouth of the living room. Rodney nudged me sharply with his elbow.

"Hello, Mrs. Davis," Rodney said.

I was just about to attach a pair of snub-nosed pliers. I cupped them in my hand like a guilty, smoldering cigarette and turned. Mom was standing there, watching us, her face glowing, wearing the big blue robe I had bought her for Mother's Day.

Mom was looking at Dad's face as if it were the face of a child in a photograph. Her eyes steadfastly refused to look at any of the things I had begun doing to him.

"When you're finished in here, baby, I want you to leave," Mom said. The fingertips of one hand were poised upon her stomach, as if it were gauging delicate reactions down there, secret chords and melodies, Morses of blood and plasma, protein and bone. "I don't want you around the baby. You can take the car, and all your father's money. But go far away, and I'll say I don't know what happened. I was asleep in my room. I woke up in the morning and found him. I hadn't heard a thing all night. I'll still love you, Phillip, but I don't want you around anymore. I've tried hard to understand, but I'm afraid I just can't understand anymore."

It was cold static moonlight. Outside, in the distance, I heard the helicopter beating past again. Somewhere in the night a police car radio sounded, and then its brief momentary eruption of inhuman voices: *"Not in the alley, over"*; *"Roger, Sam-six."* I was thinking, Just fine. You go where you want to go, Mom. I'll go where I want to go. I was staring her in the eye. I had nothing to be ashamed of. She, on the other hand, wasn't looking at me. She couldn't look at me, because she knew it too. She knew that this was my night, the night of my stark ascension. Dad wasn't going anywhere without me. Mom was the one who would be left behind. Everything was going to turn out exactly the way I wanted it to turn out, and there was nothing Mom, or Dad, or anybody else could do about it. I was going to have my way, simply because I finally understood in which direction my way led.

"I knew I lost you in San Luis," Mom said. She was watching the can of 7UP in Rodney's hand. "You'll never change, Phillip. You are the way you are, and that's that, I guess. I didn't say anything but I knew, and you knew I knew. Whatever your father knew isn't any of my business. Your father simply shouldn't have gotten involved. He knew better. He knew me. He couldn't have been that naive about you. I don't know what he expected when he came here, but we never invited him, we never made him any promises. Now, if you and your friend don't mind, I'm going back to bed. I'm going to sleep for about a hundred years. When you leave, remember to lock up. Don't leave any lights on. You won't be able to write me, because I won't let you know where I've gone."

Mom turned, paused with one hand on the wall, the

other on her stomach. Then, cautiously, she conducted my unborn sibling down the hall to her warm and silent bed.

There wasn't any time for reflection. I attached the snub-nosed pliers. Nobody was going to tell me what to do anymore. Nobody could send me away or leave me. Not even Mom. Not even Dad.

"Jesus," Rodney said. His hands were trembling, his voice faint, his eyes intent on my work now with either concealed admiration or blank distrust. "Your family's too much, guy."

"I always wanted to be good," I said as I feverishly worked, feeling vast geologic plates and fissures expanding in the earth deep under my feet. "I always wanted to go to Heaven. Now I don't care. I'll go anywhere. It's quite a relief, you know. It's like having all your appointments canceled and knowing you can spend the whole day in bed with a good book."

"You're really something, Phillip," Rodney said. "You really are."

"In order to free the self, one must abandon all preconceptions about what the self is." As I worked, the words arose in me without my volition. They were like the hard intricate tools I wielded, they were like the dense yielding body of Dad. Associative, crystalline, buzzing, hard. Next to these words, the world itself seemed to reliquefy itself, dissolving in the blood of some archetypal Christ. "Make no mistake about it—the self exists, Rodney, and this is it. *This* is the self. This is the self here." I showed Rodney something on the end of one stubby screwdriver. "Blood, tissue, bone, cartilage, marrow, mass, gravity, liquid, sound, light. It moves or it doesn't move. It lives or it doesn't live. This is the history of luminous motion, Rodney. This is the flux and convection of sudden light. We're all the same but we're all not the same too. What you know is not what I know. What you prefer is not what I prefer. There's just this—and this—and this"—Dad's body gave a sudden, galvanic kick—"or *this,*" I said, enraged by the still pulsing life in him, "or this or this or this or this. This here, or this *here. This* is all we are, this warm and fragile envelope, this thin impacted tissue. It's not that we exist but that we know we exist that makes our lives so miserable. And this—this is nothing. And this, and this, and this. This is all nothing too."

"And this," Pedro echoed. "And this, and this, and this."

"This is the progress men and women make alone in the world of light," I chanted, the words filling me with heat and rage. "This is all we are, Rodney. This is all we'll ever be . . ." They were my words but they were somebody else's words too. Mom couldn't leave me. Only I could leave Mom. I was dizzy with fierce excitement. The blood coursed and raced in my head. I was moving too, through these humming veins, down these moist undulating corridors. I was moving into the world of Dad's body, a place even Dad had never been before. I would show them. I was going to show all of them. Mom and Dad, Rodney and Beatrice, Ethel and the world. The whole world, the whole vast and intricate world. And Pedro. Pedro, of course . . . I was going to show all of them. "This is it, Rodney. This is the light. This is Dad's light—but now it's mine. Now it's my light. Now it's Mom's light too . . ."

Rodney said, "Hey, Phillip. What's that noise?"

"This is the history of motion, Rodney. The history of motion. Look—the history of motion. The history, the history of motion . . ." I could feel it now. I knew it was coming. I could feel the pulse of it in my bones and skin. It raced in my blood. It raced in Dad's blood too. Something spurted into my eye and I wiped it away with the back of my wrist.

"Hey, Phillip. Something's wrong, man. Phillip. Hey—get it together, guy. I think somebody's outside—"

It was mine and it was Dad's, and someday it would be the baby's too. Me and Mom and the baby and Dad. And the light, the light—

and then suddenly there was just the awful thundering noise of it, descending outside in the ruined and brilliant white sky. Finally I saw it. The light, the hard bright white light flashing through the cracked venetian blinds into our living room, beating and flashing, fast and sudden and secure, roaring and louder like massive engines driving and obliterating everything, even the night. It was all life, it was all living. This was my life. I was doing it now. I was living my own life now—

"Jesus Christ!" Rodney shouted, grabbing my hands, pulling at me. "Phillip—we gotta get out of here!"

But nobody pushed me, nobody made me do anything I didn't want to do. Not tonight and not ever again.

"Rodney!" I shouted. I was disentangling my hands from Dad's clinging warmth. I even tried to lift Dad in my arms to show him. I wanted Dad to see too. I wanted everyone to see. "Look there! At the window!"

It burned through the window blinds. It was life. It was white. It was coming for me, for me.

"Rodney! Look!"

I was shouting over the noise of the beating helicopter rotors. Everything was so simple now. All the hard eternal light of it was burning in our blood and our bones and our brains . . .

"Rodney!" I called. I turned around the room, alone in the whirling hallway. The back door to the garage stood wide open.

The light thundered through everything, beating back drapes and curtains. The entire house was rattling and trembling, the light swirling and turning. Pedro, darkness, Pedro, darkness. And then just the darkness. And then just the light. And Dad's life hot on my hands and my clothes and my face, and the hard beating light outside like a summons, celestial and vast, like Jesus or God, Buddha or Muhammad. Like Dad's voice. Like Mom's love. Like light and motion, motion and light—

"Rodney!" I cried. "Come back! This is it! It's over! They're here!"

"*ROGER, TEN-FOUR*" the shortwave outside blared, its cessation as suddenly loud as the world around it. Massive car doors opened and slammed, footsteps sounded heavy and fast on the front stairs, I heard a flowerpot crash into the cold alleyway. "Open up!" they shouted. "Open up in there!" And then that loud peremptory knock at my front door and, as I turned, the door exploding open with a crash of dark large-bodied men in dark blue uniforms. Their badges and flashlights gleamed, their weapons flashed, but I wasn't afraid, because I wasn't going anywhere I didn't want to go. They were mine—I wasn't theirs. My arms were even outstretched to embrace them, my hands and face stained with the sacred blood. *Totem, totem, totem*, the hard beating wings resounded outside our fragile home. *Totem, totem, totem* . . . and the light streaming through me like the rain and the wind and the sky. We would all taste the Eucharist, we would all ingest the flesh and suffer strange transubstantiations. We would all find God, we would all live forever. I knew she would tell them. I knew all along she'd never leave me or send me away. My mom loved me. They were here. I was saved. It was the police.

THE
HARD SONG

2 6

While undergoing three weeks of isolated observation at Valley Youth Correctional Facilities I was allowed some books, a pen and notepad, and a few choice hours each afternoon of strictly regulated media privileges. I was also granted, almost as an official afterthought, what seemed to me at the time like virtually acres of soft, casual introspection. They tell me I slept nearly two full days and nights upon my arrival, awaking only to take slow bites at the facility's tepid, customized meals. I don't, however, remember those first two days at all. I only remember waking one bright spring morning to the harsh sun flashing outside my window, the glass of which was inlaid with a fine protective wire mesh. The thin bed and walls of my room seemed drab by comparison. I heard a few singing birds, eccentric, anxious and shrill. I was confronted by a long mirror in which I sat on my bed, observing myself with a sort of cool diffidence, as if I were warden to my own reflection. I assumed that invisible behind the mirror sat my more official audience. My reflected face was lined and bruised from excessive sleep, and I poured a glass of water from the blue plastic pitcher beside me on the weak, clumsy bureau. My room was like the rooms of the motels in which I had been raised, at once transient and profane, fleeting and ill-designed. After months of strange vacation I was finally home again. No matter how much fun you have on vacation, it's always good to be home again.

"Do you know what you did?" Officer Henrietta asked me soon after my arrival. My afternoon sessions with Officer Henrietta, a trained and certified psychotherapist, became the only certain ritual of my day beyond mere self-maintenance. Officer Henrietta was a bluff, affable man, but one who wanted it known he wasn't about to take any nonsense, and especially not from a child.

"I don't remember," I confessed. "But I'm sure that, whatever it was, it was wrong. Or else I wouldn't be here, would I, Officer Henrietta?"

"What you did was very, very wrong," Officer Henrietta said. "What you did endangered the lives of people you loved. What you did frightened a lot of people. It frightened you, so you can't even remember what happened. Do you believe you're capable of that? Do you believe you're capable of doing things so horrible you can frighten yourself that bad?"

The office in which we met six days each week was cluttered with papers, Styrofoam coffee cups and crumpled Hershey's wrappers. I always felt comfortable in that office, and actually looked forward to the rather easy, meaningless conversations Officer Henrietta was kind enough to conduct with me. Officer Henrietta's distinct, often provocative questions never startled me or made me feel ill at ease. Instead they always implied what my own obvious responses simply had to be, responses I did not utter so much as activate, like functions in a computer. Graphs, data, production, profit, loss. Anger, love, resentment, sadness, pain. The world of the self and the world of machines. During these days and nights of slow, unhurried reflection, I began to realize that those were the two worlds I always seemed to be getting confused. The world of the self and the world of machines.

"I believe the human mind is capable of anything," I told Officer Henrietta. "The mind is its own place, just like Milton's heaven. It sounds like something Blake would have said, doesn't it? I'm talking William Blake, now. Do you know who William Blake is, Officer Henrietta?" Officer Henrietta's black felt pen sat poised at the edge of the paper, but his unresponsive brown eyes were trained upon me with a remote, unfocused expression, as if they were staring into something both vital and abstract, like the weather. "And as for me," I said, "I believe I'm capable of anything I'm capable of doing. I can be anybody I want to be, because only I have the power to decide. Not the world, not this institution, not you and your framed documents. Only me and my conceptions of me. My mom taught me that. I can grow up to be a doctor, an astronaut, or even the president of the United States. I can be a bird, a rock, a cloud. I can be anything I want to be, Officer Henrietta. And I'm afraid there's not really anything you can do to stop me."

Every once in a while Officer Henrietta emitted long, mystical sighs, vague punctuations which indicated vaster and cooler worlds than ours filled with sunny, padded white clouds and sparkling blue beaches. He leisurely chain-smoked Marlboros or Winstons and drank vile, bitter coffee just dimly discolored by Cremora. He showed me ink blots and asked me what they meant (though I suspect he may have known already without my help). I described for Officer Henrietta bats, abattoirs, leering faces and dark twisted passages filled with incessant and secret motion. He asked me abstract questions. If you drew a picture of yourself on a piece of paper, what color paper would you choose? If a strange man came up to you on the street and asked you to love him, what would you say? If you were on a sinking ship, who would you save first—the women or the children? These were all fine questions, and I answered them the best I could. I told him I would choose a sheet of beige paper, because that was the color of my mom's car. I told him I would tell the strange man to love himself, and let me get on with my own life. I told him in the event of a shipwreck I wouldn't try to save anybody, I would let the whole world drown. We would all return to the deep earth together, drifting down through the intricate seaweed and glistening blue water, women and children all together at last, journeying into a safer and warmer world than the one of broken ships.

One day Officer Henrietta began showing me photographs of a beautiful woman smiling with white, white teeth. He showed me photographs of a man tied up on a nice sofa in the living room of a nice house. Strange things had been done to his body, from which the clothing had been torn in places, like the paper windows in a Christmas Advent calendar. The pictures seemed slightly familiar to me in a dozy, unimperative way. I thought vaguely I might like to meet these people. But then I also thought it wouldn't matter to me that much if I never met them at all.

"Is there anyone you'd like to see?" Officer Henrietta asked, laying the photos facedown on his desk, shuffling and stacking them meaninglessly like a deck of cards. "Can you think of anybody offhand? A relative, maybe. Somebody you especially love."

I thought. I thought about silent places where darkness covered everything with an oily film. These were uninhabited and soundless places, like hidden chambers of the moon. You could see no faces there, you could hear no names. Like Officer Henrietta's photographs, these places didn't matter to me that much one way or the other.

Officer Henrietta was looking at me. I looked at the sheet of unmarked white paper on the desk before him, at his upraised and ineffective pen, at a photograph of his beaming family in a cheap plastic frame.

"Is Rodney around?" I asked him after a while. "Is there any possibility I might be able to see my friend Rodney for a few minutes or so? I'd like to know how's he doing, you know. I'd just feel a lot better if I knew my friend Rodney was all right."

Alone in my discrete room I would lie on the bed for hours gazing at the stale ceiling and talking to the figures who sat observing me behind the mirror. I could hear efficient machines whirring back there, official documents being filed into sliding cabinet drawers, the occasional hum of a word processor, the brief interjections of a clattering typewriter. "I think I'm learning to take things a lot easier than I used to," I told these invisible people. "In the past, I may have been too quick to make judgments. I couldn't seem to feel satisfied to accept the way things were. I think I've learned a lot about myself in the past few days or so, and I may be on the verge of some real sustained growth—both intellectually and emotionally. I'm growing more and more interested in Eastern religions, for example. Yoga, Brāhmanism, Buddhism, Tantrism, Oriental alchemy, mystical erotism. We're very much a thing-oriented culture—the West in general, I mean. We're into making things, changing things, moving things from one place to another. Sometimes I think it's best just to let everything lie. To not keep banging and bumping away at the world, to accept things for what they are. I guess in a way that might sound sort of escapist to you. I'm sure my friend Beatrice would probably be quick to agree. To imagine the world and all its suffering as a sort of necessary trial, one which presumably conditions us to understand our true *being,* is to imagine that the world itself doesn't matter, nor the conditions in it. That means, in a way, accepting the world's cruelty and its pain. That means just leaving it alone to get on with its own alien and material processes, however wrong and unjust they may be. I'm sure that could sound rather self-centered, even pretty ambivalent or smug. But I think there often comes a time in your life when you stop worrying about whether the way you think is right or proper or not. You just get tired, and start accepting the way of thinking that's easiest and least worrisome. Maya, the world as illusion. Karma, that duplicity and evanescence of mere physical life, the incessant beat and blur of material repetition. Then nirvana, the self's final liberation, a dream of nonbeing as pure being. We find our way out of this world within this world, I guess that's what it all boils down to. Now that I've got your attention, maybe I can ask you to send me a few books. I could use one or two on Vedantic philosophy. Then of course *The Upanishads*, and the *Bhagavad Gita*. I could use a general edition of Patañjali's *Yoga-sūtras*, while we're at it. I don't mean to hurry you, but whenever you get time. I was thinking they might even make a good permanent addition to the library here. I mean, when kids get screwed up like I do, I think they need to turn to some sort of traditional wisdom in order to work through their confusion. Kids who try to break the rules are only trying to find better rules they can live by, and I think the best rules are always the ones you carry within yourself. Kids need to learn they can't expect anything from anybody. They need to learn that everything they'll ever have is already inside them, is simply waiting there to be recognized.''

As I lay in my bed talking, I could hear doors opening up and down the hallway outside. I could hear toilets being flushed, and gurneys squeaking and clattering along the polished tile floors. The halls were filled with the bright, audible noise of institutional fluorescents, that hypnotic artificial sort of light you might discover like atmosphere in some alien space station.

"Of course, you know what Beatrice would say about all this, don't you?" I shrugged, affecting a smug disconcern. I couldn't remember if I'd told these invisible people anything about my friend Beatrice or not. "She'd say all my talk about some spiritual liberation's just a big con, that I'm trying to disavow ontology. You can't disavow ontology—that's what Beatrice would say. Ontology's what happens when you're hit by a bus. It's not something you can just disavow."

I wanted redemption in these days of my slow recuperation, the warm equatorial haze of samadhi, the total cessation of all transformations. They never brought me the books I requested, however. Whenever I reminded him, Officer Henrietta avoided the issue. Instead I received a few "world classics." *Les Misérables*, *David Copperfield*, *War and Peace*, all of them abridged and illustrated for some theoretical "young adult" reader. These books lay casually disregarded on my bureau while I lay on my bed thinking. If I could not learn redemption, I could at least imagine or even reinvent it. I gathered what fragments of Oriental wisdom I could recall and tried to generate larger worlds around them, vaster pictures into which these fragments might tidily fit, like pieces in a jigsaw puzzle. The mind was just a reaction of pure spiritual being to the world's material force. The mind was a whirlpool, constant and uncontainable, which spun off into the world knocking into other things, inciting other spirits to move. This was karma then, I decided: the constant push of objects which tried to make of spirit an object too—a sort of cosmic bullying, a rushing and herding of things into other things. These forces made life, death, people, pain, suffering, cities and, worst of all, human emotions. They made anger. They made hate. For years now I had been filled with this hot and irreproachable anger that burned and flared in me without warning—this anger I could not contain, which had caused me to do something, or perhaps even a series of things, for which I had been legally incarcerated. I had been incarcerated in order to protect the people I loved, and as a result of this real burning drive in me, this raging drive to hurt, to conquer, to create a more material and corrupted world, I had harmed people—people I loved, Officer Henrietta liked to remind me—and I had consequently harmed myself as well. You can't direct your hate at other people; hate is a force that burns him who uses it too. Hate never does anyone any good, I thought. This was the lesson I had been brought here to learn, and I was amazed at the effortless and benign nature of its composition. It had simply grown in me, blossomed like flowers. It actually took root and grew from the very rage and anger it was intent on eliminating. Everything carries within it the fuel of its own driving antithesis, I thought. Anger is the stuff from which real love and knowledge grow. In order to grow and learn, we must permit the world to betray itself.

On a Friday morning before lunch I was permitted two visitors. Beatrice and Ethel, both immaculately buffed and manicured, lipsticked and glossed, sat on cracked vinyl chairs in a small Visitors' Lounge which included a wobbly, unvarnished pasteboard coffee table, some magazines and an additional cracked chair for me. Ethel wore a gauzy hat and was potent with cheap perfume. Beatrice wore a dress which at first appeared very bright on her, and then, after a few minutes, as I grew inured to this uncustomary sight, began to appear slightly cheap and shiny, like polyester or cheap lacquer. Her hair was washed, her lipstick excessively bright. As I sat down in the empty chair, we all regarded one another uneasily, like strangers brought formally together by some parent-teacher committee or charity bazaar. Ethel cleared her throat and I examined my pale hands in my lap. Beatrice could not remain silent very long. She shifted nervously in her seat, adjusting and readjusting the hem of her awkward skirt.

"I don't think I owe you any apologies, Phillip," she said. "Don't think I came here to apologize."

I wanted to tell her about my anger, how it had departed suddenly, become a force of mere matter. I, meanwhile, was growing more ethereal and abstract. I thought she might like me better now, this "new" Phillip.

"That's OK, Beatrice," I said. "I didn't expect you to."

"Then you expected right." Beatrice's blue eyes flashed

at me. "What I did I did for your own good. I don't give a damn about your father. You could have drawn and quartered that SOB for all I care—"

"*Betty,*" Ethel cautioned her abruptly.

"—and I really *mean* that," Beatrice continued, cautioning Ethel back. "What I *do* care about is you and Rodney. I was damned if I was going to watch you both throw your lives away over your stupid father. He wasn't worth it, Phillip. You're trying to kill the only person in the world you love because the world won't love you. You're a patent narcissist, that's what *you* are. You gaze at the world and expect the world to gaze dreamily right back at you. You've got to grow up, Phillip. You've got to learn to relax. You've got to start showing some real concern for people in the world who weren't born with all the advantages you've had. Think of the children in Soweto and Afghanistan. Think of the political prisoners throughout Latin America and Eastern Europe. The world's not reflective, Phillip. It's dynamic and blind and stupid and correctable and utterly forlorn, just like you. Just like me and just like Rodney and just like Ethel here—" Ethel blushed slightly, as if she were flattered simply to hear her name mentioned in any context at all. "It's a world with real problems, that causes real pain, that promises real pleasure and abundance. I haven't been able to sleep all week. I knew you knew, even without me telling. I just hope you know too that it's not because I don't love you. I love you and Rodney very much. You're my family, and if I had to, I'd call the cops again today, right this very minute, if I thought you and Rodney were about to do something you'd both regret later. You can bet on it. If you tried to pull the same crap all over again, I'd have the cops all over you in a second. I'd see to it they were all over you like a cheap suit."

Meanwhile Ethel snuffled behind a dingy Kleenex. Her eyes had grown moist, and her mascara was starting to run in places.

"Where's Rodney?" I asked. It wasn't as if I were addressing her with my question, but rather trying to push her out of my way. "When am I supposed to see him, anyway?"

The Kleenex in Ethel's hand began violently shaking. Obviously flustered, Ethel looked from Beatrice to me, and then at Beatrice again. Her face was very pale.

"They caught him climbing over the back fence into a neighbor's yard," Beatrice said. "He's in a holding cell here, just like yours. But early next week he'll be transferred to a separate facility altogether. They don't want you and Rodney seeing each other again for quite a while, Phillip."

"It's my fault," Ethel said. Finally she was looking at me. Her damp hand touched mine. "I shouldn't have let him near you. I know you don't understand what you do to people, Phillip. But you were a terrible influence on Rodney. I should have paid more attention to you, Phillip. I should have gotten to know you better."

"When you get out, Phillip, I want you to call me." Beatrice leaned forward earnestly in her chair. It was the

252

customary intensity of her expression now which made her
stiff dress seem more and more like a disguise. "I want you
to call me and tell me where you are. I left word with your
parents, but they're not responding. When you get out,
Phillip, I want to see you. Call me, promise? Call me first
thing."

I promised I would. I went to the door and asked the
guard to take me back to my room. But already I knew I
would never call her. We were all moving off into separate
worlds and galaxies now. We were all journeying off to find
the only redemption any of us could afford. I didn't owe
Beatrice anything and she didn't owe me. And I certainly
never wanted to be betrayed by Beatrice ever again.

A few nights later, while I was lying on my bed trying to
design my own mantra, Rodney came and tapped at my
door.

"Phillip," he whispered. "Hey, Phillip. It's me."

My room was dark, and a mantra to me was just a fault-
ily remembered notion. A mantra was a puzzle which drew
your mind into the deeper, more complicated puzzle of the
world itself. Or so I understood it. You are hanging from a
rope in a dark pit. At the bottom of the pit a lion roars at
you. At the top, a mouse gnaws silently at your rope. This
is just the universe you've landed in. Even salvation doesn't
last very long.

"Hey, Phillip. I've just got a minute. Are you up?"

I climbed out of bed and went to the door. I could sense

the pressure of Rodney's fingertips on the outer side of my hard steel doorknob. In my dark room with the door bolted from the outside, I thought of Dad.

"Rodney, I don't think I'm supposed to talk to you."

"Look, I only got a minute. I gave the guard twenty bucks from the cash Ethel smuggled in for me. Here, something else."

I felt Rodney's body brush lightly against the outer surface of my door. Then I heard something strike the air vent over my head. Rodney's feet landed softly on the outer hall. Then I heard Rodney jump again, and a pack of Winstons popped through the air vent and ricocheted off the dark, wide-screen mirror.

"You get them?"

"I think so."

"Just one thing, Phillip—and listen to me real carefully now. Tell these fuckers anything they want to hear. You got me? Anything. Be anybody they want you to be, and get the fuck out of here. This place is full of crap, man. Have you gotten a look at that Officer Henrietta, Boy's Best Friend? I never met anybody filled with more crap in my entire life. So do what they say, right? Say whatever they want to hear."

"Rodney—I have to ask you something—"

"Hold on a second—" Rodney whispered. Then his voice grew dim, harder and echoing as he leaned away from the door. "What?" he asked, in a louder voice. "Just one minute."

"Did we hurt anybody, Rodney?" I asked quickly, afraid

my question might go unanswered. "I'm beginning to suspect we may have done something we shouldn't have—"

"*Fuck*, lady!" Rodney told the echoing hallway. "I told you *one minute!*"

Then, as if the institution itself was hurrying to divide Rodney from my vital inquiry, I heard the dark weighted body of a guard sweep down the hall and Rodney's elbows knocking loudly against my hollow door.

"*Fuck* you, lady. You fucking *cunt*, I *said* I'm coming. Watch it there, will you? *Shit!*"

"Rodney, keep in touch," I said, but he didn't hear me. His voice was steadily diminishing down the long corridor, as if someone were slowly turning down the volume on a radio.

"Tell the fuckers anything, Phillip! You hear me? Tell them whatever the fuck they want to hear and get yourself out of this dump. *Hey*, lady. That's my *arm* you've got there. Know what you just did, lady? You just *screwed* yourself out of twenty fucking bucks—that's what you just did. You blew it, lady, because I'm going to *eat* it, you hear me. I'm going to *eat* your twenty fucking dollars before I'll let you see a piece of it."

"I'll do my best," I whispered secretly, as if Rodney and I were conferring in one of the unoccupied, transgressed homes of our childhood. "I'll tell them anything—as soon as I figure out what it is they want to hear."

I would call Rodney's house months later after my release, but his number was long disconnected by then. My letters were returned by the post office, no forwarding address available. I didn't blame Ethel, really. I was not the only man in her life.

Then, just before it disappeared forever from my world, Rodney's voice said, "Hey, lady. I thought you were supposed to be letting me out to take a piss."

27

The following Thursday I was escorted to the Youth Facility's remotest, somberest corridor for what Officer Henrietta called an "informal prelim." Escorted by a young woman in a patently unattractive and bulky blue uniform, I saw for the first time the general design of the institution, filled with its atmosphere of harsh fluorescent light, bracketed by white ungleaming tile floors and lacquered beige walls. In one corridor I heard the monotonous, aggressive clocking of a Ping-Pong ball, and in another a sports program on TV. We passed a cafeteria where young Chicano men wore white aprons and black hair nets. They had tattoos on their muscular arms and lean, mustached faces, and swabbed down the floors with tall wet mops. They rested the mops against their shoulders and looked at me as I passed. I felt very uneasy looking back. They scratched under their arms and continued watching me go by. Then they scratched roughly between their legs.

In the distant and official temperature of the Deposition Room (or so the plastic sign said on its door) I was seated in a stiff chair at a table with three men who wore modest navy-blue suits with modestly patterned ties. They were introduced as a judge, a prosecuting attorney, and a Youth Offense Adviser, who, I assumed, was sort of like my lawyer. When they spoke, however, I could never distinguish who was saying what, or from what official position.

"There's no prior record, then."

"None."

"If the parents aren't making any charges, what are we holding him for?"

"We found illegal substances on his friend. Everybody thought it might be a good idea to keep him under observation for a while."

"Who's everybody?"

"Joe, Harry, Delacruz. Me."

"That's not everybody, is it?"

"No, I guess not."

"How old is he?"

"Eight years old."

I sat a little forward in my chair. "Almost eight and a half," I said, but they didn't seem to hear.

"What does the psychological profile say?"

One man opened a manila folder and read to us. "Severe amnesiac reaction to stress and poor body management. Perhaps a paranoid schizophrenic, with delusions of grandeur and competitive reality disorder." The man closed the file. "The doctor thinks the kid could grow out of it."

One of the men tapped his pencil against the flimsy Formica table.

"If we keep him, where are we going to keep him?"

"Here, I guess."

"What about a foster home?"

"I don't think this case is exactly cut out for your usual foster home."

"What do the parents think?"

"The father wants to take him to his home in Bel Air. He's pretty well off. He says he'll bring in hired help. He promises to keep a close eye on the kid for the next few years or so. He's going to hire private tutors and keep him out of school. He's going to bring in clinical psychologists. One doctor he's hired already wants to try some things on the kid with insulin. I say we give the kid back to his parents."

The men grew silent for a while. I sat quietly in my chair, trying not to look at any of them.

"What do you think, Phillip?" the most self-confident of the men asked me after a while. He crossed his hands on the thick manila folder. His hands formed a wedge which was aimed at my heart. "You've heard us discussing your future. Have any ideas about where you'd like to spend the next few years of your life?"

I looked at the man. His dark hair was cut short in a bland, official style. He wore thick plastic-framed glasses.

"I guess I don't really," I said. "I guess I'll be happy to do whatever you gentlemen think best."

The warm reality of my small, institutional room was growing dimmer and more fluid each day while I lay on my bed, contemplating my freshly designed mantras and the world's annihilation and rebirth in the form of pure, rarefied and immaculate spirit. I was no longer concerned with what crimes I had committed, nor what penalties I might suffer for them. Life itself was a penalty of sorts, and the wide world its own infallible crime. We were all in it, we all lived it. Perhaps we weren't all responsible for this awful mess, but if we weren't responsible, then I thought it pretty safe to assume that responsibility in itself didn't really mean anything. Like Mom, we did not die or cease to exist so much as awaken to a more enduring and unfathomable life. Once we awoke, this world wouldn't matter anymore. We wouldn't even know where we were. We wouldn't remember who we had been, or care too much about what we were to become. Being would only matter then, and nothing else. Now that I was saved, now that Mom had sacrificed herself in exchange for my firm redemption, I believed salvation was possible for the world too. I believed anyone could find ultimate happiness, just like my mom had, just like I was finding it now.

"Tall," Officer Henrietta told me.

"Short," I said quickly. I liked this game because when I played it I could feel myself starting to disappear, leaving nothing but my automatic words behind. I could briefly glimpse the world into which Mom had vanished. If you played the game long enough, you completely forgot you were playing any game at all.

"Big."

"Little."

"Dog."

"Cold."

"Friend."

"Suffering."

"Hurt."

"House."

"Desire."

"Warmth."

"Father."

"Blood."

Officer Henrietta put down his stack of file cards and made a succinct notation on the plywood clipboard. He took his cigarette from the ashtray and looked at me.

"Mother," he said. He took a long drag from his cigarette. He did not exhale right away. He squinted a little, as if he were trying to peer inside me.

I looked at Officer Henrietta. I deeply desired one of his menthol cigarettes, but I had recently decided to give up nicotine, as well as all earthly substances which made me indebted to mere matter.

"The history of motion," I said after a while.

Officer Henrietta exhaled the smoke slowly. A fine, gritty mist expanded in the flat spaces between us and then evaporated. "What's that?" he asked. He was talking more slowly now. We had begun playing a different sort of game entirely.

I held my folded hands braced between my legs. This room was very cold all of a sudden. I suspected someone in some deep, secluded and inviolate security nexus had activated the formidable air-conditioning.

Officer Henrietta and I continued to gaze at one another for almost a full minute.

"Nothing," I said. I watched Officer Henrietta crush out his Kool in the glass Denny's ashtray. "Can I please go back to my room now?"

Officer Henrietta sighed. Times like this I felt very sorry for Officer Henrietta.

One morning I was escorted not to Officer Henrietta's office but rather to a wide asphalt parking lot where a gray, nondescript car awaited me. Without further ceremony or discussion I was transported to the busy corridors of a Valley hospital, through avenues of pale sunlight and fading adobe shopfronts and streets filled with cars and potholes and roaring buses. From the outside the hospital appeared very dark and ominous, like some corporate office building with dark cement walls and reflecting glass windows. I was taken into a cool lobby and then into an elevator's tinkling Muzak. Women and nurses smiled at me, then frowned at the stern obdurate guard beside me who gripped my pale hand. I was taken to a private room where a beautiful woman lay exhausted in a bed, and a man and another woman stood at the window beside the bed. When I entered the room, everybody looked at me.

"I'll be right outside," the guard said. She was a woman. She went outside and closed the door.

"How are you, Phillip?" the man said. The man wore a

large bandage across the right side of his face, and there were a few visible lines of stitches across the bridge of his nose and down one side of his neck. A second woman with sun-blond hair like the man's stood beside him, her arms folded, and glared menacingly at me. This was her room, she seemed to be telling me. These were her friends, this was her family. I wasn't really wanted here. At any moment, she could ask me to leave.

The man stepped forward, and I heard other bandages brushing dryly underneath his clothes. He stepped with a slight limp. He held his body stiffly. He took my hand and sat down with me on a pair of chairs beside the bed. "Your mother's still asleep," the man said. "She's all right, though. Don't be frightened. At three thirty this morning your mother gave birth to a nine-and-a-half-pound baby boy. Isn't that exciting, sport? I wish you could have been there. It's such a miracle, watching a baby being born."

The man sat there staring at me, but I just looked at the sleeping woman in the bed. She was very beautiful, for those who like women with dark hair and rather fair skin. Her hair was a mess, though. And without any makeup she probably looked a lot older than she really was.

"This is my sister," the man said, indicating the severe woman beside the window. "This is your Aunt Sally from Phoenix."

Aunt Sally hadn't taken her eyes off me yet. She was packing a cigarette against the ledge of the window, just sitting there and looking at me. Her cigarette went tap tap tap. A sign over the sleeping woman's bed said NO SMOKING

PLEASE. If Aunt Sally doesn't like the way I look, maybe *she's* the one who should leave, I thought.

Aunt Sally showed the man her cigarette. "I'm going outside for one of these," she said. It was as if she had read my mind.

The man nodded at her and she left.

"I'll be right outside," Aunt Sally added, and closed the door behind her.

The man and I sat together for a while and watched the sleeping woman. The man held my hand in his, and I didn't mind. I knew he was trying to tell me something. He was waiting for the right moment. He thought he might be able to detect that right moment in the pulse of my hand.

"We're all going home together, sport. It's a great house. It's in the best part of Bel Air. I'm sorry you've had to spend so much time in that awful place, but I didn't really have any choice. I've had a couple of good lawyers on it, and you should be able to go home with your mother and me tomorrow. I know things have been very confusing for you, sport. No hard feelings, I promise. But if we're going to sort things out, we're going to have to sort them out together, if you know what I mean. We're going to have to work through things together in our own house, just between us three—us *four* now, I should say—and not give up until we get it right. You follow me, sport? Are you with me on this?"

I didn't answer. I was already growing bored with looking at the sleeping woman, so instead I gazed outside the window at the white, cottony sunlight suffusing the San Fernando Valley. There was no color out there anywhere today, I thought. It was one of the Valley's white days.

"Would you like to go with me and see the baby?" the man asked. "We could do that right now, if you want. Before they take you back."

I didn't like this man very much. I knew that right away. I didn't really dislike him that much, either, though. I tried to be as tactful as possible.

"Let's just not rush things, OK?" I said. Out in the distance, I saw an oblique dark shape beginning to emerge from the white sky. After another moment I recognized it. It was the Goodyear blimp.

Two days later Officer Henrietta shook my hand and gave me a little lecture about growing into manhood and all the responsibilities a young man faces. Growing up is never easy, and young men face difficult problems every day, problems like sex and drugs and peer pressure. It was important to remember, Officer Henrietta explained, that a young man must learn to find truth within himself and his family, and that if a young man only knew that people around him really did love him, he'd also know that no matter how hard the problems or how difficult the choices, he would still find his way safely through any unpleasantness the world might have to offer. "Even when you're an adult," Officer Henrietta said, "it doesn't get any easier. You keep thinking it's going to get easier, but it doesn't. I think you just get used to the pressure after a while. I think you just become a better judge of your own character."

In the long pause that followed, I said, "I'm sure you're probably very right, Officer Henrietta. And I'll keep your good advice firmly in mind. I really will."

"Good boy, Phillip. Now you go along and pack your things. And if you ever have any problems, or if you ever have *any* questions and you don't know who to turn to, you can always call me. OK? Now get going. And keep in touch."

"I will, Officer Henrietta," I said, gazing for the last time around his blithe, cluttered office. I would miss it here. Here the games were always clearly games, and never really mattered that much. "And I will keep in touch. I promise you. I really will."

2 8

Beatrice was right, of course. I was going to grow up.

I moved to the big house in Bel Air with the man and woman from the hospital and was enrolled in a private school. I was given my own room, color television and VCR, and three times a week I was visited by a battery of psychologists and dieticians who examined me with very clinical smiles. I grew accustomed to the spaces and geometries that lay around my large house, and for the first few months I was occasionally allowed to explore these spaces, by foot or by bike. I was never alone, however, for wherever I went covert men and women followed me in slow, very obvious automobiles. Sometimes I even saw these men and women parked beside the schoolyard where I would sit during lunchtime recesses and watch my addled, utterly inefficient classmates run their races and enact their imaginary dramas of pirates, cowboys and tycoons. The covert men and women never bothered or oppressed me. I knew they were only there to protect me. Eventually they stopped coming around and I felt a certain calm emptiness surround me; I even missed those covert men and women in a way. It was as if I had lost the only authentic family I had ever known.

This was my home and this was my family where I did not really live so much as circulate among things, events and strangers like a sort of atmosphere. Here was the man in the chair by the fire. Here was the woman in the bed near the TV. Here was the baby in the room filled with bright plastic toys. The baby was very remarkable, and everybody always said so. It never cried or raised a fuss, and whenever you spoke to it, it seemed to know exactly what you were saying. "My name is Phillip," I would say some nights after everybody else had fallen asleep, standing alone over the baby's dark crib. "I live in the next room. Your parents support me and see to my education. When you grow up, you will be very happy. You will exercise and eat right, and be involved in all sorts of extramural sports at your school. You will fill this room of yours with many sports trophies and citations of scholastic excellence. You will eventually become involved with a pretty girl from your high school, and you will often bring her by the house. I will always live here, too, but I will never bother you. I will always be in the next room. I will always be a moment away, in case you ever need anything, or in case any sort of emergency arises. But otherwise, I think, it would be best if we didn't see each other too much. I'm not trying to be antisocial. I'm just considering all the complicated logistics involved in people living together over a long period of time." The small, intelligent baby would look up at me as

I talked. Its dark, attentive eyes concentrated on my moving lips. This was a baby the man and woman of my house would eventually be very proud of. They would never have to feel nervous about a child like this. They would always know where it was, and generally what it was thinking. They could engage in casual conversations with it, without worrying so much about what they said, or what it might say back.

I had a future now, as firm and incontrovertible as my house and my family. I would complete grammar school, junior high, high school. Perhaps I would attend USC or UCLA, and earn my degree in law, medicine or journalism. I would marry a lovely, patient woman who would bear me no more than three lovely children. I would acquire a good job, my own big house, and two cars in a two-car garage. A Pontiac and a Volvo. My wife and I would send the kids to summer camp every year, to give us a little time to be together. On Christmas, we would take everybody to the house of the man and woman who had raised me in Bel Air. We would drink and sing Christmas carols. Every other year or so either I or my wife would have an affair with someone, usually someone I worked with or my wife met at one of the various regional political and charity functions she often attended. We would consider calling everything off. The house, the marriage, the formal avowals. But then we would start to grow more anxious and uncertain the further and further we grew apart from one another. We would begin to feel ourselves verging on vast unlabeled places that seemed to open up out of the earth under our feet. We would come to tearful and sudden reconciliations, reconciliations that grew quickly more formal and sensible as succeeding weeks passed. Our children would grow up. Just like me, they would raise families of their own.

I have never been truly unhappy since I have settled down to a more normal childhood, but perhaps, at times, I do feel a little restless. On these nights, when my parents are asleep, I take out the little red sports car the man recently purchased, an MG convertible with a hard, racy little engine and quick catlike traction. I drive it out along the coast highway, or across Sunset into Hollywood, where the tacky streets are empty and somehow magical late at night after all the hookers and junkies have gone home, like the stage of an abandoned movie set. Some nights I drive south to Orange County on Highway 5, or even as far as San Clemente. The air is always pleasant at night that far south, clear and warm. There are still a few rolling hills and green pastures that have not been converted to barnaclelike condominiums, shopping plazas, hotels or bowling alleys. It is always nice just to drive and relax and not feel in a hurry to be going anywhere. It's nice just to drive aimlessly around for a while with my own abstract thoughts and dim, fading memories of a life that has always seemed to me rather formless and abstract to begin with.

Some nights, though, I drive to the San Fernando Valley and the house where Mom and I once lived together. The front yard has been reseeded, and a number of pine and fig saplings have been planted around the front yard, where they have already grown into substantial trees. The basement window-latch can still be slipped open with a flat screwdriver and, inside, the garage has recently been swabbed out with solvent. Cleansed of its familiar smells, even the familiar angles and architecture of that garage seem strange and unfamiliar to me now. A large Ford Galaxy automobile stands in the middle of everything like an animal presence, rusted and spackled with Bondo, serene and almost majestic. A cat with luminous green eyes observes me from the perfect darkness between a matching washer and dryer. I go up the back stairs. The stairs have been carpeted with individual strips of green shag; the strips have been fastened down with bright red and yellow thumbtacks. I unlock the back door with a paperclip. Then I'm standing in the redecorated kitchen. Everything gleams in the darkness, aided by moonlight which falls through the cafe-style curtains. Nothing looks familiar here either, and I move into the living room.

We learn the rules when we get older, and that's what helps us get by. We're not uncertain anymore. We're not startled by the slightest sounds. As I step into the living room the only thing I find familiar here are the floorboards, which do not creak when I don't want them to. I feel like a spider on its home web, exerting texture, balance and pressure, gliding across the surface of spaces and silver fabric. Small children never know. They don't know why people do things, or even what they're going to do next. Small children invent their own reasons for things and things that happen. Children are reasonable too, just like adults. It's just that children don't know the acceptable rules of reason yet. Children can get lost. They need someone strong to lead them. Otherwise, they can be easily led astray by the convolutions of their own minds. Childhood is not a glorious thing. Childhood does not comfort or instruct. Childhood isolates people. Sometimes, children make mistakes which they regret later on in their lives.

This living room was not filled with fine furniture, but it was clean and functional and what is often referred to as homey. Flowers in vases, framed photographs on shelves, a crushed velvet family portrait of the Kennedys, dull paisley wallpaper, a large waiting television console, the whirling dust and fading, sun-bleached curtains. Only this linked me with the past, this whirling dust. This was the vast sound into which Mom had vanished. I thought I heard something and I turned. A tiny rectangle of light escaped from underneath one of the bedroom doors.

"The history of motion," I whispered. "The history of motion. Light, sound, heat, gravity, mass, life. Motion, the history of motion," I whispered, over and over again, but I couldn't remember, the fundamental weight of the words didn't work. "The history, the history of light. Light and history, history and motion, motion and history . . ." The words were like the dust. They whirled without the frame of sentences or that dark ritual meaning which would call her forth again, out of the shadows of this lost house. The words would make the house ours again. The words would bring Mom back to earth. "The history of motion. The history of motion, Mom . . ." My family was very far away and inaccessible to me now. But I didn't want to be with them. I wanted to be here. I wanted to stay here forever. I couldn't stop crying, but I didn't have to stop crying either. It wasn't that I wasn't happy. It wasn't that I didn't know my life had turned out for the best. But I was growing up now, and so I could cry all I wanted to, even while my hands filled with the tears, even while I felt the icy wet turning in my stomach and my heart. "The history, the history of motion." And then, as if by magic, the door in the hallway opened. A mist of pale yellow light poured out.

The child rubbed its eyes with its fists and looked at me.

"*¿Quien es?*" she asked. She was a dark formless shape, looking for the bathroom. I must have looked enormous to her.

She pulled her tiny fists away from her dark eyes, peering at me, incredibly tiny and perfect like a tiny robot. "*¿Eres tu mi padre? ¿Eres tu?*"

This was it. I was about to find what I could not find in my own big house with all the strong, independent and well-designed furniture I possessed there. If only I could remember, I could stay. I wouldn't have to go back. Everything would be better again, it would all make perfect sense: the history, the history of motion, something about light, and living one's own life in a world where everything is always moving, and the way time takes you away from people, even people you love. . . . But I couldn't remember how it went.

I couldn't remember the tone or the light of it, the chords or the melody. . . . The words wouldn't come and I couldn't make them.

We stood looking at one another in the dark hallway. She was not that much smaller than I. In some ways, however, she was very much smaller.

"Mi madre es en la cama. La cama de mi madre es azul."

There was no way back unless I could remember. And I couldn't. I couldn't remember. I couldn't remember.

"Carmelita?" a woman's voice said. "Carmelita? *¿Qué pasa, pobrecita?* What are you doing?" The woman's voice was growing larger and more indistinct.

I continued to cry, without any reason. I wasn't even sad. I didn't feel lost or lonely or forlorn. I just stood there in the heavy darkness and saw the light click on in the open doorway down the hall. I heard slippers being pulled onto feet, then the feet on the floor. In a moment, the child's mother would appear at the bedroom door.

A NOTE ABOUT THE AUTHOR

Scott Bradfield is thirty-four years old. He has a
Ph.D. in American Literature from the University of
California at Irvine, where he taught for five years.
Born and raised in California, Bradfield lived for several years in London, where he reviewed regularly for
newspapers and magazines; his work has appeared in
the Los Angeles *Times*, the Washington *Post*, the
Times Literary Supplement and *The Sunday Times*
(London). He is currently teaching at the University
of Connecticut at Storrs, and is working on a
second novel.

A NOTE ON THE TYPE

This book was set in a digitized version of Janson. The hot-metal version of Janson was a recutting made direct from type cast from matrices long thought to have been made by the Dutchman Anton Janson, who was a practicing type founder in Leipzig during the years 1668–1687. However, it has been conclusively demonstrated that these types are actually the work of Nicholas Kis (1650–1702), a Hungarian, who most probably learned his trade from the master Dutch type founder Dirk Voskens. The type is an excellent example of the influential and sturdy Dutch types that prevailed in England up to the time William Caslon (1692–1766) developed his own incomparable designs from them.

Composed by Creative Graphics, Inc.
Allentown, Pennsylvania

Printed and bound by Fairfield Graphics,
Fairfield, Pennsylvania

Designed by Valarie Jean Astor

A Year in Provence

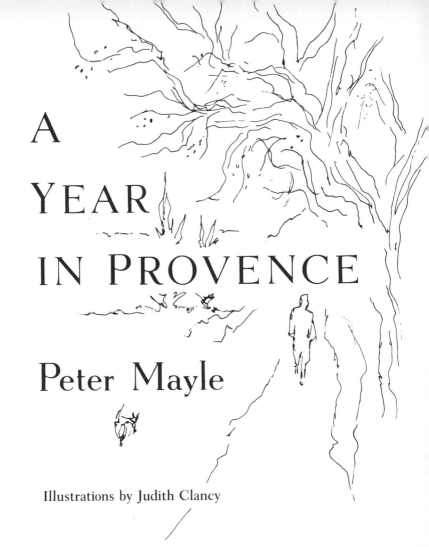

A
YEAR
IN PROVENCE

Peter Mayle

Illustrations by Judith Clancy

ALFRED A. KNOPF

NEW YORK

THIS IS A BORZOI BOOK
PUBLISHED BY ALFRED A. KNOPF, INC.

Copyright © 1989 by Peter Mayle
Illustrations copyright © 1990 by Judith Clancy
All rights reserved under International and Pan-American
Copyright Conventions. Published in the United States
by Alfred A. Knopf, Inc., New York, Distributed by
Random House, Inc., New York. Originally published in
Great Britain by Hamish Hamilton, Ltd.,
London, in 1989.

Library of Congress information available upon request

Manufactured in the United States of America in 2009

ISBN: 978-0-307-29162-2
9 8 7 6 5 4 3 2 1

To Jennie,

with love and thanks

A Year in Provence

JANUARY

THE YEAR BEGAN with lunch.

We have always found that New Year's Eve, with its eleventh-hour excesses and doomed resolutions, is a dismal occasion for all the forced jollity and midnight toasts and kisses. And so, when we heard that over in the village of Lacoste, a few miles away, the proprietor of Le Simiane was offering a six-course lunch with pink champagne to his amiable clientele, it seemed like a much more cheerful way to start the next twelve months.

By 12:30 the little stone-walled restaurant was full. There were some serious stomachs to be seen—entire families with the *embonpoint* that comes from spending two or three diligent hours every day at the table, eyes down and conversation postponed in the observance of France's favorite ritual. The proprietor of the restaurant, a man who had somehow perfected the art of hovering despite his considerable size, was dressed for the day in a velvet smoking jacket and bow tie. His mustache, sleek with pomade, quivered with enthusiasm as he rhapsodized over the menu: foie gras, lobster mousse, beef *en croûte*, salads dressed in virgin oil, hand-picked cheeses, desserts of a miraculous lightness, *digestifs*. It was a gastronomic aria which he performed at each table, kissing the tips of his fingers so often that he must have blistered his lips.

The final *"bon appétit"* died away and a companionable near-silence descended on the restaurant as the food received its due attention. While we ate, my wife and I thought of previous New Year's Days, most of them spent under impenetrable cloud in England. It was hard to associate the sunshine and dense blue sky outside with the first of January but, as everyone kept telling us, it was quite normal. After all, we were in Provence.

We had been here often before as tourists, desperate for our annual ration of two or three weeks of true heat and sharp light. Always when we left, with peeling noses and regret, we promised ourselves that one day we would live here. We had talked about it during the long gray winters and the damp green summers, looked with an addict's longing at photographs of village markets and vineyards, dreamed of being woken up by the sun slanting through the bedroom window. And now, somewhat to our surprise, we had done it. We had committed ourselves. We had bought a house, taken French lessons, said our good-byes, shipped over our two dogs, and become foreigners.

In the end, it had happened quickly—almost impulsively— because of the house. We saw it one afternoon and had mentally moved in by dinner.

It was set above the country road that runs between the two medieval hill villages of Ménerbes and Bonnieux, at the end of a dirt track through cherry trees and vines. It was a *mas*, or farmhouse, built from local stone which two hundred years of wind and sun had weathered to a color somewhere between pale honey and pale gray. It had started life in the eighteenth century

as one room and, in the haphazard manner of agricultural buildings, had spread to accommodate children, grandmothers, goats,
and farm implements until it had become an irregular three-story
house. Everything about it was solid. The spiral staircase which
rose from the wine *cave* to the top floor was cut from massive
slabs of stone. The walls, some of them a meter thick, were built
to keep out the winds of the Mistral which, they say, can blow
the ears off a donkey. Attached to the back of the house was an
enclosed courtyard, and beyond that a bleached white stone swimming pool. There were three wells, there were established shade
trees and slim green cypresses, hedges of rosemary, a giant almond
tree. In the afternoon sun, with the wooden shutters half-closed
like sleepy eyelids, it was irresistible.

It was also immune, as much as any house could be, from
the creeping horrors of property development. The French have
a weakness for erecting *jolies villas* wherever building regulations
permit, and sometimes where they don't, particularly in areas of
hitherto unspoiled and beautiful countryside. We had seen them
in a ghastly rash around the old market town of Apt, boxes made
from that special kind of livid pink cement which remains livid
no matter what the weather may throw at it. Very few areas of
rural France are safe unless they have been officially protected,
and one of the great attractions of this house was that it sat
within the boundaries of a national park, sacred to the French
heritage and out of bounds to concrete mixers.

The Lubéron Mountains rise up immediately behind the
house to a high point of nearly 3,500 feet and run in deep folds
for about forty miles from west to east. Cedars and pines and
scrub oak keep them perpetually green and provide cover for boar,
rabbits, and game birds. Wild flowers, thyme, lavender, and
mushrooms grow between the rocks and under the trees, and
from the summit on a clear day the view is of the Basses-Alpes
on one side and the Mediterranean on the other. For most of the
year, it is possible to walk for eight or nine hours without seeing
a car or a human being. It is a 247,000-acre extension of the

back garden, a paradise for the dogs and a permanent barricade against assault from the rear by unforeseen neighbors.

Neighbors, we have found, take on an importance in the country that they don't begin to have in cities. You can live for years in an apartment in London or New York and barely speak to the people who live six inches away from you on the other side of a wall. In the country, separated from the next house though you may be by hundreds of yards, your neighbors are part of your life, and you are part of theirs. If you happen to be foreign and therefore slightly exotic, you are inspected with more than usual interest. And if, in addition, you inherit a long-standing and delicate agricultural arrangement, you are quickly made aware that your attitudes and decisions have a direct effect on another family's well-being.

We had been introduced to our new neighbors by the couple from whom we bought the house, over a five-hour dinner marked by a tremendous goodwill on all sides and an almost total lack of comprehension on our part. The language spoken was French, but it was not the French we had studied in textbooks and heard on cassettes; it was a rich, soupy patois, emanating from somewhere at the back of the throat and passing through a scrambling process in the nasal passages before coming out as speech. Half-familiar sounds could be dimly recognized as words through the swirls and eddies of Provençal: *demain* became *demang, vin* became *vang, maison* became *mesong.* That by itself would not have been a problem had the words been spoken at normal conversational speed and without further embroidery, but they were delivered like bullets from a machine gun, often with an extra vowel tacked on to the end for good luck. Thus an offer of more bread—page-one stuff in French for beginners—emerged as a single twanging question. *Encoredupanga?*

Fortunately for us, the good humor and niceness of our neighbors were apparent even if what they were saying was a mystery. Henriette was a brown, pretty woman with a permanent smile and a sprinter's enthusiasm for reaching the finish line of

each sentence in record time. Her husband, Faustin—or Faus-
tang, as we thought his name was spelled for many weeks—was
large and gentle, unhurried in his movements and relatively slow
with his words. He had been born in the valley, he had spent
his life in the valley, and he would die in the valley. His father,
Pépé André, who lived next to him, had shot his last boar at the
age of eighty and had given up hunting to take up the bicycle.
Twice a week he would pedal to the village for his groceries and
his gossip. They seemed to be a contented family.

They had, however, a concern about us, not only as neighbors but as prospective partners, and, through the fumes of *marc*
and black tobacco and the even thicker fog of the accent, we
eventually got to the bottom of it.

Most of the six acres of land we had bought with the house
was planted with vines, and these had been looked after for years
under the traditional system of *métayage*: the owner of the land
pays the capital costs of new vine stock and fertilizer, while the
farmer does the work of spraying, cropping, and pruning. At the
end of the season, the farmer takes two-thirds of the profits and
the owner one-third. If the property changes hands, the arrangement comes up for review, and there was Faustin's concern. It
was well known that many of the properties in the Lubéron were
bought as *résidences secondaires*, used for holidays and amusement,
their good agricultural land turned into elaborately planted gardens. There were even cases of the ultimate blasphemy, when
vines had been grubbed up to make way for tennis courts. Tennis
courts! Faustin shrugged with disbelief, shoulders and eyebrows
going up in unison as he contemplated the extraordinary idea of
exchanging precious vines for the curious pleasures of chasing a
little ball around in the heat.

He needn't have worried. We loved the vines—the ordered
regularity of them against the sprawl of the mountain, the way
they changed from bright green to darker green to yellow and red
as spring and summer turned to autumn, the blue smoke in the
pruning season as the clippings were burned, the pruned stumps

studding the bare fields in the winter—they were meant to be here. Tennis courts and landscaped gardens weren't. (Nor, for that matter, was our swimming pool, but at least it hadn't replaced any vines.) And, besides, there was the wine. We had the option of taking our profit in cash or in the bottle, and in an average year our share of the crop would be nearly a thousand litres of good ordinary red and pink. As emphatically as we could in our unsteady French, we told Faustin that we would be delighted to continue the existing arrangement. He beamed. He could see that we would all get along very well together. One day, we might even be able to talk to each other.

THE PROPRIETOR of Le Simiane wished us a happy new year and hovered in the doorway as we stood in the narrow street, blinking into the sun.

"Not bad, eh?" he said, with a flourish of one velvet-clad arm which took in the village, the ruins of the Marquis de Sade's château perched above, the view across to the mountains and the bright, clean sky. It was a casually possessive gesture, as if he was showing us a corner of his personal estate. "One is fortunate to be in Provence."

Yes indeed, we thought, one certainly was. If this was winter we wouldn't be needing all the foul-weather paraphernalia—boots and coats and inch-thick sweaters—that we had brought over from England. We drove home, warm and well fed, making bets on how soon we could take the first swim of the year, and feeling a smug sympathy for those poor souls in harsher climates who had to suffer real winters.

Meanwhile, a thousand miles to the north, the wind that had started in Siberia was picking up speed for the final part of its journey. We had heard stories about the Mistral. It drove people, and animals, mad. It was an extenuating circumstance in crimes of violence. It blew for fifteen days on end, uprooting trees, overturning cars, smashing windows, tossing old ladies into the gutter, splintering telegraph poles, moaning through houses like a cold and baleful ghost, causing *la grippe*, domestic squabbles, absenteeism from work, toothache, migraine—every problem in Provence that couldn't be blamed on the politicians was the fault of the *sâcré vent* which the Provençaux spoke about with a kind of masochistic pride.

Typical Gallic exaggeration, we thought. If they had to put up with the gales that come off the English Channel and bend the rain so that it hits you in the face almost horizontally, then they might know what a real wind was like. We listened to their stories and, to humor the tellers, pretended to be impressed.

And so we were poorly prepared when the first Mistral of the year came howling down the Rhône valley, turned left, and smacked into the west side of the house with enough force to skim roof tiles into the swimming pool and rip a window that had carelessly been left open off its hinges. The temperature dropped twenty degrees in twenty-four hours. It went to zero, then six below. Readings taken in Marseilles showed a wind speed of 180 kilometers an hour. My wife was cooking in an overcoat. I was trying to type in gloves. We stopped talking about our first swim and thought wistfully about central heating. And then one morning, with the sound of branches snapping, the pipes burst one after the other under the pressure of water that had frozen in them overnight.

They hung off the wall, swollen and stopped up with ice, and Monsieur Menicucci studied them with his professional plumber's eye.

"*Oh là là,*" he said. "*Oh là là.*" He turned to his young apprentice, whom he invariably addressed as *jeune homme* or *jeune*. "You see what we have here, *jeune*. Naked pipes. No insulation. Côte d'Azur plumbing. In Cannes, in Nice, it would do, but here . . ."

He made a clucking sound of disapproval and wagged his finger under *jeune*'s nose to underline the difference between the soft winters of the coast and the biting cold in which we were now standing, and pulled his woolen bonnet firmly down over his ears. He was short and compact, built for plumbing, as he would say, because he could squeeze himself into constricted spaces that more ungainly men would find inaccessible. While we waited for *jeune* to set up the blowtorch, Monsieur Menicucci delivered the first of a series of lectures and collected *pensées* which I would listen to with increasing enjoyment throughout the coming year. Today, we had a geophysical dissertation on the increasing severity of Provençal winters.

For three years in a row, winters had been noticeably harder than anyone could remember—cold enough, in fact, to kill ancient olive trees. It was, to use the phrase that comes out in Provence whenever the sun goes in, *pas normal*. But why? Monsieur Menicucci gave me a token two seconds to ponder this phenomenon before warming to his thesis, tapping me with a finger from time to time to make sure I was paying attention.

It was clear, he said, that the winds which brought the cold down from Russia were arriving in Provence with greater velocity than before, taking less time to reach their destination and therefore having less time to warm up en route. And the reason for this—Monsieur Menicucci allowed himself a brief but dramatic pause—was a change in the configuration of the earth's crust. *Mais oui*. Somewhere between Siberia and Ménerbes the curvature of the earth had flattened, enabling the wind to take a more direct route south. It was entirely logical. Unfortunately, part two of the lecture (Why the Earth Is Becoming Flatter) was interrupted by a crack of another burst pipe, and my education was put aside for some virtuoso work with the blowtorch.

The effect of the weather on the inhabitants of Provence is immediate and obvious. They expect every day to be sunny, and their disposition suffers when it isn't. Rain they take as a personal affront, shaking their heads and commiserating with each other in the cafés, looking with profound suspicion at the sky as though a plague of locusts is about to descend, and picking their way with distaste through the puddles on the pavement. If anything worse than a rainy day should come along, such as this sub-zero snap, the result is startling: most of the population disappears.

As the cold began to bite into the middle of January, the towns and villages became quiet. The weekly markets, normally jammed and boisterous, were reduced to a skeleton crew of intrepid stallholders who were prepared to risk frostbite for a living, stamping their feet and nipping from hip flasks. Customers moved briskly, bought and went, barely pausing to count their change. Bars closed their doors and windows tight and conducted their business in a pungent fog. There was none of the usual dawdling on the streets.

Our valley hibernated, and I missed the sounds that marked the passing of each day almost as precisely as a clock: Faustin's rooster having his morning cough; the demented clatter—like nuts and bolts trying to escape from a biscuit tin—of the small Citroën van that every farmer drives home at lunchtime; the hopeful fusillade of a hunter on afternoon patrol in the vines on the opposite hillside; the distant whine of a chainsaw in the forest; the twilight serenade of farm dogs. Now there was silence. For hours on end the valley would be completely still and empty, and we became curious. What was everybody doing?

Faustin, we knew, traveled around the neighboring farms as a visiting slaughterer, slitting the throats and breaking the necks of rabbits and ducks and pigs and geese so that they could be turned into terrines and hams and *confits*. We thought it an uncharacteristic occupation for a softhearted man who spoiled his dogs, but he was evidently skilled and quick and, like any true countryman, he wasn't distracted by sentiment. We might treat a rabbit as a pet or become emotionally attached to a goose, but we had come from cities and supermarkets, where flesh was hygienically distanced from any resemblance to living creatures. A shrink-wrapped pork chop has a sanitized, abstract appearance that has nothing whatever to do with the warm, mucky bulk of a pig. Out here in the country there was no avoiding the direct link between death and dinner, and there would be many occasions in the future when we would be grateful for Faustin's winter work.

But what did everyone else do? The earth was frozen, the vines were clipped and dormant, it was too cold to hunt. Had they all gone on holiday? No, surely not. These were not the kind of gentlemen farmers who spent their winters on the ski slopes or yachting in the Caribbean. Holidays here were taken at home during August, eating too much, enjoying siestas and resting up before the long days of the *vendange*. It was a puzzle, until we realized how many of the local people had their birthdays in September or October, and then a possible but unverifiable answer suggested itself: they were busy indoors making babies. There is a season for everything in Provence, and the first two months of the year must be devoted to procreation. We have never dared ask.

The cold weather brought less private pleasures. Apart from the peace and emptiness of the landscape, there is a special smell about winter in Provence which is accentuated by the wind and the clean, dry air. Walking in the hills, I was often able to smell a house before I could see it, because of the scent of woodsmoke coming from an invisible chimney. It is one of the most primitive smells in life, and consequently extinct in most cities, where fire regulations and interior decorators have combined to turn fireplaces into blocked-up holes or self-consciously lit "architectural features." The fireplace in Provence is still used—to cook on, to sit around, to warm the toes, and to please the eye—and fires are laid in the early morning and fed throughout the day with scrub oak from the Lubéron or beech from the foothills of Mont Ventoux. Coming home with the dogs as dusk fell, I always stopped to look from the top of the valley at the long zigzag of smoke ribbons drifting up from the farms that are scattered along the Bonnieux road. It was a sight that made me think of warm kitchens and well-seasoned stews, and it never failed to make me ravenous.

The well-known food of Provence is summer food—the melons and peaches and asparagus, the courgettes and aubergines, the peppers and tomatoes, the *aioli* and bouillabaisse and monumental salads of olives and anchovies and tuna and hard-boiled eggs and sliced, earthy potatoes on beds of multicoloured lettuce glistening with oil, the fresh goat's cheeses—these had been the memories that came back to torment us every time we looked at the limp and shriveled selection on offer in English shops. It had never occurred to us that there was a winter menu, totally different but equally delicious.

The cold-weather cuisine of Provence is peasant food. It is made to stick to your ribs, keep you warm, give you strength, and send you off to bed with a full belly. It is not pretty, in the way that the tiny and artistically garnished portions served in fashionable restaurants are pretty, but on a freezing night with the Mistral coming at you like a razor there is nothing to beat it. And on the night one of our neighbors invited us to dinner it was cold enough to turn the short walk to their house into a short run.

We came through the door and my glasses steamed up in the heat from the fireplace that occupied most of the far wall of the room. As the mist cleared, I saw that the big table, covered in checked oilcloth, was laid for ten; friends and relations were coming to examine us. A television set chattered in the corner, the radio chattered back from the kitchen, and assorted dogs and cats were shooed out of the door as one guest arrived, only to sidle back in with the next. A tray of drinks was brought out, with pastis for the men and chilled, sweet muscat wine for the women, and we were caught in a crossfire of noisy complaints about the weather. Was it as bad as this in England? Only in the summer, I said. For a moment they took me seriously before someone saved me from embarrassment by laughing. With a great deal of jockeying for position—whether to sit next to us or as far away as possible, I wasn't sure—we settled ourselves at the table.

It was a meal that we shall never forget; more accurately, it was several meals that we shall never forget, because it went beyond the gastronomic frontiers of anything we had ever experienced, both in quantity and length.

It started with homemade pizza—not one, but three: anchovy, mushroom, and cheese, and it was obligatory to have a slice of each. Plates were then wiped with pieces torn from the two-foot loaves in the middle of the table, and the next course came out. There were pâtés of rabbit, boar, and thrush. There was a chunky, pork-based terrine laced with *marc*. There were *saucissons* spotted with peppercorns. There were tiny sweet onions marinated in a fresh tomato sauce. Plates were wiped once more and duck was brought in. The slivers of *magret* that appear, arranged in fan formation and lapped by an elegant smear of sauce on the refined tables of nouvelle cuisine—these were nowhere to be seen. We had entire breasts, entire legs, covered in a dark, savory gravy and surrounded by wild mushrooms.

We sat back, thankful that we had been able to finish, and watched with something close to panic as plates were wiped yet again and a huge, steaming casserole was placed on the table. This was the speciality of Madame our hostess—a rabbit *civet* of the richest, deepest brown—and our feeble requests for small portions were smilingly ignored. We ate it. We ate the green salad with knuckles of bread fried in garlic and olive oil, we ate the plump round *crottins* of goat's cheese, we ate the almond and cream gâteau that the daughter of the house had prepared. That night, we ate for England.

With the coffee, a number of deformed bottles were produced which contained a selection of locally made *digestifs*. My heart would have sunk had there been any space left for it to sink to, but there was no denying my host's insistence. I must try one particular concoction, made from an eleventh-century recipe by an alcoholic order of monks in the Basses-Alpes. I was asked to close my eyes while it was poured, and when I opened them a tumbler of viscous yellow fluid had been put in front of me. I looked in despair around the table. Everyone was watching me; there was no chance of giving whatever it was to the dog or letting it dribble discreetly into one of my shoes. Clutching the table for support with one hand, I took the tumbler with the other, closed my eyes, prayed to the patron saint of indigestion, and threw it back.

Nothing came out. I had been expecting at best a scalded tongue, at worst permanently cauterized taste buds, but I took in nothing but air. It was a trick glass, and for the first time in my adult life I was deeply relieved not to have a drink. As the laughter of the other guests died away, genuine drinks were threatened, but we were saved by the cat. From her headquarters on top of a large *armoire*, she took a flying leap in pursuit of a moth and crash-landed among the coffee cups and bottles on the table. It seemed like an appropriate moment to leave. We walked home pushing our stomachs before us, oblivious to the cold, incapable of speech, and slept like the dead.

Even by Provençal standards, it had not been an everyday meal. The people who work on the land are more likely to eat well at noon and sparingly in the evening, a habit that is healthy and sensible and, for us, quite impossible. We have found that there is nothing like a good lunch to give us an appetite for dinner. It's alarming. It must have something to do with the novelty of living in the middle of such an abundance of good things to eat, and among men and women whose interest in food verges on obsession. Butchers, for instance, are not content merely to sell you meat. They will tell you, at great length, while the queue backs up behind you, how to cook it, how to serve it, and what to eat and drink with it.

The first time this happened, we had gone into Apt to buy veal for the Provençal stew called *pebronata*. We were directed towards a butcher in the old part of town who was reputed to have the master's touch and to be altogether *très sérieux*. His shop was small, he and his wife were large, and the four of us constituted a crowd. He listened intently as we explained that we wanted to make this particular dish; perhaps he had heard of it.

He puffed up with indignation, and began to sharpen a large

knife so energetically that we stepped back a pace. Did we realize, he said, that we were looking at an expert, possibly the greatest *pebronata* authority in the Vaucluse? His wife nodded admiringly. Why, he said, brandishing ten inches of sharp steel in our faces, he had written a book about it—a *definitive* book—containing twenty variations of the basic recipe. His wife nodded again. She was playing the rôle of senior nurse to his eminent surgeon, passing him fresh knives to sharpen prior to the operation.

We must have looked suitably impressed, because he then produced a handsome piece of veal and his tone became professorial. He trimmed the meat, cubed it, filled a small bag with chopped herbs, told us where to go to buy the best peppers (four green and one red, the contrast in color being for aesthetic reasons), went through the recipe twice to make sure we weren't going to commit a *bêtise*, and suggested a suitable Côtes du Rhône. It was a fine performance.

Gourmets are thick on the ground in Provence, and pearls of wisdom have sometimes come from the most unlikely sources. We were getting used to the fact that the French are as passionate about food as other nationalities are about sport and politics, but even so it came as a surprise to hear Monsieur Bagnols, the floor cleaner, handicapping three-star restaurants. He had come over from Nîmes to sand down a stone floor, and it was apparent from the start that he was not a man who trifled with his stomach. Each day precisely at noon he changed out of his overalls and took himself off to one of the local restaurants for two hours.

He judged it to be not bad, but of course nothing like the Beaumanière at Les Baux. The Beaumanière has three Michelin stars and a 17 out of 20 rating in the Gault-Millau Guide and there, he said, he had eaten a truly exceptional sea bass *en croûte*. Mind you, the Troisgros in Roanne was a superb establishment too, although being opposite the station the setting wasn't as pretty as Les Baux. The Troisgros has three Michelin stars and a 19½ out of 20 rating in the Gault-Millau Guide. And so it went on, as he adjusted his knee pads and scrubbed away at the floor, a personal guide to five or six of the most expensive restaurants in France that Monsieur Bagnols had visited on his annual treats.

He had once been in England, and had eaten roast lamb at a hotel in Liverpool. It had been gray and tepid and tasteless. But of course, he said, it is well known that the English kill their lamb twice; once when they slaughter it, and once when they cook it. I retreated in the face of such withering contempt for my national cuisine, and left him to get on with the floor and dream of his next visit to Bocuse.

T HE WEATHER continued hard, with bitter but extravagantly starry nights and spectacular sunrises. One early morning, the sun seemed abnormally low and large, and walking into it everything was either glare or deep shadow. The dogs were running well ahead of me, and I heard them barking long before I could see what they had found.

We had come to a part of the forest where the land fell away to form a deep bowl in which, a hundred years before, some misguided farmer had built a house that was almost permanently in the gloom cast by the surrounding trees. I had passed it many times. The windows were always shuttered, and the only sign of human habitation was smoke drifting up from the chimney. In the yard outside, two large and matted Alsatians and a black mongrel were constantly on the prowl, howling and straining against their chains in their efforts to savage any passers-by. These dogs were known to be vicious; one of them had broken loose and laid open the back of grandfather André's leg. My dogs, full of valor when confronted by timid cats, had wisely decided against passing too close to three sets of hostile jaws, and had developed the habit of making a detour around the house and over a small steep hill. They were at the top now, barking in that speculative, nervous manner that dogs adopt to reassure themselves when they encounter something unexpected in familiar territory.

I reached the top of the hill with the sun full in my eyes, but I could make out the backlit silhouette of a figure in the trees, a nimbus of smoke around his head, the dogs inspecting him noisily from a safe distance. As I came up to him, he extended a cold, horny hand.

"*Bonjour.*" He unscrewed a cigarette butt from the corner of his mouth and introduced himself. "Massot, Antoine."

He was dressed for war. A stained camouflage jacket, an army jungle cap, a bandolier of cartridges, and a pump-action shotgun. His face was the color and texture of a hastily cooked steak, with a wedge of nose jutting out above a ragged, nicotine-stained mustache. Pale blue eyes peered through a sprouting tangle of ginger eyebrows, and his decayed smile would have brought despair to the most optimistic dentist. Nevertheless, there was a certain mad amiability about him.

I asked if his hunting had been successful. "A fox," he said, "but too old to eat." He shrugged, and lit another of his fat Boyards cigarettes, wrapped in yellow maize paper and smelling like a young bonfire in the morning air. "Anyway," he said, "he won't be keeping my dogs awake at night," and he nodded down toward the house in the hollow.

I said that his dogs seemed fierce, and he grinned. Just playful, he said. But what about the time one of them had escaped and attacked the old man? Ah, that. He shook his head at the painful memory. The trouble is, he said, you should never turn your back on a playful dog, and that had been the old man's mistake. *Une vraie catastrophe.* For a moment, I thought he was regretting the wound inflicted on grandfather André, which had punctured a vein in his leg and required a visit to the hospital for injections and stitches, but I was mistaken. The real sadness was that Massot had been obliged to buy a new chain, and those robbers in Cavaillon had charged him 250 francs. That had bitten deeper than teeth.

To save him further anguish, I changed the subject and asked him if he really ate fox. He seemed surprised at such a stupid question, and looked at me for a moment or two without replying, as though he suspected me of making fun of him.

"One doesn't eat fox in England?" I had visions of the members of the Belvoir Hunt writing to *The Times* and having a collective heart attack at such an unsporting and typically foreign idea.

"No, one doesn't eat fox in England. One dresses up in a red coat and one chases after it on horseback with several dogs, and then one cuts off its tail."

He cocked his head, astonished. *"Ils sont bizarres, les Anglais."* And then, with great gusto and some hideously explicit gestures, he described what civilized people did with a fox.

Civet de renard à la façon Massot

Find a young fox, and be careful to shoot it cleanly in the head, which is of no culinary interest. Buckshot in the edible parts of the fox can cause chipped teeth— Massot showed me two of his—and indigestion.

Skin the fox, and cut off its *parties*. Here, Massot made a chopping motion with his hand across his groin, and followed this with some elaborate twists and tugs of the hand to illustrate the gutting process.

Leave the cleaned carcass under cold running water for twenty-four hours to eliminate the *goût sauvage*. Drain it, bundle it up in a sack, and hang it outdoors overnight, preferably when there is frost.

The following morning, place the fox in a casserole of cast iron and cover with a mixture of blood and red wine. Add herbs, onions, and heads of garlic, and simmer for a day or two. (Massot apologized for his lack of precision but said that the timing varied according to size and age of fox.)

In the old days, this was eaten with bread and boiled potatoes, but now, thanks to progress and the invention of the deep-fat fryer, one could enjoy it with *pommes frites.*

By now, Massot was in a talkative mood. He lived alone, he told me, and company was scarce in the winter. He had spent his life in the mountains, but maybe it was time to move into the village, where he could be among people. Of course, it would be a tragedy to leave such a beautiful house, so calm, so sheltered from the Mistral, so perfectly situated to escape the heat of the midday sun, a place where he had passed so many happy years. It would break his heart, unless—he looked at me closely, pale eyes watery with sincerity—unless he could render me a service by making it possible for one of my friends to buy his house.

I looked down at the ramshackle building huddled in the shadows, with the three dogs padding endlessly to and fro on their rusting chains, and thought that in the whole of Provence it would be difficult to find a less appealing spot to live. There was no sun, no view, no feeling of space, and almost certainly a dank and horrid interior. I promised Massot that I would bear it in mind, and he winked at me. "A million francs," he said. "A sacrifice." And in the meantime, until he left this little corner of paradise, if there was anything I wanted to know about the rural life, he would advise me. He knew every centimeter of the forest, where the mushrooms grew, where the wild boar came to drink, which gun to choose, how to train a hound—there was nothing he didn't know, and this knowledge was mine for the asking. I thanked him. *"C'est normal,"* he said, and stumped off down the hill to his million-franc residence.

WHEN I TOLD a friend in the village that I had met Massot, he smiled.

"Did he tell you how to cook a fox?"

I nodded.

"Did he try to sell his house?"

I nodded.

"The old *blagueur*. He's full of wind."

I didn't care. I liked him, and I had a feeling that he would be a rich source of fascinating and highly suspect information. With him to initiate me into the joys of rustic pursuits and Monsieur Menicucci in charge of more scientific matters, all I needed now was a navigator to steer me through the murky waters of French bureaucracy, which in its manifold subtleties and inconveniences can transform a molehill of activity into a mountain of frustration.

We should have been warned by the complications attached to the purchase of the house. We wanted to buy, the proprietor wanted to sell, a price was agreed, it was all straightforward. But then we became reluctant participants in the national sport of paper gathering. Birth certificates were required to prove we existed; passports to prove that we were British; marriage certificates to enable us to buy the house in our joint names; divorce certificates to prove that our marriage certificates were valid; proof that we had an address in England. (Our driver's licenses, plainly addressed, were judged to be insufficient; did we have more formal evidence of where we were living, like an old electricity bill?) Back and forth between France and England the pieces of paper went—every scrap of information except blood type and fingerprints—until the local lawyer had our lives contained in a dossier. The transaction could then proceed.

We made allowances for the system because we were foreigners buying a tiny part of France, and national security clearly had to be safeguarded. Less important business would doubtless be quicker and less demanding of paperwork. We went to buy a car.

It was the standard Citroën *deux chevaux*, a model that has changed very little in the past twenty-five years. Consequently, spare parts are available in every village. Mechanically it is not much more complicated than a sewing machine, and any reasonably competent blacksmith can repair it. It is cheap, and has a comfortingly low top speed. Apart from the fact that the suspension is made of blancmange, which makes it the only car in the world likely to cause seasickness, it is a charming and practical vehicle. And the garage had one in stock.

The salesman looked at our driver's licenses, valid throughout the countries of the Common Market until well past the year 2000. With an expression of infinite regret, he shook his head and looked up.

"*Non.*"

"*Non?*"

"*Non.*"

We produced our secret weapons: two passports.

"*Non.*"

We rummaged around in our papers. What could he want? Our marriage certificate? An old English electricity bill? We gave up, and asked him what else, apart from money, was needed to buy a car.

"You have an address in France?"

We gave it to him, and he noted it down on the sales form with great care, checking from time to time to make sure that the third carbon copy was legible.

"You have proof that this is your address? A telephone bill? An electricity bill?"

We explained that we hadn't yet received any bills because we had only just moved in. He explained that an address was necessary for the *carte grise*—the document of car ownership. No address, no *carte grise*. No *carte grise*, no car.

Fortunately, his salesman's instincts overcame his relish for a bureaucratic impasse, and he leaned forward with a solution: If we would provide him with the deed of sale of our house, the whole affair could be brought to a swift and satisfactory conclusion, and we could have the car. The deed of sale was in the lawyer's office, fifteen miles away. We went to get it, and placed it triumphantly on his desk, together with a check. Now could we have the car?

"Malheureusement, non." We must wait until the check had been cleared, a delay of four or five days, even though it was drawn on a local bank. Could we go together to the bank and clear it immediately? No, we couldn't. It was lunchtime. The two areas of endeavor in which France leads the world —bureaucracy and gastronomy—had combined to put us in our place.

It made us mildly paranoid, and for weeks we never left home without photocopies of the family archives, waving passports and birth certificates at everyone from the checkout girl at the supermarket to the old man who loaded the wine into the car at the cooperative. The documents were always regarded with interest, because documents are holy things here and deserve respect, but we were often asked why we carried them around. Was this the way one was obliged to live in England? What a strange and tiresome country it must be. The only short answer to that was a shrug. We practiced shrugging.

The cold lasted until the final days of January, and then turned perceptibly warmer. We anticipated spring, and I was anxious to hear an expert forecast. I decided to consult the sage of the forest.

Massot tugged reflectively at his mustache. There were signs, he said. Rats can sense the coming of warmer weather before any of those complicated satellites, and the rats in his roof had been unusually active these past few days. In fact, they had kept him awake one night and he had loosed off a couple of shots into the ceiling to quieten them down. *Eh, oui.* Also, the new moon was due, and that often brought a change at this time of year. Based on these two significant portents, he predicted an early, warm spring. I hurried home to see if there were any traces of blossom on the almond tree, and thought about cleaning the swimming pool.

FEBRUARY

THE FRONT PAGE of our newspaper, *Le Provençal*, is usually
devoted to the fortunes of local football teams, the windy pro-
nouncements of minor politicians, breathless reports of supermarket holdups in Cavaillon—*"le Chicago de Provence"*—and the
occasional ghoulish account of sudden death on the roads caused
by drivers of small Renaults trying to emulate Alain Prost.

This traditional mixture was put aside, one morning in early
February, for a lead story which had nothing to do with sport,
crime, or politics: PROVENCE UNDER BLANKET OF SNOW! shouted
the headline with an undercurrent of glee at the promise of
the follow-up stories which would undoubtedly result from
Nature's unseasonable behavior. There would be mothers and
babies miraculously alive after a night in a snowbound car, old
men escaping hypothermia by inches thanks to the intervention

of public-spirited and alert neighbors, climbers plucked from the side of Mont Ventoux by helicopter, postmen battling against all odds to deliver electricity bills, village elders harking back to previous catastrophes—there were days of material ahead, and the writer of that first story could almost be seen rubbing his hands in anticipation as he paused between sentences to look for some more exclamation marks.

Two photographs accompanied the festive text. One was of a line of white, feathery umbrellas—the snow-draped palm trees along the Promenade des Anglais in Nice. The other showed a muffled figure in Marseilles dragging a mobile radiator on its wheels through the snow at the end of a rope, like a man taking an angular and obstinate dog for a walk. There were no pictures of the countryside under snow because the countryside was cut off; the nearest snowplow was north of Lyon, three hundred kilometers away, and to a Provençal motorist—even an intrepid journalist—brought up on the sure grip of baking tarmac, the horror of waltzing on ice was best avoided by staying home or holing up in the nearest bar. After all, it wouldn't be for long. This was an aberration, a short-lived climatic hiccup, an excuse for a second *café crème* and perhaps something a little stronger to get the heart started before venturing outside.

Our valley had been quiet during the cold days of January, but now the snow had added an extra layer of silence, as though the entire area had been soundproofed. We had the Lubéron to ourselves, eerie and beautiful, mile after mile of white icing marked only by occasional squirrel and rabbit tracks crossing the footpaths in straight and purposeful lines. There were no human footprints except ours. The hunters, so evident in warmer weather with their weaponry and their arsenals of salami, baguettes, beer, Gauloises, and all the other necessities for a day out braving nature in the raw, had stayed in their burrows. The sounds we mistook for gunshots were branches snapping under the weight of great swags of snow. Otherwise it was so still that, as Massot observed later, you could have heard a mouse fart.

Closer to home, the drive had turned into a miniature mountainscape where wind had drifted the snow into a range of knee-deep mounds, and the only way out was on foot. Buying a loaf of bread became an expedition lasting nearly two hours—into Ménerbes and back without seeing a single moving vehicle, the white humps of parked cars standing as patiently as sheep by the side of the hill leading up to the village. The Christmas-card weather had infected the inhabitants, who were greatly amused by their own efforts to negotiate the steep and treacherous streets, either teetering precariously forward from the waist or leaning even more precariously backward, placing their feet with the awkward deliberation of intoxicated roller-skaters. The municipal cleaning squad, two men with brooms, had cleared the access routes to essential services—butcher, baker, *épicerie*, and café— and small knots of villagers stood in the sunshine congratulating one another on their fortitude in the face of calamity. A man on skis appeared from the direction of the Mairie and, with marvelous inevitability, collided with the only other owner of assisted transport, a man on an ancient sled. It was a pity the journalist from *Le Provençal* wasn't there to see it: SNOW CLAIMS VICTIMS IN HEAD-ON COLLISION, he could have written, and he could have watched it all from the steamy comfort of the café.

The dogs adapted to the snow like young bears, plunging into the drifts to emerge with white whiskers and bucking their way across the fields in huge, frothy leaps. And they learned to skate. The pool, that just days before I had been planning to clean and make ready for some early spring swimming, was a block of blue-green ice, and it seemed to fascinate them. Onto the ice would go the two front paws, then a tentative third paw, and finally the remaining leg would join the rest of the dog. There would be a moment or two of contemplation at the curiosity of a life in which you can drink something one day and stand on it the next before the tail would start whirring with excitement and a form of progress could be made. I had always thought that dogs were engineered on the principle of four-wheel–drive vehicles, with equal propulsion coming from each leg, but the power appears to be concentrated in the back. Thus the front half of the skating dog may have the intention of proceeding in a straight line, but the rear half is wildly out of control, fishtailing from side to side and sometimes threatening to overtake.

The novelty of being marooned in the middle of a picturesque sea was, during the day, a great pleasure. We walked for miles, we chopped wood, we ate enormous lunches, and we stayed warm. But at night, even with fires and sweaters and yet more food, the chill came up from the stone floors and out of the stone walls, making the toes numb and the muscles tight with cold. We were often in bed by nine o'clock and often, in the early morning, our breath was visible in small clouds over the breakfast table. If the Menicucci theory was correct and we were living in a flatter world, all future winters were going to be like this. It was time to stop pretending we were in a subtropical climate and give in to the temptations of central heating.

I called Monsieur Menicucci, and he asked anxiously about my pipes. I told him they were holding up well. "That pleases me," he said, "because it is minus five degrees, the roads are perilous, and I am fifty-eight years old. I am staying at home." He paused, then added, "I shall play the clarinet." This he did every day to keep his fingers nimble and to take his mind off the hurly-burly of plumbing, and it was with some difficulty that I managed to steer the conversation away from his thoughts on the baroque composers and toward the mundane subject of our cold house. Eventually, we agreed that I should pay him a visit as soon as the roads had cleared. He had all kinds of installations at his house, he said—gas, oil, electricity, and, his latest acquisition, a revolving solar-heating panel. He would show them all to me and I could also meet Madame his wife, who was an accomplished soprano. I was obviously going to have a musical time among the radiators and stopcocks.

The prospect of being warm made us think of summer, and we started to make plans for turning the enclosed courtyard at the back of the house into an open-air living room. There was already a barbecue and a bar at one end, but what it lacked was a large, solid, permanent table. As we stood in six inches of snow, we tried to picture lunchtime in mid-August, and traced on the flagstones a five-foot square, large enough to seat eight bronzed and barefooted people and with plenty of room in the middle for giant bowls of salad, pâtés and cheese, cold roasted peppers, olive bread, and chilled bottles of wine. The Mistral gusted through the courtyard and obliterated the shape in the snow, but by then we had decided: the table would be square and the top a single slab of stone.

Like most people who come to the Lubéron, we had been impressed by the variety and versatility of the local stone. It can be *pierre froide* from the quarry at Tavel, a smooth, close-grained pale beige; it can be *pierre chaude* from Lacoste, a rougher, softer off-white, or it can be any one of twenty shades and textures in between. There is a stone for fireplaces, for swimming pools, for staircases, for walls and floors, for garden benches and kitchen sinks. It can be rough or polished, hard-edged or rolled, cut square or in voluptuous curves. It is used where, in Britain or America, a builder might use wood or iron or plastic. Its only disadvantage, as we were finding out, is that it is cold in winter.

What came as a real surprise was the price. Meter for meter, stone was cheaper than linoleum, and we were so delighted by this rather misleading discovery—having conveniently overlooked the cost of laying stone—that we decided to risk the elements and go to the quarry without waiting for spring. Friends had suggested a man called Pierrot at Lacoste, whose work was good and whose prices were correct. He was described to us as *un original*, a character, and a rendezvous was made with him for 8:30 in the morning, while the quarry would still be quiet.

We followed a signpost off the side road out of Lacoste and along a track through the scrub oak toward the open countryside. It didn't look like a light industrial zone, and we were just about to turn back when we nearly fell into it—a huge hole bitten out of the ground, littered with blocks of stone. Some were raw, some worked into tombstones, memorials, giant garden urns, winged angels with intimidating blind stares, small triumphal arches, or stocky round columns. Tucked away in a corner was a hut, its windows opaque with years of quarry dust.

We knocked and went in, and there was Pierrot. He was shaggy, with a wild black beard and formidable eyebrows. A piratical man. He made us welcome, beating the top layer of dust from two chairs with a battered trilby hat which he then placed carefully over the telephone on the table.

"English, eh?"

We nodded, and he leaned toward us with a confidential air.

"I have an English car, a vintage Aston Martin. *Magnifique*."

He kissed the tips of his fingers, speckling his beard with white, and poked among the papers on his table, raising puffs from every pile. Somewhere there was a photograph.

The phone started to make gravelly noises. Pierrot rescued it from under his hat and listened with an increasingly serious face before putting the phone down.

"Another tombstone," he said. "It's this weather. The old ones can't take the cold." He looked around for his hat, retrieved it from his head, and covered the phone again, hiding the bad news.

He returned to the business at hand. "They tell me you want a table."

I had made a detailed drawing of our table, marking all the measurements carefully in meters and centimeters. For someone with the artistic flair of a five-year-old, it was a masterpiece. Pierrot looked at it briefly, squinting at the figures, and shook his head.

"*Non*. For a piece of stone this size, it needs to be twice as thick. Also, your base would collapse—*pouf!*—in five minutes, because the top will weigh . . ." he scribbled some calculations on my drawing ". . . between three and four hundred kilos." He turned the paper over, and sketched on the back. "There. That's what you want." He pushed the sketch across to us. It was much better than mine, and showed a graceful monolith: simple, square, well proportioned. "A thousand francs, including delivery."

We shook hands on it, and I promised to come back later in the week with a check. When I did, it was at the end of a working day, and I found that Pierrot had changed color. From the top of his trilby down to his boots he was stark white, dusted all over as though he had been rolling in confectioner's sugar, the only man I have ever seen who aged twenty-five years in the course of a working day. According to our friends, whose information I didn't entirely trust, his wife ran the vacuum cleaner over him every night when he came home, and all the furniture in his house, from armchairs to bidets, was made from stone.

At the time, it was easy enough to believe. Deep winter in Provence has a curiously unreal atmosphere, the combination of silence and emptiness creating the feeling that you are separated from the rest of the world, detached from normal life. We could imagine meeting trolls in the forest or seeing two-headed goats by the light of a full moon, and for us it was a strangely enjoyable contrast to the Provence we remembered from summer holidays. For others, winter meant boredom or depression, or worse; the suicide rate in the Vaucluse, so we were told, was the highest in France, and it became more than a statistic when we heard that a man who lived two miles from us had hanged himself one night.

A local death brings sad little announcements, which are posted in the windows of shops and houses. The church bell tolls, and a procession dressed with unfamiliar formality makes its slow way up to the cemetery, which is often one of the most commanding sites in the village. An old man explained why this was so. "The dead get the best view," he said, "because they are there for such a long time." He cackled so hard at his own joke that he had a coughing fit, and I was worried that his turn had come to join them. When I told him about the cemetery in California where you pay more for a tomb with a view than for more modest accommodation he was not at all surprised. "There are always fools," he said, "dead or alive."

Days passed with no sign of a thaw, but the roads were now showing strips of black where farmers and their tractors had cleared away the worst of the snow, making a single-lane passage through the drifts on either side. This brought out a side of the French motorist that I had never expected to see; he displayed patience, or at least a kind of mulish obstinacy that was far removed from his customary Grand Prix behavior behind the wheel. I saw it on the roads around the village. One car would be driving cautiously along the clear middle lane and would meet another coming from the opposite direction. They would stop, snout to snout. Neither would give way by reversing. Neither would pull over to the side and risk getting stuck in a drift. Glaring through the windscreens at each other, the drivers would wait in the hope that another car would come up behind them, which would constitute a clear case of *force majeure* and oblige the single car to back down so that superior numbers could proceed.

And so it was with a light foot on the accelerator that I went off to see Monsieur Menicucci and his treasure house of heating appliances. He met me at the entrance to his storeroom, woolen bonnet pulled down to cover his ears, scarf wound up to his chin, gloved, booted, the picture of a man who took the challenge of keeping warm as a scientific exercise in personal insulation. We exchanged politenesses about my pipes and his clarinet and he ushered me inside to view a meticulously arranged selection of tubes and valves and squat, mysterious machines crouched in corners. Menicucci was a talking catalogue, reeling off heating coefficients and therms which were so far beyond me that all I could do was to nod dumbly at each new revelation.

At last the litany came to an end. "*Et puis voilà*," said Menicucci, and looked at me expectantly, as though I now had the world of central heating at my fingertips, and could make an intelligent and informed choice. I could think of nothing to say except to ask him how he heated his own house.

"Ah," he said, tapping his forehead in mock admiration, "that is not a stupid thing to ask. What kind of meat does the butcher eat?" And, with that mystical question hanging unanswered in the air, we went next door to his house. It was undeniably warm, almost stuffy, and Monsieur Menicucci made a great performance of removing two or three outer layers of clothing, mopping his brow theatrically and adjusting his bonnet to expose his ears to the air.

He walked over to a radiator and patted it on the head. "Feel that," he said, "cast iron, not like the *merde* they use for radiators nowadays. And the boiler—you must see the boiler. But *attention*"—he stopped abruptly and prodded me with his lecturer's finger—"it is not French. Only the Germans and the Belgians know how to make boilers." We went into the boiler room, and I dutifully admired the elderly, dial-encrusted machine which was puffing and snorting against the wall. "This gives twenty-one degrees throughout the house, even when the temperature outside is minus six," and he threw open the outside door to let in some minus-six air on cue. He had the good instructor's gift for illustrating his remarks wherever possible with practical demonstration, as though he was talking to a particularly dense child. (In my case, certainly as far as plumbing and heating were concerned, this was quite justified.)

Having met the boiler, we went back to the house and met Madame, a diminutive woman with a resonant voice. Did I want a *tisane*, some almond biscuits, a glass of Marsala? What I really wanted was to see Monsieur Menicucci in his bonnet playing his clarinet, but that would have to wait until another day. Meanwhile, I had been given much to think about. As I left to go to the car, I looked up at the revolving solar heating apparatus on the roof and saw that it was frozen solid, and I had a sudden longing for a houseful of cast-iron radiators.

I arrived home to discover that a scale model of Stonehenge had been planted behind the garage. The table had arrived—five feet square, five inches thick, with a massive base in the form of a cross. The distance between where it had been delivered and where we wanted it to be was no more than fifteen yards, but it might as well have been fifty miles. The entrance to the courtyard was too narrow for any mechanical transport, and the high wall and tiled half-roof that made a sheltered area ruled out the use of a crane. Pierrot had told us that the table would weigh between six and eight hundred pounds. It looked heavier.

He called that evening.

"Are you pleased with the table?"

Yes, the table is wonderful, but there is a problem.

"Have you put it up yet?"

No, that's the problem. Did he have any helpful suggestions?

"A few pairs of arms," he said. "Think of the Pyramids."

Of course. All we needed were fifteen thousand Egyptian slaves and it would be done in no time.

"Well, if you get desperate, I know the rugby team in Carcassonne."

And with that he laughed and hung up.

We went to have another look at the monster, and tried to work out how many people would be needed to manhandle it into the courtyard. Six? Eight? It would have to be balanced on its side to pass through the doorway. We had visions of crushed toes and multiple hernias, and belatedly understood why the previous owner of the house had put a light, folding table in the place we had chosen for our monument. We took the only reasonable course of action open to us, and sought inspiration in front of the fire with a glass of wine. It was unlikely that anyone would steal the table overnight.

As it turned out, a possible source of help was not long in coming. Weeks before, we had decided to rebuild the kitchen, and had spent many enlightening hours with our architect as we were introduced to French building terminology, to *coffres* and *rehausses* and *faux-plafonds* and *vide-ordures*, to *plâtrage* and *dallage* and *poutrelles* and *coins perdus*. Our initial excitement had turned into anticlimax as the plans became more and more dog-eared and, for one reason or another, the kitchen remained untouched. Delays had been caused by the weather, by the plasterer going skiing, by the chief *maçon* breaking his arm playing football on a motorbike, by the winter torpor of local suppliers. Our architect, an expatriate Parisian, had warned us that building in Provence was very similar to trench warfare, with long periods of boredom interrupted by bursts of violent and noisy activity, and we had so far experienced the first phase for long enough to look forward to the second.

The assault troops finally arrived, with a deafening clatter, while the morning was still hesitating between dawn and daylight. We went outside with bleary eyes to see what had fallen down, and could just make out the shape of a truck, spiked with scaffolding. A cheerful bellow came from the driver's seat.

"Monsieur Mayle?"

I told him he'd found the right house.

"Ah bon. On va attaquer la cuisine. Allez!"

The door opened, and a cocker spaniel jumped out, followed by three men. There was an unexpected whiff of aftershave as the chief *maçon* mangled my hand and introduced himself and his team: Didier, the lieutenant Eric, and the junior, a massive young man called Claude. The dog, Pénélope, declared the site open by relieving herself copiously in front of the house, and battle commenced.

We had never seen builders work like this. Everything was done on the double: scaffolding was erected and a ramp of planks was built before the sun was fully up, the kitchen window and sink disappeared minutes later, and by ten o'clock we were standing in a fine layer of preliminary rubble as Didier outlined his plans for destruction. He was brisk and tough, with the cropped hair and straight back of a military man; I could see him as a drill instructor in the Foreign Legion, putting young layabouts through their paces until they whimpered for mercy. His speech was percussive, full of the onomatopoeic words like *tok* and *crak* and *boum* that the French like to use when describing any form of collision or breakage—and there was to be plenty of both. The ceiling was coming down, the floor was coming up and all the existing fittings coming out. It was a gutting job, the entire kitchen to be evacuated—*chut!*—through the hole that used to be a window. A wall of polythene sheeting was nailed up to screen the area from the rest of the house, and domestic catering operations were transferred to the barbecue in the courtyard.

It was startling to see and hear the joyful ferocity with which the three masons pulverized everything within sledgehammer range. They thumped and whistled and sang and swore amid the falling masonry and sagging beams, stopping (with some reluctance, it seemed to me) at noon for lunch. This was demolished with the same vigor as a partition wall—not modest packets of sandwiches, but large plastic hampers filled with chickens and sausage and *choucroute* and salads and loaves of bread, with proper crockery and cutlery. None of them drank alcohol, to our relief. A tipsy mason nominally in charge of a forty-pound hammer was a frightening thought. They were dangerous enough sober.

Pandemonium resumed after lunch, and continued until nearly seven o'clock without any break. I asked Didier if he regularly worked a ten- or eleven-hour day. Only in the winter, he said. In the summer it was twelve or thirteen hours, six days a week. He was amused to hear about the English timetable of a late start and an early finish, with multiple tea breaks. "*Une petite journée*" was how he described it, and asked if I knew any English masons who would like to work with him, just for the experience. I couldn't imagine a rush of volunteers.

When the masons had gone for the day, we dressed for a picnic in the Arctic and started to prepare our first dinner in the temporary kitchen. There was a barbecue fireplace and a fridge. A sink and two gas rings were built into the back of the bar. It had all the basic requirements except walls, and with the temperature still below zero walls would have been a comfort. But the fire of vine clippings was burning brightly, the smell of lamb chops and rosemary was in the air, the red wine was doing noble work as a substitute for central heating, and we felt hardy and adventurous. This delusion lasted through dinner until it was time to go outside and wash the dishes.

THE FIRST true intimations of spring came not from early blossom or the skittish behavior of the rats in Massot's roof, but from England. With the gloom of January behind them, people in London were making holiday plans, and it was astonishing how many of those plans included Provence. With increasing regularity, the phone would ring as we were sitting down to dinner —the caller having a cavalier disregard for the hour's time difference between France and England—and the breezy, half-remembered voice of a distant acquaintance would ask if we were swimming yet. We were always noncommittal. It seemed unkind to spoil their illusions by telling them that we were sitting in a permafrost zone with the Mistral screaming through the hole in the kitchen wall and threatening to rip open the polythene sheet which was our only protection against the elements.

The call would continue along a course that quickly became predictable. First, we would be asked if we were going to be at home during Easter or May, or whichever period suited the caller. With that established, the sentence which we soon came to dread —"We were thinking of coming down around then . . ."— would be delivered, and would dangle, hopeful and unfinished, waiting for a faintly hospitable reaction.

It was difficult to feel flattered by this sudden enthusiasm to see us, which had lain dormant during the years we had lived in England, and it was difficult to know how to deal with it. There is nothing quite as thick-skinned as the seeker after sunshine and free lodging; normal social sidesteps don't work. You're booked up that week? Don't worry—we'll come the week after. You have a house full of builders? We don't mind; we'll be out by the pool anyway. You've stocked the pool with barracuda and put a tank trap in the drive? You've become teetotal vegetarians?

You suspect the dogs of carrying rabies? It didn't matter what we said; there was a refusal to take it seriously, a bland determination to overcome any feeble obstacle we might invent.

We talked about the threatened invasions to other people who had moved to Provence, and they had all been through it. The first summer, they said, is invariably hell. After that, you learn to say no. If you don't, you will find yourselves running a small and highly unprofitable hotel from Easter until the end of September.

Sound but depressing advice. We waited nervously for the next phone call.

LIFE HAD CHANGED, and the masons had changed it. If we got up at 6:30 we could have breakfast in peace. Any later, and the sound effects from the kitchen made conversation impossible. One morning when the drills and hammers were in full song, I could see my wife's lips move, but no words were reaching me. Eventually she passed me a note: Drink your coffee before it gets dirty.

But progress was being made. Having reduced the kitchen to a shell, the masons started, just as noisily, to rebuild, bringing all their materials up the plank ramp and through a window-sized space ten feet above the ground. Their stamina was extraordinary, and Didier—half-man, half fork-lift truck—was somehow able to run up the bouncing ramp pushing a wheelbarrow of wet cement, a cigarette in one side of his mouth and breath enough to whistle out of the other. I shall never know how the three of them were able to work in a confined space, under cold and difficult conditions, and remain so resolutely good-humored.

Gradually, the structure of the kitchen took shape and the follow-up squad came to inspect it and to coordinate their various contributions. There was Ramon the plasterer, with his plaster-covered radio and basketball boots, Mastorino the painter, Trufelli the tile-layer, Zanchi the carpenter, and the *chef-plombier* himself, with *jeune* two paces behind him on an invisible lead, Monsieur Menicucci. There were often six or seven of them all talking at once among the debris, arguing about dates and availabilities while Christian, the architect, acted as referee.

It occurred to us that, if this energy could be channeled for an hour or so, we had enough bodies and biceps to shift the stone table into the courtyard. When I suggested this, there was instant cooperation. Why not do it now? they said. Why not indeed? We clambered out of the kitchen window and gathered around the table, which was covered with a white puckered skin of frost. Twelve hands grasped the slab and twelve arms strained to lift it. There was not the slightest movement. Teeth were sucked thoughtfully, and everyone walked around the table looking at it until Menicucci put his finger on the problem. The stone is porous, he said. It is filled with water like a sponge. The water has frozen, the stone has frozen, the ground has frozen. *Voilà!* It is immovable. You must wait until it has thawed. There was some desultory talk about blowtorches and crowbars, but Menicucci put a stop to that, dismissing it as *patati-patata*, which I took to mean nonsense. The group dispersed.

With the house full of noise and dust six days a week, the oasis of Sunday was even more welcome than usual. We could lie in until the luxurious hour of 7:30 before the dogs began agitating for a walk, we could talk to each other without having to go outside, and we could console ourselves with the thought that we were one week closer to the end of the chaos and disruption. What we couldn't do, because of the limited cooking facilities, was to celebrate Sunday as it should always be celebrated in France, with a long and carefully judged lunch. And so, using the temporary kitchen as an excuse, we leaped rather than fell into the habit of eating out on Sunday.

As an appetizer, we would consult the oracular books, and came to depend more and more on the Gault-Millau guide. The Michelin is invaluable, and nobody should travel through France without it, but it is confined to the bare bones of prices and grades and specialities. Gault-Millau gives you the flesh as well. It will tell you about the chef—if he's young, where he was trained; if he's established, whether he's resting on his past success or still trying hard. It will tell you about the chef's wife, whether she is welcoming or *glaciale*. It will give you some indication of the style of the restaurant, and if there's a view or a pretty terrace. It will comment on the service and the clientele, on the prices and the atmosphere. And, often in great detail, on the food and the wine list. It is not infallible, and it is certainly not entirely free from prejudice, but it is amusing and always interesting and, because it is written in colloquial French, good homework for novices in the language like us.

The 1987 guide lists 5,500 restaurants and hotels in a suitably orotund and well-stuffed volume, and picking through it we came across a local entry that sounded irresistible. It was a restaurant at Lambesc, about half an hour's drive away. The chef was a woman, described as *"l'une des plus fameuses cuisinières de Provence,"* her dining room was a converted mill, and her cooking was *"pleine de force et de soleil."* That would have been enough of a recommendation in itself, but what intrigued us most was the age of the chef. She was eighty.

It was gray and windy when we arrived in Lambesc. We still suffered twinges of guilt if we stayed indoors on a beautiful day, but this Sunday was bleak and miserable, the streets smeared with old snow, the inhabitants hurrying home from the bakery with bread clutched to the chest and shoulders hunched against the cold. It was perfect lunch weather.

We were early, and the huge vaulted dining room was empty. It was furnished with handsome Provençal antiques, heavy and dark and highly polished. The tables were large and so well-spaced that they were almost remote from one another, a luxury usually reserved for grand and formal restaurants. The sound of voices and the clatter of saucepans came from the kitchen, and something smelled delicious, but we had obviously anticipated opening time by a few minutes. We started to tiptoe out to find a drink in a café.

"Who are you?" a voice said.

An old man had emerged from the kitchen and was peering at us, screwing up his eyes against the light coming through the door. We told him we'd made a reservation for lunch.

"Sit down, then. You can't eat standing up." He waved airily at the empty tables. We sat down obediently, and waited while he came slowly over with two menus. He sat down with us.

"American? German?"

English.

"Good," he said, "I was with the English in the war."

We felt that we had passed the first test. One more correct answer and we might be allowed to see the menus which the old man was keeping to himself. I asked him what he would recommend.

"Everything," he said. "My wife cooks everything well."

He dealt the menus out and left us to greet another couple, and we dithered enjoyably between lamb stuffed with herbs, *daube*, veal with truffles, and an unexplained dish called the *fantaisie du chef*. The old man came back and sat down, listened to the order, and nodded.

"It's always the same," he said. "It's the men who like the *fantaisie*."

I asked for a half bottle of white wine to go with the first course, and some red to follow.

"No," he said, "you're wrong." He told us what to drink, and it was a red Côtes du Rhône from Visan. Good wine and good women came from Visan, he said. He got up and fetched a bottle from a vast dark cupboard.

"There. You'll like that." (Later, we noticed that everybody had the same wine on their table.)

He went off to the kitchen, the oldest head waiter in the world, to pass our order to perhaps the oldest practicing chef in France. We thought we heard a third voice from the kitchen, but there were no other waiters, and we wondered how two people with a combined age of over 160 managed to cope with the long hours and hard work. And yet, as the restaurant became busier, there were no delays, no neglected tables. In his unhurried and stately way, the old man made his rounds, sitting down from time to time for a chat with his clients. When an order was ready, Madame would clang a bell in the kitchen and her husband would raise his eyebrows in pretended irritation. If he continued talking, the bell would clang again, more insistently, and off he would go, muttering *"j'arrive, j'arrive."*

The food was everything the Gault-Millau guide had promised, and the old man had been right about the wine. We did like it. And, by the time he served the tiny rounds of goat's cheese marinated in herbs and olive oil, we had finished it. I asked for another half bottle, and he looked at me disapprovingly.

"Who's driving?"

"My wife."

He went again to the dark cupboard. "There are no half-bottles," he said, "you can drink as far as here." He drew an imaginary line with his finger halfway down the new bottle.

The kitchen bell had stopped clanging and Madame came out, smiling and rosy faced from the heat of the ovens, to ask us if we had eaten well. She looked like a woman of sixty. The two of them stood together, his hand on her shoulder, while she talked about the antique furniture, which had been her dowry, and he interrupted. They were happy with each other and they loved their work, and we left the restaurant feeling that old age might not be so bad after all.

RAMON THE PLASTERER was lying on his back on a precarious platform, an arm's length below the kitchen ceiling. I passed a beer up to him, and he leaned sideways on one elbow to drink it. It looked like an uncomfortable position, either for drinking or working, but he said he was used to it.

"Anyway," he said, "you can't stand on the floor and throw stuff up. That one who did the ceiling of the Sistine Chapel— you know, that Italian—he must have been on his back for weeks."

Ramon finished the beer, his fifth of the day, handed down the empty bottle, belched lightly, and returned to his labors. He had a slow, rhythmical style, flicking the plaster on to the ceiling with his trowel and working it into a chunky smoothness with a roll of his wrist. He said that, when it was finished, it would look as though it had been there for a hundred years. He didn't believe in rollers or sprayers or instruments of any sort apart from his trowel and his eye for a line and a curve, which he said was infallible. One evening after he had gone I checked his surfaces with a level. They were all true, and yet they were unmistakably the work of a hand rather than a machine. The man was an artist, and well worth his beer ration.

A breeze was coming through the hole in the kitchen wall, and it felt almost mild. I could hear something dripping. When I went outside I found that the seasons had changed. The stone table was oozing water, and spring had arrived.

MARCH

THE ALMOND TREE was in tentative blossom. The days were longer, often ending with magnificent evenings of corrugated pink skies. The hunting season was over, with hounds and guns put away for six months. The vineyards were busy again as the well-organized farmers treated their vines and their more lackadaisical neighbors hurried to do the pruning they should have done in November. The people of Provence greeted spring with uncharacteristic briskness, as if nature had given everyone an injection of sap.

The markets changed abruptly. On the stalls, fishing tackle and ammunition belts and waterproof boots and long brushes with steel bristles for amateur chimney sweeps were replaced by displays of ferocious-looking agricultural implements—machetes and grubbing tools, scythes and hoes with sharp curved prongs, spraying equipment that was guaranteed to bring the rain of death down on any weed or insect foolhardy enough to threaten the grapes. Flowers and plants and tiny new season vegetables were everywhere, and café tables and chairs sprouted on the pavements. There was a feeling of activity and purpose in the air, and one or two optimists were already buying espadrilles from the multicolored racks outside the shoe shops.

In contrast to this bustle, work on the house had come to a standstill. Following some primeval springtime urge, the builders had migrated, leaving us with some token sacks of plaster and piles of sand as proof of their intention to come back—one day —and finish what they had so nearly finished. The phenomenon of the vanishing builder is well known throughout the world, but in Provence the problem has its own local refinements and frustrations, and its own clearly defined seasons.

Three times a year, at Easter, August, and Christmas, the owners of holiday homes escape from Paris and Zürich and Düsseldorf and London to come down for a few days or weeks of the simple country life. Invariably, before they come, they think of something that is crucial to the success of their holiday: a set of Courrèges bidets, a searchlight in the swimming pool, a retiled terrace, a new roof for the servants' quarters. How can they possibly enjoy their rustic interlude without these essentials? In panic, they telephone the local builders and craftsmen. Get it done—it *must* be done—before we arrive. Implicit in these urgent instructions is the understanding that generous payments will be forthcoming if the work is done at once. Speed is of the essence; money isn't.

It is too tempting to ignore. Everyone remembers when Mitterrand first came to power; the rich went into financial paralysis, and sat on their cash. Building work was scarce in Provence then, and who knows when bad times might come again? So the jobs are accepted, and less clamorous clients suddenly find themselves with dormant concrete mixers and forlorn, uncompleted rooms.

Faced with this situation, there are two ways to respond. Neither of them will produce immediate results, but one way will reduce the frustration, and the other will add to it.

We tried both. To begin with, we made a conscious effort to become more philosophical in our attitude to time, to treat days and weeks of delays in the Provençal fashion—that is, to enjoy the sunshine and to stop thinking like city people. This month, next month, what's the difference? Have a pastis and relax. It worked well enough for a week or two, and then we noticed that the building materials at the back of the house were turning green with the first growth of spring weeds. We decided to change our tactics and get some firm dates out of our small and elusive team of workmen. It was an educational experience.

We learned that time in Provence is a very elastic commodity, even when it is described in clear and specific terms. *Un petit quart d'heure* means sometime today. *Demain* means sometime this week. And, the most elastic time segment of all, *une quinzaine* can mean three weeks, two months, or next year, but never, ever does it mean fifteen days. We learned also to interpret the hand language that accompanies any discussion of deadlines. When a Provençal looks you in the eye and tells you that he will be hammering on your door ready to start work next Tuesday for certain, the behavior of his hands is all-important. If they are still, or patting you reassuringly on the arm, you can expect him on Tuesday. If one hand is held out at waist height, palm downwards, and begins to rock from side to side, adjust the timetable to Wednesday or Thursday. If the rocking develops into an agitated waggle, he's really talking about next week or God knows when, depending on circumstances beyond his control. These unspoken disclaimers, which seem to be instinctive and therefore more revealing than speech, are occasionally reinforced by the magic word *normalement*, a supremely versatile escape clause worthy of an insurance policy. *Normalement*—providing it doesn't rain, providing the truck hasn't broken down, providing the brother-in-law hasn't borrowed the tool box—is the Provençal builder's equivalent of the fine print in a contract, and we came to regard it with infinite suspicion.

But, despite their genial contempt for punctuality and their absolute refusal to use the telephone to say when they were coming or when they weren't, we could never stay irritated with them for long. They were always disarmingly cheerful, they worked long and hard when they were with us, and their work was excellent. In the end, they were worth waiting for. And so, little by little, we reverted to being philosophical, and came to terms with the Provençal clock. From now on, we told ourselves, we would assume that nothing would be done when we expected it to be done; the fact that it happened at all would be enough.

FAUSTIN was behaving curiously. For two or three days he had been clanking up and down on his tractor, towing a contraption of metal intestines which spewed fertilizer to either side as he passed between the rows of vines. He kept stopping to get off the tractor and walk over to a field, now empty and overgrown, which had been planted with melons. He studied the field from one end, remounted his tractor, sprayed some more vines, and returned to study the other end. He paced, he pondered, he scratched his head. When he went home for lunch, I walked down to see what it was he found so fascinating, but to me it looked like any other fallow melon field—a few weeds, some tatters of plastic left over from the strips that had protected last year's crop, half an acre of nothing. I wondered if Faustin suspected it of harboring buried treasure, because we had already dug up two gold Napoleon coins nearer the house, and he had told us that there were probably more to be found. But peasants don't hide their gold in the middle of cultivated land when it can be squirreled away more securely under the flagstones or down a well. It was odd.

He came visiting that evening with Henriette, looking unusually spruce and businesslike in his white shoes and orange shirt, and bearing jars of homemade rabbit pâté. Half way through his first pastis, he leaned forward confidentially. Did we know that the wine produced from our vineyards—Côtes du Lubéron —was about to be given *Appellation Contrôlée* status? He leaned back, nodding slowly, and said *"Eh oui"* several times while we absorbed the news. Clearly, said Faustin, the wine would become more expensive and vineyard owners would make more money. And, clearly, the more vines one has the more money one makes.

There was no arguing with that, so Faustin moved on to a second drink—he drank in an efficient, unobtrusive way, and always reached the bottom of his glass before I expected—and put forward his proposition. It seemed to him that our melon field could be more profitably employed. He inhaled some pastis while Henriette produced a document from her bag. It was a *droit d'implantation*, giving us the right to plant vines, a privilege accorded to us by the government itself. While we looked at the paper, Faustin demolished the nonsensical idea of continuing to grow melons, dismissing them with a wave of his glass as being too demanding in terms of time and water, and always vulnerable to attack by the wild boar who come down from the mountains in the summer. Only last year, Faustin's brother Jacky had lost a third of his melon crop. Eaten by the boars! The profit disappearing into a pig's belly! Faustin shook his head at the painful memory, and had to be revived by a third large pastis.

By chance, he said, he had made some calculations. Our field would accommodate 1,300 new vines in place of the tiresome melons. My wife and I looked at each other. We were equally fond of wine and Faustin, and he obviously had his heart set on progress and expansion. We agreed that the extra vines sounded like a good idea, but thought no more about it after he had left. Faustin is a ruminant among men, not given to hasty action, and in any case, nothing happens quickly in Provence. Perhaps next spring he would get around to it.

At seven o'clock the following morning, a tractor was plowing up the melon field, and two days later the planting team arrived—five men, two women, and four dogs, under the direction of the *chef des vignes* Monsieur Beauchier, a man with forty years' experience of planting vines in the Lubéron. He personally pushed the small plow behind the tractor, making sure that lines were straight and correctly spaced, trudging up and down in his canvas boots, his leathery face rapt in concentration. The lines were staked at each end by bamboo rods and marked by lengths of twine. The field was now stripped and ready to be turned into a vineyard.

The new vines, about the size of my thumb and tipped with red wax, were unloaded from the vans while Monsieur Beauchier inspected his planting equipment. I had assumed that the planting would be done mechanically, but all I could see were a few hollow steel rods and a large triangle made of wood. The planting team gathered around and were assigned their duties, then jostled untidily into formation.

Beauchier led the way with the wooden triangle, which he used like a three-sided wheel, the points making equidistant marks in the earth. Two men followed him with steel rods, plunging them into the marks to make holes for the vines, which were planted and firmed in by the rear guard. The two women, Faustin's wife and daughter, dispensed vines, advice, and fashion comments on the assortment of hats worn by the men, particularly Faustin's new and slightly rakish yachting cap. The dogs enjoyed themselves by getting in everyone's way, dodging kicks and tangling themselves in the twine.

As the day wore on, the planters became more widely spaced, with Beauchier often two hundred yards in front of the stragglers at the back, but distance was no barrier to conversation. It appears to be part of the ritual that lengthy discussions are always conducted between the two people farthest away from each other, while the intervening members of the team curse the dogs and argue about the straightness of the lines. And so the raucous procession moved up and down the field until mid-afternoon, when Henriette produced two large baskets and work stopped for the Provençal version of a coffee break.

The team sat on a grassy bank above the vines, looking like a scene from Cartier-Bresson's scrapbook, and attacked the contents of the baskets. There were four liters of wine and an enormous pile of the sugared slices of fried bread called *tranches dorées*, dark gold in color and crisp and delicious to taste. Grandfather André arrived to inspect what had been done, and we saw him poking the earth critically with his stick and then nodding his head. He came over for a glass of wine and sat in the sun, a benign old lizard, scratching a dog's stomach with the end of his muddy stick and asking Henriette what was for dinner. He wanted to eat early so that he could watch *Santa Barbara*, his favorite television soap opera.

The wine had all gone. The men stretched and brushed the crumbs from their mouths and went back to work. By late evening it was finished, and the ragged old melon field was now impeccable, the tiny dots of new vines just visible against the setting sun. The team gathered in our courtyard to unkink their backs and make inroads on the pastis, and I took Faustin to one side to ask him about payment. We'd had the tractor for three days, and dozens of hours of labor. What did we owe them? Faustin was so anxious to explain that he put down his glass. We would pay for the vines, he said, but the rest was taken care of by the system which operated in the valley, with everyone contributing their time free when major replanting had to be done. It all evened out in the end, he said, and it avoided paperwork and tedious dealings with *les fiscs* about taxes. He smiled and tapped the side of his nose with a finger and then, as though it was a small matter hardly worth mentioning, he asked if we would like 250 asparagus plants put in while we still had the use of the tractor and the men. It was done the next day. So much for our theory that nothing happens fast in Provence.

· · ·

THE LUBÉRON sounded different in spring. Birds who had been ducking all winter came out of hiding now that the hunters were gone, and their song replaced gunfire. The only jarring noise I could hear as I walked along the path toward the Massot residence was a furious hammering, and I wondered if he had decided to put up a For Sale notice in preparation for the beginning of the tourist season.

I found him on the track beyond his house, contemplating a five-foot stake that he had planted at the edge of a clearing. A rusty piece of tin had been nailed to the top of the stake, with a single angry word daubed in white paint: PRIVÉ! Three more stakes and notices were lying on the track, together with a pile of boulders. Massot was obviously intending to barricade the clearing. He grunted good morning and picked up another stake, hammering it into the ground as if it had just insulted his mother.

I asked him what he was doing.

"Keeping out the Germans," he said, and started to roll boulders into a rough cordon between the stakes.

The piece of land that he was sealing off was some distance from his house, and on the forest side of the track. It couldn't possibly belong to him, and I said I thought it was part of the national park.

"That's right," he said, "but I'm French. So it's more mine than the Germans'." He moved another boulder. "Every summer they come here and put up their tents and make *merde* all over the forest."

He straightened up and lit a cigarette, tossing the empty packet into the bushes. I asked him if he had thought that maybe one of the Germans might buy his house.

"Germans with tents don't buy anything except bread," he said with a sniff of disdain. "You should see their cars—stuffed with German sausage, German beer, tins of sauerkraut. They bring it all with them. Mean? They're real *pisse-vinaigres*."

Massot, in his new role as protector of the countryside and authority on the economics of tourism, went on to explain the problem of the peasant in Provence. He admitted that tourists— even German tourists—brought money to the area, and that people who bought houses provided work for local builders. But look what they had done to property prices! It was a scandal. No farmer could afford to pay them. We tactfully avoided any discussion of Massot's own attempts at property speculation, and he sighed at the injustice of it all. Then he cheered up, and told me a house-buying story that had ended to his complete satisfaction.

There was a peasant who for years had coveted his neighbor's house; not for the house itself, which was almost a ruin, but for the land that was attached to it. He offered to buy the property, but his neighbor, taking advantage of the sharp rise in house prices, accepted a higher offer from a Parisian.

During the winter, the Parisian spent millions of francs renovating the house and installing a swimming pool. Finally, the work is finished, and the Parisian and his chic friends come down for the long First of May weekend. They are charmed by the house and amused by the quaint old peasant who lives next door, particularly by his habit of going to bed at eight o'clock.

The Parisian household is awakened at four in the morning by Charlemagne, the peasant's large and noisy cockerel, who crows nonstop for two hours. The Parisian complains to the peasant. The peasant shrugs. It is the country. Cocks must crow. That is normal.

The next morning, and the morning after that, Charlemagne is up and crowing at four o'clock. Tempers are getting frayed, and the guests return to Paris early, to catch up on their sleep. The Parisian complains again to the peasant, and again the peasant shrugs. They part on hostile terms.

In August, the Parisian returns with a houseful of guests. Charlemagne wakes them punctually every morning at four. Attempts at afternoon naps are foiled by the peasant, who is doing some work on his house with a jackhammer and a loud concrete mixer. The Parisian insists that the peasant silence his cockerel. The peasant refuses. After several heated exchanges, the Parisian takes the peasant to court, seeking an injunction to restrain Charlemagne. The verdict is in favor of the peasant, and the cockerel continues his early morning serenades.

Visits to the house eventually become so intolerable that the Parisian puts it up for sale. The peasant, acting through a friend, manages to buy most of the land.

The Sunday after the purchase goes through, the peasant and his friend celebrate with a huge lunch, the main course of which is Charlemagne, turned into a delicious *coq au vin*.

Massot thought that this was a fine story—defeat for the Parisian, victory and more land for the peasant, a good lunch— it had everything. I asked him if it was true, and he looked at me sideways, sucking on the ragged end of his moustache. "It doesn't do to cross a peasant" was all he would say, and I thought that if I were a German camper I'd try Spain this summer.

EVERY DAY, as the weather stayed mild, there was fresh evidence of growth and greenery, and one of the most verdant patches of all was the swimming pool, which had turned a bilious emerald in the sunshine. It was time to call Bernard the *pisciniste* with his algae-fighting equipment before the plant life started crawling out of the deep end and through the front door.

A job like this is never done in Provence simply on the basis of a phone call and a verbal explanation. There has to be a preliminary visit of inspection—to walk around the problem, to nod knowingly, to have a drink or two, and then to make another rendezvous. It is a kind of limbering-up exercise, only to be skipped in cases of real emergency.

On the evening Bernard arrived to look at the pool, I was scrubbing at the garland of green fur that had developed just above the water line, and he watched me for a few moments before squatting down on his haunches and wagging a finger under my nose. Somehow I knew what his first word would be.

"*Non*," he said, "you mustn't scrub it. You must treat it. I will bring a product." We abandoned the green fur and went indoors for a drink, and Bernard explained why he hadn't been able to come earlier. He had been suffering from toothache, but couldn't find a local dentist who was prepared to treat him, because of his strange affliction: he bites dentists. He can't stop himself. It is an incurable reflex. The moment he feels an exploratory finger in his mouth—*tak!*—he bites. He had so far bitten the only dentist in Bonnieux, and four dentists in Cavaillon, and had been obliged to go to Avignon, where he was unknown in dental circles. Fortunately, he had found a dentist who fought back with anesthetic, knocking Bernard out completely while the repair work was done. The dentist told him afterwards that he had a mouthful of eighteenth-century teeth.

Eighteenth century or not, they looked very white and healthy against Bernard's black beard as he laughed and talked. He was a man of great charm and, although born and raised in Provence, not at all a country bumpkin. He drank scotch, the older the better, rather than pastis, and had married a girl from Paris whom we suspected of having a hand in the contents of his wardrobe. Not for him the canvas boots and the old blue trousers and frayed and faded shirts that we were used to seeing; Bernard was dapper, from his soft leather shoes to his large assortment of designer sunglasses. We wondered what kind of ensemble he would wear for the work of chlorinating and barnacle-scraping that was needed before the pool was ready for human occupation.

The day of the spring clean arrived, and Bernard bounded up the steps in sunglasses, gray flannels, and blazer, twirling an umbrella in case the rain promised by the weather forecast should come our way. Following him with some difficulty was the secret of his continued elegance, a small, scruffy man weighed down with tubs of chlorine, brushes, and a suction pump. This was Gaston, who was actually going to do the job under Bernard's supervision.

Later that morning, I went out to see how they were getting on. A fine drizzle had set in, and the sodden Gaston was wrestling with the serpentine coils of the suction hose while Bernard, blazer slung nonchalantly around his shoulders, was directing operations from the shelter of his umbrella. There, I thought, is a man who understands how to delegate. If anyone could help us move our stone table into the courtyard, surely it was Bernard. I took him away from his duties at the poolside and we went to study the situation.

The table looked bigger, heavier and more permanently settled in its garnish of weeds than ever, but Bernard was not discouraged. "*C'est pas méchant*," he said, "I know a man who could do it in half an hour." I imagined a sweating giant heaving the great slabs around as a change from winning tug-of-war contests with teams of horses, but it was more prosaic than that. Bernard's man had just acquired a machine called *un bob*, a scaled-down version of a fork-lift truck, narrow enough to pass through the courtyard doorway. *Voilà!* It sounded easy.

The owner of *le bob* was telephoned and arrived within half an hour, eager to put his new machine into active service. He measured the width of the doorway and assessed the weight of the table. No problem; *le bob* could do it. There was a small adjustment to be made here and there, but a mason could take care of that. It was merely a question of removing the lintel over the doorway—just for five minutes—to provide sufficient height for the load to pass through. I looked at the lintel. It was another piece of stone, four feet wide, nine inches thick, and deeply embedded in the side of the house. It was major demolition, even to my inexpert eye. The table stayed where it was.

The wretched thing had become a daily frustration. Here we were with hot weather and the outdoor eating season just around the corner—the days we had dreamed about back in

England and through the winter—and we had nowhere to put a bowl of olives, let alone a five-course lunch. We seriously considered calling Pierrot at the quarry and asking for an introduction to the Carcassonne rugby team, and then Providence arrived with a screech of brakes and a dusty cocker spaniel.

Didier had been working at a house on the other side of Saint-Rémy, and had been approached by a uniformed *gendarme*. Would there be any interest, the *gendarme* wondered, in a load of weathered stone, the old, lichen-covered stuff, that could be used to give a new wall instant antiquity? It so happened that one of the jobs on Didier's long list was to build a wall at the front of our house, and he thought of us. The officer of the law wanted to be paid *au noir*, in cash, but stone like that was not easy to find. Would we like it?

We would happily have agreed to half a ton of bird droppings if it meant getting Didier and his entourage back; we had often thought of them as movers of the table before they disappeared, and this seemed like a wink from the gods. Yes, we would have the stone, and could he give us a hand with the table? He looked at it and grinned. "Seven men," he said. "I'll come on Saturday with two when I bring the stone if you can find the rest." We had a deal, and soon we would have a table. My wife started planning the first outdoor lunch of the year.

We lured three more-or-less able-bodied young men with the promise of food and drink, and when Didier and his assistants arrived the seven of us took up our positions around the table to go through the ritual of spitting on hands and deciding how best to negotiate the fifteen-yard journey. In circumstances like these, every Frenchman is an expert, and various theories were advanced: the table should be rolled on logs; no, it should be pulled on a wooden pallet; nonsense, it could be pushed most of the way by truck. Didier let everyone finish, and then ordered us to pick it up, two to each side, with him taking one side on his own.

With a reluctant squelch, the slab came out of the ground, and we staggered the first five yards, veins popping with effort while Didier kept up a running commentary of directions. Another five yards, and then we had to stop to turn it so that it could get through the doorway. The weight was brutal, and we were already sweating and aching, and at least one of us thought that he was getting a little old for this kind of work, but the table was now on its side and ready to be inched into the courtyard.

"This," said Didier, "is the amusing part." There was only enough room for two men on either side of the slab, and they would have to take the weight while the others pushed and pulled. Two enormous webbing straps were passed under the table, there was more spitting on hands, and my wife disappeared into the house, unable to watch the mashing of feet and four men having simultaneous ruptures. "Whatever you do," said Didier, "don't drop it. *Allez!*" And with curses and skinned knuckles and a chorus of grunts that would have done credit to an elephant in labor, the table slowly crossed the threshold and at long last entered the courtyard.

We compared wounds and sprains before setting up the base—a relatively insignificant structure weighing no more than 300 pounds—and coating its top with cement. One final heave, and the slab went on, but Didier wasn't satisfied; it was a hair's-breadth off center. Eric, the chief assistant, was required to kneel under the table on all fours. He supported most of the weight on his back while the top was centered, and I wondered if my insurance covered death on the premises by crushing. To my relief, Eric surfaced without any visible injury, although, as Didier said cheerfully, it's the internal damage that slows a man down in his line of work. I hoped he was joking.

Beers were passed around, and the table was admired. It looked just as we'd imagined on that afternoon in February when we had traced the outline in the snow. It was a good size, and handsome against the stone of the courtyard wall. The perspiration stains and smudges of blood would soon dry off, and then lunch could be served.

In our anticipation of all the pleasures of long outdoor meals there was only one slight regret, because we were coming to the very end of the season for that ugly but delicious fungus which is almost worth its weight in gold, the fresh Vaucluse truffle.

The truffle world is secretive, but strangers can get a glimpse of it by going to one of the villages round Carpentras. There, the cafés do a brisk trade in breakfast jolts of *marc* and Calvados, and an unknown face coming through the door brings muttered conversations to a sudden stop. Outside, men stand in tight, preoccupied groups looking, sniffing, and finally weighing wart-encrusted, earth-covered lumps that are handled with reverential care. Money passes, fat, grimy wads of it, in 100-, 200-, and 500-franc notes, which are double-checked with much licking of thumbs. Attention from outsiders is not welcomed.

This informal market is an early stage in the process that leads to the tables of three-star restaurants and the counters of ruinously expensive Parisian delicatessens like Fauchon and Hédiard. But even here in the middle of nowhere, buying directly from men with dirt under their fingernails and yesterday's garlic on their breath, with dented, wheezing cars, with old baskets or plastic bags instead of smart attaché cases—even here, the prices are, as they like to say, *très sérieux*. Truffles are sold by weight, and the standard unit is the kilo. At 1987 prices, a kilo of truffles bought in the village market cost at least 2,000 francs, payable in cash. Checks are not accepted, receipts are never given, because the *truffiste* is not anxious to participate in the crackpot government scheme the rest of us call income tax.

So the starting price is 2,000 francs a kilo. With a little massaging along the way from various agents and middlemen, by the time the truffle reaches its spiritual home in the kitchens of Bocuse or Troisgros the price will probably have doubled. At Fauchon, it could easily have reached 5,000 francs a kilo, but at least they accept checks.

There are two reasons why these absurd prices continue to be paid, and continue to rise—the first, obviously, being that nothing in the world smells or tastes like fresh truffles except fresh truffles. The second is that, despite all the effort and ingenuity that the French have brought to bear on the problem, they haven't been able to cultivate the truffle. They continue to try, and it is not uncommon in the Vaucluse to come across fields that have been planted with truffle-oaks and keep-off notices. But the propagation of truffles seems to be a haphazard affair which is only understood by nature—thus adding to the rarity and the price—and human attempts at truffle breeding haven't come to much. Until they do, there is only one way to enjoy truffles without spending a small fortune, and that is to find them yourself.

We were lucky enough to be given a free course in truffle-hunting techniques by our almost resident expert, Ramon the plasterer. He had tried everything over the years, and admitted to some modest success. He was generous with his advice and, as he smoothed on his plaster and drank his beer, he told us exactly what to do. (He didn't tell us where to go, but then no truffle man would.)

It all depends, he said, on timing, knowledge, and patience, and the possession of a pig, a trained hound, or a stick. Truffles grow a few centimeters under the ground, on the roots of certain oak or hazelnut trees. During the season, from November until March, they can be tracked down by nose, providing you have sensitive enough equipment. The supreme truffle detector is the pig, who is born with a fondness for the taste, and whose sense of smell in this case is superior to the dog's. But there is a snag: the pig is not content to wag his tail and point when he has discovered a truffle. He wants to eat it. In fact, he is desperate to eat it. And, as Ramon said, you cannot reason with a pig on the brink of gastronomic ecstasy. He is not easily distracted, nor is he of a size you can fend off with one hand while you rescue the truffle with the other. There he is, as big as a small tractor, rigid with porcine determination and refusing to be budged. Given this fundamental design fault, we weren't surprised when Ramon told us that the lighter and more amenable dog had become increasingly popular.

Unlike pigs, dogs do not instinctively root for truffles; they have to be trained, and Ramon favoured the *saucisson* method. You take a slice and rub it with a truffle, or dip it in truffle juice, so that the dog begins to associate the smell of truffles with a taste of heaven. Little by little, or by leaps and bounds if the dog is both intelligent and a gourmet, he will come to share your enthusiasm for truffles, and he will be ready for field trials. If your training has been thorough, if your dog is temperamentally suited to the work, and if you know where to go, you might find yourself with a *chien truffier* who will point the way to the buried treasure. Then, just as he begins to dig for it, you bribe him away with a slice of treated sausage and uncover what you hope will be a lump of black gold.

Ramon himself had eventually settled on another method, the stick technique, which he demonstrated for us, tiptoeing across the kitchen with an imaginary wand held in front of him. Once again, you have to know where to go, but this time you have to wait for the right weather conditions as well. When the sun is shining on the roots of a likely-looking oak, approach cautiously and, with your stick, prod gently around the base of the tree. If a startled fly should rise vertically from the vegetation, mark the spot and dig. You might have disturbed a member of the fly family whose genetic passion is to lay its eggs on the truffle (doubtless adding a certain *je ne sais quoi* to the flavor). Many peasants in the Vaucluse had adopted this technique because walking around with a stick is less conspicuous than walking around with a pig, and secrecy can be more easily preserved. Truffle hunters like to protect their sources.

The finding of truffles, chancy and unpredictable though it is, began to seem almost straightforward when compared with the skulduggery that goes on in the sales and distribution department. With the relish of an investigative reporter, and frequent winks and nudges, Ramon took us through the most common of the murky practices.

With everything edible in France, certain areas have the reputation for producing the best—the best olives from Nyons, the best mustard from Dijon, the best melons from Cavaillon, the best cream from Normandy. The best truffles, it is generally agreed, come from the Périgord, and naturally one pays more for them. But how do you know that the truffle you buy in Cahors hasn't been dug up several hundred kilometers away in the Vaucluse? Unless you know and trust your supplier, you can't be sure, and Ramon's inside information was that 50 percent of the truffles sold in the Périgord were born elsewhere and "naturalized."

Then there is the uncanny business of the truffle that somehow gains weight between leaving the ground and arriving on the scales. It could be that it has been gift wrapped in an extra coating of earth. On the other hand, it could be that a heavier substance altogether has found its way inside the truffle itself—invisible until, in mid-slice, your knife lays bare a sliver of metal. *Ils sont vilains, ces types!* Even if you are prepared to sacrifice the flavor of fresh truffles for the protection offered by the canned variety—even then, you can't be sure. One hears rumors. It has been hinted that some French cans with French labels actually contain Italian or Spanish truffles. (Which, if true, must be one of the most profitable and least publicized acts of cooperation ever between Common Market countries.)

Yet, for all the whispers of chicanery and prices that become more ridiculous each year, the French continue to follow their noses and dig into their pockets, and we found ourselves doing the same when we heard that the last truffles of the season were being served at one of our favorite local restaurants.

Chez Michel is the village bar of Cabrières and the headquarters of the *boules* club, and not sufficiently upholstered or pompous to attract too much attention from the Guide Michelin inspectors. Old men play cards in the front; clients of the restaurant eat very well in the back. The owner cooks, Madame his wife takes the orders, members of the family help at table and in the kitchens. It is a comfortable neighborhood *bistrot* with no apparent intention of joining the culinary merry-go-round which turns talented cooks into brand names and pleasant restaurants into temples of the expense account.

Madame sat us down and gave us a drink, and we asked how the truffles were. She rolled her eyes and an expression close to pain crossed her face. For a moment we thought they had all gone, but it was simply her reaction to one of life's many unfairnesses, which she then explained to us.

Her husband, Michel, loves to cook with fresh truffles. He has his suppliers, and he pays, as everyone must, in cash, without the benefit of a receipt. For him, this is a substantial and legitimate business cost which cannot be set against the profits because there is no supporting evidence on paper to account for the outlay. Also, he refuses to raise the price of his menus, even when they are studded with truffles, to a level which might offend his regular customers. (In winter, the clientele is local, and careful with its money; the big spenders don't usually come down until Easter.)

This was the problem, and Madame was doing her best to be philosophical about it as she showed us a copper pan containing several thousand francs' worth of nondeductible truffles. We asked her why Michel did it, and she gave a classic shrug— shoulders and eyebrows going upwards in unison, corners of the mouth turning down. *"Pour faire plaisir,"* she said.

We had omelettes. They were moist and fat and fluffy, with a tiny deep black nugget of truffle in every mouthful, a last rich taste of winter. We wiped our plates with bread and tried to guess what a treat like this would cost in London, and came to the conclusion that we had just eaten a bargain. Comparison with London is a sure way of justifying any minor extravagance in Provence.

Michel came out of the kitchen to make his rounds and

noticed our bone-clean plates. "They were good, the truffles?" Better than good, we said. He told us that the dealer who had sold them to him—one of the old rogues in the business—had just been robbed. The thief had taken a cardboard box stuffed with cash, more than 100,000 francs, but the dealer hadn't dared to report the loss for fear that embarrassing questions might be asked about where the money had come from. Now he was pleading poverty. Next year his prices would be higher. *C'est la vie.*

We got home to find the telephone ringing. It is a sound that both of us detest, and there is always a certain amount of maneuvering to see who can avoid answering it. We have an innate pessimism about telephone calls; they have a habit of coming at the wrong time, and they are too sudden, catapulting you into a conversation you weren't expecting. Letters, on the other hand, are a pleasure to receive, not least because they allow you to consider your reply. But people don't write letters anymore. They're too busy, they're in too much of a hurry or, dismissing the service that manages to deliver bills with unfailing reliability, they don't trust the post. We were learning not to trust the telephone, and I picked it up as I would a long-dead fish.

"How's the weather?" asked an unidentified voice.

I said that the weather was good. It must have made all the difference, because the caller then introduced himself as Tony. He wasn't a friend, or even a friend of a friend, but an acquaintance of an acquaintance. "Looking for a house down there," he said, in the clipped, time-is-money voice that executives adopt when they talk on their car phones to their wives. "Thought you could give me a hand. Want to get in before the Easter rush and the frogs put up the prices."

I offered to give him the names of some property agents. "Bit of a problem there," he said. "Don't speak the language. Order a meal, of course, but that's about it." I offered to give him the name of a bilingual agent, but that wouldn't do. "Don't want to get tied up with one firm. Bad move. No leverage."

We had reached the moment in the conversation when I

was supposed to offer my services, or else say something to terminate this budding relationship before it could bud any further, but the chance was denied me.

"Must go. Can't chat all night. Plenty of time for that when I get down next week." And then those awful words that put an end to any hopes of hiding: "Don't worry. I've got your address. I'll find you."

The line went dead.

APRIL

IT WAS ONE of those mornings when the early mist hung in wet sheets along the valley under a band of bright blue sky and, by the time we came home from walking, the dogs were sleek with damp, whiskers glittering in the sun. They saw the stranger first, and pranced around him pretending to be fierce.

He stood by the swimming pool, fending off their attentions with a handbag of masculine design and backing ever closer to the deep end. He seemed relieved to see us.

"Dogs all right, are they? Not rabid or anything?" The voice was recognizable as that of our telephone caller, Tony from London, and he and his handbag joined us for breakfast. He was large and prosperously padded around the waistline, with tinted glasses, carefully tousled hair and the pale-colored casual clothes that English visitors wear in Provence regardless of the weather.

He sat down and produced from his bag a bulging Filofax, a gold pen, a packet of duty-free Cartier cigarettes, and a gold lighter. His watch was also gold. I was sure that gold medallions nestled in his chest hair. He told us he was in advertising.

He gave us a brief but extremely complimentary account of his business history. He had started his own advertising agency, built it up—"tough business, bloody competitive"—and had just sold a controlling interest for what he described as heavy money and a five-year contract. Now, he said, he was able to relax, although one would never have guessed from his behavior that he was a man who had left the cares of office behind. He was in a constant fidget, looking at his watch, arranging and rearranging his trinkets on the table in front of him, adjusting his glasses and smoking in deep, distracted drags. Suddenly, he stood up.

"Mind if I make a quick call? What's the code for London?"

My wife and I had come to expect this as an inevitable part of welcoming the Englishman abroad into our home. He comes in, he has a drink or a cup of coffee, he makes a phone call to check that his business has not collapsed during the first few hours of his absence. The routine never varies, and the substance of the call is as predictable as the routine.

"Hi, it's me. Yes, I'm calling from Provence. Everything okay? Any messages? Oh. None? David didn't call back? Oh shit. Look, I'll be moving around a bit today, but you can reach me on (what's the number here?) Got that? What? Yes, the weather's fine. Call you later."

Tony put the phone down and reassured us about the state of his company, which was managing to stumble along without him. He was now ready to devote his energies, and ours, to the purchase of property.

Buying a house in Provence is not without its complications, and it is easy to understand why busy and efficient people from cities, used to firm decisions and quickly struck deals, often give up after months of serpentine negotiations that have led nowhere. The first of many surprises, always greeted with alarm and disbelief, is that all property costs more than its advertised price. Most of this is because the French government takes a cut of about 8 percent on all transactions. Then there are the legal fees, which are high. And it is sometimes a condition of the sale that the purchaser pays the agent's commission of 3 to 5 percent. An unlucky buyer could end up paying as much as 15 percent on top of the price.

There is, however, a well-established ritual of respectable cheating which has the double attractions, so dear to every French heart, of saving money and screwing the government. This is the two-price purchase, and a typical example would work as follows: Monsieur Rivarel, a businessman in Aix, wishes to sell an old country house that he inherited. He wants a million francs. As it is not his principal residence, he will be liable for tax on the proceeds of the sale, a thought that causes him great distress. He therefore decides that the official, recorded price—the *prix déclaré*—will be 600,000 francs, and he will grit his teeth and pay tax on that. His consolation is that the balance of 400,000 francs will be paid in cash, under the table. This, as he will point out, is an *affaire intéressante* not only for him, but for the buyer, because the official fees and charges will be based on the lower, declared price. *Voilà!* Everyone is happy.

The practical aspects of this arrangement call for a sense of timing and great delicacy on the part of the lawyer, or *notaire*, when the moment comes to sign the act of sale. All the interested parties—the buyer, the seller, and the property agent—are gathered in the *notaire's* office, and the act of sale is read aloud, line by interminable line. The price marked on the contract is 600,000 francs. The 400,000 in cash which the buyer has brought along has to be passed to the seller, but it would be highly improper if this were to happen in front of the *notaire*. Consequently, he feels a pressing need to go to the lavatory, where he stays until the cash has been counted and has changed hands. He can then return, accept the check for the declared price, and supervise the signing ceremony without having compromised his legal reputation. It has been said, rather unkindly, that two basic requirements for a rural *notaire* are a blind eye and a diplomatic bladder.

But there can be many obstacles to overcome before the visit to the *notaire*, and one of the most common is the problem of multiple ownership. Under French law, property is normally inherited by the children, with each child having an equal share. All of them must be in agreement before their inheritance is sold, and the more children there are the less likely this becomes, as is the case with an old farmhouse not far from us. It has been passed down from one generation to the next, and ownership is now divided between fourteen cousins, three of whom are of Corsican extraction and thus, according to our French friends, impossible to deal with. Prospective buyers have made their offers, but at any given time nine cousins might accept, two would be undecided, and the Corsicans would say no. The farm remains unsold, and will doubtless pass to the thirty-eight children of the fourteen cousins. Eventually, it will be owned by 175 distant relatives who don't trust one another.

Even if the property should be owned outright by a single acquisitive peasant, such as Massot, there is no guarantee of a straightforward transaction. The peasant may set a price which he thinks is absurdly high, and which will keep him in drink and lottery tickets for the rest of his days. A buyer comes along and agrees to the inflated price. The peasant immediately suspects trickery. It's too easy. The price must be too low. He withdraws the house from the market for six months before trying again at a higher figure.

And then there are the trifling inconveniences that are mentioned casually at the last minute: an outbuilding that has been lost to a neighbor in a card game; an ancient right of way that technically permits the passage of herds of goats through the kitchen twice a year; a dispute over well water that has been bitter and unresolved since 1958; the venerable sitting tenant who is bound to die before next spring—there is always something unexpected, and a buyer needs patience and a sense of humor to see the business through.

I tried to prepare Tony for these local oddities as we drove to the office of a property agent whom we knew, but I should have saved my breath. He was, by his own modest admission, a shrewd and resourceful negotiator. He had played hardball with the big boys on Madison Avenue, and it would take more than bureaucracy or a French peasant to get the better of him. I began to doubt the wisdom of introducing him to anyone who didn't have a car phone and a personal business manager.

The agent met us at the door of her office, and sat us down with two thick files of property details and photographs. She spoke no English and Tony spoke vestigial French, and since direct communication was impossible he behaved as if she wasn't there. It was a particularly arrogant form of bad manners, made worse by the assumption that even the most derogatory language can be used without the risk of it being understood. And so I passed an embarrassing half hour as Tony flicked through the files, muttering "Fuck me!" and "They must be joking" at intervals while I made feeble attempts to translate his comments into some nonsense about his being impressed by the prices.

He had started with the firm intention of finding a village house with no land. He was far too busy to bother with a garden. But as he went through the properties I could see him mentally becoming the Provençal squire with acres of vines and olives. By the time he had finished he was worrying about where he should put his tennis court. To my disappointment, there were three properties that he thought worthy of his attention.

"We'll do those this afternoon," he announced, making notes in his Filofax and looking at his watch. I thought he was going to commandeer the agent's phone for an international call, but he was just reacting to a signal from his stomach. "Let's hit a restaurant," he said, "and we can be back here by two." The agent smiled and nodded as Tony waved two fingers at her and we left the poor woman to recover.

At lunch, I told Tony that I wouldn't be going with him and the agent that afternoon. He was surprised that I had anything better to do, but ordered a second bottle of wine and told me that money was an international language and he didn't anticipate having any difficulties. Unfortunately, when the bill arrived he discovered that neither his gold American Express card nor the wad of traveler's checks that he hadn't had time to change were of any interest to the restaurant's proprietor. I paid, and made some remark about the international language. Tony was not amused.

I left him with mixed feelings of relief and guilt. Boors are always unpleasant, but when you're in a foreign country and they are of your own nationality you feel some kind of vague responsibility. The next day, I called the agent to apologize. "Don't worry," she said, "Parisians are often just as bad. At least I couldn't understand what he was saying."

A FINAL CONFIRMATION that warmer weather was here to stay was provided by Monsieur Menicucci's wardrobe. He had come to carry out the preliminary *études* for his summer project, which was our central heating. His woolen bonnet had been replaced by a lightweight cotton model decorated with a slogan advertising sanitary fittings, and instead of his thermal snowshoes he was wearing brown canvas boots. His assistant, *jeune*, was in a guerrilla outfit of army fatigues and jungle cap, and the two of them marched through the house taking measurements as Menicucci delivered himself of assorted *pensées*.

Music was his first subject today. He and his wife had just attended an official artisans' and plumbers' lunch, followed by ballroom dancing, which was one of his many accomplishments. "Yes, Monsieur Peter," he said, "we danced until six. I had the feet of a young man of eighteen." I could picture him, nimble and exact, whirling Madame around the floor, and I wondered if he had a special ballroom bonnet for these occasions, because it was impossible to think of him bareheaded. I must have smiled at the thought. "I know," he said, "you're thinking that the waltz is not serious music. For that one must listen to the great composers."

He then expounded a remarkable theory, which had occurred to him while he was playing the clarinet during one of the power cuts that the French electricity board arranges at regular intervals. Electricity, he said, is a matter of science and logic. Classical music is a matter of art and logic. *Vous voyez?* Already one sees a common factor. And when you listen to the disciplined and logical progression of some of Mozart's work, the conclusion is inescapable: Mozart would have made a formidable electrician.

I was saved from replying by *jeune*, who had finished counting up the number of radiators we would need, and had arrived at a figure of twenty. Menicucci received the news with a wince, shaking his hand as if he'd burned his fingers. "*Oh là là.* This will cost more than *centimes.*" He mentioned several million francs, saw my shocked expression and then divided by a hundred; he had been quoting in old money. Even so, it was a considerable amount. There was the high cost of cast iron, plus the government sales tax, or TVA, of 18.6 percent. This led him to mention an outrageous fiscal irregularity which typified the villainy of politicians.

"You buy a bidet," he said, jabbing me with his finger, "and you pay full TVA. The same for a washer or a screw. But I will tell you something *scandaleux* and altogether wrong. You buy a pot of caviar, and you will pay only 6 percent TVA, because it is classified as *nourriture*. Now tell me this: Who eats caviar?" I pleaded not guilty. "I will tell you. It is the politicians, the millionaires, the *grosses légumes* in Paris—they are the ones who eat caviar. It's an outrage." He stumped off, fulminating about caviar orgies in the Elysée Palace, to check *jeune's* radiator arithmetic.

The thought of Menicucci occupying the premises for five or six weeks, burrowing his way through the thick old walls with a drill that was almost as big as he was and filling the air with

dust and running commentaries, was not a treat to look forward
to. It would be a dirty and tedious process involving almost every
room in the house. But one of the joys of Provence, we told
ourselves, was that we could live outdoors while this was going
on. Even this early in the year, the days were very nearly hot,
and we decided to start the outdoor season in earnest one Sunday
morning when the sun coming through the bedroom window woke
us up at seven o'clock.

All good Sundays include a trip to the market, and we were
in Coustellet by eight. The space behind the disused station was
lined with elderly trucks and vans, each with a trestle table set
up in front. A blackboard showed the day's prices for vegetables.
The stall holders, already tanned from the fields, were eating
croissants and brioches that were still warm from the bakery
across the street. We watched as one old man sliced a baguette
lengthways with a wooden-handled pocket knife and spread on
fresh goat's cheese in a creamy layer before pouring himself a
glass of red wine from the liter bottle that would keep him going
until lunchtime.

The Coustellet market is small compared to the weekly markets in Cavaillon and Apt and Isle-sur-la-Sorgue, and not yet
fashionable. Customers carry baskets instead of cameras, and only
in July and August are you likely to see the occasional haughty
woman down from Paris with her Dior track suit and small,
nervous dog. For the rest of the season, from spring until autumn,
it is just the local inhabitants, and the peasants who bring in
what they have taken from the earth or the greenhouse a few
hours earlier.

We walked slowly along the rows of trestle tables, admiring
the merciless French housewife at work. Unlike us, she is not
content merely to look at the produce before buying. She gets to
grips with it—squeezing aubergines, sniffing tomatoes, snapping
the matchstick-thin *haricots verts* between her fingers, poking
suspiciously into the damp green hearts of lettuces, tasting
cheeses and olives—and, if they don't come up to her private

standards, she will glare at the stall holder as if she has been betrayed before taking her custom elsewhere.

At one end of the market, a van from the wine cooperative was surrounded by men rinsing their teeth thoughtfully in the new rosé. Next to them, a woman was selling free-range eggs and live rabbits, and beyond her the tables were piled high with vegetables, small and fragrant bushes of basil, tubs of lavender honey, great green bottles of first pressing olive oil, trays of hot-house peaches, pots of black *tapenade*, flowers and herbs, jams and cheeses—everything looked delicious in the early morning sun.

We bought red peppers to roast and big brown eggs and basil and peaches and goat's cheese and lettuce and pink-streaked on-ions. And, when the basket could hold no more, we went across the road to buy half a yard of bread—the *gros pain* that makes such a tasty mop for any olive oil or vinaigrette sauce that is left on the plate. The bakery was crowded and noisy, and smelled of warm dough and the almonds that had gone into the morning's cakes. While we waited, we remembered being told that the French spend as much of their income on their stomachs as the English do on their cars and stereo systems, and we could easily believe it.

Everyone seemed to be shopping for a regiment. One round, jolly woman bought six large loaves—three yards of bread—a chocolate brioche the size of a hat, and an entire wheel of apple tart, the thin slices of apple packed in concentric rings, shining under a glaze of apricot sauce. We were aware that we had missed breakfast.

Lunch made up for it: cold roasted peppers, slippery with olive oil and speckled with fresh basil, tiny mussels wrapped in bacon and barbecued on skewers, salad, and cheese. The sun was hot and the wine had made us sleepy. And then we heard the phone.

It is a rule of life that, when the phone rings between noon and three on a Sunday, the caller is English; a Frenchman wouldn't dream of interrupting the most relaxed meal of the week. I should have let it ring. Tony from advertising was back, and judging by the absence of static on the line he was hideously close.

"Just thought I'd touch base with you." I could hear him taking a drag on his cigarette, and I made a mental note to buy an answering machine to deal with anyone else who might want to touch base on a Sunday.

"I think I've found a place." He didn't pause to hear the effect of his announcement, and so missed the sound of my heart sinking. "Quite a way from you, actually, nearer the coast." I told him that I was delighted; the nearer the coast he was, the better. "Needs a lot doing to it, so I'm not going to pay what he's asking. Thought I'd bring my builders over to do the work. They did the office in six weeks, top to bottom. Irish, but bloody good. They could sort this place out in a month."

I was tempted to encourage him, because the idea of a gang of Irish workmen exposed to the pleasures of a building site in Provence—the sun, cheap wine, endless possibilities for delay, and a proprietor too far away to be a daily nuisance—had the makings of a fine comic interlude, and I could see Mr. Murphy and his team stretching the job out until October, maybe getting the family over from Donegal for a holiday during August and generally having a grand time. I told Tony he might be better advised to hire local labor, and to get an architect to hire it for him.

"Don't need an architect," he said, "I know exactly what I want." He would. "Why should I pay him an arm and a leg for a couple of drawings?" There was no helping him. He knew best. I asked him when he was going back to England. "This evening," he said, and then guided me through the next hectic pages of his Filofax: a client meeting on Monday, three days in New York, a sales conference in Milton Keynes. He reeled it off with the mock weariness of the indispensable executive, and he was welcome to every second of it. "Anyway," he said, "I'll keep in touch. I won't finalize on the house for a week or two, but I'll let you know as soon as I've inked it."

My wife and I sat by the pool and wondered, not for the first time, why we both found it so difficult to get rid of thick-skinned and ungracious people. More of them would be coming down during the summer, baying for food and drink and a bedroom, for days of swimming and lifts to the airport. We didn't think of ourselves as antisocial or reclusive, but our brief experience with the thrustful and dynamic Tony had been enough to remind us that the next few months would require firmness and ingenuity. And an answering machine.

The approach of summer had obviously been on Massot's mind as well, because when I saw him a few days later in the forest he was busy adding a further refinement to his anticamper defenses. Under the signs he had nailed up saying PRIVÉ! he was fixing a second series of unwelcoming messages, short but sinister: *Attention! Vipères!* It was the perfect deterrent—full of menace, but without the need for visible proof that is the great drawback of other discouragements such as guard dogs, electrified fences, and patrols armed with submachine guns. Even the most resolute camper would think twice before tucking himself up in a sleeping bag which might have one of the local residents coiled at the bottom. I asked Massot if there really were vipers in the Lubéron, and he shook his head at yet another example of the ignorance of foreigners.

"*Eh oui*," he said, "not big"—he held his hands up, about twelve inches apart—"but if you're bitten you need to get to a doctor within forty-five minutes, or else . . ." He pulled a dreadful face, head to one side, tongue lolling from the side of his mouth, "They say that when a viper bites a man, the man dies. But when a viper bites a woman"—he leaned forward and waggled his eyebrows—"the viper dies." He snorted with amusement and offered me one of his fat yellow cigarettes. "Don't ever go walking without a good pair of boots."

The Lubéron viper, according to Professor Massot, will normally avoid humans, and will attack only if provoked. When this happens, Massot's advice was to run in zigzags, and preferably uphill, because an enraged viper can sprint—in short, straight bursts on level ground—as fast as a running man. I looked nervously around me, and Massot laughed. "Of course, you can always try the peasant's trick: Catch it behind the head and squeeze until its mouth is wide open. Spit hard into the mouth and *plok!*—he's dead." He spat in demonstration, hitting one of the dogs on the head. "But best of all," said Massot, "is to take a woman with you. They can't run as fast as men, and the viper will catch them first." He went home to his breakfast leaving me to pick my way cautiously through the forest and practice my spitting.

EASTER WEEKEND arrived, and our cherry trees—about thirty of them—blossomed in unison. From the road, the house looked as if it were floating on a pink-and-white sea, and motorists were stopping to take photographs or walking tentatively up the drive until barking from the dogs turned them back. One group, more adventurous than the rest, drove up to the house in a car with Swiss plates and parked on the roadside. I went to see what they wanted.

"We will picnic here," the driver told me.

"I'm sorry, it's a private house."

"No, no," he said, waving a map at me, "this is the Lubéron."

"No, no," I said, "that's the Lubéron," and pointed to the mountains.

"But I can't take my car up *there*."

Eventually he drove off, puffing with Swiss indignation and leaving deep wheel marks in the grass we were trying to turn into a lawn. The tourist season had begun.

Up in the village on Easter Sunday, the small parking area was full, and not one of the cars had local plates. The visitors explored the narrow streets, looking curiously into people's houses and posing for photographs in front of the church. The young man who spends all day sitting on a doorstep next to the *épicerie* was asking everyone who passed for ten francs to make a phone call and taking the proceeds into the café.

The Café du Progrès has made a consistent and successful effort to avoid being picturesque. It is an interior decorator's nightmare, with tables and chairs that wobble and don't match, gloomy paintwork, and a lavatory that splutters and gurgles often and noisily next to a shabby ice-cream cabinet. The proprietor is gruff, and his dogs are indescribably matted. There is, however, a long and spectacular view from the glassed-in terrace next to the lavatory, and it's a good place to have a beer and watch the play of light on the hills and villages that stretch away toward the Basses-Alpes. A hand-lettered notice warns you not to throw cigarette ends out of the window, following complaints from the clientele of the open-air restaurant below, but if you observe this rule you will be left undisturbed. The regulars stay at the bar; the *terrasse* is for tourists, and on Easter Sunday it was crowded.

There were the Dutch, wholesome in their hiking boots and backpacks; the Germans, armed with Leicas and heavy costume jewelery; the Parisians, disdainful and smart, inspecting their glasses carefully for germs; an Englishman in sandals and an open-necked striped business shirt, working out his holiday finances on a pocket calculator while his wife wrote postcards to neighbors in Surrey. The dogs nosed among the tables looking for sugar lumps, causing the hygiene-conscious Parisians to shrink away. An Yves Montand song on the radio fought a losing battle with the sanitary sound effects, and empty pastis glasses were banged on the bar as the locals started to drift off toward home and lunch.

Outside the café, three cars had converged and were growling at one another. If one of them had reversed ten yards, they could all have passed, but a French driver considers it a moral defeat to give way, just as he feels a moral obligation to park wherever he can cause maximum inconvenience and to overtake on a blind bend. They say that Italians are dangerous drivers, but for truly lethal insanity I would back a Frenchman hurtling down the N100, late and hungry, against all comers.

I drove back from the village and just missed the first accident of the season. An old white Peugeot had gone backwards into a wooden telegraph pole at the bottom of the drive with sufficient force to snap the pole in two. There was no other car to be seen, and the road was dry and dead straight. It was difficult to work out how the back of the car and the pole had contrived to meet with such force. A young man was standing in the middle of the road, scratching his head. He grinned as I pulled up.

I asked him if he was hurt. "I'm fine," he said, "but I think the car is *foutu*." I looked at the telegraph pole, which was bent over the car, kept from falling by the sagging phone line. That also was *foutu*.

"We must hurry," said the young man. "Nobody must know." He put a finger to his lips. "Can you give me a lift home? It's just up the road. I need the tractor." He got into the car, and the cause of the accident became clear; he smelled as though he had been marinated in Ricard. He explained that the car had to be removed with speed and secrecy. If the post office found that he had attacked one of their poles they would make him pay for it. "Nobody must know," he repeated, and hiccupped once or twice for emphasis.

I dropped him off and went home. Half an hour later, I went out to see if the stealthy removal of the car had been accomplished, but it was still there. So was a group of peasants, arguing noisily. Also two other cars and a tractor, which was blocking the road. As I watched, another car arrived and the driver sounded his horn to get the tractor to move. The man on the tractor pointed at the wreck and shrugged. The horn sounded again, this time in a continuous blare that bounced off the mountains and must have been audible in Ménerbes, two kilometers away.

The commotion lasted for another half hour before the Peugeot was finally extracted from the ditch and the secret motorcade disappeared in the direction of the local garage, leaving the telegraph pole creaking ominously in the breeze. The post office men came to replace it the following week, and attracted a small crowd. They asked one of the peasants what had happened. He shrugged innocently. "Who knows?" he said. "Woodworm?"

OUR FRIEND from Paris examined his empty glass with surprise, as if evaporation had taken place while he wasn't looking. I poured some more wine and he settled back in his chair, face tilted up to the sun.

"We still have the heating on in Paris," he said, and took a sip of the cool, sweet wine from Beaumes de Venise. "And it's been raining for weeks. I can see why you like it here. Mind you, it wouldn't suit me."

It seemed to be suiting him well enough, basking in the warmth after a good lunch, but I didn't argue with him.

"You'd hate it," I said. "You'd probably get skin cancer from the sun and cirrhosis of the liver from too much plonk, and if you were ever feeling well enough you'd miss the theater. And anyway, what would you do all day?"

He squinted at me drowsily, and put his sunglasses on. "Exactly."

It was part of what had become a familiar litany:

Don't you miss your friends?

No. They come and see us here.

Don't you miss English television?

No.

There must be *something* about England you miss?

Marmalade.

And then would come the real question, delivered half-humorously, half-seriously: what do you *do* all day? Our friend from Paris put it another way.

"Don't you get bored?"

We didn't. We never had time. We found the everyday curiosities of French rural life amusing and interesting. We were enjoying the gradual process of changing the house around so that it suited the way we lived. There was the garden to be designed and planted, a *boules* court to be built, a new language to be learned, villages and vineyards and markets to be discovered —the days went quickly enough without any other distractions, and there were always plenty of those. The previous week, as it happened, had been particularly rich in interruptions.

They started on Monday with a visit from Marcel the Parcel, our postman. He was irritated, barely pausing to shake hands before demanding to know where I had hidden the mailbox. He had his rounds to do, it was almost noon, how could I expect him to deliver letters if he had to play *cache-cache* with the mailbox? But we hadn't hidden it. So far as I knew, it was down at the end of the drive, firmly planted on a steel post. "*Non*," said the postman, "it has been moved." There was nothing for it but to walk down the drive together and spend a fruitless five minutes searching the bushes to see if it had been knocked over. There was no sign that a mailbox had ever been there except a small post hole in the ground. "*Voilà*," said the postman, "it is as I told you." I found it hard to believe that anyone would steal a mailbox, but he knew better. "It is quite normal," he said, "people around here are *mal fini*." I asked him what that meant. "Mad."

Back to the house we went, to restore his good humor with a drink and to discuss the installation of a new mailbox that he would be happy to sell me. We agreed that it should be built into the side of an old well, positioned at the regulation height of seventy centimeters above the ground so that he could drop letters in without having to leave his van. Obviously, the well had to be studied and measurements taken, and by then it was time for lunch. Post office business would be resumed at two o'clock.

A couple of days later, I was summoned from the house by a car horn, and found the dogs circling a new white Mercedes.

The driver wasn't prepared to leave the safety of his car, but risked a half-open window. I looked in and saw a small brown couple beaming at me nervously. They complimented me on the ferocity of the dogs and requested permission to get out. They were both dressed for the city, the man in a sharply cut suit, his wife in hat and cloak and patent-leather boots.

How fortunate to find me at home, they said, and what a beautiful house. Had I lived here long? No? Then I would undoubtedly be needing some genuine Oriental carpets. This was indeed my lucky day, because they had just come from an important carpet exhibition in Avignon, and by chance a few choice items remained unsold. Before taking them up to Paris—where people of taste would fight to buy them—the couple had decided to take a drive in the country, and fate had led them to me. To mark the happy occasion, they were prepared to let me choose from their most exquisite treasures at what they described as *very interesting* prices.

While the natty little man had been telling me the good news, his wife had been unloading carpets from the car and arranging them artistically up and down the drive, commenting loudly on the charms of each one: "Ah, what a beauty!" and "See the colors in the sun" and "This one—oh, I shall be sad to see it go." She trotted back to join us, patent boots twinkling, and she and her husband looked at me expectantly.

The carpet seller does not enjoy a good reputation in Provence, and to describe a man as a *marchand de tapis* is to imply that he is at best shifty and at worst someone who would steal the corset from your grandmother. I had also been told that traveling carpet sellers often acted as reconnaissance parties, spying out the land for their burglar associates. And there was always the possibility that the carpets would be fakes, or stolen.

But they didn't look like fakes, and there was one small rug that I thought was very handsome. I made the mistake of saying so, and Madame looked at her husband in well-rehearsed surprise. "Extraordinary!" she said. "What an eye Monsieur has. This is indisputably our favorite too. But why not have something a little bigger as well?" Alas, I said, I was penniless, but this was brushed aside as a minor and temporary inconvenience. I could always pay later, with a substantial discount for cash. I looked again at the rug. One of the dogs was lying on it, snoring gently. Madame crooned with delight. "You see, Monsieur? The *toutou* has chosen it for you." I gave in. After three minutes of inexpert haggling on my part, the original price was reduced by 50 percent, and I went to fetch the checkbook. They watched closely while I made out the check, telling me to leave the payee's name blank. With a promise to return next year, they drove slowly around our new rug and the sleeping dog, Madame smiling and waving regally from her nest of carpets. Their visit had taken up the entire morning.

The final interruption ended the week on a sour note. A truck had come to deliver gravel and, as I watched it backing toward the spot the driver had chosen to unload, the rear wheels suddenly sank into the ground. There was a crack, and the truck tilted backwards. A pungent and unmistakable smell filled the air. The driver got out to inspect the damage and said, with unconscious accuracy, the single most appropriate word for the occasion.

"*Merde!*" He had parked in the septic tank.

"So you see," I said to our friend from Paris, "one way or another, there's never a dull moment."

He didn't reply, and I reached over and took off his sunglasses. The sun in his eyes woke him up.

"What?"

MAY

LE PREMIER MAI started well, with a fine sunrise, and as it was a national holiday we thought we should celebrate in correct French fashion by paying homage to the summer sport and taking to our bicycles.

Tougher and more serious cyclists had been training for weeks, muffled against the spring winds in thick black tights and face masks, but now the air was warm enough for delicate amateurs like us to go out in shorts and sweaters. We had bought two lightweight and highly strung machines from a gentleman in Cavaillon called Edouard Cunty—'*Vélos de Qualité!*'—and we were keen to join the brightly colored groups from local cycling clubs as they swooped gracefully and without any apparent effort up and down the back country roads. We assumed that our legs, after a winter of hard walking, would be in good enough condition

for a gentle ten-mile spin up to Bonnieux and over to Lacoste—
an hour of light exercise to limber up, nothing too strenuous.

It was easy enough to begin with, although the narrow, hard
saddles made an early impression, and we realized why some
cyclists slip a pound of rump steak inside the back of their shorts
to cushion the coccyx from the road. But for the first couple of
miles there was nothing to do except glide along and enjoy the
scenery. The cherries were ripening, the winter skeletons of the
vines had disappeared under a cover of bright green leaves, the
mountains looked lush and soft. The tires made a steady thrumming sound, and there were occasional whiffs of rosemary and
lavender and wild thyme. This was more exhilarating than walking, quieter and healthier than driving, not too taxing, and altogether delightful. Why hadn't we done it before? Why didn't
we do it every day?

· The euphoria lasted until we began to climb up to Bonnieux.
My bicycle suddenly put on weight. I could feel the muscles in
my thighs complaining as the gradient became steeper, and my
unseasoned backside was aching. I forgot about the beauties of
nature and wished I had worn steak in my shorts. By the time
we reached the village it hurt to breathe.

The woman who runs the Café Clerici was standing outside
with her hands on her ample hips. She looked at the two red-
faced, gasping figures bent over their handlebars. *"Mon Dieu!
The Tour de France is early this year."* She brought us beer,
and we sat in the comfort of chairs designed for human bottoms.
Lacoste now seemed rather far away.

The hill that twists up to the ruins of the Marquis de Sade's
château was long and steep and agonizing. We were halfway up
and flagging when we heard a whirr of *dérailleur* gears, and we
were overtaken by another cyclist—a wiry, brown man who
looked to be in his mid-sixties. *"Bonjour,"* he said brightly, *"bon
vélo,"* and he continued up the hill and out of sight. We labored
on, heads low, thighs burning, regretting the beer.

The old man came back down the hill, turned, and cruised

along next to us. "*Courage,*" he said, not even breathing hard, "*c'est pas loin. Allez!*" And he rode with us into Lacoste, his lean old legs, shaved bare in case of falls and grazes, pumping away with the smoothness of pistons.

We collapsed on the terrace of another café, which overlooked the valley. At least it would be downhill most of the way home, and I gave up the idea of calling an ambulance. The old man had a peppermint *frappé*, and told us that he had done thirty kilometers so far, and would do another twenty before lunch. We congratulated him on his fitness. "It's not what it was. I had to stop doing the Mont Ventoux ride when I turned sixty. Now I just do these little *promenades.*" Any slight satisfaction we felt at climbing the hill disappeared.

The ride back was easier, but we were still hot and sore when we reached home. We dismounted and walked stiff-legged to the pool, discarding clothes as we went, and dived in. It was like going to heaven. Lying in the sun afterwards with a glass of wine we decided that cycling would be a regular part of our summer lives. It was, however, some time before we could face the saddles without flinching.

THE FIELDS around the house were inhabited every day by figures moving slowly and methodically across the landscape, weeding the vineyards, treating the cherry trees, hoeing the sandy earth. Nothing was hurried. Work stopped at noon for lunch in the shade of a tree, and the only sounds for two hours were snatches of distant conversation that carried hundreds of yards on the still air.

Faustin was spending most of his days on our land, arriving just after seven with his dog and his tractor and usually contriving to organize his work so that it ended near the house—close enough to hear the sound of bottles and glasses. One drink to settle the dust and be sociable was his normal ration but, if the visit stretched to two drinks, it meant business—some new step forward in agricultural cooperation which he had been mulling over during his hours among the vines. He never approached a subject directly, but edged toward it, crabwise and cautious.

"Do you like rabbits?"

I knew him well enough to understand that he wasn't talking about the charms of the rabbit as a domestic pet, and he confirmed this by patting his belly and muttering reverently about *civets* and *pâtés*. But the trouble with rabbits, he said, was their appetites. They ate like holes, kilos and kilos. I nodded, but I was at a loss to know where our interests and those of the hungry rabbit coincided.

Faustin stood up and beckoned me to the door of the courtyard. He pointed at two small terraced fields. "Lucerne," he said. "Rabbits love it. You could get three cuts from those fields between now and autumn." My knowledge of local plant life was far from complete, and I had thought that the fields were covered in some kind of dense Provençal weed which I had been meaning to clear. It was fortunate I hadn't; Faustin's rabbits would never have forgiven me. It was an unexpected triumph for gardening by neglect. In case I had missed the point, Faustin waved his glass at the fields and said again, "Rabbits love lucerne." He made nibbling noises. I told him he could have as much as his rabbits could eat, and he stopped nibbling.

"*Bon.* If you're sure you won't need it." Mission accomplished, he stumped off toward his tractor.

Faustin is slow in many ways, but quick with his gratitude. He was back the following evening with an enormous bouquet of asparagus, neatly tied with red, white, and blue ribbon. His wife, Henriette, was behind him carrying a pickax, a ball of string, and a tub filled with young lavender plants. They should have been planted long before, she said, but her cousin had only just brought them down from the Basses-Alpes. They must be planted at once.

Labor was divided rather unfairly, it seemed to us. Faustin was in charge of keeping the string straight and drinking pastis;

Henriette swung the pickaxe, each planting hole a pick handle's distance from the next. Offers to help were refused. "She's used to it," said Faustin proudly, as Henriette swung and measured and planted in the twilight, and she laughed. "Eight hours of this and you sleep like a baby." In half an hour it was done—a bed of fifty plants that would be the size of hedgehogs in six months, knee high in two years, arranged with meticulous symmetry to mark the boundary of the rabbits' lucerne factory.

Whatever had been on the menu for dinner was forgotten, and we prepared the asparagus. There was too much for one meal, more than I could get both hands around, the patriotic tricolor ribbon printed with Faustin's name and address. He told us that it was the law in France for the producer to be identified like this, and we hoped one day to have our own ribbon when our asparagus plants grew up.

The pale shoots were as fat as thumbs, delicately colored and patterned at the tips. We ate them warm, with melted butter. We ate bread that had been baked that afternoon in the old *boulangerie* at Lumières. We drank the light red wine from the vineyards in the valley. We supported local industry with every mouthful.

Through the open door we could hear the croaking of our resident frog, and the long, sliding song of a nightingale. We took a final glass of wine outside and looked by the light of the moon at the new lavender bed while the dogs rooted for mice in the lucerne fields. The rabbits would eat well this summer and, Faustin had promised, would taste all the better for it in the winter. We realized we were becoming as obsessive about food as the French, and went back indoors to attend to some unfinished business with a goat's cheese.

BERNARD the *pisciniste* had brought us a present, and he was assembling it with great enthusiasm. It was a floating armchair for the pool, complete with a drinks compartment. It had come all the way from Miami, Florida, which in Bernard's opinion was the capital of the world for pool accessories. "The French don't understand these things," he said disparagingly. "There are companies making air cushions, but how can you drink on a floating cushion?" He tightened the last wing nut on the frame and stood back to admire the chair in all its Miami dazzle, a vivid block of styrofoam, plastic, and aluminium. "There. The glass fits here in the armrest. You can repose in great comfort. *C'est une merveille.*" He launched the chair into the water, careful not to splash his pink shirt and white trousers. "You must put it away every night," he said. "The gypsies will be here soon for the cherry picking. They'll steal anything."

It was a reminder that we had been intending to get some insurance arranged for the house, but with the builders making holes in the walls I couldn't imagine any insurance company taking the risk. Bernard removed his sunglasses in horror. Didn't we know? There was a higher burglary rate in the Vaucluse than anywhere else in France except Paris. He looked at me as if I had committed an act of terminal lunacy. "You must be protected immediately. I will send a man this afternoon. Stay *en garde* until he comes."

I thought this was perhaps a little dramatic, but Bernard seemed convinced that robber bands were lurking close by, waiting only for us to go to the village butcher before swooping down in a pantechnicon to pick the house bare. Only last week, he told me, he had found his car jacked up outside his own front door with all four wheels removed. These people were *salauds.*

One reason, apart from idleness, why we had neglected the matter of insurance was that we detested insurance companies, with their weasel words and evasions and extenuating circumstances, and their conditional clauses set in minuscule, illegible type. But Bernard was right. It was stupid to trust to luck. We resigned ourselves to spending the afternoon with a gray man in a suit who would tell us to put a lock on our refrigerator.

It was early evening when the car pulled up in a cloud of

dust. The driver had obviously come to the wrong house. He was young and dark and good-looking, resplendent in the costume of a 1950s saxophone player—a wide-shouldered drape jacket shot through with gleaming threads, a lime-green shirt, capacious trousers that narrowed to hug his ankles, shoes of dark blue suede with bulbous crêpe soles, a flash of turquoise socks.

"Fructus, Thierry. *Agent d'assurance.*" He walked into the house with short, jaunty steps. I half expected him to start snapping his fingers and make a few mean moves across the floor. I offered him a beer while I got over my surprise, and he sat down and gave me the benefit of his vibrant socks.

"*Une belle mesong.*" He had a strong Provençal accent which contrasted strangely with the clothes, and which I found reassuring. He was businesslike and serious, and asked if we were living in the house all year round; the high rate of burglaries in the Vaucluse, he said, was partly due to the large number of holiday homes. When houses are left empty for ten months a year, well . . . the shoulders of his jacket escalated in an upholstered shrug. The stories one heard in his profession made you want to live in a safe.

But that needn't concern us. We were permanent. And, furthermore, we had dogs. This was good, and it would be taken into account when he assessed the premium. Were they vicious? If not, perhaps they could be trained. He knew a man who could turn poodles into lethal weapons.

He made some notes in a neat, small hand and finished his beer. We went on a tour of the house. He approved of the heavy wooden shutters and solid old doors, but stopped and sucked his teeth in front of a small window—a *fenestron* that was less than a foot square. The modern professional burglar, he told us, will often work like Victorian chimney sweeps used to, sending a child through openings that would be impossible for adults. Since we were in France, there was an official, established size for juvenile burglars; they were all more than 12 centimeters wide, and narrower gaps were therefore childproof. Quite how this had been calculated Monsieur Fructus didn't know, but the little window would have to be barred to make it safe from the depredations of anorexic five-year-olds.

For the second time that day, the itinerant cherry pickers were held up as a threat to domestic security—Spaniards or Italians, Monsieur Fructus said, working for a pittance of three francs a kilo, here today and gone tomorrow, a grave risk. One cannot be too careful. I promised to stay on the alert and to barricade the window as soon as possible, and to talk to the dogs about being vicious. Reassured, he drove off into the sunset with the sound of Bruce Springsteen bellowing from the car stereo.

The cherry pickers had started to hold an awful fascination for us. We wanted to see some of these light-fingered scoundrels in the flesh; surely it would be any day now that they would descend on us, because the cherries were certainly ready to pick. We'd tasted them. We now had breakfast on a small terrace which faced the early sun, twenty yards from an old tree bowed down with fruit. While my wife made coffee, I picked cherries. They were cool and juicy, almost black, and they were our first treat of the day.

We knew that organized picking had begun the morning we heard a radio playing somewhere between the house and the road. The dogs went to investigate, bristling and noisy with self-importance, and I followed, expecting to find a gang of swarthy strangers and their larcenous children. The leaves on the trees hid their bodies from the waist upward. All I could see were various pairs of legs balanced on triangular wooden ladders, and then a great brown moon of a face under a straw trilby poked through the foliage.

"*Sont bonnes, les cerises.*" He offered me a finger, with a pair of cherries dangling from the end. It was Faustin. He and Henriette and assorted relatives had decided to gather the fruit themselves because of the wages demanded by outside labor. Someone had actually asked for five francs a kilo. Imagine! I tried to: an uncomfortable ten-hour working day perched on a ladder and tormented by fruit flies, nights sleeping rough in a barn or the back of a van—it didn't sound like overgenerous pay to me. But Faustin was adamant. It was daylight robbery, *mais enfin*, what could you expect from cherry pickers? He reckoned to get about two tons of fruit for the jam factory in Apt, and the proceeds would be kept in the family.

The orchards were well stocked with pickers of all shapes and sizes during the next few days, and I stopped to give two of them a ride into Bonnieux one evening. They were students from Australia, red from the sun and stained with cherry juice. They were exhausted, and complained about the hours and the tedium and the stinginess of the French peasant.

"Well, at least you're seeing a bit of France."

"France?" said one of them. "All I've seen is the inside of a flaming cherry tree."

They were determined to go back to Australia with no good memories of their time in Provence. They didn't like the people. They were suspicious of the food. French beer gave them the runs. Even the scenery was small by Australian standards. They couldn't believe I had chosen to live here. I tried to explain, but we were talking about two different countries. I dropped them off at the café, where they would spend the evening being home-sick. They were the only miserable Australians I had ever met, and it was depressing to hear a place that I loved being so thoroughly condemned.

Bernard cheered me up. I had come to his office in Bonnieux with the translation of a letter that he had received from an English client, and he was laughing as he opened the door.

His friend Christian, who was also our architect, had just been asked to redesign a brothel in Cavaillon. There were, *naturellement*, many unusual requirements to be met. The placing of mirrors, for instance, was of crucial importance. Certain fittings not normally found in polite bedrooms would have to be accommodated. The bidets would be working overtime, and they would have to function impeccably. I thought of Monsieur Menicucci and *jeune* trying to adjust their taps and washers while traveling salesmen from Lille chased scantily clad young ladies through the corridors. I thought of Ramon the plasterer, a man with a definite twinkle in his eye, let loose among the *filles de joie*. He'd stay there for the rest of his life. It was a wonderful prospect.

Unfortunately, said Bernard, although Christian regarded it as an interesting architectural challenge, he was going to turn it down. Madame who ran the enterprise wanted the work finished in an impossibly short time, and she wasn't prepared to close the premises while it was being done, which would place severe demands on the workmen's powers of concentration. Nor was she prepared to pay the TVA, arguing that she didn't charge her clients a sales tax, so why should she have to pay one? In the end, she would hire a couple of renegade masons who would do a fast and clumsy job, and the chance of getting Cavaillon's brothel photographed for the pages of the *Architectural Digest* would be lost. A sad day for posterity.

WE WERE LEARNING what it was like to live more or less permanently with guests. The advance guard had arrived at Easter, and others were booked in until the end of October. Half-forgotten invitations, made in the distant safety of winter, were coming home to roost and drink and sunbathe. The girl in the laundry assumed from our sheet count that we were in the hotel business, and we remembered the warnings of more experienced residents.

As it turned out, the early visitors must have taken a course in being ideal guests. They rented a car, so that they weren't dependent on us to ferry them around. They amused themselves during the day, and we had dinner together in the evening. They left when they had said they were going to. If they were all like that, we thought, the summer would pass very pleasantly.

The greatest problem, as we soon came to realize, was that

our guests were on holiday. We weren't. We got up at seven. They were often in bed until ten or eleven, sometimes finishing breakfast just in time for a swim before lunch. We worked while they sunbathed. Refreshed by an afternoon nap, they came to life in the evening, getting into high social gear as we were falling asleep in the salad. My wife, who has a congenitally hospitable nature and a horror of seeing people underfed, spent hours in the kitchen, and we washed dishes far into the night.

Sundays were different. Everybody who came to stay with us wanted to go to one of the Sunday markets, and they start early. For once in the week, we and the guests kept the same hours. Bleary-eyed and unusually quiet, they would doze in the back of the car during the twenty-minute ride to breakfast in the café overlooking the river at Isle-sur-la-Sorgue.

We parked by the bridge and woke our friends. They had gone to bed, reluctant and still boisterous, at two in the morning, and the bright light was having savage effects on their hangovers. They hid behind sunglasses and nursed big cups of *café crème*. At the dark end of the bar, a *gendarme* swallowed a surreptitious pastis. The man selling lottery tickets promised instant wealth to anyone who hesitated by his table. Two overnight truck drivers with blue sandpaper chins attacked their breakfasts of steak and *pommes frites* and shouted for more wine. The fresh smell of the river came through the open door, and ducks trod water while they waited for crumbs to be swept off the terrace.

We set off for the main square, running the gauntlet between groups of sallow gypsy girls in tight, shiny black skirts selling lemons and long plaits of garlic, hissing at one another in competition. The stalls were crammed haphazardly along the street —silver jewelery next to flat wedges of salt cod, wooden barrels of gleaming olives, hand-woven baskets, cinnamon and saffron and vanilla, cloudy bunches of gypsophila, a cardboard box full of mongrel puppies, lurid Johnny Hallyday T-shirts, salmon-pink corsets and brassières of heroic proportions, rough country bread and dark terrines.

A lanky blue-black Senegalese loped through the turmoil of the square, festooned with his stock of authentic African tribal leatherware, made in Spain, and digital watches. There was a roll of drums. A man in a flat-topped peaked hat, accompanied by a dog dressed in a red jacket, cleared his throat and adjusted his portable loudspeaker system to an unbearable whine. Another drum roll. "*Prix choc!* Lamb from Sisteron! Charcuterie! Tripe! Go at once to Boucherie Crassard, Rue Carnot. *Prix choc!*" He fiddled again with his loudspeaker and consulted a clipboard. He was the town's mobile broadcasting service, announcing everything from birthday greetings to the local cinema programs, complete with musical effects. I wanted to introduce him to Tony from advertising; they could have had an interesting time comparing promotional techniques.

Three Algerians with deeply rutted brown faces stood gossiping in the sun, their lunches hanging upside down from their hands. The live chickens they were holding by the legs had a fatalistic air about them, as if they knew that their hours were numbered. Everywhere we looked, people were eating. Stall holders held out free samples—slivers of warm pizza, pink ringlets of ham, sausage dusted with herbs and spiced with green peppercorns, tiny, nutty cubes of nougat. It was a dieter's vision of hell. Our friends started asking about lunch.

We were hours away from lunch, and before that we had to see the nonedible side of the market, the *brocanteurs* with their magpie collections of bits and pieces of domestic history rescued from attics all over Provence. Isle-sur-la-Sorgue has been an antique dealers' town for years; there is a huge warehouse by the station where thirty or forty dealers have permanent pitches, and where you can find almost anything except a bargain. But it was too sunny a morning to spend in the gloom of a warehouse, and we stayed among the outside stalls under the plane trees where the purveyors of what they like to call *haut bric-à-brac* spread their offerings on tables and chairs or on the ground, or hung them from nails in the tree trunks.

Faded sepia postcards and old linen smocks were jumbled up with fistfuls of cutlery, chipped enamel signs advertising purgatives and pomade for unruly mustaches, fire irons and chamber pots, Art Deco brooches and café ashtrays, yellowing books of poetry and the inevitable Louis Quatorze chair, perfect except for a missing leg. As it got closer to noon the prices went down and haggling began in earnest. This was the moment for my wife, who is close to professional standard at haggling, to strike. She had been circling a small plaster bust of Delacroix. The dealer marked it down to seventy-five francs, and she moved in for the kill.

"What's your best price?" she asked the dealer.

"My *best* price, Madame, is a hundred francs. However, this now seems unlikely, and lunch approaches. You can have it for fifty."

We put Delacroix in the car, where he gazed thoughtfully out of the back window, and we joined the rest of France as the entire country prepared itself for the pleasures of the table.

One of the characteristics which we liked and even admired about the French is their willingness to support good cooking, no matter how remote the kitchen may be. The quality of the food is more important than convenience, and they will happily drive for an hour or more, salivating en route, in order to eat well. This makes it possible for a gifted cook to prosper in what might appear to be the most unpromising of locations, and the restaurant we had chosen was so isolated that on our first visit we'd taken a map.

Buoux is barely large enough to be called a village. Hidden in the hills about ten miles from Bonnieux, it has an ancient Mairie, a modern telephone kiosk, fifteen or twenty scattered houses, and the Auberge de la Loube, built into the side of the hill with an empty, beautiful valley below it. We had found it with some difficulty in the winter, doubting the map as we went deeper and deeper into the wilderness. We had been the only clients that night, eating in front of a huge log fire while the wind rattled the shutters.

There could hardly have been a greater contrast between that raw night and a hot Sunday in May. As we came around the bend in the road leading to the restaurant we saw that the small parking area was already full, half of it taken up by three horses tethered to the bumper of a decrepit Citroën. The restaurant cat sprawled on the warm roof tiles, looking speculatively at some chickens in the next field. Tables and chairs were arranged along the length of an open-fronted barn, and we could hear the ice buckets being filled in the kitchen.

Maurice the chef came out with four glasses of peach champagne, and took us over to see his latest investment. It was an old open carriage with wooden wheels and cracked leather seats, large enough for half a dozen passengers. Maurice was planning to organize horse-drawn coach excursions through the Lubéron, stopping, *bien sûr*, for a good lunch on the way. Did we think it was an amusing idea? Would we come? Of course we would. He gave us a pleased, shy smile and went back to his ovens.

He had taught himself to cook, but he had no desire to become the Bocuse of Buoux. All he wanted was enough business to allow him to stay in his valley with his horses. The success of his restaurant was based on value for money and good, simple food rather than flights of gastronomic fancy, which he called *cuisine snob*.

There was one menu, at 110 francs. The young girl who serves on Sundays brought out a flat basketwork tray and put it in the middle of the table. We counted fourteen separate hors d'oeuvres—artichoke hearts, tiny sardines fried in batter, perfumed *tabouleh*, creamed salt cod, marinated mushrooms, baby calamari, *tapenade*, small onions in a fresh tomato sauce, celery and chick-peas, radishes and cherry tomatoes, cold mussels. Balanced on the top of the loaded tray were thick slices of pâté and gherkins, saucers of olives and cold peppers. The bread had a fine crisp crust. There was white wine in the ice bucket, and a bottle of Châteauneuf-du-Pape left to breathe in the shade.

The other customers were all French, people from the neighboring villages dressed in their clean, somber Sunday clothes, and one or two more sophisticated couples looking fashionably out of place in their bright boutique colors. At a big table in the corner, three generations of a family piled their plates high and wished each other *bon appétit*. One of the children, showing remarkable promise for a six-year-old gourmet, said that he preferred this pâté to the one he ate at home, and asked his grandmother for a taste of her wine. The family dog waited patiently by his side, knowing as all dogs do that children drop more food than adults.

The main course arrived—rosy slices of lamb cooked with whole cloves of garlic, young green beans, and a golden potato-and-onion *galette*. The Châteauneuf-du-Pape was poured, dark and heady, "a wine with shoulders," as Maurice had said. We abandoned plans for an active afternoon, and drew lots to see who would get Bernard's floating armchair.

The cheese was from Banon, moist in its wrapping of vine leaves, and then came the triple flavors and textures of the desserts—lemon sorbet, chocolate tart, and *crème anglaise* all sharing a plate. Coffee. A glass of *marc* from Gigondas. A sigh of contentment. Where else in the world, our friends wondered, could you eat so well in such unfussy and relaxed surroundings? Italy, perhaps, but very few other places. They were used to London, with its overdecorated restaurants, its theme food, and its grotesque prices. They told us about a bowl of pasta in Mayfair that cost more than the entire meal each of us had just had. Why was it so difficult to eat well and cheaply in London? Full of easy after-lunch wisdom, we came to the conclusion that the English eat out less often than the French, and when they do they want to be impressed as well as fed; they want bottles of wine in baskets, and finger bowls, and menus the length of a short novel, and bills they can boast about.

Maurice came over and asked if his cooking had pleased us. He sat down while he did some addition on a scrap of paper. "*La douloureuse*," he said, pushing it over the table. It came to just over 650 francs, or about what two people would pay for a smart lunch in Fulham. One of our friends asked him if he'd ever thought of moving somewhere more accessible, like Avignon or even Ménerbes. He shook his head. "It's good here. I have everything I want." He could see himself there and cooking in twenty-five years' time, and we hoped we would still be in a fit state to totter up and enjoy it.

On the way home, we noticed that the combination of food and Sunday has a calming influence on the French motorist. His stomach is full. He is on his weekly holiday. He dawdles along without being tempted by the thrills of overtaking on a blind bend. He stops to take the air and relieve himself in the bushes by the roadside, at one with nature, nodding companionably at passing cars. Tomorrow he will take up the mantle of the kamikaze pilot once again, but today it is Sunday in Provence, and life is to be enjoyed.

JUNE

THE LOCAL advertising industry was in bloom. Any car parked near a market for longer than five minutes became a target for roving Provençal media executives, who swooped from windscreen to windscreen stuffing small, excitable posters under the wipers. We were constantly returning to our car to find it flapping with messages—breathless news of forthcoming attractions, unmissable opportunities, edible bargains, and exotic services.

There was an accordion contest in Cavaillon, with the added delights of "*Les Lovely Girls Adorablement Déshabillées* (*12 Tableaux*)" to entertain us in between numbers. A supermarket was launching *Opération Porc*, which promised every conceivable part of a pig's anatomy at prices so low that we would rub our eyes in disbelief. There were *boules* tournaments and *bals dansants*, bicycle races and dog shows, mobile discothèques complete with *disc jockeys*, firework displays, and organ recitals. There was Madame Florian, clairvoyant and alchemist, who was so confident of her supernatural powers that she provided a guarantee of satisfaction with every séance. There were the working girls—from Eve, who described herself as a delicious creature available for saucy rendezvous, to Mademoiselle Roz, who could realize all our fantasies over the telephone, a service that she proudly announced had been banned in Marseilles. And there was, one day, a desperate and hastily written note asking not for our money but for our blood.

The smudged photocopy told the story of a small boy who was waiting to go to America for a major operation, and who needed constant transfusions to keep him alive until the hospital could accept him. *"Venez nombreux et vite,"* said the note. The blood unit would be at the village hall in Gordes at eight the next morning.

When we arrived at 8:30 the hall was already crowded. A dozen beds were arranged along the wall, all occupied, and from the row of upturned feet we could see that a good cross-section of the local population had turned out, easily identified by their footwear: sandals and espadrilles for the shopkeepers, high heels for the young matrons, canvas ankle boots for the peasants, and carpet slippers for their wives. The elder women kept a firm grip on their shopping baskets with one hand while they clenched and unclenched the other fist to speed the flow of blood into the plastic bags, and there was considerable debate about whose contribution was the darkest, richest, and most nourishing.

We lined up for a blood test behind a thick-set old man with a florid nose, a frayed cap, and overalls, who watched with amusement as the nurse made unsuccessful attempts to prick the toughened skin of his thumb.

"Do you want me to fetch the butcher?" he asked. She jabbed once more, harder. *"Merde."* A swelling drop of blood appeared, and the nurse transferred it neatly into a small tube, added some liquid, and shook the mixture vigorously. She looked up from the tube with a disapproving expression.

"How did you come here?" she asked the old man.

He stopped sucking his thumb. "Bicycle," he said, "all the way from Les Imberts."

The nurse sniffed. "It astonishes me that you didn't fall off." She looked at the tube again. "You're technically drunk."

"Impossible," said the old man. "I may have had a little red wine with breakfast, *comme d'habitude*, but that's nothing. And furthermore," he said, wagging his bloodstained thumb under her nose, "a measure of alcohol enriches the corpuscles."

The nurse was not convinced. She sent the old man away to have a second breakfast, this time with coffee, and told him to come back at the end of the morning. He lumbered off grumbling, holding the wounded thumb before him like a flag of battle.

We were pricked, pronounced sober, and shown to our beds. Our veins were plumbed into the plastic bags. We clenched and unclenched dutifully. The hall was noisy and good-humored, and people who would normally pass one another on the street without acknowledgment were suddenly friendly, in the way that often happens when strangers are united in their performance of a good deed. Or it might have had something to do with the bar at the end of the room.

In England, the reward for a bagful of blood is a cup of tea and a biscuit. But here, after being disconnected from our tubes, we were shown to a long table manned by volunteer waiters. What would we like? Coffee, chocolate, croissants, brioches, sandwiches of ham or garlic sausage, mugs of red or rosé wine? Eat up! Drink up! Replace those corpuscles! The stomach must be served! A young male nurse was hard at work with a corkscrew, and the supervising doctor in his long white coat wished us all *bon appétit*. If the steadily growing pile of empty bottles behind the bar was anything to go by, the appeal for blood was an undoubted success, both clinically and socially.

Some time later, we received through the post our copy of *Le Globule*, the official magazine for the blood donors. Hundreds of liters had been collected that morning in Gordes, but the other statistic that interested me—the number of liters that had been drunk—was nowhere to be found, a tribute to medical discretion.

OUR FRIEND the London lawyer, a man steeped in English reserve, was watching what he called the antics of the frogs from the Fin de Siècle café in Cavaillon. It was market day, and the pavement was a human traffic jam, slow moving, jostling and chaotic.

"Look over there," he said, as a car stopped in the middle of the street while the driver got out to embrace an acquaintance, "they're always mauling each other. See that? *Men kissing.* Damned unhealthy, if you ask me." He snorted into his beer, his sense of propriety outraged by such deviant behavior, so alien to the respectable Anglo-Saxon.

It had taken me some months to get used to the Provençal delight in physical contact. Like anyone brought up in England, I had absorbed certain social mannerisms. I had learned to keep my distance, to offer a nod instead of a handshake, to ration kissing to female relatives and to confine any public demonstrations of affection to dogs. To be engulfed by a Provençal welcome, as thorough and searching as being frisked by airport security guards, was, at first, a startling experience. Now I enjoyed it, and I was fascinated by the niceties of the social ritual, and the sign language which is an essential part of any Provençal encounter.

When two unencumbered men meet, the least there will be is the conventional handshake. If the hands are full, you will be offered a little finger to shake. If the hands are wet or dirty, you will be offered a forearm or an elbow. Riding a bicycle or driving a car does not excuse you from the obligation to *toucher les cinq sardines*, and so you will see perilous contortions being performed on busy streets as hands grope through car windows and across handlebars to find each other. And this is only at the first and most restrained level of acquaintance. A closer relationship requires more demonstrative acknowledgment.

As our lawyer friend had noticed, men kiss other men. They squeeze shoulders, slap backs, pummel kidneys, pinch cheeks. When a Provençal man is truly pleased to see you, there is a real possibility of coming away from his clutches with superficial bruising.

The risk of bodily damage is less where women are concerned, but an amateur can easily make a social blunder if he miscalculates the required number of kisses. In my early days of *See also* discovery, I would plant a single kiss, only to find that the other cheek was being proffered as I was drawing back. Only snobs kiss once, I was told, or those unfortunates who suffer from congenital *froideur*. I then saw what I assumed to be the correct procedure—the triple kiss, left-right-left, so I tried it on a Parisian friend. Wrong again. She told me that triple-kissing was a low Provençal habit, and that two kisses were enough among civilized people. The next time I saw my neighbor's wife, I kissed her twice. *"Non,"* she said, *"trois fois."*

I now pay close attention to the movement of the female head. If it stops swiveling after two kisses, I am almost sure I've filled my quota, but I stay poised for a third lunge just in case the head should keep moving.

It's a different but equally tricky problem for my wife, who is on the receiving end and has to estimate the number of times she needs to swivel, or indeed if she needs to swivel at all. One morning she heard a bellow in the street, and turned to see Ramon the plasterer advancing on her. He stopped, and wiped his hands ostentatiously on his trousers. My wife anticipated a handshake, and held out her hand. Ramon brushed it aside and kissed her three times with great gusto. You never can tell.

Once the initial greeting is over, conversation can begin.

Shopping baskets and packages are put down, dogs are tied to café tables, bicycles and tools are leaned up against the nearest wall. This is necessary, because for any serious and satisfactory discussion both hands must be free to provide visual punctuation, to terminate dangling sentences, to add emphasis, or simply to decorate speech which, as it is merely a matter of moving the mouth, is not on its own sufficiently physical for the Provençal. So the hands and the eternally eloquent shoulders are vital to a quiet exchange of views, and in fact it is often possible to follow the gist of a Provençal conversation from a distance, without hearing the words, just by watching expressions and the movements of bodies and hands.

There is a well-defined silent vocabulary, starting with the hand waggle which had been introduced to us by our builders. They used it only as a disclaimer whenever talking about time or cost, but it is a gesture of almost infinite flexibility. It can describe the state of your health, how you're getting on with your mother-in-law, the progress of your business, your assessment of a restaurant, or your predictions about this year's melon crop. When it is a subject of minor importance, the waggle is perfunctory, and is accompanied by a dismissive raising of the eyebrows. More serious matters—politics, the delicate condition of one's liver, the prospects for a local rider in the Tour de France—are addressed with greater intensity. The waggle is in slow motion, with the upper part of the body swaying slightly as the hand rocks, a frown of concentration on the face.

The instrument of warning and argument is the index finger, in one of its three operational positions. Thrust up, rigid and unmoving, beneath your conversational partner's nose, it signals caution—watch out, *attention*, all is not what it seems. Held just below face level and shaken rapidly from side to side like an agitated metronome, it indicates that the other person is woefully ill informed and totally wrong in what he has just said. The correct opinion is then delivered, and the finger changes from its sideways motion into a series of jabs and prods, either tapping the chest if the unenlightened one is a man or remaining a few discreet centimeters from the bosom in the case of a woman.

Describing a sudden departure needs two hands: the left, fingers held straight, moves upwards from waist level to smack into the palm of the right hand moving downward—a restricted version of the popular and extremely vulgar bicep crunch. (Seen at its best during midsummer traffic jams, when disputing drivers will leave their cars to allow themselves the freedom of movement necessary for a left-arm uppercut stopped short by the right hand clamping on the bicep.)

At the end of the conversation, there is the promise to stay in touch. The middle three fingers are folded into the palm and the hand is held up to an ear, with the extended thumb and little finger imitating the shape of a telephone. Finally, there is a parting handshake. Packages, dogs, and bicycles are gathered up until the whole process starts all over again fifty yards down the street. It's hardly surprising that aerobics never became popular in Provence. People get quite enough physical exercise in the course of a ten-minute chat.

These and other everyday amusements of life in nearby towns and villages were not doing much for our spirit of exploration and adventure. With so many distractions on our doorstep, we were neglecting the more famous parts of Provence, or so we were told by our friends in London. In the knowledgeable and irritating manner of seasoned armchair travelers, they kept pointing out how conveniently placed we were for Nîmes and Arles and Avignon, for the flamingoes of the Camargue and the *bouillabaisse* of Marseilles. They seemed surprised and mildly disapproving when we admitted that we stayed close to home, not believing our excuses that we could never find the time to go anywhere, never felt a compulsion to go church crawling or monument spotting, didn't want to be tourists. There was one exception to this rooted existence, and one excursion that we were always happy to make. We both loved Aix.

The corkscrew road we take through the mountains is too narrow for trucks and too serpentine for anyone in a hurry. Apart from a single farm building with its ragged herd of goats, there is nothing to see except steep and empty landscapes of gray rock and green scrub oak, polished into high definition by the extraordinary clarity of the light. The road slopes down through the foothills on the south side of the Lubéron before joining up with the amateur Grand Prix that takes place every day on the RN7, the *Nationale Sept* that has eliminated more motorists over the years than is comfortable to think about as one waits for a gap in the traffic.

The road leads into Aix at the end of the most handsome main street in France. The Cours Mirabeau is beautiful at any time of the year, but at its best between spring and autumn, when the plane trees form a pale green tunnel five hundred yards long. The diffused sunlight, the four fountains along the center of the Cours' length, the perfect proportions which follow da Vinci's rule to "let the street be as wide as the height of the houses"—the arrangement of space and trees and architecture is so pleasing that you hardly notice the cars.

Over the years, a nice geographical distinction has evolved between work and more frivolous activities. On the shady side of the street, appropriately, are the banks and insurance companies and property agents and lawyers. On the sunny side are the cafés.

I have liked almost every café that I have ever been to in France, even the ratty little ones in tiny villages where the flies are more plentiful than customers, but I have a soft spot for the sprawling cafés of the Cours Mirabeau, and the softest spot of all for the Deux Garçons. Successive generations of proprietors have put their profits under the mattress and resisted all thoughts of redecoration, which in France usually ends in a welter of plastic and awkward lighting, and the interior looks much the same as it must have looked fifty years ago.

The ceiling is high, and toasted to a caramel color by the smoke from a million cigarettes. The bar is burnished copper, the tables and chairs gleam with the patina bestowed by countless bottoms and elbows, and the waiters have aprons and flat feet, as all proper waiters should. It is dim and cool, a place for reflection and a quiet drink. And then there is the terrace, where the show takes place.

Aix is a university town, and there is clearly something in the curriculum that attracts pretty students. The terrace of the Deux Garçons is always full of them, and it is my theory that they are there for education rather than refreshment. They are taking a degree course in café deportment, with a syllabus divided into four parts.

One: The Arrival

One must always arrive as conspicuously as possible, preferably on the back of a crimson Kawasaki 750 motorcycle driven by a young man in head-to-toe black leather and three-day stubble. It is not done to stand on the pavement and wave him good-bye as he booms off down the Cours to visit his hairdresser. That is for *gauche* little girls from the Auvergne. The sophisticated student is too busy for sentiment. She is concentrating on the next stage.

Two: The Entrance

Sunglasses must be kept on until an acquaintance is identified at one of the tables, but one must not appear to be looking for company. Instead, the impression should be that one is heading into the café to make a phone call to one's titled Italian admirer, when—*quelle surprise!*—one sees a friend. The sunglasses can then be removed and the hair tossed while one is persuaded to sit down.

Three: Ritual Kissing

Everyone at the table must be kissed at least twice, often three times, and in special cases four times. Those being kissed should remain seated, allowing the new arrival to bend and swoop around the table, tossing her hair, getting in the way of the waiters, and generally making her presence felt.

Four: Table Manners

Once seated, sunglasses should be put back on to permit the discreet study of one's own reflection in the café windows—not for reasons of narcissism, but to check important details of technique: the way one lights a cigarette, or sucks the straw in a Perrier *menthe*, or nibbles daintily on a sugar lump. If these are satisfactory, the glasses can be adjusted downward so that they rest charmingly on the end of the nose, and attention can be given to the other occupants of the table.

This performance continues from mid-morning until early evening, and never fails to entertain me. I imagine there must be the occasional break for academic work in between these hectic periods of social study, but I have never seen a textbook darken the café tables, nor heard any discussion of higher calculus or political science. The students are totally absorbed in showing form, and the Cours Mirabeau is all the more decorative as a result.

It would be no hardship to spend most of the day café hopping, but as our trips to Aix are infrequent we feel a pleasant obligation to squeeze in as much as possible during the morning—to pick up a bottle of *eau-de-vie* from the man in the rue d'Italie and some cheeses from Monsieur Paul in the rue des Marseillais, to see what new nonsense is in the windows of the boutiques which are crammed, chic by jowl, next to older and less transient establishments in the narrow streets behind the

Cours, to join the crowds in the flower market, to take another look at the tiny, beautiful place d'Albertas, with its cobbles and its fountain, and to make sure that we arrive in the rue Frédéric Mistral while there are still seats to be had at Chez Gu.

There are larger, more decorative, and more gastronomically distinguished restaurants in Aix, but ever since we ducked into Gu one rainy day we have kept coming back. Gu himself presides over the room—a genial, noisy man with the widest, jauntiest, most luxuriant and ambitious mustache I have ever seen, permanently fighting gravity and the razor in its attempts to make contact with Gu's eyebrows. His son takes the orders and an unseen woman with a redoubtable voice—Madame Gu, perhaps—is audibly in charge of the kitchen. The customers are made up of local businessmen, the girls from Agnes B. round the corner, smart women with their shopping bags and dachshunds, and the occasional furtive and transparently illicit couple murmuring intently and ignoring their *aioli*. The wine is served in jugs, a good three-course meal costs 80 francs, and all the tables are taken by 12:30 every day.

As usual, our good intentions to have a quick and restrained lunch disappear with the first jug of wine, and, as usual, we justify our self-indulgence by telling each other that today is a holiday. We don't have businesses to get back to or diaries full of appointments, and our enjoyment is heightened, in a shamefully unworthy way, by the knowledge that the people around us will be back at their desks while we are still sitting over a second cup of coffee and deciding what to do next. There is more of Aix to see, but lunch dulls the appetite for sightseeing, and our bag of cheeses would take a smelly revenge on the way home if they were jostled through the heat of the afternoon. There is a vineyard outside Aix that I have been meaning to visit. Or there is a curiosity that we noticed on the way into town, a kind of medieval junkyard, littered with massive relics and wounded garden statuary. There, surely, we will find the old stone garden bench we've been looking for, and they'll probably pay us to take it away.

Matériaux d'Antan takes up a plot the size of an important cemetery by the side of the RN7. Unusually, in a country so determined to safeguard its possessions from robbers that it has the highest padlock population in Europe, the site was completely open to the road: no fences, no threatening notices, no greasy Alsatians on chains, and no sign of any proprietor. How trusting, we thought as we parked, to conduct a business without any obvious means of protecting the stock. And then we realized why the owner could afford to be so relaxed about security; nothing on display could have weighed less than five tons. It would have taken ten men and a hydraulic winch to lift anything, and a car transporter to take it away.

If we had been planning to build a replica of Versailles we could have done all our shopping there in one afternoon. A full-size bath, cut from a single slab of marble? Over in the corner, with brambles growing through the plug hole. A staircase for the entrance hall? There were three, of varying lengths, gracefully curved arrangements of worn stone steps, each step as large as a dining table. Great snakes of iron balustrading lay next to them, with or without the finishing touches of giant pineapples. There were entire balconies complete with gargoyles, marble cherubs the size of stout adults, who seemed to be suffering from mumps, terra-cotta amphorae eight feet long, lying in a drunken muddle on their sides, mill wheels, columns, architraves, and plinths. Everything one could imagine in stone, except a plain bench.

"Bonjour." A young man appeared from behind a scaled-up version of the Winged Victory of Samothrace and asked if he could help us. A bench? He hooked his index finger over the bridge of his nose while he thought, then shook his head apologetically. Benches were not his specialty. However, he did have an exquisite eighteenth-century gazebo in wrought iron, or, if we had a sufficiently large garden, there was a fine mock-Roman triumphal arch he could show us, ten meters high and wide enough for two chariots abreast. Such pieces were rare, he said. For a moment, we were tempted by the thought of Faustin driving

his tractor through a triumphal arch on his way to the vineyard, a wreath of olive leaves around his straw trilby, but my wife could see the impracticalities of a 250-ton impulse purchase. We left the young man with promises to come back if we ever bought a château.

The answering machine welcomed us home, winking its little red eye to show that people had been talking to it. There were three messages.

A Frenchman whose voice I didn't recognize conducted a suspicious, one-sided conversation, refusing to accept the fact that he was talking to a machine. Our message, asking callers to leave a number where they could be reached, set him off. Why must I give you my number when I am already talking to you? He waited for a reply, breathing heavily. Who is there? Why do you not answer? More heavy breathing. *Allo? Allo? Merde. Allo?* His allotted span on the tape ran out while he was in mid-grumble, and we never heard from him again.

Didier, brisk and businesslike, informed us that he and his team were ready to resume work, and would be attacking two rooms at the bottom of the house. *Normalement*, they would certainly arrive tomorrow, or perhaps the day after. And how many puppies did we want? Pénélope had fallen pregnant to a hairy stranger in Goult.

And then there was an English voice, a man we remembered meeting in London. He had seemed pleasant, but we hardly knew him. This was about to change, because he and his wife were going to drop in. He didn't say when, and he didn't leave a number. Probably, in the way of the itinerant English, they would turn up one day just before lunch. But we'd had a quiet month so far, with few guests and fewer builders, and we were ready for a little company.

They arrived at dusk, as we were sitting down to dinner in the courtyard—Ted and Susan, wreathed in apologies and loud in their enthusiasm for Provence, which they had never seen before, and for our house, our dogs, us, everything. It was all, so they said several times in the first few minutes, super. Their breathless jollity was disarming. They talked in tandem, a seamless dialogue which neither required nor allowed any contribution from us.

"Have we come at a bad time? Typical of us, I'm afraid."

"Absolutely typical. You must *loathe* people dropping in like this. A glass of wine would be lovely."

"Darling, look at the pool. Isn't it *pretty*."

"Did you know the post office in Ménerbes has a little map showing how to find you? *Les Anglais*, they call you, and they fish out this map from under the counter."

"We'd have been here earlier, except that we bumped into this sweet old man in the village . . ."

". . . well, his car, actually . . ."

"Yes, his car, but he was sweet about it, darling, wasn't he, and it wasn't really a shunt, more a scrape."

"So we took him into the café and bought him a drink . . ."

"Quite a few drinks, wasn't it, darling?"

"And some for those funny friends of his."

"Anyway, we're here now, and I must say it's *absolutely* lovely."

"And so kind of you to put up with us barging in on you like this."

They paused to drink some wine and catch their breath, looking around and making small humming noises of approval. My wife, acutely conscious of the slightest symptoms of undernourishment, noticed that Ted was eyeing our dinner, which was still untouched on the table. She asked if they would like to eat with us.

"Only if it's absolutely no trouble—just a crust and a scrap of cheese and maybe *one* more glass of wine."

Ted and Susan sat down, still chattering, and we brought out sausage, cheeses, salad, and some slices of the cold vegetable omelette called *crespaou* with warm, fresh tomato sauce. It was received with such rapture that I wondered how long it had been since their last meal, and what arrangements they had made for their next one.

"Where are you staying while you're down here?"

Ted filled his glass. Well, nothing had actually been booked—"Typical of us, absolutely typical"—but a little *auberge*, they thought, somewhere clean and simple and not too far away because they'd adore to see the house in the daytime if we could bear it. There must be half a dozen small hotels we could recommend.

There were, but it was past ten, getting close to bedtime in Provence, and not the moment to be banging on shuttered windows and locked doors and dodging the attentions of hotel guard dogs. Ted and Susan had better stay the night and find somewhere in the morning. They looked at each other, and began a duet of gratitude that lasted until their bags had been taken upstairs. They cooed a final good night from the guest-room window, and we could still hear them chirruping as we went off to bed. They were like two excited children, and we thought it would be fun to have them stay for a few days.

The barking of the dogs woke us just after three. They were intrigued by noises coming from the guest room, heads cocked at the sound of someone being comprehensively sick, interspersed with groans and the splash of running water.

I always find it difficult to know how best to respond to other people's ailments. I prefer to be left alone when I'm ill, remembering what an uncle had told me long ago. "Puke in private, dear boy," he had said. "Nobody else is interested in seeing what you ate." But there are other sufferers who are comforted by the sympathy of an audience.

The noises persisted, and I called upstairs to ask if there was anything we could do. Ted's worried face appeared around the door. Susan had eaten something. Poor old thing had a delicate stomach. All this excitement. There was nothing to be done except to let nature take its course, which it then loudly did again. We retreated to bed.

The thunder of falling masonry started shortly after seven. Didier had arrived as promised, and was limbering up with a sawed-off sledgehammer and an iron spike while his assistants tossed sacks of cement around and bullied the concrete mixer into life. Our invalid felt her way slowly down the stairs, clutching her brow against the din and the bright sunlight, but insisting that she was well enough for breakfast. She was wrong, and had to leave the table hurriedly to return to the bathroom. It was a perfect morning with no wind, no clouds, and a sky of true blue. We spent it finding a doctor who would come to the house, and then went shopping for suppositories in the pharmacy.

Over the next four or five days, we came to know the chemist well. The unlucky Susan and her stomach were at war. Garlic made her bilious. The local milk, admittedly rather curious stuff, put her bowels in an uproar. The oil, the butter, the water, the wine—nothing agreed with her, and twenty minutes in the sun turned her into a walking blister. She was allergic to the south.

It's not uncommon. Provence is such a shock to the northern system; everything is full-blooded. Temperatures are extreme, ranging from over a hundred degrees down to minus twenty. Rain, when it comes, falls with such abandon that it washes roads away and closes the autoroute. The Mistral is a brutal, exhausting wind, bitter in winter and harsh and dry in summer. The food is full of strong, earthy flavors that can overwhelm a digestion used to a less assertive diet. The wine is young and deceptive, easy to drink but sometimes higher in alcoholic content than older wines that are treated with more caution. The combined effects of the food and climate, so different from England, take time to get used to. There is nothing bland about Provence, and it can poleaxe people as it had poleaxed Susan. She and Ted left us to convalesce in more temperate surroundings.

Their visit made us realize how fortunate we were to have the constitutions of goats and skins that accepted the sun. The routine of our days had changed, and we were living outdoors. Getting dressed took thirty seconds. There were fresh figs and melons for breakfast, and errands were done early, before the warmth of the sun turned to heat in mid-morning. The flagstones around the pool were hot to the touch, the water still cool enough to bring us up from the first dive with a gasp. We slipped into the habit of that sensible Mediterranean indulgence, the siesta.

The wearing of socks was a distant memory. My watch stayed in a drawer, and I found that I could more or less tell the time by the position of the shadows in the courtyard, although I seldom knew what the date was. It didn't seem important. I was turning into a contented vegetable, maintaining sporadic contact with real life through telephone conversations with people in faraway offices. They always asked wistfully what the weather was like, and were not pleased with the answer. They consoled themselves by warning me about skin cancer and the addling effect of sun on the brain. I didn't argue with them; they were probably right. But addled, wrinkled, and potentially cancerous as I might have been, I had never felt better.

The masons were working stripped to the waist, enjoying the weather as much as we were. Their main concession to the heat was a slightly extended lunch break, which was monitored to the minute by our dogs. At the first sound of hampers being opened and plates and cutlery coming out, they would cross the courtyard at a dead run and take their places by the table, something they never did with us. Patient and unblinking, they would watch every mouthful with underprivileged expressions. Invariably, it worked. At the end of lunch they would skulk back to their lairs under the rosemary hedge, their cheeks bulging guiltily with Camembert or cous-cous. Didier claimed that it fell off the table.

Work on the house was going according to schedule—that is, each room was taking three months from the day the masons moved in to the day that we could move in. And we had the prospect of Menicucci and his radiators to look forward to in August. In another place, in less perfect weather, it would have been depressing, but not here. The sun was a great tranquilizer, and time passed in a haze of well-being; long, slow, almost torpid days when it was so enjoyable to be alive that nothing else mattered. We had been told that the weather often continued like this until the end of October. We had also been told that July and August were the two months when sensible residents left Provence for somewhere quieter and less crowded, like Paris. Not us.

JULY

MY FRIEND had rented a house in Ramatuelle, a few kilometers from Saint-Tropez. We wanted to see each other, despite a mutual reluctance to brave the bad-tempered congestion of high summer traffic. I lost the toss, and said I'd be there by lunchtime.

After driving for half an hour I found myself in a different country, inhabited mostly by trailers. They were wallowing toward the sea in monstrous shoals, decked out with curtains of orange and brown and window stickers commemorating past migrations. Groups of them rested in the parking areas by the side of the autoroute, shimmering with heat. Their owners, ignoring the open countryside behind them, set up picnic tables and chairs with a close and uninterrupted view of the passing trucks, and within easy breathing distance of the diesel fumes. As I turned off the autoroute to go down to Sainte-Maxime, I could see more trailers stretching ahead in a bulbous, swaying convoy, and I gave up any thoughts of an early lunch. The final five kilometers of the journey took an hour and a half. Welcome to the Côte d'Azur.

It used to be beautiful, and rare and expensive pockets of it still are. But compared with the peace and relative emptiness of the Lubéron it seemed like a madhouse, disfigured by overbuilding, overcrowding, and overselling: villa developments, *steack pommes frites*, inflatable rubber boats, genuine Provençal souvenirs made from olive wood, pizzas, water-skiing lessons, nightclubs, go-kart tracks—the posters were everywhere, offering everything.

The people whose business it is to make a living from the Côte d'Azur have a limited season, and their eagerness to take your money before autumn comes and the demand for inflatable rubber boats stops is palpable and unpleasant. Waiters are impatient for their tips, shopkeepers snap at your heels so that you won't take too long to make up your mind, and then refuse to accept 200-franc notes because there are so many forgeries. A hostile cupidity hangs in the air, as noticeable as the smell of Ambre Solaire and garlic. Strangers are automatically classified as tourists and treated like nuisances, inspected with unfriendly eyes and tolerated for cash. According to the map, this was still Provence. It wasn't the Provence I knew.

My friend's house was in the pine forests outside Ramatuelle, at the end of a long private track, completely detached from the lunacy three kilometers away on the coast. He was not surprised to hear that a two-hour drive had taken more than four hours. He told me that to be sure of a parking spot for dinner in Saint-Tropez it was best to be there by 7:30 in the morning, that going down to the beach was an exercise in frustration, and that the only guaranteed way to get to Nice airport in time to catch a plane was by helicopter.

As I drove back home in the evening against the trailer tide,

I wondered what it was about the Côte d'Azur that continued to attract such hordes every summer. From Marseilles to Monte Carlo, the roads were a nightmare and the seashore was covered with a living carpet of bodies broiling in the sun, flank to oily flank for mile after mile. Selfishly, I was glad they wanted to spend their holidays there rather than in the open spaces of the Lubéron, among more agreeable natives.

Some natives, of course, were less agreeable than others, and I met one the next morning. Massot was *en colère*, kicking at the undergrowth in the small clearing near his house and chewing at his mustache in vexation.

"You see this?" he said. "Those *salauds*. They come like thieves in the night and leave early in the morning. *Saloperie* everywhere." He showed me two empty sardine cans and a wine bottle which proved beyond any reasonable doubt that his arch-enemies, the German campers, had been trespassing in his private section of the national park. That in itself was bad enough, but the campers had treated his elaborate defense system with contempt, rolling back boulders to make a gap in the barricade and —*sales voleurs!*—stealing the notices that warned of the presence of vipers.

Massot took off his jungle cap and rubbed the bald spot on the back of his head as he considered the enormity of the crime. He looked in the direction of his house, standing on tiptoe first on one side of the path, then on the other. He grunted.

"It might work," he said, "but I'd have to cut down the trees."

If he removed the small forest that stood between his house and the clearing, he would be able to see the headlights of any car coming down the track and loose off a couple of warning shots from his bedroom window. But, then again, those trees were extremely valuable, and added to the general desirability of the house he was trying to sell. No buyer had yet been found, but it was only a matter of time before somebody recognized it for the bargain it was. The trees had better stay. Massot thought again, and suddenly brightened up. Maybe the answer was *pièges à feu*. Yes, he liked that.

I had heard about *pièges à feu*, and they sounded horrendous —concealed snares that exploded when they were disturbed, like miniature mines. The thought of fragments of German camper flying through the air was alarming to me, but clearly very amusing to Massot, who was pacing round the clearing saying *boum!* every three or four yards as he planned his mine field.

Surely he wasn't serious, I said, and in any case I thought that *pièges à feu* were illegal. Massot stopped his explosions and tapped the side of his nose, sly and conspiratorial.

"That may be true," he said, "but there's no law against notices." He grinned, and raised both arms above his head. "*Boum!*"

Where were you twenty years ago, I thought, when they needed you on the Côte d'Azur?

Perhaps Massot's antisocial instincts were being intensified by the heat. It was often in the nineties by mid-morning, and the sky turned from blue to a burnt white by noon. Without consciously thinking about it, we adjusted to the temperature by getting up earlier and using the cool part of the day to do anything energetic. Any sudden or industrious activity between midday and early evening was out of the question; like the dogs, we sought out the shade instead of the sun. Cracks appeared in the earth, and the grass gave up trying to grow. For long periods during the day the only sounds were those made by the *cigales* round the house, the bees in the lavender, and bodies toppling into the pool.

I walked the dogs each morning between six and seven, and they discovered a new sport, more rewarding than chasing rabbits and squirrels. It had started when they came across what they thought was a large animal made of bright blue nylon. Circling it at a safe distance, they barked until it stirred and finally woke. A rumpled face appeared from one end, followed a few moments later by a hand offering a biscuit. From then on, the sight of a sleeping bag among the trees meant food. For the campers, it must have been disquieting to wake up and see two whiskery faces only inches away, but they were amiable enough about it once they had recovered from the shock.

Strangely enough, Massot was half-right. They were mostly Germans, but not the indiscriminate rubbish-tippers that he complained about. These Germans left no trace; everything was bundled into giant backpacks before they shuffled off like two-legged snails into the heat of the day. In my short experience of litter in the Lubéron, the French themselves were the most likely offenders, but no Frenchman would accept that. At any time of the year, but particularly in the summer, it was well known that foreigners of one stripe or another were responsible for causing most of the problems in life.

The Belgians, so it was said, were to blame for the majority of accidents because of their habit of driving in the middle of the road, forcing the famously prudent French driver into ditches to avoid being *écrasé*. The Swiss and the noncamping section of the German population were guilty of monopolizing hotels and restaurants and pushing up property prices. And the English —ah, the English. They were renowned for the frailty of their digestive systems and their preoccupation with drains and plumbing. "They have a talent for diarrhea," a French friend observed. "If an Englishman hasn't got it, he is looking for somewhere to have it."

There is just enough of a hint of truth in these national insults to sustain their currency, and I was witness to an interlude in one of Cavaillon's busiest cafés that must have confirmed the French in their opinion of English sensitivities.

A couple with their small son were having coffee, and the boy indicated his need to go to the lavatory. The father looked up from his two-day-old copy of the *Daily Telegraph*.

"You'd better make sure it's all right," he said to the boy's mother. "Remember what happened in Calais?"

The mother sighed, and made her way dutifully into the

gloom at the rear of the café. When she reappeared it was at high speed, and she looked as if she had just eaten a lemon.

"It's *disgusting*. Roger is not to go in there."

Roger became immediately interested in exploring a forbidden lavatory.

"I've got to go," he said, and played his trump card. "It's number two. I've got to go."

"There isn't even a seat. It's just a *hole*."

"I don't care. I've got to go."

"You'll have to take him," said the mother. "I'm not going in there again."

The father folded his newspaper and stood up, with young Roger tugging at his hand.

"You'd better take the newspaper," said the mother.

"I'll finish it when I get back."

"There's no paper," she hissed.

"Ah. Well, I'll try to save the crossword."

The minutes passed, and I was wondering if I could ask the mother exactly what had happened in Calais, when there was a loud exclamation from the back of the café.

"Poo!"

It was the emerging Roger, followed by his ashen-faced father holding the remnants of his newspaper. Conversation in the café stopped as Roger gave an account of the expedition at the top of his voice. The *patron* looked at his wife and shrugged. Trust the English to make a spectacle out of a simple visit to the *wa-wa*.

The equipment that had caused such consternation to Roger and his parents was a *toilette à la Turque*, which is a shallow porcelain tray with a hole in the middle and footrests at each side. It was designed, presumably by a Turkish sanitary engineer, for maximum inconvenience, but the French had added a refinement of their own—a high-pressure flushing device of such velocity that unwary users can find themselves soaked from the shins down. There are two ways of avoiding sodden feet: the first is to operate the flushing lever from the safety of dry land in the doorway, but since this requires long arms and the balance of an acrobat, the second option—not to flush at all—is unfortunately much more prevalent. To add to the problem, some establishments install an energy-saving device which is peculiar to the French. The light switch, always located on the outside of the lavatory door, is fitted with an automatic timer that plunges the occupant into darkness after thirty-eight seconds, thus saving precious electricity and discouraging loiterers.

Amazingly enough, *à la Turque* lavatories are still being manufactured, and the most modern café is quite likely to have a chamber of horrors in the back. But, when I mentioned this to Monsieur Menicucci, he leapt to the defense of French sanitary ware, insisting that at the other end of the scale were lavatories of such sophistication and ergonometric perfection that *even an American* would be impressed. He suggested a meeting to discuss two lavatories we needed for the house. He had some marvels to show us, he said, and we would be ravished by the choice.

He arrived with a valise full of catalogues, and unloaded them onto the table in the courtyard as he made some mystifying remarks about vertical or horizontal evacuation. As he had said, there was a wide choice, but they were all aggressively modern in design and color—squat, sculptural objects in deep burgundy or burnt apricot. We were looking for something simple and white.

"*C'est pas facile,*" he said. People nowadays wanted new forms and colors. It was all part of the French sanitary revolution. The traditional white was not favored by the designers. There was, however, one model he had seen recently which might be exactly what we wanted. He rummaged through his catalogues and—yes, he was sure of it—this was the one for us.

"*Voilà! Le W.C. haute couture!*" He pushed the catalogue over to us and there, lit and photographed like an Etruscan vase, was the Pierre Cardin lavatory.

"You see?" said Menicucci. "It is even signed by Cardin."
And so it was, up on the top and well out of harm's way. Apart
from the signature it was perfect, a handsome design that looked
like a lavatory and not like a giant goldfish bowl. We ordered two.

It was a saddened Menicucci who telephoned a week later
to tell us that the House of Cardin no longer made our lavatories.
Une catastrophe but he would continue his researches.

A further ten days passed before he reappeared, now in
triumph, coming up the steps to the house waving another catalogue above his head.

"*Toujours couture!*" he said. "*Toujours couture!*"

Cardin may have left the bathroom, but his place had been
taken by the gallant Courrèges, whose design was very similar
and who had exercised remarkable restraint in the matter of the
signature, leaving it off altogether. We congratulated Menicucci,
and he allowed himself a celebratory Coca-Cola. He raised his
glass.

"Today the lavatories, tomorrow the central heating," he
said, and we sat for a while in the 90-degree sunshine while he
told us how warm we were going to be and went through his plan
of attack. Walls were to be broken, dust would be everywhere,
the noise of the jackhammer would take over from the bees and
the crickets. There was only one bright spot about it, said Menicucci. It would keep the guests away for a few weeks. *Eh, oui.*

But before this period of enforced and ear-splitting seclusion
we were expecting one last guest, a man so maladroit and disaster-
prone, so absentminded and undomesticated, so consistently involved in household accidents that we had specifically asked him
to come on the eve of demolition so that the debris of his visit
could be buried under the rubble of August. It was Bennett, a
close friend for fifteen years who cheerfully admitted to being
the World's Worst Guest. We loved him, but with apprehension.

He called from the airport, several hours after he was due
to arrive. Could I come down and pick him up? There had been
a slight problem with the car hire company, and he was stranded.

I found him in the upstairs bar at Marignane, comfortably installed with a bottle of champagne and a copy of the French edition of *Playboy*. He was in his late forties, slim and extremely good-looking, dressed in an elegant suit of off-white linen with badly scorched trousers. "Sorry to drag you out," he said, "but they've run out of cars. Have some champagne."

He told me what had happened and, as usual with Bennett, it was all so unlikely that it had to be true. The plane had arrived on time, and the car he had reserved, a convertible, was waiting for him. The top was down, it was a glorious afternoon and Bennett, in an expansive mood, had lit a cigar before heading toward the autoroute. It had burned quickly, as cigars do when fanned by a strong breeze, and Bennett had tossed it away after twenty minutes. He became aware that passing motorists were waving at him, so in return he waved to them; how friendly the French have become, he thought. He was some miles up the autoroute before he realized that the back of the car was burning, set on fire by the discarded cigar butt that had lodged in the upholstery. With what he thought was tremendous presence of mind, he pulled on to the hard shoulder, stood up on the front seat, and urinated into the flames. And that was when the police had found him.

"They were terribly nice," he said, "but they thought it would be best if I brought the car back to the airport, and then the car rental people had a fit and wouldn't give me another one."

He finished his champagne and gave me the bill. What with all the excitement, he said, he hadn't managed to change his traveler's checks. It was good to see him again, still the same as ever, charming, terminally clumsy, beautifully dressed, permanently short of funds. My wife and I had once pretended to be his maid and manservant at a dinner party when we were all so broke that we shared out the tip afterwards. We always had fun with Bennett, and dinner that night lasted into the early hours of the morning.

The week passed as uneventfully as could be expected, given

that our guest was a man who could, and often did, spill his drink over himself while looking at his watch, and whose immaculate white trousers never survived the first course of dinner unsoiled. There were one or two breakages, the odd drowned towel in the swimming pool, a sudden panic when he realized that he had sent his passport to the dry cleaners, some worrying moments when he thought he had eaten a wasp, but no true calamities. We were sad to see him go, and hoped he would come back soon to finish the four half-empty glasses of Calvados we found under his bed, and to pick up the underpants that he had left hanging decoratively from the hat rack.

IT WAS BERNARD who had told us about the old station café in Bonnieux. Solid and serious was how he described it, a family restaurant of the kind that used to exist all over France before food became fashionable and *bistrots* started serving slivers of duckling instead of *daube* and tripe. Go soon, Bernard said, because *la patronne* talks about retiring, and take a big appetite with you. She likes to see clean plates.

The station at Bonnieux has been closed for more than forty years, and the path that leads to it is potholed and neglected. From the road there is nothing to see—no signs, no menus. We had passed by dozens of times, assuming that the building was unoccupied, not knowing that a crowded car park was hidden behind the trees.

We found a space between the local ambulance and a mason's scarred truck, and stood for a moment listening to the clatter of dishes and the murmur of conversation that came through the open windows. The restaurant was fifty yards from the station, foursquare and unpretentious, with faded lettering just legible in hand-painted capitals: Café de la Gare.

A small Renault van pulled into the car park, and two men in overalls got out. They washed their hands at the old sink against the outside wall, using the yellow banana of soap that was mounted over the taps on its bracket, and elbowed the door open, hands still wet. They were regulars, and went straight to the towel that hung from a hook at the end of the bar. By the time they had dried their hands two glasses of pastis and a jug of water were waiting for them.

It was a big, airy room, dark at the front and sunny at the back, where windows looked over fields and vineyards toward the hazy bulk of the Lubéron. There must have been forty people, all men, already eating. It was only a few minutes past noon, but the Provençal has a clock in his stomach, and lunch is his sole concession to punctuality. *On mange à midi*, and not a moment later.

Each table had its white paper cover and two unlabeled bottles of wine, a red and a pink, from the Bonnieux cooperative two hundred yards away on the other side of the road. There was no written menu. Madame cooked five meals a week, lunch from Monday to Friday, and customers ate what she decided they would eat. Her daughter brought us a basket of good, chewy bread, and asked us if we wanted water. No? Then we must tell her when we wanted more wine.

Most of the other customers seemed to know one another, and there were some spirited and insulting exchanges among the tables. An enormous man was accused of slimming. He looked up from his plate and stopped eating long enough to growl. We saw our electrician and Bruno, who lays the stone floors, eating together in a corner, and recognized two or three other faces that we hadn't seen since work had stopped on the house. The men were sunburned, looking fit and relaxed as if they had been on holiday. One of them called across to us.

"*C'est tranquille chez vous?* Peaceful without us?"

We said we hoped they would be coming back when work started again in August.

"*Normalement, oui.*" The hand waggled. We knew what that meant.

Madame's daughter returned with the first course, and explained that it was a light meal today because of the heat. She put down an oval dish covered with slices of *saucisson* and cured ham, with tiny gherkins, some black olives, and grated carrots in a sharp marinade. A thick slice of white butter to dab on the *saucisson*. More bread.

Two men in jackets came in with a dog and took the last empty table. There was a rumor, so Madame's daughter said, that the older of the two men had been the French ambassador to a country in the Middle East. *Un homme distingué.* He sat there among the masons and plumbers and truck drivers, feeding his dog small pieces of sausage.

Salad arrived in glass bowls, the lettuce slick with dressing, and with it another oval dish. Noodles in a tomato sauce and slices of roast loin of pork, juicy in a dark onion gravy. We tried to imagine what Madame would serve up in the winter, when she wasn't toying with these light meals, and we hoped that she would have second thoughts about retiring. She had taken up her position behind the bar, a short, comfortably proportioned woman, her hair still dark and thick. She looked as though she could go on forever.

Her daughter cleared away, emptied the last of the red wine into our glasses and, unasked, brought another bottle with the cheese. The early customers were starting to leave to go back to work, wiping their mustaches and asking Madame what she proposed to give them tomorrow. Something good, she said.

I had to stop after the cheese. My wife, who has never yet been defeated by a menu, had a slice of *tarte au citron*. The room began to smell of coffee and Gitanes, and the sun coming through the window turned the smoke blue as it drifted above the heads of the three men sitting over thimble-sized glasses of *marc*. We ordered coffee and asked for a bill, but bills were not part of the routine. Customers settled up at the bar on the way out.

Madame told us what we owed. Fifty francs each for the food, and four francs for the coffee. The wine was included in the price. No wonder the place was full every day.

Was it really true she was going to retire?

She stopped polishing the bar. "When I was a little girl," she said, "I had to choose whether to work in the fields or in the kitchen. Even in those days I hated the land. It's hard, dirty work." She looked down at her hands, which were well kept and surprisingly young-looking. "So I chose the kitchen, and when I married we moved here. I've been cooking for thirty-eight years. It's enough."

We said how sorry we were, and she shrugged.

"One becomes tired." She was going to live in Orange, she said, in an apartment with a balcony, and sit in the sun.

It was two o'clock, and the room was empty except for an old man with white stubble on his leather cheeks, dipping a sugar lump into his Calvados. We thanked Madame for a fine lunch.

"*C'est normal*," she said.

The heat outside was like a blow on the skull and the road back to the house was a long mirage, liquid and rippling in the glare, the leaves on the vines drooping, the farm dogs silent, the countryside stunned and deserted. It was an afternoon for the pool and the hammock and an undemanding book, a rare afternoon without builders or guests, and it seemed to pass in slow motion.

By the evening, our skins prickling from the sun, we were sufficiently recovered from lunch to prepare for the sporting event of the week. We had accepted a challenge from some friends who, like us, had become addicted to one of the most pleasant games ever invented, and we were going to try to uphold the honor of Ménerbes on the *boules* court.

Long before, during a holiday, we had bought our first set of *boules* after watching the old men in Roussillon spend an enjoyably argumentative afternoon on the village court below the post office. We had taken our *boules* back to England, but it is not a game that suits the damp, and they gathered cobwebs in a barn. They had been almost the first things we unpacked when we came to live in Provence. Smooth and tactile, they fitted into the palm of the hand, heavy, dense, gleaming spheres of steel that made a satisfying *chock* when tapped together.

We studied the techniques of the professionals who played every day next to the church at Bonnieux—men who could drop a *boule* on your toe from twenty feet away—and came home to practice what we had seen. The true aces, we noticed, bent their knees in a crouch and held the *boule* with the fingers curled around and the palm facing downward, so that when the *boule* was thrown, friction from the fingers provided backspin. And there were the lesser elements of style—the grunts and encouragements that helped every throw on its way, and the shrugs and muttered oaths when it landed short or long. We soon became experts in everything except accuracy.

There were two basic types of delivery: the low, rolling throw that skittered along the ground, or the high-trajectory drop shot, aimed to knock the opponent's *boule* off the court. The precision of some of the players we watched was remarkable, and for all our crouching and grunting it would take years of applied effort before we would be welcomed to a serious court like the one in Bonnieux.

Boules is an essentially simple game, which a beginner can enjoy from the first throw. A small wooden ball, the *cochonnet*, is tossed up the court. Each player has three *boules*, identified by different patterns etched into the steel, and at the end of the round the closest to the *cochonnet* is the winner. There are different systems of scoring, and all kinds of local bylaws and variations. These, if carefully planned, can be of great advantage to the home team.

We were playing on our own court that evening, and the game was therefore subject to Lubéron Rules:

1. Anyone playing without a drink is disqualified.
2. Incentive cheating is permitted.
3. Disputes concerning the distance from the *cochonnet* are mandatory. Nobody's word is final.

4. Play stops when darkness falls unless there is no clear winner, in which case blind man's *boules* are played until there is a torchlight decision or the *cochonnet* is lost.

We had gone to some trouble to construct a court with deceptive slopes and shallow hollows to baffle visitors, and had roughened the playing surface so that our luck would have a sporting chance against superior skill. We were quietly confident, and I had the added advantage of being in charge of the pastis; any signs of consistent accuracy from the visiting team would be countered by bigger drinks, and I knew from personal experience what big drinks did to one's aim.

Our opponents included a girl of sixteen who had never played before, but the other three had at least six weeks of practice between them, and were not to be treated lightly. As we inspected the playing surface, they made disparaging comments about its lack of regularity, complained about the angle of the setting sun, and made a formal request for dogs to be banned from the court. The old stone roller was trundled up and down to humor them. Moistened fingers were held in the air to gauge the strength of the breeze, and play commenced.

There is a distinct, if slow, rhythm to the game. A throw is made, and play stops while the next to throw strolls up for a closer look and tries to decide whether to bomb or whether to attempt a low, creeping delivery that will sidle round the other *boules* to kiss the *cochonnet*. A contemplative sip of pastis is taken, the knees are flexed, the *boule* loops through the air, thuds to earth, and rolls with a soft crunching sound to its resting place. There are no hurried movements and almost no sporting injuries. (One exception being Bennett, who had scored a broken roof tile and self-inflicted concussion of the toe during his first and last game.)

Intrigue and gamesmanship make up for the lack of athletic drama, and the players that evening behaved abominably. *Boules* were moved by stealth, with accidental nudges of the foot. Players poised to throw were distracted by comments on their stance, offers of more pastis, accusations of stepping over the throwing line, warnings of dogs crossing the court, sightings of imaginary grass snakes, and conflicting bad advice from every side. There were no clear winners at halftime, when we stopped to watch the sunset.

To the west of the house, the sun was centered in the V made by two mountain peaks in a spectacular display of natural symmetry. Within five minutes it was over, and we played on in the *crépuscule*, the French word that makes twilight sound like a skin complaint. Measuring distances from the *cochonnet* became more difficult and more contentious, and we were about to agree on a dishonorable draw when the young girl whose first game it was put three *boules* in a nine-inch group. Foul play and alcohol had been defeated by youth and fruit juice.

We ate out in the courtyard, the flagstones sun-warm under our bare feet, the candlelight flickering on red wine and brown faces. Our friends had rented their house to an English family for August, and they were going to spend the month in Paris on the proceeds. According to them, all the Parisians would be down in Provence, together with untold thousands of English, Germans, Swiss, and Belgians. Roads would be jammed; markets and restaurants impossibly full. Quiet villages would become noisy, and everyone without exception would be in a filthy humor. We had been warned.

We had indeed. We had heard it all before. But July had been far less terrible than predicted, and we were sure that August could be dealt with very easily. We would unplug the phone, lie down by the pool, and listen, whether we liked it or not, to the concerto for jackhammer and blowtorch, conducted by Maestro Menicucci.

AUGUST

"THERE IS a strong rumor," said Menicucci, "that Brigitte Bardot has bought a house in Roussillon." He put his spanner down on the wall and moved closer so that there was no chance of *jeune* overhearing any more of Miss Bardot's personal plans.

"She intends to leave Saint-Tropez." Menicucci's finger was poised to tap me on the chest. "And I don't blame her. Do you know"—tap, tap, tap went the finger—"that at any given moment during any day in the month of August there are five thousand people making *pipi* in the sea?"

He shook his head at the unsanitary horror of it all. "Who would be a fish?"

We stood in the sun sympathizing with the plight of any marine life unfortunate enough to be resident in Saint-Tropez while *jeune* toiled up the steps carrying a cast-iron radiator, a garland of copper piping slung around his shoulders, his Yale University T-shirt dark with sweat. Menicucci had made a significant sartorial concession to the heat, and had discarded his usual heavy corduroy trousers in favor of a pair of brown shorts that matched his canvas boots.

It was the opening day of *les grands travaux*, and the area in front of the house resembled a scrapyard. Piled around an oily workbench of great antiquity were some of the elements of our central heating system—boxes of brass joints, valves, soldering guns, gas canisters, hacksaws, radiators, drilling bits, washers and spanners, and cans of what looked like black treacle. This was only the first delivery; the water tank, the fuel tank, the boiler, and the burner were still to come.

Menicucci took me on a guided tour of the components, emphasizing their quality. *"C'est pas de la merde, ça."* He then pointed out which walls he was going to burrow through, and full realization of the weeks of dust and chaos ahead sunk in. I almost wished I could spend August in Saint-Tropez with the half-million incontinent holidaymakers already there.

They and millions more had come down from the north in the course of a single massively constipated weekend. Twenty-mile traffic jams had been reported on the autoroute at Beaune, and anyone getting through the tunnel at Lyon in less than an hour was considered lucky. Cars and tempers became overheated. The breakdown trucks had their best weekend of the year. Fatigue and impatience were followed by accidents and death. It was a traditionally awful start to the month, and the ordeal would be repeated four weeks later in the opposite direction during the exodus weekend.

Most of the invaders passed us by on their way to the coast, but there were thousands who made their way into the Lubéron, changing the character of markets and villages and giving the local inhabitants something new to philosophize about over their pastis. Café regulars found their usual places taken by foreigners, and stood by the bar grizzling over the inconveniences of the holiday season—the bakery running out of bread, the car parked outside one's front door, the strange late hours that visitors kept. It was admitted, with much nodding and sighing, that tourists brought money into the region. Nevertheless, it was generally agreed that they were a funny bunch, these natives of August.

It was impossible to miss them. They had clean shoes and indoor skins, bright new shopping baskets and spotless cars. They drifted through the streets of Lacoste and Ménerbes and Bonnieux in a sightseer's trance, looking at the people of the village as if they too were quaint rustic monuments. The beauties of nature were loudly praised every evening on the ramparts of Ménerbes, and I particularly liked the comments of an elderly English couple as they stood looking out over the valley.

"What a marvelous sunset," she said.

"Yes," replied her husband. "Most impressive for such a small village."

Even Faustin was in fine holiday humor. His work on the vines was finished for the time being, and there was nothing he could do but wait for the grapes to ripen and try out his repertoire of English jokes on us. "What is it," he asked me one morning, "that changes from the color of a dead rat to the color of a dead lobster in three hours?" His shoulders started to shake as he tried to suppress his laughter at the unbearably funny answer. "*Les Anglais en vacances,*" he said, "*vous comprenez?*" In case I hadn't fully grasped the richness of the joke, he then explained very carefully that the English complexion was known to be so fair that the slightest exposure would turn it bright red. "*Même sous un rayon de lune,*" he said, shuddering with mirth, "even a moonbeam makes them pink."

Faustin in waggish mood early in the morning was transformed into Faustin the somber by the evening. He had heard news from the Côte d'Azur, which he told to us with a terrible relish. There had been a forest fire near Grasse, and the Canadair planes had been called out. These operated like pelicans, flying out to sea and scooping up a cargo of water to drop on the flames inland. According to Faustin, one of the planes had scooped up a swimmer and dropped him into the fire, where he had been *carbonisé*.

Curiously, there was no mention of the tragedy in *Le Provençal*, and we asked a friend if he had heard anything about it. He looked at us and shook his head. "It's the old August story," he said. "Every time there's a fire someone starts a rumor like that. Last year they said a water-skier had been picked up. Next year it could be a doorman at the Negresco in Nice. Faustin was pulling your leg."

It was difficult to know what to believe. Odd things were possible in August, and so we were not at all surprised when some friends who were staying in a nearby hotel told us that they had seen an eagle at midnight in their bedroom. Well, perhaps not the eagle itself, but the unmistakable and huge *shadow* of an eagle. They called the man on night duty at the desk, and he came up to their room to investigate.

Did the eagle seem to come from the wardrobe in the corner of the room? Yes, said our friends. *Ah bon*, said the man, the mystery is solved. He is not an eagle. He is a bat. He has been seen leaving that wardrobe before. He is harmless. Harmless he may be, said our friends, but we would prefer not to sleep with a bat, and we would like another room. *Non*, said the man. The hotel is full. The three of them stood in the bedroom and discussed bat-catching techniques. The man from the hotel had an idea. Stay there, he said. I shall return with the solution. He reappeared a few minutes later, gave them a large aerosol can of fly killer, and wished them good night.

THE PARTY was being held in a house outside Gordes, and we had been asked to join a few friends of the hostess for dinner before the other guests arrived. It was an evening that we anticipated with mixed feelings—pleased to be invited, but far from confident about our ability to stay afloat in a torrent of dinner party French. As far as we knew, we were going to be the only English speakers there, and we hoped we wouldn't be separated from each other by too many breakneck Provençal conversations. We had been asked to arrive at what for us was the highly sophisticated hour of nine o'clock, and we drove up the hill toward Gordes with stomachs rumbling at being kept waiting so late. The parking area behind the house was full. Cars lined the road outside for fifty yards, and every other car seemed to have a Parisian 75 number plate. Our fellow guests were not going to be a few friends from the village. We began to feel we should have worn less casual clothes.

We walked inside and found ourselves in magazine country, decorated by *House and Garden* and dressed by *Vogue*. Candlelit tables were arranged on the lawn and the terrace. Fifty or sixty people, cool and languid and wearing white, held glasses of champagne in jeweled fingers. The sound of Vivaldi came through the open doorway of a floodlit barn. My wife wanted to go home and change. I was conscious of my dusty shoes. We had blundered into a *soirée*.

Our hostess saw us before we could escape. She at least was reassuringly dressed in her usual outfit of shirt and trousers.

"You found somewhere to park?" She didn't wait for an answer. "It's a little difficult in the road because of that ditch."

We said it didn't seem at all like Provence, and she shrugged. "It's August." She gave us a drink and left us to mingle with the beautiful people.

We could have been in Paris. There were no brown, weathered faces. The women were fashionably pallid, the men carefully barbered and sleek. Nobody was drinking pastis. Conversation was, by Provençal standards, whisper-quiet. Our perceptions had definitely changed. At one time, this would have seemed normal. Now it seemed subdued and smart and vaguely uncomfortable. There was no doubt about it; we had turned into bumpkins.

We gravitated toward the least chic couple we could see, who were standing detached from the crowd with their dog. All three were friendly, and we sat down together at one of the tables on the terrace. The husband, a small man with a sharp, Norman face, told us that he had bought a house in the village twenty years before for 3,000 francs, and had been coming down every summer since then, changing houses every five or six years. He had just heard that his original house was back on the market, overrestored and decorated to death and priced at a million francs. "It's madness," he said, "but people like *le tout Paris*"—he nodded toward the other guests—"they want to be with their friends in August. When one buys, they all buy. And they pay Parisian prices."

They had begun to take their places at the tables, carrying bottles of wine and plates of food from the buffet. The women's high heels sank into the gravel of the terrace, and there were some refined squeals of appreciation at the deliciously primitive setting—*un vrai dîner sauvage*—even though it was only marginally more primitive than a garden in Beverly Hills or Kensington.

The Mistral started, suddenly and most inconveniently, while there was still plenty of uneaten shrimp salad on the tables. Lettuce leaves and scraps of bread became airborne, plucked from plates and blown among the snowy bosoms and silk trousers, scoring the occasional direct hit on a shirt front. Tablecloths snapped and billowed like sails, tipping over candles and wine-glasses. Carefully arranged coiffures and composures were ruffled. This was a little too *sauvage*. There was a hasty retreat, and dinner was resumed under shelter.

More people arrived. The sound of Vivaldi from the barn was replaced by a few seconds of electronic hissing, followed by the shrieks of a man undergoing heart surgery without anesthetic: Little Richard was inviting us to get down and boogie.

We were curious to see what effect the music would have on such an elegant gathering. I could imagine them nodding their heads in time to a civilized tune, or dancing in that intimate crouch the French adopt whenever they hear Charles Aznavour, but *this*—this was a great sweating squawk from the jungle.

AWOPBOPALOOWOPAWOPBAMBOOM! We climbed the steps to the barn to see what they would make of it.

Colored strobe lighting was flashing and blinking, synchronized with the drumbeat and bouncing off the mirrors propped against the walls. A young man, shoulders hunched and eyes half-closed against the smoke of his cigarette, stood behind the twin turntables, his fingers coaxing ever more bass and volume from the knobs on the console.

GOOD GOLLY MISS MOLLY! screamed Little Richard. The young man went into a spasm of delight, and squeezed out an extra decibel. *YOU SURE LOVE TO BALL!* The barn vibrated, and *le tout Paris* vibrated with it, arms and legs and buttocks and breasts jiggling and shaking and grinding and flailing around, teeth bared, eyes rolling, fists pumping the air, jewelery out of control, buttons bursting under the strain, elegant façades gone to hell as everyone writhed and jerked and twitched and *got down.*

Most of them didn't bother with partners. They danced with their own reflections, keeping one eye, even in the midst of ecstasy, fixed on the mirrors. The air was filled with the smell of warm and scented flesh, and the barn turned into one huge throb, seething and frenzied and difficult to cross without being spiked by elbows or lashed by a whirling necklace.

Were these the same people who had been behaving so decorously earlier in the evening, looking as though their idea of a wild time might be a second glass of champagne? They were bouncing away like amphetamine-stuffed teenagers, and they seemed set for the night. We dodged and sidestepped through the squirming mass and left them to it. We had to be up early in the morning. We had a goat race to go to.

We had first seen the poster a week before, taped to the window of a *tabac.* There was to be a *Grande Course de Chèvres* through the streets of Bonnieux, starting from the Café César. The ten runners and their drivers were listed by name. There were numerous prizes, bets could be placed, and, said the poster, animation would be assured by a grand orchestra. It was clearly going to be a sporting event of some magnitude, Bonnieux's answer to the Cheltenham Gold Cup or the Kentucky Derby. We arrived well before the race to be sure of a good position.

By nine o'clock it was already too hot to wear a watch, and the terrace in front of the Café César was spilling over with customers having their breakfast of *tartines* and cold beer. Against the wall of the steps leading down to the rue Voltaire, a large woman had established herself at a table, shaded by a parasol that advertised *Véritable Jus de Fruit*. She beamed at us, riffling a book of tickets and rattling a cash box. She was the official bookmaker, although there was a man taking off-track bets in the back of the café, and she invited us to try our luck. "Look before you bet," she said. "The runners are down there."

We knew they weren't far away; we could smell them and their droppings, aromatic as they cooked in the sun. We looked over the wall, and the contestants looked back at us with their mad, pale eyes, masticating slowly on some prerace treat, their chins fringed with wispy beards. They would have looked like dignified mandarins had it not been for the blue and white jockey caps that each of them was wearing, and their racing waistcoats, numbered to correspond with the list of runners. We were able to identify Bichou and Tisane and all the rest of them by name, but it was not enough to bet on. We needed inside information, or at least some help in assessing the speed and staying power of the runners. We asked the old man who was leaning on the wall next to us, confident in the knowledge that he, like every Frenchman, would be an expert.

"It's a matter of their *crottins*," he said. "The goats who make the most droppings before the race are likely to do well. An empty goat is faster than a full goat. *C'est logique.*" We studied form for a few minutes, and No. 6, Totoche, obliged with a generous effort. "*Voilà*," said our tipster, "now you must examine the drivers. Look for a strong one."

Most of the drivers were refreshing themselves in the café.

Like the goats, they were numbered and wore jockey caps, and we were able to pick out the driver of No. 6, a brawny, likely looking man who seemed to be pacing himself sensibly with the beer. He and the recently emptied Totoche had the makings of a winning team. We went to place our bet.

"*Non.*" Madame the bookmaker explained that we had to get first, second, and third in order to collect, which ruined our calculations. How could we know what the dropping rate had been while we were away looking at the drivers? A certainty had dwindled into a long shot, but we went for No. 6 to win, the only female driver in the race to come second, and a goat called Nénette, whose trim fetlocks indicated a certain fleetness of hoof, to come in third. Business done, we joined the sporting gentry in the little *place* outside the café.

The grand orchestra promised by the poster—a van from Apt with a sound system in the back—was broadcasting Sonny and Cher singing "I've Got You, Babe." A thin, high-chic Parisienne we recognized from the night before started to tap one dainty white-shod foot, and an unshaven man with a glass of pastis and a heavy paunch asked her to dance, swiveling his substantial hips as an inducement. The Parisienne gave him a look that could have turned butter rancid, and became suddenly interested in the contents of her Vuitton bag. Aretha Franklin took over from Sonny and Cher, and children played hopscotch among the goat droppings. The *place* was packed. We wedged ourselves between a German with a video camera and the man with the paunch to watch as the finishing line was prepared.

A rope was strung across the *place*, about eight feet above the ground. Large balloons, numbered from one to ten, were filled with water and tied at regular intervals along the length of the rope. Our neighbor with the paunch explained the rules: Each of the drivers was to be issued a sharp stick, which had two functions. The first was to provide a measure of encouragement for any goats reluctant to run; the second was to burst their balloons at the end of the race to qualify as finishers. *Evidemment*, he said, the drivers would get soaked, which would be droll.

The drivers had now emerged from the café, and were swaggering through the crowd to collect their goats. Our favorite driver, No. 6, had his pocket knife out, and was putting a fine point on each end of his stick, which I took to be a good sign. One of the other drivers immediately lodged a complaint with the organizers, but the dispute was cut short by the arrival of a car which had somehow managed to creep down through one of the narrow streets. A young woman got out. She was holding a map. She looked extremely puzzled. She asked the way to the autoroute.

The way to the autoroute, unfortunately, was blocked by ten goats, two hundred spectators, and a musical van. Nevertheless, said the young woman, that is where I am going. She got back in the car and started inching forward.

Consternation and uproar. The organizers and some of the drivers surrounded the car, banging on the roof, brandishing sticks, rescuing goats and children from certain death beneath the barely moving wheels. Spectators surged forward to see what was going on. The car, embedded in humanity, was forced to stop, and the young woman sat looking straight ahead, tight-lipped with exasperation. *Reculez!* shouted the organizers, pointing back in the direction the car had come from, and waving at the crowd to make way. With a vicious crunch of gears, the car reversed, whining angrily up the street to the sound of applause.

The contestants were called to the starting line, and drivers checked the fastening of the cords around the goats' necks. The goats themselves were unaffected by the drama of the occasion. No. 6 was trying to eat the waistcoat worn by No. 7. No. 9, our outsider, Nénette, insisted on facing backwards. The driver picked her up by her horns and turned her around, jamming her between his knees to keep her pointing in the right direction. Her jockey cap had been knocked over one eye, giving her a rakish and demented air, and we wondered about the wisdom of our bet. We were counting on her to take third place, but with impaired vision and no sense of geography this seemed unlikely.

They were under starter's orders. Weeks, maybe months, of training had prepared them for this moment. Horn to horn, waistcoat to waistcoat, they waited for the starting signal. One of the drivers belched loudly, and they were off.

Within fifty yards, it became apparent that these goats were not instinctive athletes, or else they had misunderstood the purpose of the event. Two of them applied their brakes firmly after a few yards, and had to be dragged along. Another remembered what it should have done half an hour before, and paused at the first bend to answer a call of nature. Nénette, possibly because she was half-blinkered by her cap, overshot the turn and pulled her driver into the crowd. The other runners straggled up the hill, stimulated by various methods of persuasion.

"Kick them up the arse!" shouted our friend with the paunch. The Parisienne, who was hemmed in next to us, winced. This encouraged him to give her the benefit of his local knowledge. "Did you know," he said, "that the last one to finish gets eaten? Roasted on a spit. *C'est vrai.*" The Parisienne pulled her sunglasses from their nest in her hair and put them on. She didn't look well.

The course followed a circuit around the high part of the village, looping back down to the old fountain which had been transformed into a water obstacle with a plastic sheet stretched between some hay bales. This had to be waded or swum just before the final sprint to the line of balloons outside the café— a brutal test of coordination and stamina.

Progress reports were being shouted down by spectators at the halfway mark, and news reached us that No. 1 and No. 6 were fighting it out in the lead. Only nine goats had been counted going past; the tenth had *disparu.* "Probably having its throat cut," said the man with the paunch to the Parisienne. She made a determined effort, and pushed through the crowd to find less offensive company near the finishing line.

There was a splash from the fountain, and the sound of a woman's voice raised to scold. The water obstacle had claimed its first victim—a little girl who had miscalculated the depth, and who stood waist-deep in the water, bedraggled and bawling with surprise.

"Elles viennent, les chèvres!"

The girl's mother, in desperation at the thought of her child being trampled to a pulp by the contestants, hitched up her skirt and plunged into the water. "What thighs!" said the man with the paunch, kissing the tips of his fingers.

With a clatter of hoofs, the leading runners approached the fountain and skidded into the hay bales, showing very little enthusiasm for getting wet. Their drivers grunted and cursed and tugged and finally manhandled their goats into the water and out the other side to the finishing straight, their sodden espadrilles squelching on the tarmac, their sticks poised like lances. The positions at the halfway mark had been maintained, and it was still No. 1 and No. 6, Titine and Totoche, skittering up to the line of balloons.

No. 1, with an enormous backhand swipe, exploded his balloon first, showering the Parisienne, who stepped smartly backwards into a pile of droppings. No. 6, for all his stick sharpening before the race, had more difficulty, just managing to burst his balloon before the next runners reached the line. One by one, or in dripping groups, they staggered in until all that remained was a single swollen balloon hanging from the line. No. 9, the wayward Nénette, had not completed the course. "The butcher's got her," said the man with the paunch.

We saw her as we walked back to the car. She had broken her cord and escaped from her driver, and was perched high above the street in a tiny walled garden, her cap hanging from one horn, eating geraniums.

. . .

"*BONJOUR, maçon.*"

"*Bonjour, plombier.*"

The team had arrived for another loud, hot day, and were exchanging greetings and handshakes with the formality of people who had never met before, addressing each other by *métier* rather than by name. Christian, the architect, who had worked with them for years, never referred to them by their first names, but always by a rather grand and complicated hyphenation which combined surname with profession; thus Francis, Didier, and Bruno became Menicucci-Plombier, Andreis-Maçon, and Trufelli-Carreleur. This occasionally achieved the length and solemnity of an obscure aristocratic title, as with Jean-Pierre the carpet layer, who was officially known as Gaillard-Poseur de Moquette.

They were gathered around one of many holes that Menicucci had made to accommodate his central-heating pipes, and were discussing dates and schedules in the serious manner of men whose lives were governed by punctuality. There was a strict sequence to be followed: Menicucci had to complete laying his pipes; the masons were then to move in and repair the damage, followed by the electrician, the plasterer, the tile layer, the carpenter, and the painter. Since they were all good Provençaux, there was no chance at all that dates would be observed, but it provided the opportunity for some entertaining speculation.

Menicucci was enjoying his position of eminence as the key figure, the man whose progress would dictate the timetable of everyone else.

"You will see," he said, "that I have been obliged to make a Gorgonzola of the walls, but what is that, *maçon?* Half a day to repair?"

"Maybe a day," said Didier. "But when?"

"Don't try to rush me," said Menicucci. "Forty years as a

plumber have taught me that you cannot hurry central heating. It is *très, très délicat*."

"Christmas?" suggested Didier.

Menicucci looked at him, shaking his head. "You joke about it, but think of the winter." He demonstrated winter for us, wrapping an imaginary overcoat around his shoulders. "It is minus ten degrees." He shivered, pulling his bonnet over his ears. "All of a sudden, the pipes start to leak! And why? Because they have been placed too quickly and without proper attention." He looked at his audience, letting them appreciate the full drama of a cold and leaking winter. "Who will be laughing then? Eh? Who will be making jokes about the plumber?"

It certainly wouldn't be me. The central heating experience so far had been a nightmare, made bearable only by the fact that we could stay outside during the day. Previous construction work had at least been confined to one part of the house, but this was everywhere. Menicucci and his copper tentacles were unavoidable. Dust and rubble and tortured fragments of piping marked his daily passage like the spoor of an iron-jawed termite. And, perhaps worst of all, there was no privacy. We were just as likely to find *jeune* in the bathroom with a blowtorch as to come across Menicucci's rear end sticking out of a hole in the living room wall. The pool was the only refuge, and even there it was best to be completely submerged so that the water muffled the relentless noise of drills and hammers. We sometimes thought that our friends were right, and that we should have gone away for August, or hidden in the deep freeze.

The evenings were such a relief that we usually stayed at home, convalescing after the din of the day, and so we missed most of the social and cultural events that had been organized for the benefit of summer visitors to the Lubéron. Apart from a bottom-numbing evening in the Abbey of Senanque, listening to Gregorian chants as we sat on benches of appropriately monastic discomfort, and a concert held in a floodlit ruin above Oppède, we didn't move from the courtyard. It was enough just to be alone and to be quiet.

Hunger eventually forced us out one night when we discovered that what we had planned to have for dinner had acquired a thick coating of grit from the day's drilling. We decided to go to a simple restaurant in Goult, a small village with an invisible population and no tourist attractions of any kind. It would be like eating at home, but cleaner. We beat a layer of dust from our clothes and left the dogs to guard the holes in the walls.

It had been a still, oppressively hot day, and the village smelled of heat, of baked tarmac and dried-out rosemary and warm gravel. And people. We had chosen the night of the annual fête.

We should have known, because every village celebrated August in one way or another—with a *boules* tournament or a donkey race or a barbecue or a fair, with colored lights strung in the plane trees and dance floors made from wooden planks laid across scaffolding, with gypsies and accordion players and souvenir sellers and rock groups from as far away as Avignon. They were noisy, enjoyable occasions unless, like us, you were suffering from the mild concussion brought on by spending the day in a construction site. But we were there and we wanted the dinner that we had already mentally ordered. What were a few extra people compared to the delights of a salad made with warm mussels and bacon, chicken tickled with ginger, and the chef's clinging and delicious chocolate cake?

At any other time of the year, the sight of more than a dozen people in the village streets would indicate an event of unusual interest—a funeral, perhaps, or a price-cutting war between the two butchers who had adjacent shops a few yards from the café. But this was an exceptional night; Goult was playing host to the world, and the world was obviously as hungry as we were. The restaurant was full. The terrace outside the restaurant was full. Hopeful couples lurked in the shadows under the trees, waiting for a free table. The waiters looked harassed. The proprietor, Patrick, looked tired but satisfied, a man with a temporary gold mine. "You should have called," he said. "Come back at ten and I'll see what I can do."

Even the café, which was large enough to hold the entire population of Goult, could offer standing room only. We took our drinks across the road, where stalls had been set up in a hollow square around the monument honoring the men of the village who had fought and died in the wars, fallen for the glory of France. Like most war memorials we had seen, it was respectfully well kept, with a cluster of three new *tricolore* flags sharp and clean against the gray stone.

The windows in the houses around the square were open and the occupants leaned out, their flickering television sets forgotten behind them as they watched the slow-moving confusion below. It was more of a market than anything else, local artisans with their carved wood and pottery, wine growers and honey makers, a few antique dealers and artists. The heat of the day could be felt in the stone walls and seen in the way that the lazy, drifting crowd was walking, weight back on the heels, stomachs out, shoulders relaxed in a holiday slouch.

Most of the stands were trestle tables, with artifacts displayed on print tablecloths, often with a notice propped up saying that the owner could be found in the café if there was any risk of a sale. One stand, larger and more elaborate than the others, looked like an outdoor sitting room, furnished with tables and chairs and chaises longues and decorated with potted palms. A dark, stocky man in shorts and sandals sat at one of the tables with a bottle of wine and an order book. It was Monsieur Aude, the artist *ferronnier* of Saint-Pantaléon, who had done some work on the house. He beckoned us to sit down with him.

The *ferronnier* is a man who works with iron and steel, and in rural France he is kept busy making bars and gates and shutters and grilles to keep out the burglars who are assumed to be behind every bush. Monsieur Aude had progressed beyond these simple security devices, and had discovered that there was a market for replicas of classical eighteenth- and nineteenth-century steel furniture. He had a book of photographs and designs, and if you wanted a park bench or a baker's grill or a folding campaign bed such as Napoleon might have used, he would make it for you, then season it, being a superb judge of rust, to the required state of antiquity. He worked with his brother-in-law and a small beagle bitch and he could be relied upon to quote a delivery time of two weeks for anything, and to arrive with it three months later. We asked him if business was good.

He tapped his order book. "I could open a factory—Germans, Parisians, Belgians. This year they all want the big round tables and these garden chairs." He moved the chair next to him so that we could see the graceful arch of the legs. "The problem is that they think I can make everything in a couple of days, and as you know . . ." he left the sentence unfinished, and chewed reflectively on a mouthful of wine. A couple who had been circling the stand came up and asked about a campaign bed. Monsieur Aude opened his book and licked the point of his pencil, then looked up at them. "I have to tell you," he said with a completely straight face, "that it might take two weeks."

It was almost eleven by the time we started to eat, and well past midnight when we got home. The air was warm and heavy and abnormally still. It was a night for the pool, and we slipped into the water to float on our backs and look at the stars—the perfect end to a sweltering day. A long way off, from the direction of the Côte d'Azur, there was a mutter of thunder and the brief flicker of lightning, distant and ornamental, somebody else's storm.

It reached Ménerbes in the dark and early hours of the morning, waking us with a clap that shook the windows and startled the dogs into a chorus of barking. For an hour or more it seemed to stay directly above the house, rolling and exploding and floodlighting the vineyard. And then it rained with the intensity of a burst dam, crashing on the roof and in the courtyard, dripping down the chimney and seeping under the front door. It stopped just after dawn and, as if nothing had happened, the sun came up as usual.

We had no electricity. A little later, when we tried to call the Electricité de France office, we found we had no phone line. When we walked around the house to see what the storm had destroyed we saw that half the drive had been washed into the road, leaving ruts as wide as tractor wheels and deep enough to be dangerous to any normal car. But there were two silver linings: It was a beautiful morning, and there were no workmen. They were undoubtedly too busy with their own leaks to worry about our central heating. We went for a walk in the forest, to see what the storm had done there.

It was dramatic, not because of any uprooted trees, but because of the effects of the deluge on earth that had been baked for weeks. Wraiths of steam rose among the trees, and with them a continuous hissing sound as the heat of the new day started to dry the undergrowth. We came back for a late breakfast filled with the optimism that sunshine and blue sky can inspire, and we were rewarded by a working phone, with Monsieur Fructus on the end of it. He had called to see if his insurance policy had suffered any damage.

We told him that the only casualty had been the drive.

"*C'est bieng*," he said, "I have a client who has fifty centimeters of water in his kitchen. It sometimes happens. August is bizarre."

He was right. It had been a strange month, and we were glad it was over so that life could return to the way it had been before, with empty roads and uncrowded restaurants and Menicucci back in long trousers.

SEPTEMBER

OVERNIGHT, the population of the Lubéron dwindled. The *résidences secondaires*—some fine old houses among them—were locked and shuttered, their gateposts manacled with rusting lengths of chain. The houses would stay empty now until Christmas, so obviously, visibly empty that it was easy to understand why housebreaking in the Vaucluse had achieved the importance of a minor industry. Even the most poorly equipped and slow-moving of burglars could count on several undisturbed months in which to do his work, and in past years there had been some highly original thefts. Entire kitchens had been dismantled and taken away, old Roman roof tiles, an antique front door, a mature olive tree—it was as if a discerning burglar was setting up house with the choicest items he could find, selected with a connoisseur's eye from a variety of properties. Maybe he was the villain who had taken our mailbox.

We began to see our local friends again as they emerged from the summer siege. Most of them were recovering from a surfeit of guests, and there was a certain awful similarity in the stories they told. Plumbing and money were the main topics, and it was astonishing how often the same phrases were used by mystified, apologetic, or tightfisted visitors. Unwittingly, they had compiled between them The Sayings of August.

"What do you mean, they don't take credit cards? Everyone takes credit cards."

"You've run out of vodka."

"There's a very peculiar smell in the bathroom."

"Do you think you could take care of this? I've only got a five hundred-franc note."

"Don't worry. I'll send you a replacement as soon as I get back to London."

"I didn't realize you had to be so careful with a septic tank."

"Don't forget to let me know how much those calls to Los Angeles were."

"I feel terrible watching you slave away like that."

"You've run out of whisky."

As we listened to the tales of blocked drains and guzzled brandy, of broken wineglasses in the swimming pool, of sealed wallets and prodigious appetites, we felt that we had been very kindly treated during August. Our house had suffered considerable damage, but from the sound of it our friends' houses had suffered too. At least we hadn't had to provide food and lodging for Menicucci while he was wreaking havoc.

In many ways, the early part of September felt like a second spring. The days were dry and hot, the nights cool, the air wonderfully clear after the muggy haze of August. The inhabitants of the valley had shaken off their torpor and were getting down to the main business of the year, patrolling their vineyards every morning to examine the grapes that hung for mile after mile in juicy and orderly lines.

Faustin was out there with the rest of them, cupping the bunches in his hand and looking up at the sky, sucking his teeth in contemplation as he tried to second-guess the weather. I asked him when he thought he was going to pick.

"They should cook some more," he said. "But the weather in September is not to be trusted."

He had made the same gloomy comment about the weather every month of the year so far, in the resigned and plaintive tones used by farmers all over the world when they tell you how hard it is to scratch a living from the land. Conditions are never right. The rain, the wind, the sunshine, the weeds, the insects, the government—there is always at least one fly in their ointment, and they take a perverse pleasure in their pessimism.

"You can do everything right for eleven months a year," said Faustin, "and then—*pouf*—a storm comes and the crop is hardly fit for grape juice." *Jus de raiseng*—he said it with such scorn that I could imagine him leaving a spoiled crop to rot on the vines rather than waste his time picking grapes that couldn't even aspire to become *vin ordinaire*.

As if his life were not already filled with grief, Nature had put a further difficulty in his way: the grapes on our land would have to be picked at two separate times, because about five hundred of our vines produced table grapes which would be ready before the *raisins de cuve*. This was *un emmerdement*, made tolerable only because of the good price that table grapes fetched. Even so, it meant that there were two possible occasions when disappointment and disaster could strike and, if Faustin knew anything about it, strike they undoubtedly would. I left him shaking his head and grumbling to God.

To make up for the mournful predictions of Faustin, we received a daily ration of joyful news from Menicucci, now coming to the end of his labors on the central heating system and almost beside himself with anticipation as the day of firing up the boiler approached. Three times he reminded me to order the oil, and then insisted on supervising the filling of the tank to make sure that the delivery was free from foreign bodies.

"*Il faire très attention*," he explained to the man who brought the oil. "The smallest piece of *cochonnerie* in your fuel will affect my burner and clog the electrodes. I think it would be prudent to filter it as you pump it into the tank."

The fuel man drew himself up in outrage, parrying Menicucci's wagging finger with his own, oily and black-rimmed at the tip. "My fuel is already triple-filtered. *C'est impeccable.*" He made as if to kiss his fingertips and then thought better of it.

"We shall see," said Menicucci. "We shall see." He looked with suspicion at the nozzle before it was placed inside the tank, and the fuel man wiped it ostentatiously on a filthy rag. The filling ceremony was accompanied by a detailed technical discourse on the inner workings of the burner and the boiler which the fuel man listened to with scant interest, grunting or saying *Ah bon?* whenever his participation was required. Menicucci turned to me as the last few liters were pumped in. "This afternoon we will have the first test." He had an anxious moment as a dreadful possibility occurred to him. "You're not going out? You and Madame will be here?" It would have been an act of supreme unkindness to deprive him of his audience. We promised to be ready and waiting at two o'clock.

We gathered in what had once been a dormitory for donkeys, now transformed by Menicucci into the nerve center of his heating complex. Boiler, burner, and water tank were arranged side by side, joined together by umbilical cords of copper, and an impressive array of painted pipes—red for hot water, blue for cold, *très logique*—fanned out from the boiler and disappeared into the ceiling. Valves and dials and switches, bright and incongruous against the rough stone of the walls, awaited the master's touch. It looked extremely complicated, and I made the mistake of saying so.

Menicucci took it as a personal criticism, and spent ten minutes demonstrating its astonishing simplicity, flicking switches, opening and closing valves, twiddling dials and gauges, and making me thoroughly bewildered. *"Voilà!"* he said after a final flourish on the switches. "Now that you understand the apparatus, we will start the test. *Jeune!* Pay attention."

The beast awoke with a series of clicks and snuffles. *"Le brûleur,"* said Menicucci, dancing around the boiler to adjust the controls for the fifth time. There was a thump of air, and then a muffled roar. "We have combustion!" He made it sound as dramatic as the launch of a space shuttle. "Within five minutes, every radiator will be hot. Come!"

He scuttled around the house, insisting that we touch each radiator. "You see? You will be able to pass the entire winter *en chemise.*" By this time, we were all sweating profusely. It was eighty degrees outside, and the indoor temperature with the heating full on was insufferable. I asked if we could turn it off before we dehydrated.

"Ah non. You must leave it on for twenty-four hours so that we can verify all the joints and make sure there are no leaks. Touch nothing until I return tomorrow. It is most important that everything remains at maximum." He left us to wilt, and to enjoy the smell of cooked dust and hot iron.

THERE IS ONE September weekend when the countryside sounds as though rehearsals are being held for World War Three. It is the official start of the hunting season, and every red-blooded Frenchman takes his gun, his dog, and his murderous inclinations into the hills in search of sport. The first sign that this was about to happen came through the post—a terrifying document from a gunsmith in Vaison-la-Romaine, offering a complete range of artillery at preseason prices. There were sixty or seventy models to choose from, and my hunting instincts, which had been dormant since birth, were aroused by the thought of owning a Verney Carron Grand Bécassier, or a Ruger .44 Magnum with an electronic sight. My wife, who has a well-founded lack of confidence in my ability to handle any kind of dangerous equipment, pointed out that I hardly needed an electronic sight to shoot myself in the foot.

We had both been surprised at the French fondness for guns. Twice we had visited the homes of outwardly mild and unwarlike men, and twice we had been shown the family arsenal; one man had five rifles of various calibers, the other had eight, oiled and polished and displayed in a rack on the dining room wall like a lethal piece of art. How could anyone need eight guns? How would you know which one to take with you? Or did you take them all, like a bag of golf clubs, selecting the .44 Magnum for leopard or moose and the Baby Bretton for rabbit?

After a while, we came to realize that the gun mania was only part of a national fascination with outfits and accoutrements, a passion for looking like an expert. When a Frenchman takes up cycling or tennis or skiing, the last thing he wants is for the world to mistake him for the novice that he is, and so he accessorizes himself up to professional standard. It's instant. A few thousand francs and there you are, indistinguishable from any other seasoned ace competing in the Tour de France or Wimbledon or the Winter Olympics. In the case of *la chasse*, the accessories are almost limitless, and they have the added attraction of being deeply masculine and dangerous in their appearance.

We were treated to a preview of hunting fashions in Cavaillon market. The stalls had stocked up for the season, and looked like small paramilitary depots: there were cartridge bandoliers and plaited leather rifle slings; jerkins with myriad zippered pockets and game pouches that were washable and therefore *très pratique*, because bloodstains could be easily removed; there were wilderness boots of the kind used by mercenaries parachuting into the Congo; fearsome knives with nine-inch blades and compasses set into the handle; lightweight aluminium water bottles which would probably see more pastis than water; webbing belts with D-rings and a special sling to hold a bayonet, presumably in case the ammunition ran out and game had to be attacked with cold steel; forage caps and commando trousers, survival rations and tiny collapsible field stoves. There was everything a man might need for his confrontation with the untamed beasts of the forest except that indispensable accessory with four legs and a nose like radar, the hunting dog.

Chiens de chasse are too specialized to be bought and sold across a counter, and we were told that no serious hunter would consider buying a pup without first meeting both parents. Judging by some of the hunting dogs we had seen, we could imagine that finding the father might have been difficult, but among all the hybrid curiosities there were three more or less identifiable types—the liver-colored approximation of a large spaniel, the stretched beagle, and the tall, rail-thin hound with the wrinkled, lugubrious face.

Every hunter considers his dog to be uniquely gifted, and he will have at least one implausible story of stamina and prowess to tell you. To hear the owners talk, you would think that these dogs were supernaturally intelligent creatures, trained to a hair and faithful unto death. We looked forward with interest to seeing them perform on the opening weekend of the season. Perhaps their example would inspire our dogs to do something more useful than stalk lizards and attack old tennis balls.

Hunting in our part of the valley started shortly after seven o'clock one Sunday morning, with salvos coming from either side of the house and from the mountains behind. It sounded as though anything that moved would be at risk, and when I went out for a walk with the dogs I took the biggest white handkerchief I could find in case I needed to surrender. With infinite caution, we set off along the footpath that runs behind the house toward the village, assuming that any hunter worth his gun license would have moved well away from the beaten track and into the tangled undergrowth farther up the mountain.

There was a noticeable absence of birdsong; all sensible or experienced birds had left at the sound of the first shot for somewhere safer, like North Africa or central Avignon. In the bad old days, hunters used to hang caged birds in the trees to lure other birds close enough for a point-blank shot, but that had been made illegal, and the modern hunter now had to rely on woodcraft and stealth.

I didn't see much evidence of that, but I did see enough hunters and dogs and weaponry to wipe out the entire thrush and rabbit population of southern France. They hadn't gone up into the forest; in fact, they had barely left the footpath. Knots of them were gathered in the clearings—laughing, smoking, taking nips from their khaki-painted flasks and cutting slices of *saucisson*—but of active hunting—man versus thrush in a battle of wits—there was no sign. They must have used up their ration of shells during the early morning fusillade.

Their dogs, however, were anxious to get to work. After months of confinement in kennels, they were delirious with liberty and the scents of the forest, tracking back and forth, noses close to the ground and twitching with excitement. Each dog wore a thick collar with a small brass bell—the *clochette*—hanging from it. We were told that this had a double purpose. It signaled the dog's whereabouts so that the hunter could position himself for the game that was being driven toward him, but it was also a precaution against shooting at something in the bushes that sounded like a rabbit or a boar and finding that you had shot your own dog. No responsible hunter, *naturellement*, would ever shoot at anything he couldn't see—or so I was told. But I had my doubts. After a morning with the pastis or the *marc*, a rustle in the bushes might be too much to resist, and the cause of the rustle might be human. In fact, it might be me. I thought about wearing a bell, just to be on the safe side.

Another benefit of the *clochette* became apparent at the end of the morning: it was to help the hunter avoid the humiliating experience of losing his dog at the end of the hunt. Far from the disciplined and faithful animals I had imagined them to be, hunting dogs are wanderers, led on by their noses and oblivious of the passage of time. They have not grasped the idea that hunting stops for lunch. The bell doesn't necessarily mean that the dog will come when called, but at least the hunter can tell roughly where he is.

Just before noon, camouflage-clad figures started to make their way to the vans parked at the side of the road. A few had dogs with them. The rest were whistling and shouting with increasing irritation, making a bad-tempered hissing noise—"*Vieng ici! Vieng ici!*"—in the direction of the symphony of bells that could be heard coming from the forest.

Response was patchy. The shouts became more bad tempered, degenerating into bellows and curses. After a few minutes the hunters gave up and went home, most of them dogless.

We were joined a little later for lunch by three abandoned hounds who came down to drink at the swimming pool. They were greatly admired by our two bitches for their devil-may-care manner and exotic aroma, and we penned them all in the courtyard while we wondered how we could get them back to their owners. We consulted Faustin.

"Don't bother," he said. "Let them go. The hunters will be back in the evening. If they don't find their dogs, they'll leave a *coussin.*"

It always worked, so Faustin said. If the dog was in the forest, one simply left something with the scent of the kennel on it—a cushion or, more likely, a scrap of sacking—near the spot where the dog had last been seen. Sooner or later, the dog would come back to its own scent and wait to be picked up.

We let the three hounds out, and they loped off, baying with excitement. It was an extraordinary, doleful sound, not a bark or a howl but a lament, like an oboe in pain. Faustin shook his head. "They'll be gone for days." He himself didn't hunt, and regarded hunters and their dogs as intruders who had no right to be nosing around his precious vines.

He had decided, he told us, that the moment had come to pick the table grapes. They would start as soon as Henriette had finished servicing the *camion*. She was the mechanically minded member of the family, and every September she had the job of coaxing another few kilometers out of the grape truck. It was at least thirty years old—maybe more, Faustin couldn't remember exactly—blunt-nosed and rickety, with open sides and bald tires. It had ceased to be roadworthy years ago, but there was no question of buying a new truck. And why waste good money having it serviced at a garage when you had a mechanic for a wife? It was only used for a few weeks a year, and Faustin was careful to take it on the back roads to avoid meeting any of those officious little *flics* from the police station at Les Baumettes, with their absurd regulations about brakes and valid insurance.

Henriette's ministrations were successful, and the old truck gasped up the drive early one morning, loaded with shallow wooden grape trays, just deep enough for a single layer of bunches. Stacks of trays were placed along each line of vines, and the three of them—Faustin, Henriette, and their daughter—took their scissors and set to work.

It was a slow and physically uncomfortable business. Because the appearance of table grapes is almost as important as their taste, every bunch had to be examined, every bruised or wrinkled grape snipped off. The bunches grew low, sometimes touching the earth and hidden by leaves, and the pickers' progress was in yards per hour—squatting down, cutting, standing up, inspecting, snipping, packing. The heat was fierce, coming up from the ground as well as beating down on the necks and shoulders. No shade, no breeze, no relief in the course of a ten-hour day except the break for lunch. Never again would I look at a bunch of grapes in a bowl without thinking of backache and sunstroke. It was past seven when they came in for a drink, exhausted and radiating heat, but satisfied. The grapes were good and three or four days would see them all picked. I said to Faustin that he must be pleased with the weather. He pushed back his hat and I could see the line sharp across his forehead where the burned brown skin turned white.

"It's too good," he said. "It won't last." He took a long pull at his pastis as he considered the spectrum of misfortunes that could occur. If not storms, there might be a freak frost, a plague of locusts, a forest fire, a nuclear attack. Something was bound to go wrong before the second batch of grapes was picked. And, if it didn't, he could console himself with the fact that his doctor had put him on a diet to reduce his cholesterol level. Yes, that was certainly a grave problem. Reassured at having remembered that fate had recently dealt him a black card, he had another drink.

IT HAD taken me some time to get used to having a separate purpose-built room devoted exclusively to wine—not a glorified cupboard or a cramped cavity under the stairs, but a genuine *cave*. It was buried in the bottom of the house, with permanently cool stone walls and a floor of gravel, and there was space for three or four hundred bottles. I loved it. I was determined to fill it up. Our friends were equally determined to empty it. This gave me the excuse to make regular visits—errands of social mercy—to the vineyards so that guests should never go thirsty.

In the interests of research and hospitality, I went to Gigondas and Beaumes-de-Venise and Châteauneuf-du-Pape, none of them bigger than a large village, all of them single-minded in their dedication to the grape. Everywhere I looked, there were signs advertising the *caves* that seemed to be at fifty-yard intervals. *Dégustez nos vins!* Never has a invitation been accepted with more enthusiasm. I had *dégustations* in a garage in Gigondas and a château above Beaumes-de-Venise. I found a powerful and velvety Châteauneuf-du-Pape for thirty francs a liter, squirted into plastic containers with a marvelous lack of ceremony from what looked like a garage pump. In a more expensive and more pretentious establishment, I asked to try the *marc*. A small cut-glass bottle was produced, and a drop was dabbed on the back of my hand, whether to sniff or to suck I wasn't quite sure.

After a while, I bypassed the villages and started to follow the signs, often half-hidden by vegetation, that pointed deep into the countryside where the wines baked in the sun, and where I could buy directly from the men who made the wine. They were, without exception, hospitable and proud of their work and, to me at least, their sales pitch was irresistible.

It was early afternoon when I turned off the main road leading out of Vacqueyras and followed the narrow, stony track through the vines. I had been told that it would lead me to the maker of the wine I had liked at lunchtime, a white Côtes-du-Rhône. A case or two would fill the void in the *cave* that had been made by the last raiding party we had entertained. A quick stop, no more than ten minutes, and then I would get back home.

The track led to a sprawl of buildings, arranged in a square U around a courtyard of beaten earth, shaded by a giant plane tree and guarded by a drowsy Alsatian who welcomed me with a halfhearted bark, doing his duty as a substitute for a doorbell. A man in overalls, holding an oily collection of spark plugs, came over from his tractor. He gave me his forearm to shake.

I wanted some white wine? Of course. He himself was busy nursing his tractor, but his uncle would take care of me. *"Edouard! Tu peux servir ce monsieur?"*

The curtain of wooden beads hanging across the front door parted, and Uncle Edward came blinking into the sunshine. He was wearing a sleeveless vest, cotton *bleu de travail* trousers, and carpet slippers. His girth was impressive, comparable with the trunk of the plane tree, but even that was overshadowed by his nose. I had never seen a nose quite like it—wide, fleshy, and seasoned to a color somewhere between rosé and claret, with fine purple lines spreading out across his cheeks. Here was a man who clearly enjoyed every mouthful of his work.

He beamed, the lines on his cheeks looking like purple whiskers. *"Bon. Une petite dégustation."* He led me across the courtyard and slid back the double doors of a long, windowless building, telling me to stay just inside the door while he went to switch on the light. After the glare outside, I could see nothing, but there was a reassuring smell, musty and unmistakable, the air itself tasting of fermented grapes.

Uncle Edward turned on the light and closed the doors against the heat. A long trestle table and half a dozen chairs were placed under the single light bulb with its flat tin shade. In a dark corner, I could make out a flight of stairs and a concrete ramp leading down into the cellar. Crates of wine were stacked on wooden pallets around the walls, and an old refrigerator hummed quietly next to a cracked sink.

Uncle Edward was polishing glasses, holding each one up to the light before placing it on the table. He made a neat line of seven glasses, and began to arrange a variety of bottles behind them. Each bottle was accorded a few admiring comments: "The white monsieur knows, yes? A very agreeable young wine. The rosé, not at all like those thin rosés one finds on the Côte d'Azur. Thirteen degrees of alcohol, a proper wine. There's a light red —one could drink a bottle of that before a game of tennis. That one, *par contre*, is for the winter, and he will keep for ten years or more. And then . . ."

I tried to stop him. I told him that all I wanted were two cases of the white, but he wouldn't hear of it. Monsieur had taken the trouble to come personally, and it would be unthinkable not to taste a selection. Why, said Uncle Edward, he himself would join me in a progress through the vintages. He clapped a heavy hand on my shoulder and sat me down.

It was fascinating. He told me the precise part of the vine-yard that each of the wines had come from, and why certain slopes produced lighter or heavier wines. Each wine we tasted was accompanied by an imaginary menu, described with much lip smacking and raising of the eyes to gastronomic heaven. We mentally consumed *écrevisses*, salmon cooked with sorrel, rosemary-flavored chicken from Bresse, roasted baby lamb with a creamy garlic sauce, an *estouffade* of beef and olives, a *daube*, loin of pork spiked with slivers of truffle. The wines tasted progressively better and became progressively more expensive; I was being traded up by an expert, and there was nothing to be done except sit back and enjoy it.

"There is one more you should try," said Uncle Edward, "although it is not to everybody's taste." He picked up a bottle and poured a careful half glass. It was deep red, almost black. "A wine of great character," he said. "Wait. It needs *une bonne bouche.*" He left me surrounded by glasses and bottles, feeling the first twinges of an afternoon hangover.

"*Voilà.*" He put a plate in front of me—two small round goat's cheeses, speckled with herbs and shiny with oil—and gave me a knife with a worn wooden handle. He watched as I cut off a piece of cheese and ate it. It was ferociously strong. My palate, or what was left of it, had been perfectly primed and the wine tasted like nectar.

Uncle Edward helped me load the cases into the car. Had I really ordered all this? I must have. We had been sitting in the convivial murk for nearly two hours, and one can make all kinds of expansive decisions in two hours. I left with a throbbing head and an invitation to come back next month for the *vendange.*

Our own *vendange*, the agricultural highlight of the year, took place during the last week of September. Faustin would have liked it to be a few days later, but he had some private information about the weather which convinced him that it would be a wet October.

The original party of three that had picked the table grapes was reinforced by Cousin Raoul and Faustin's father. His contribution was to walk slowly behind the pickers, prodding among the vines with his stick until he found a bunch of grapes that had been overlooked and then shouting—he had a good, carrying bellow for a man of eighty-four—for someone to come back and do the job properly. In contrast to the others in their shorts and vests, he was dressed for a brisk November day in a sweater, a cap, and a suit of heavy cotton. When my wife appeared with a camera, he took off his cap, smoothed his hair, put his cap back on and struck a pose, waist deep in vines. Like all our neighbors, he loved having his portrait taken.

Slowly and noisily, the rows were picked clean, the grapes piled into plastic crates and stacked in the back of the truck. Every evening now, the roads were busy with vans and tractors towing their purple mountains to the wine cooperative at Maubec, where they were weighed and tested for alcoholic content.

To Faustin's surprise, the crop was gathered without incident, and to celebrate he invited us to go with him to the cooperative when he made the last delivery. "Tonight we will see the final figures," he said, "and then you will know how much you can drink next year."

We followed the truck as it swayed off into the sunset at twenty miles an hour, keeping to narrow roads that were stained with fallen, squashed grapes. There was a queue waiting to unload. Burly men with roasted faces sat on their tractors until it was their turn to back up to the platform and tip their loads down the chute—the first stage of their journey to the bottle.

Faustin finished unloading, and we went with him into the building to see our grapes going into the huge stainless-steel vats. "Watch that dial," he said. "It shows the degrees of alcohol." The needle swung up, quivered, and settled at 12.32 percent. Faustin grunted. He would have liked 12.50 and an extra few days in the sun might have done it, but anything above 12 was reasonable. He took us over to the man who kept the tallies of each delivery and peered at a line of figures on a clipboard, matching them with a handful of slips of paper he pulled from his pocket. He nodded. It was all correct.

"You won't go thirsty." He made the Provençal drinking gesture, fist clenched and thumb pointing towards his mouth. "Just over one thousand two hundred liters."

It sounded like a good year to us, and we told Faustin we were pleased. "Well," he said, "at least it didn't rain."

OCTOBER

THE MAN stood peering into the moss and light undergrowth around the roots of an old scrub oak tree. His right leg was encased up to the thigh in a green rubber fishing wader; on the other foot was a running shoe. He held a long stick in front of him and carried a blue plastic shopping basket.

He turned sideways on to the tree, advanced the rubber-clad leg, and plunged his stick nervously into the vegetation, in the manner of a fencer expecting a sudden and violent riposte. And again, with the rubber leg pushed forward: on guard, thrust, withdraw, thrust. He was so absorbed by his duel that he had no idea that I was watching, equally absorbed, from the path. One of the dogs went up behind him and gave his rear leg an exploratory sniff.

He jumped—*merde!*—and then saw the dog, and me, and looked embarrassed. I apologized for startling him.

"For a moment," he said, "I thought I was being attacked."

I couldn't imagine who he thought was going to sniff his leg before attacking him, and I asked what he was looking for. In reply, he held up his shopping basket. *"Les champignons."*

This was a new and worrying aspect of the Lubéron. It was, as I already knew, a region full of strange things and even stranger people. But surely mushrooms, even wild mushrooms, didn't attack fully grown men. I asked him if the mushrooms were dangerous.

"Some can kill you," he said.

That I could believe, but it didn't explain the rubber boot or the extraordinary performance with the stick. At the risk of being made to feel like the most ignorant of city-reared dunces, I pointed at his right leg.

"The boot is for protection?"

"Mais oui."

"But against what?"

He slapped the rubber with his wooden sword and swaggered down toward me, D'Artagnan with a shopping basket. He delivered a backhand cut at a clump of thyme and came closer.

"Les serpents." He said it with just the trace of a hiss. "They are preparing for winter. If you disturb them—*sssst!*—they attack. It can be very grave."

He showed me the contents of his shopping basket, snatched from the forest at the risk of life and limb. To me, they looked highly poisonous, varying in color from blue-black to rust to violent orange, not at all like the civilized white mushrooms sold in the markets. He held the basket under my nose, and I breathed in what he called the essence of the mountains. To my surprise, it was good—earthy, rich, slightly nutty—and I looked at the mushrooms more closely. I had seen them in the forest, in evil-looking clusters under the trees, and had assumed that they were instant death. My booted friend assured me that they were not only safe, but delicious.

"But," he said, "you must know the deadly species. There are two or three. If you're not sure, take them to the pharmacy."

It had never occurred to me that a mushroom could be clinically tested before being permitted to enter an omelette but, since the stomach is by far the most influential organ in France, it made perfect sense. The next time I went into Cavaillon, I toured the pharmacies. Sure enough, they had been converted into mushroom guidance centers. The window displays, normally devoted to surgical trusses and pictures of young women reducing the cellulite on their slim bronzed thighs, now featured large mushroom identification charts. Some pharmacies went even further, and filled their windows with piles of reference books which described and illustrated every species of edible fungus known to man.

I saw people going into the pharmacies with grubby bags which they presented at the counter rather anxiously, as though they were undergoing tests for a rare disease. The small, muddy objects in the bags were solemnly inspected by the resident white-coated expert, and a verdict was pronounced. I suppose it made an interesting change from the usual daily round of suppositories and liver tonics. I found it so distracting that I almost forgot why I had come to Cavaillon—not to loiter around pharmacies but to shop for bread at the local shrine of baking.

Living in France had turned us into bakery addicts, and the business of choosing and buying our daily bread was a recurring pleasure. The village bakery in Ménerbes, with its erratic opening hours—"Madame will reopen when she has finished making her *toilette*," I was told one day—had first encouraged us to visit other bakeries in other villages. It was a revelation. After years of taking bread for granted, more or less as a standard commodity, it was like discovering a new food.

We tried the dense, chewy loaves from Lumières, fatter and flatter than the ordinary *baguette*, and the dark-crusted *boules*, as big as squashed footballs, from Cabrières. We learned which breads would keep for a day, and which would be stale in three hours; the best bread for making *croûtons* or for spreading with *rouille* to launch into a sea of fish soup. We became used to the delightful but initially surprising sight of bottles of champagne offered for sale next to the tarts and tiny individual pastries that were made fresh every morning and gone by noon.

Most of the bakeries had their own touches which distinguished their loaves from mass-produced supermarket bread: slight variations from conventional shapes, an extra whorl of crusty decoration, an elaborate pattern, the artist baker signing his work. It was as if the sliced, wrapped, machine-made loaf had never been invented.

In Cavaillon, there are seventeen bakers listed in the *Pages Jaunes*, but we had been told that one establishment was ahead of all the rest in terms of choice and excellence, a veritable *palais de pain*. At Chez Auzet, so they said, the baking and eating of breads and pastries had been elevated to the status of a minor religion.

When the weather is warm, tables and chairs are placed on the pavement outside the bakery so that the matrons of Cavaillon can sit with their hot chocolate and almond biscuits or strawberry tarts while they give proper, leisurely consideration to the bread they will buy for lunch and dinner. To help them, Auzet has printed a comprehensive bread menu, the *Carte des .Pains*. I took a copy from the counter, ordered coffee, sat in the sun, and started to read.

It was another step in my French education. Not only did it introduce me to breads I had never heard of before, it told me with great firmness and precision what I should be eating with them. With my *apéritif*, I could choose between the tiny squares called *toasts*, a *pain surprise* which might be flavored with finely chopped bacon, or the savory *feuillets salés*. That was simple. The decisions became more complicated when the meal itself was being chosen. Supposing, for example, I wanted to start with *crudités*. There were four possible accompaniments: onion bread, garlic bread, olive bread, or roquefort bread. Too difficult? In that case, I could have seafood, because the gospel according the Auzet authorized only one bread to eat with seafood, and that was thinly sliced rye.

And so it went on, listing with uncompromising brevity what I should eat with *charcuterie*, foie gras, soup, red and white meat, game with feathers and game with fur, smoked meats, mixed salads (not to be confused with the separately listed green salads), and three different consistencies of cheese. I counted eighteen varieties of bread, from thyme to pepper, from nuts to bran. In a fog of indecision, I went inside the shop and consulted Madame. What would she recommend with calves' liver?

She set off on a short tour of the shelves, and then selected a stubby brown *banette*. While she was counting out my change, she told me about a restaurant where the chef serves a different bread with each of the five courses on his menu. There's a man who understands bread, she said. Not like some.

I was beginning to understand it, just as I was beginning to understand mushrooms. It had been an instructive morning.

M A S S O T was in a lyrical mood. He had just left his house to go into the forest and kill something when I met him on a hill overlooking a long stretch of vineyards. With his gun under his arm and one of his yellow cigarettes screwed into the corner of his mouth, he stood contemplating the valley.

"Look at those vines," he said. "Nature is wearing her prettiest clothes."

The effect of this unexpectedly poetic observation was slightly spoiled when Massot cleared his throat noisily and spat, but he was right; the vines were spectacular, field after field of russet and yellow and scarlet leaves, motionless in the sunlight. Now that the grapes had all been picked there were no tractors or human figures to interfere with our appreciation of the view.

Work on the vines wouldn't start again until the leaves had fallen and the pruning began. It was a space between seasons, still hot, but not quite summer and not yet autumn.

I asked Massot if there had been any progress in the sale of his property, maybe a nice German couple who had fallen in love with the house while camping nearby.

He bristled at the mention of campers. "They couldn't afford a house like mine. In any case, I have taken it off the market until 1992. You'll see. When the frontiers are abolished, they'll all be looking for houses down here—English, Belgians . . ." He waved his hand airily to include the other Common Market nationalities. "Prices will become much more important. Houses in the Lubéron will be *très recherchées*. Even your little place might fetch a million or two."

It was not the first time that 1992 had been mentioned as the year when the whole of Provence would be showered with foreign money, because in 1992 the Common Market would come into its own. Nationalities would be forgotten as we all became one big happy family of Europeans. Financial restrictions would be lifted—and what would the Spaniards and Italians and the rest of them do? What else but hurry down to Provence waving their checkbooks and looking for houses.

It was a popular thought, but I couldn't see why it should happen. Provence already had a considerable foreign population; they had found no problem buying houses. And, for all the talk of European integration, a date on a piece of paper wasn't going to stop the bickering and bureaucracy and jockeying for special preference which all the member countries—notably France— used when it suited them. Fifty years might see a difference; 1992 almost certainly would not.

But Massot was convinced. In 1992, he was going to sell up and retire, or possibly buy a little *bar-tabac* in Cavaillon. I asked him what he'd do with his three dangerous dogs, and for a moment I thought he was going to burst into tears.

"They wouldn't be happy in a town," he said. "I'd have to shoot them."

He walked along with me for a few minutes, and cheered himself up by muttering about the profits that were certain to come his way, and about time too. A lifetime of hard work should be rewarded. A man should spend his old age in comfort, not breaking his back on the land. As it happened, his land was exceptional in the valley for its ill-kempt appearance, but he always spoke of it as though it were a cross between the gardens at Villandry and the manicured vineyards of Château Lafite. He turned off the path to go into the forest and terrorize some birds, a brutal, greedy, and mendacious old scoundrel. I was becoming quite fond of him.

The way home was littered with spent shotgun cartridges fired by the men whom Massot dismissed as *chasseurs du sentier*, or footpath hunters—miserable namby-pambies who didn't want to get their boots dirty in the forest, and who hoped that birds would somehow fly into their buckshot. Among the scattered shell cases were crushed cigarette packets and empty sardine cans and bottles, souvenirs left by the same nature lovers who complained that the beauty of the Lubéron was being ruined by tourists. Their concern for conservation didn't extend to removing their own rubbish. A messy breed, the Provençal hunter.

I arrived at the house to find a small conference taking place around the electricity meter which was hidden behind some trees in the back garden. The man from Electricité de France had opened the meter to read it, and had discovered that a colony of ants had made a nest. The figures were obscured. It was impossible to establish our consumption of electricity. The ants must be removed. My wife and the man from the EDF had been joined by Menicucci, whom we now suspected of living in the boiler room, and who liked nothing better than to advise us on any domestic problem that might arise.

"*Oh là là.*" A pause while Menicucci bent down for a closer look at the meter. *"Ils sont nombreux, les fourmis."* For once, he had made an understatement. The ants were so numerous that they appeared as one solid black block, completely filling the metal box that housed the meter.

"I'm not touching them," said the EDF man. "They get into your clothes and bite you. The last time I tried to brush away an ants' nest I had them with me all afternoon."

He stood looking at the squirming mass, tapping his screwdriver against his teeth. He turned to Menicucci. "Do you have a blowtorch?"

"I'm a plumber. Of course I have a blowtorch."

"*Bon.* Then we can burn them off."

Menicucci was aghast. He took a step backwards and crossed himself. He smote his forehead. He raised his index finger to the position that indicated either extreme disagreement, or the start of a lecture, or both.

"I cannot believe what I have just heard. A blowtorch? Do you realize how much current passes through here?"

The EDF man looked offended. "Of course I know. I'm an electrician."

Menicucci affected to be surprised. "*Ah bon?* Then you will know what happens when you burn a live cable."

"I would be very prudent with the flame."

"Prudent! Prudent! *Mon Dieu,* we could all perish with the ants."

The EDF man sheathed his screwdriver and crossed his arms. "Very well. I will not occupy myself with the ants. You remove them."

Menicucci thought for a moment and then, like a magician setting up a particularly astonishing trick, he turned to my wife. "If Madame could possibly bring me some fresh lemons—two or three will be enough—and a knife?"

Madame the magician's assistant came back with the knife and lemons, and Menicucci cut each into four quarters. "This is an *astuce* that I was taught by a very old man," he said, and muttered something impolite about the stupidity of using a blowtorch—*"putain de chalumeau"*—while the EDF man sulked under a tree.

When the lemons were all quartered, Menicucci advanced on the nest and started to squeeze lemon juice back and forth over the ants, pausing between squeezes to observe the effect that the downpour of citric acid was having.

The ants surrendered, evacuating the meter box in panic-stricken clumps, climbing over one another in their haste to escape. Menicucci enjoyed his moment of triumph. *"Voilà, jeune homme,"* he said to the EDF man, "ants cannot support the juice of fresh lemons. That is something you have learned today. If you leave slices of lemon in your meters you will never have another infestation."

The EDF man took it with a marked lack of graciousness, complaining that he was not a lemon supplier and that the juice had made the meter sticky. "Better sticky than burned to a cinder," was Menicucci's parting shot as he returned to his boiler. *"Beh oui.* Better sticky than burned."

THE DAYS were warm enough for swimming, the nights cool enough for fires, Indian summer weather. It finally ended in the excessive style that was typical of the Provençal climate. We went to bed in one season and woke up in another.

The rain had come in the night, and continued for most of the following day; not the fat, warm drops of summer, but gray sheets that fell in a vertical torrent, sluicing through the vine-yards, flattening shrubs, turning flower beds into mud and mud into brown rivers. It stopped in the late afternoon, and we went to look at the drive—or, rather, where the drive had been the previous day.

It had already suffered in the big storm of August, but the ruts made then were scratches compared to what we now saw: a succession of craters led down to the road, where most of the drive had been deposited in sodden piles. The rest of it was in the melon field opposite the house. Some of the gravel and stones had traveled more than a hundred yards. A recently detonated mine field could hardly have looked worse, and nobody except a man who hated his car would have attempted to drive to the house from the road. We needed a bulldozer just to tidy up the mess, and several tons of gravel to replace what the rain had washed away.

I called Monsieur Menicucci. Over the months, he had established himself as a human version of the Yellow Pages, and, since he had a regard verging on the proprietorial for our house, his recommendations had been made, so he told us, as though it were his own money at stake. He listened as I told him of the lost drive, making interjections—*quelle catastrophe* was mentioned more than once—to show that he appreciated the extent of the problem.

I finished talking, and I could hear Menicucci making a verbal list of our requirements: *"Un bulldozer, bien sûr, un camion, une montagne de gravier, un compacteur . . ."* There were a few moments of humming, probably a snatch of Mozart to assist the mental processes, and then he made up his mind. *"Bon.* There is a young man, the son of a neighbor, who is an artist with the bulldozer, and his prices are correct. He's called Sanchez. I will ask him to come tomorrow."

I reminded Menicucci that the drive was not possible for an ordinary car.

"He's used to that," said Menicucci. "He will come on his *moto* with special tires. He can pass anywhere."

I watched him negotiate the drive the next morning, doing slalom turns to avoid the craters and standing up on his footrests as he drove over the mounds of earth. He cut the engine and looked back at the drive, a study in color-coordinated *moto chic.* His hair was black, his leather jacket was black, his bike was black. He wore aviator sunglasses with impenetrable reflective lenses. I wondered if he knew our insurance agent, the formidably hip Monsieur Fructus. They would have made a good pair.

Within half an hour, he had made a tour of the mine field on foot, estimated a price, telephoned to order the gravel, and given us a firm date, two days away, for his return with the bulldozer. We had our doubts that he was real and, when Menicucci called that evening in his capacity as supervisor of catastrophes, I said that Monsieur Sanchez had surprised us with his efficiency.

"It runs in the family," Menicucci said. "His father is a melon millionaire. The son will be a bulldozer millionaire. They are very serious, despite being Spanish." He explained that Sanchez *père* had come to France as a young man to find work, and had developed a method of producing earlier and more succulent melons than anyone else in Provence. He was now, said Menicucci, so rich that he worked for only two months a year and lived during the winter in Alicante.

Sanchez *fils* arrived as promised, and spent the day rearranging the landscape with his bulldozer. He had a delicacy of touch that was fascinating to watch, redistributing tons of earth as accurately as if he were using a trowel. When the drive was level, he smoothed the surface with a giant comb, and invited us to see what he had done. It looked too immaculate to walk on, and he had given it a slight camber so that any future downpours would run off into the vines.

"C'est bon?"

As good as the autoroute to Paris, we said.

"Bieng. Je revieng demaing." He climbed into the control tower of his bulldozer and drove off at a stately fifteen miles an hour. Tomorrow the gravel would be laid.

The first vehicle to disturb the combed perfection of the drive's surface crawled up to the house the next morning and stopped with a shudder of relief in the parking area. It was a truck that looked to be even more venerable than Faustin's grape wagon, sagging so low on its suspension that the rusty exhaust pipe nearly touched the ground. A man and a woman, both round and weatherbeaten, were standing by the truck and looking with interest at the house, obviously itinerant field workers hoping for one last job before heading further south for the winter.

They seemed a nice old couple, and I felt sorry for them.

"I'm afraid the grapes have all been picked," I said.

The man grinned and nodded. "That's good. You were lucky to get them in before the rain." He pointed up to the forest behind the house. "Plenty of mushrooms there, I should think."

Yes, I said, plenty.

They showed no sign of going. I said they were welcome to leave their truck outside the house and pick some mushrooms.

"No, no," said the man. "We're working today. My son is on his way with the gravel."

The melon millionaire opened the back doors of the truck and took out a long-handled mason's shovel and a wide-toothed wooden rake. "I'll leave the rest for him to unload," he said. "I don't want to squash my feet."

I looked inside. Packed tight up against the back of the seats and stretching the length of the truck was a miniature steam-roller, the *compacteur*.

While we waited for his son, Monsieur Sanchez talked about life and the pursuit of happiness. Even after all these years, he said, he still enjoyed the occasional day of manual labor. His work with the melons was finished by July, and he got bored with nothing to do. It was very agreeable to be rich, but one needed something else, and, as he liked working with his hands, why not help his son?

I had never employed a millionaire before. I don't have much time for them as a rule, but this one put in a good long day. Load after load of gravel was delivered and tipped onto the drive by the son. The father shoveled and spread, and Madame Sanchez followed behind with the wooden rake, pushing and smoothing. Then the *compacteur* was unloaded; it was like a massive baby carriage with handlebars, and it was wheeled ceremoniously up and down the drive with Sanchez the son at the controls, shouting instructions at his parents—another shoveful here, more raking there, mind your feet, don't tread on the vines.

It was a true family effort, and by the end of the afternoon we had a pristine ribbon of crushed, putty-colored gravel worthy of being entered for the Concours d'Elégance sponsored by *Bulldozer Magazine*. The *compacteur* was inserted into the back of the truck; the parents into the front. Young Sanchez said that the price would be less than his estimate, but he would work it out exactly and his father would come around to deliver the bill.

The next morning when I got up, there was an unfamiliar van parked outside the house. I looked for a driver, but there was nobody in the vines or in the outbuildings. It was probably an idle hunter who couldn't be bothered to walk up from the road.

We were finishing breakfast when there was a tap on the window and we saw the round brown face of Monsieur Sanchez. He wouldn't come into the house, because he said his boots were too dirty. He had been in the forest since six o'clock, and he had a present for us. From behind his back he produced his old checked cap, bulging with wild mushrooms. He gave us his favorite recipe—oil, butter, garlic, and chopped parsley—and told us a dreadful story about three men who had died after an ill-chosen mushroom supper. A neighbor had found them still at the table with wide, staring eyes—Monsieur Sanchez gave us a demonstration, rolling his eyes back in his head—completely paralyzed by malignant fungus. But we were not to worry, he said. He would stake his life on the mushrooms in his cap. *Bon appétit!*

My wife and I ate them that evening, studying each other between mouthfuls for signs of paralysis and eye rolling. They tasted so much better than ordinary mushrooms that we decided to invest in a guidebook and to share a pair of anti-snake boots.

. . .

THERE COMES a time in the restoration of an old house when the desire to see it finished threatens all those noble aesthetic intentions to see it finished properly. The temptation to settle for the shortcut nags away as the delays add up and the excuses multiply: the carpenter has severed a fingertip, the mason's truck has been stolen, the painter has *la grippe*, fittings ordered in May and promised for June don't arrive until September, and all the time the concrete mixer and the rubble and the shovels and pickaxes become more and more like permanent fixtures. During the hot months of summer, tranquilized by the sun, it had been possible to look with a patient eye at the uncompleted jobs throughout the house. Now that we were spending more time indoors with them, patience had been replaced by irritation.

With Christian the architect, we went through the rooms to establish who had to do what, and how long it would take.

"*Normalement,*" said Christian, a man of great charm and implacable optimism, "there is only six or seven days of work. A little masonry, some plastering, two days of painting, *et puis voilà. Terminé.*"

We were encouraged. As we said to Christian, there had been dark moments recently when we imagined waking up on Christmas morning still surrounded by the debris of a building site.

He threw up everything in horror—hands, eyebrows, and shoulders. What a thought. It was inconceivable that these mere finishing touches should be delayed any longer. He would telephone the various members of the *équipe* immediately to organize a week of intensive activity. Progress would be made. No, more than progress; a conclusion.

One by one, they came at odd times to the house: Didier and his dog at seven in the morning. The electrician at lunchtime, Ramon the plasterer for an evening drink. They came, not to work, but to look at the work that had to be done. They were all astonished that it had taken so long, as though people other than themselves had been responsible. Each of them told us, confidentially, that the problem was always that one had to wait for the other fellow to finish before one could start. But, when we mentioned Christmas, they roared with laughter. Christmas was *months* away; they could almost build a complete house by Christmas. There was, however, a common reluctance to name a day.

When can you come? we asked.

Soon, soon, they said.

We would have to be content with that. We went out to the front of the house, where the concrete mixer stood guard over the steps to the front door, and imagined a cypress tree standing in its place.

Soon, soon.

NOVEMBER

THE FRENCH PEASANT is an inventive man, and he hates waste. He is reluctant to discard anything, because he knows that one day the bald tractor tire, the chipped scythe, the broken hoe, and the transmission salvaged from the 1949 Renault van will serve him well and save him from disturbing the contents of that deep, dark pocket where he keeps his money.

The contraption that I found at the edge of the vineyard was a rusty monument to his ingenuity. A 100-liter oil drum had been sliced in half lengthwise and mounted on a framework of narrow-gauge iron piping. An old wheel, more oval than round, had been bolted onto the front. Two handles of unequal length protruded from the back. It was, so Faustin told me, a *brouette de vigneron*—a wheelbarrow, custom built at minimal expense for the pruning season.

All the vines had now been stripped of their leaves by the autumn winds, and the tangled shoots looked like coiled clumps of brown barbed wire. Sometime before the sap started to rise next spring they would have to be cut back to the main stem. The clippings, or *sarments*, were of no agricultural use, too fibrous to rot into the ground during the winter, and too numerous to leave piled in the corridors between the vines where the tractors would pass. They would have to be gathered up and burned; hence the *brouette de vigneron*.

It was the simplest kind of mobile incinerator. A fire was lit in the bottom of the oil drum, the *sarments* were clipped and thrown on the fire, and the barrow was pushed along to the next vine. When the drum was full, the pale grey ash was scattered on the ground and the process began again. It was, in its primitive way, a model of efficiency.

Walking back to the house just before dusk, I saw a slim plume of blue smoke rising from the corner of the field where Faustin was pruning and burning. He straightened up and rubbed his back, and his hand felt cold and stiff when I shook it. He pointed along the rows of clipped vines, twisted claws black against the sandy soil.

"Nice and clean, eh? I like to see them nice and clean." I asked him to leave some *sarments* for me to gather up to use on the barbecue next summer, and I remembered seeing them once in a shop which called itself a food boutique in New York— Genuine Vine Clippings, they were labeled, and they were guaranteed to impart That Authentic Barbecue Flavor. They had been trimmed to a standard length and neatly trussed with straw twine, and they cost two dollars for a small bunch. Faustin couldn't believe it.

"People buy them?"

He looked at the vines again, estimating how many hundreds of dollars he had burned in the course of the day, and shook his head. Another cruel blow. He shrugged.

"*C'est curieux.*"

. . .

OUR FRIEND, who lived deep in Côtes du Rhône country north of Vaison-la-Romaine, was to be honored by the winegrowers of his village and admitted to the Confrérie Saint-Vincent, the local equivalent of the Chevaliers du Tastevin. The investiture was to take place in the village hall, followed by dinner, followed by dancing. The wines would be strong and plentiful and the winegrowers and their wives would be out in force. Ties were to be worn. It was that kind of occasion.

Years before, we had been to another Chevaliers' dinner, in Burgundy. Two hundred people in full evening dress, rigid with decorum at the start of the meal, had turned into a friendly mob singing Burgundian drinking songs by the time the main course was served. We had blurred but happy memories of watching the sozzled Chevaliers after dinner, trying to find and then to unlock their cars, with the amiable assistance of the Clos Vougeot police force. It had been our first experience of an evening formally dedicated to mass intoxication, and we had enjoyed it enormously. Any friend of the grape was a friend of ours.

The village hall was officially called the *Salle des Fêtes*. It was a fairly recent construction, designed with a complete disregard for its medieval surroundings by the anonymous and overworked French architect whose mission in life is to give every village its own eyesore. This was a classic of the contemporary blockhouse school—a box of raw brick and aluminum-trimmed glass set in a garden of tarmac, devoid of charm but rich in neon light fittings.

We were greeted at the door by two substantial, rosy-faced men in white shirts, black trousers, and wide scarlet sashes. We told them we were guests of the new Confrère.

"*Bieng, bieng. Allez-y.*" Meaty hands patted us on the back and into the big room.

At one end was a raised platform, furnished with a long table

and a microphone. Smaller tables, set for dinner, were placed
down either side of the room and across the far end, leaving a
large space in the middle which was packed with winegrowers
and their friends.

The level of conversation was deafening; men and women
who are used to talking to each other across a vineyard find it
difficult to adjust their volume, and the room echoed and boomed
with voices that had been developed to compete with the Mistral.
But, if the voices had come straight in from the fields, the clothes
were definitely from the Sunday-best *armoire*: dark suits and shirts
whose collars looked uncomfortably tight around weatherbeaten
necks for the men; vividly colored and elaborate dresses for the
women. One couple, more couture conscious than the rest, had
outfits of startling splendor. The woman shimmered in a dress
of gray bugle beads, and small matching gray feathers were sewn
to the back of her stockings so that her legs appeared to flutter
when she walked. Her husband wore a white jacket trimmed
with black piping, a frilled shirt with more black piping, and
black evening trousers. Either his nerve or his resources had run
out at that point, because his shoes were sensible, thick-soled
and brown. Nevertheless, we felt sure that they were the couple
to watch when the dancing started.

We found our friend and his family. He was glancing around
the room, looking puzzled and almost ill-at-ease, and we thought
that the solemnity of the occasion had brought on an attack of
Confrère's nerves. The problem, however, was altogether more
serious.

"I can't see a bar anywhere," he said. "Can you?"

There were barrels of wine against one of the walls. There
were bottles of wine on the tables. We were in a village that
would float on a sea of Côtes du Rhône if all the *caves* were
emptied, but there was no bar. And, now that we studied our
fellow revelers, we made another worrying discovery. Nobody
was holding a glass.

We were prevented from making an indiscreet grab at a bottle on the nearest table by a fanfare on the loudspeaker system, and the Confrères filed in and took up their position behind the table on the dais—a dozen or more figures in cloaks and wide-brimmed hats, some holding parchment scrolls, one with an imposingly fat book. Any moment now, we thought, the *vin d'honneur* would be served to signal the start of the ceremony.

The mayor embraced the microphone and delivered the opening speech. The senior Confrère gave a speech. His assistant, the keeper of the fat book, gave a speech. One by one the three new Confrères were summoned to the dais and eulogized at length for their love of wine and good fellowship. One by one, they replied with speeches accepting the honors bestowed upon them. I detected a certain huskiness in the voice of our friend which others may have mistaken for emotion. I knew it to be thirst.

As a finale, we were asked to join in the singing of a song written in the Provençal language by Frédéric Mistral.

"*Coupo santo e versanto,*" we sang in praise of the sainted and overflowing goblet, "*A-de-reng beguen en troupo lou vin pur de nostre plant*"—let us all drink together the pure wine of our growth, and about time too. The investiture had taken just over an hour, and not a drop had passed anyone's lips.

There was a noticeable eagerness to be seated, and at last the sainted goblets were filled, emptied, and refilled. An air of relief spread throughout the tables, and we were able to relax and consider the menu.

Quail in aspic came first; the heads, which we were told cost two francs each, were detachable and could be used again at a future banquet. Then there was sea bass. These were mere preliminaries, the chef's limbering-up exercises before attacking the sirloin of Charolais beef *en croûte*. But, before that, there was a small and deadly item described as a *Trou Provençal*—a sorbet made with the minimum of water and the maximum of *marc*. Its purpose, so we were told, was to clear the palate; in fact it was sufficiently powerful to anesthetize not only the palate, but the sinus passages and the front portion of the skull as well. But the chef knew what he was doing. After the initial jolt of frozen alcohol wore off, I could feel a hollowness in the stomach—the *trou*—and I could face the rest of the long meal with some hope of being able to finish it.

The beef made its entrance to the strains of a second fanfare, and was paraded around the tables by the waiters and waitresses before being served. The white wine gave way to the pride of the local winegrowers, a formidably heavy red, and the courses kept coming until, after the serving of soufflés and champagne, it was time to rise up and dance.

The band was of the old school, clearly not interested in performing for people who simply like to hop up and down; they wanted to see *dancing*. There were waltzes and quicksteps and several numbers that might have been gavottes, but for me the highlight of the evening was the tango interlude. I don't think it is given to many of us to witness fifty or sixty couples in the advanced stages of inebriation attempting the swoops and turns and heel-stamping flourishes of the true tango artist, and it was a sight I shall never forget. Elbows were cocked, heads flicked from side to side, desperate and off-balance charges were made with twinkling feet from one end of the room to the other, potential collision and disaster were everywhere. One diminutive man danced blind, his head sunk into the *décolletage* of his taller partner. The couple in bugle beads and frilled shirt, molded together at the groin with their backs arching outward, lunged and dipped through the crowd with a dexterity unknown outside the tango palaces of Buenos Aires.

Miraculously, nobody was injured. When we left, sometime after one o'clock, the music was still playing and the dancers, stuffed with food and awash with wine, were still dancing. Not for the first time, we marveled at the Provençal constitution.

We arrived back at the house the following day to find that its appearance had changed; there was an unfamiliar tidiness in front of the steps that led up to the door. The cement mixer, which had for months been an integral part of the façade of the house, was no longer there.

It was an ominous sign. As much as we disliked having its hulk parked outside, it was at least a guarantee that Didier and his masons would return. Now they had crept in and taken it—*our* cement mixer—probably to use on a six-month job somewhere the other side of Carpentras. Our hopes of having a finished house by Christmas suddenly seemed like a bad attack of misplaced optimism.

Christian, as usual, was sympathetic and reassuring.

"They had to go to Mazan . . . an emergency job . . . the roof of an old widow's house . . ."

I felt guilty. What were our problems compared to the plight of a poor old widow exposed to the elements?

"Don't worry," Christian said. "Two days, maybe three, and then they'll be back to finish off. There's plenty of time before Christmas. It's weeks away."

Not many weeks away, we thought. My wife suggested kidnapping Didier's cocker spaniel, closer to his heart even than the cement mixer, and keeping it as a hostage. It was a fine, bold scheme, except that the dog never left Didier's side. Well, if not his dog, maybe his wife. We were prepared to consider almost anything.

The unfinished jobs—temporary windows and chinks in the masonry in particular—were made more apparent by the first sustained Mistral of winter. It blew for three days, bending the cypress tree in the courtyard into a green C, tearing at the tatters of plastic in the melon fields, worrying away at loose tiles and shutters, moaning through the night. It was malevolent and inescapable, a wind to lower the spirits as it threw itself endlessly against the house, trying to get in.

"Good weather for suicide," Massot said to me one morning as the wind flattened his mustache against his cheeks. "*Beh oui.* If this continues, we'll see a funeral or two."

Of course, he said, this was nothing like the Mistrals of his boyhood. In those days, the wind blew for weeks on end, doing strange and horrible things to the brain. He told me the story of Arnaud, a friend of his father's.

Arnaud's horse was old and tired and no longer strong enough for farm work. He decided to sell it and buy a fresh young horse, and walked the fifteen kilometers to Apt market one windy morning leading the old nag behind him. A buyer was found, the price was agreed, but the young horses for sale that day were poor, thin specimens. Arnaud walked home alone. He would return next week in the hope that better animals would be on sale.

The Mistral continued all that week, and was still blowing when Arnaud walked again to Apt market. This time he was lucky, and bought a big dark horse. It cost him almost double what he had made on the sale of the old horse, but, as the dealer said, he was paying for youth. The new horse had years of work in him.

Arnaud was only two or three kilometres from his farm when the horse broke free from its leading rein and bolted. Arnaud ran after it until he could run no more. He searched in the scrub and in the vineyards, shouting into the wind, cursing the Mistral that had unsettled the horse, cursing his bad luck, cursing his lost money. When it became too dark to search any longer, he made his way home, angry and despairing. Without a horse, he couldn't work the land; he would be ruined.

His wife met him at the door. An extraordinary thing had happened: a horse, a big dark horse, had come running up the track and had gone into one of the outbuildings. She had given it water and pulled a cart across the opening to block its escape.

Arnaud took a lantern and went to look at the horse. A broken lead rein hung from its head. He touched its neck, and his fingers came away stained. In the light of the lantern, he could see the sweat running down its flanks, and pale patches where the dye had worn off. He had bought back his old horse.

In rage and shame he went up into the forest behind his farm and hanged himself.

Massot lit a cigarette, hunching his shoulders and cupping his hands against the wind.

"At the inquest," he said, "someone had a sense of humor. The cause of death was recorded as suicide while the balance of the mind was disturbed by a horse."

Massot grinned and nodded. All his stories, it seemed, ended brutally.

"But he was a fool," Massot said. "He should have gone back and shot the dealer who sold him the horse—*paf!*—and blamed it on the Mistral. That's what I'd have done." His reflections on the nature of justice were interrupted by the whine of an engine in low gear, and a Toyota four-wheel-drive truck, as wide as the footpath, slowed down briefly to give us time to jump out of the way. It was Monsieur Dufour, the village grocer and scourge of the Lubéron's *sanglier* population.

We had seen the heads of *sangliers* mounted on the walls of butchers' shops, and had paid no more attention to them than to any other of the strange rustic decorations that we saw from time to time. But once or twice during the summer the *sangliers* had come down from the dry upper slopes of the mountain to drink from the swimming pool and steal melons, and we could never look a stuffed head in the eye again after seeing the living animals. They were black and stout and longer in the leg than a conventional pig, with worried, whiskery faces. We loved our rare glimpses of them, and wished that the hunters would leave them alone. Unfortunately, *sangliers* taste like venison, and are consequently chased from one end of the Lubéron to the other.

Monsieur Dufour was the acknowledged champion hunter, a modern and mechanized Nimrod. Dressed in his combat uniform, his truck bristling with high-powered armaments, he could drive up the rocky trails and reach the *sanglier*-infested upper slopes while less well equipped hunters were still coughing their way up on foot. On the flat bed of his truck was a large wooden chest containing six hounds, trained to track for days on end. The poor old pigs didn't stand much of a chance.

I said to Massot that I thought it was a shame the *sangliers* were hunted quite so relentlessly by so many hunters.

"But they taste delicious," he said. "'Specially the young ones, the *marcassins*. And besides, it's natural. The English are too sentimental about animals, except those men who chase foxes, and they are mad."

The wind was strengthening and getting colder, and I asked Massot how long he thought it would last.

"A day, a week. Who knows?" He leered at me. "Not feeling like suicide, are you?"

I said I was sorry to disappoint him, but I was well and cheerful, looking forward to the winter and Christmas.

"Usually a lot of murders after Christmas." He said it as though he was looking forward to a favorite television program, a bloody sequel to the Mistral suicides.

I heard gunfire as I walked home, and I hoped Dufour had missed. No matter how long I lived here, I would never make a true countryman. And, as long as I preferred to see a wild boar on the hoof instead of on the plate, I'd never make an adopted Frenchman. Let him worship his stomach; I would maintain a civilized detachment from the blood lust that surrounded me.

This noble smugness lasted until dinner. Henriette had given us a wild rabbit, which my wife had roasted with herbs and mustard. I had two helpings. The gravy, thickened with blood, was wonderful.

MADAME SOLIVA, the eighty-year-old chef whose *nom de cuisine* was Tante Yvonne, had first told us about an olive oil that she said was the finest in Provence. She had better credentials than anyone we knew. Apart from being a magnificent cook, she was olive oil's answer to a Master of Wine. She had tried them all, from Alziari in Nice to the United Producers of Nyons, and in her expert and considered view the oil produced in the valley of Les Baux was the best. One could buy it, she told us, from the little mill in Maussane-les-Alpilles.

When we lived in England, olive oil had been a luxury, to be saved for the making of fresh mayonnaise and the dressing of salads. In Provence, it was an abundant daily treat which we bought in five-liter *bidons* and used for cooking, for marinating goats' cheeses and red peppers, and for storing truffles. We dipped our bread in it, bathed our lettuce in it, and even used it as a hangover preventative. (One tablespoon of oil, taken neat before drinking, was supposed to coat the stomach and protect it against the effects of too much young pink wine.) We soaked up olive oil like sponges, and gradually learned to distinguish between different grades and flavors. We became fussy and no doubt insufferable about our oil, never buying it from shops or supermarkets, but always from a mill or a producer, and I looked forward to oil-buying expeditions almost as much as trips to the vineyards.

An essential part of a day out is lunch, and before going anywhere new we always studied the Gault-Millau guide as well as the map. We discovered that Maussane was perilously close to the Baumanière at Les Baux, where the bills are as memorable as the cooking, but we were saved from temptation by Madame Soliva. "Go to Le Paradou," she told us, "and have lunch at the café. And make sure you're there by noon."

It was a cold, bright day, good eating weather, and we walked into the Bistro du Paradou a few minutes before midday with appetites sharpened by the smell of garlic and woodsmoke that greeted us. An enormous fire, a long room filled with old marble-topped tables, a plain tiled bar, a busy clatter coming from the kitchen—it had everything. Except, as the *patron* explained, somewhere for us to sit.

The room was still empty, but he said it would be full within fifteen minutes. He shrugged in apology. He looked at my wife, so near and yet so far from a good lunch, her face a study in tragic deprivation. At the sight of a woman so clearly in distress, he relented, sat us at a table facing the fire, and put a thick glass carafe of red wine between us.

The regulars started coming through the door in noisy groups, going straight to the places they occupied every day. By 12:30 every seat was taken and the *patron*, who was also the only waiter, was a plate-laden blur.

The restaurant worked on the simple formula of removing the burden of decision from its customers. As in the station café at Bonnieux, you ate and drank what you were given. We had a crisp, oily salad and slices of pink country sausages, an *aioli* of snails and cod and hard-boiled eggs with garlic mayonnaise, creamy cheese from Fontvieille, and a homemade tart. It was the kind of meal that the French take for granted and tourists remember for years. For us, being somewhere between the two, it was another happy discovery to add to our list, somewhere to come back to on a cold day with an empty stomach in the certain knowledge that we would leave warm and full.

We arrived at the olive oil mill in Maussane two months early. The new crop of olives wouldn't be gathered until January, and that was the time to buy oil at its most fresh. Luckily, said the manager of the mill, last year's crop had been plentiful and there was still some oil left. If we would like to have a look around, he would pack a dozen liters for us to take away.

The official name of the establishment—Coopérative Oléicole de la Vallée des Baux—was almost too long to fit on the front of the modest building that was tucked away at the side of a small road. Inside, every surface seemed to have been rubbed with a fine coating of oil; floors and walls were slick to the touch, the stairs that led up to the sorting platform were slippery underfoot. A group of men sat at a table sticking the Coopérative's ornate gold labels onto bottles and flasks filled with the greenish-yellow oil—pure and natural, as the notice on the wall said, extracted by a single cold pressing.

We went into the office to pick up the squat, two liter jugs that the manager had packed in a carton for us, and he presented each of us with bars of olive-oil soap.

"There is nothing better for the skin," he said, and he patted his cheeks with dainty fingertips. "And, as for the oil, it is a masterpiece. You'll see."

Before dinner that night, we tested it, dripping it onto slices of bread that had been rubbed with the flesh of tomatoes. It was like eating sunshine.

THE GUESTS continued to come, dressed for high summer and hoping for swimming weather, convinced that Provence enjoyed a Mediterranean climate and dismayed to find us in sweaters, lighting fires in the evening, drinking winter wines, and eating winter food.

Is it always as cold as this in November? Isn't it hot all the year round? They would look dejected when we told them about snowdrifts and subzero nights and bitter winds, as though we had lured them to the North Pole under false tropical pretenses.

Provence has been accurately described as a cold country with a high rate of sunshine, and the last days of November were as bright and as blue as May, clean and exhilarating and, as far as Faustin was concerned, profoundly ominous. He was predicting a savage winter, with temperatures so low that olive trees would die of cold as they had in 1976. He speculated with grim enjoyment about chickens being frozen stiff and old people turning blue in their beds. He said there would undoubtedly be extended power cuts, and warned me to have the chimney swept.

"You'll be burning wood night and day," he said, "and that's when chimneys catch fire. And when the *pompiers* come to put out the fire they'll charge you a fortune unless you have a certificate from the chimney sweep."

And it could be much worse than that. If the house burned down as the result of a chimney fire, the insurance company wouldn't pay out unless one could produce a certificate. Faustin looked at me, nodding gravely as I absorbed the thoughts of being cold, homeless, and bankrupt, and all because of an unswept chimney.

But what would happen, I asked him, if the certificate had been burned with the house? He hadn't thought of that, and I think he was grateful to me for suggesting another disastrous possibility. A connoisseur of woe needs fresh worries from time to time, or he will become complacent.

I arranged for Cavaillon's premier chimney sweep, Monsieur Beltramo, to come up to the house with his brushes and suction cleaners. A tall man with a courtly manner and an aquiline, sooty profile, he had been a chimney sweep for twenty years. Not once, he told me, had a chimney cleaned by him ever caught fire. When he was finished, he made out the *certificat de ramonage*, complete with smudged fingerprints, and wished me a pleasant winter. "It won't be a cold one this year," he said. "We've had three cold winters in a row. The fourth is always mild."

I asked him if he was going to clean Faustin's chimney, and exchange weather forecasts.

"No. I never go there. His wife sweeps the chimney."

DECEMBER

THE POSTMAN drove at high speed up to the parking area
behind the house and reversed with great élan into the garage
wall, crushing a set of rear lights. He didn't appear to have noticed
the damage as he came into the courtyard, smiling broadly and
waving a large envelope. He went straight to the bar, planted his
elbow, and looked expectant.

"Bonjour, jeune homme!"

I hadn't been called young man for years, and it wasn't the
postman's normal habit to bring the mail into the house. Slightly
puzzled, I offered him the drink that he was waiting for.

He winked. "A little pastis," he said. "Why not?"

Was it his birthday? Was he retiring? Had he won the big
prize in the Loterie Nationale? I waited for him to explain the
reason for his high spirits, but he was too busy telling me about

the *sanglier* that his friend had shot the previous weekend. Did
I know how to prepare these creatures for the pot? He took me
through the whole gory process, from disembowelment to hanging, quartering, and cooking. The pastis disappeared—it wasn't,
I realized, his first of the morning—and a refill accepted. Then
he got down to business.

"I have brought you the official post office calendar," said
the postman. "It shows all the saints' days, and there are some
agreeable pictures of young ladies."

He took the calendar from its envelope and leafed through
the pages until he found a photograph of a girl wearing a pair of
coconut shells.

"*Voilà!*"

I told him that he was most kind to think of us, and thanked
him.

"It's free," he said. "Or you can buy it if you want to."

He winked again, and I finally understood the purpose of
the visit. He was collecting his Christmas tip, but since it would
be undignified simply to arrive at the front door with an outstretched hand, we had to observe the ritual of the calendar.

He took his money and finished his drink and roared off to
his next call, leaving the remnants of his rear light on the drive.

My wife was looking at the calendar when I came back into
the house.

"Do you realize," she said, "that it's only three weeks until
Christmas, and there's still no sign of the builders?"

And then she had an idea that only a woman could have
had. It was obvious, she thought, that the birthday of Jesus Christ
was not a sufficiently important deadline for the completion of
work on the house. Somehow or other, Christmas would come
and go and it would be February by the time everyone recovered
from their New Year hangovers and holidays. What we should
do was to invite the builders to a party to celebrate the end of
the job. But not just the builders; their wives must come too.

The intuitive cunning of this suggestion was based on two

assumptions. First, that the wives, who never saw the work that their husbands did in other people's houses, would be so curious that they would find the invitation irresistible. And second, that no wife would want her husband to be the one not to have finished his part of the work. This would cause loss of face among the other wives and public embarrassment, followed by some ugly recriminations in the car on the way home.

It was an inspiration. We fixed a date for the last Sunday before Christmas and sent out the invitations: champagne from 11 o'clock onward.

Within two days, the cement mixer was back in front of the house. Didier and his assistants, cheerful and noisy, resumed where they had left off as though there had never been a three-month hiatus. No excuses were made, and no direct explanation given for the sudden return to work. The closest Didier came to it was when he mentioned casually that he wanted to have everything finished before he went skiing. He and his wife, he said, would be delighted to accept our invitation.

We had worked out that if everyone came there would be twenty-two people, all with good Provençal appetites. And, as it was so close to Christmas, they would be looking for something a little more festive than a bowlful of olives and a few slices of *saucisson*. My wife started making lists of provisions, and terse footnotes and reminders were scattered throughout the house: Rabbit terrine! *Gambas* and mayonnaise! Individual pizzas! Mushroom tart! Olive bread! How many quiches?—the scraps of paper were everywhere, making my one-word list—champagne—look sparse and inadequate.

The gastronomic highlight was delivered one cold morning by a friend who had relatives in Périgord. It was an entire foie gras—raw, and therefore a fraction of the price of the prepared product. All we had to do was cook it and add some slivers of black truffle.

We unwrapped it. The previous owner must have been a bird the size of a small aircraft, because the liver was enormous

—a rich, dark yellow mass that filled both my hands when I lifted it onto the chopping board. Following our friend's instructions, I cut it up and compressed it into glass preserving jars, inserting pieces of truffle with nervous fingers. This was like cooking money.

The jars were sealed, and placed in a huge saucepan of boiling water for precisely ninety minutes. After cooling off, they were refrigerated, then laid to rest in the *cave*. My wife crossed foie gras off her list.

It felt strange to be coming to the end of the year under blue skies, and without the frenzy that characterizes the weeks before an English Christmas. The only hint of festive preparations in our valley was the strange noise coming from the house of Monsieur Poncet, about a mile away from us. On two successive mornings as I walked past, I heard terrible squawks—not cries of fear or pain, but of outrage. I didn't think they were human, but I wasn't sure. I asked Faustin if he had noticed them.

"Oh, that," he said. "Poncet is grooming his ass."

On Christmas Eve, there was to be a living *crèche* in the church in Ménerbes, and the ass of Monsieur Poncet had an important supporting role. Naturally, he had to look his best, but he had an aversion to being brushed and combed, and he was not the kind of ass to suffer grooming quietly. Doubtless he would be presentable on the night, said Faustin, but one would be wise to stay well away from his hind legs, as he was reputed to have an impressive kick.

Up in the village, casting was in progress for the Infant Jesus. Babies of a suitable age and disposition were required to present themselves, and temperament—the ability to rise to the big occasion—would be all-important, as the proceedings did not start until midnight.

Apart from that, and the cards that the postman stuffed in the mailbox, Christmas might have been months away. We did not have a television, and so we were spared the sight of those stupefyingly jolly commercials. There were no carol singers, no office parties, no strident countdowns of the remaining shopping days. I loved it. My wife was not so sure; something was missing. Where was my Christmas spirit? Where was the mistletoe? Where was the Christmas tree? We decided to go into Cavaillon to find them.

We were rewarded at once by the sight of Santa Claus. Dressed in baggy red *bouclé* trousers, a Rolling Stones T-shirt, red fur-trimmed pixie hat, and false beard, he came weaving toward us as we walked down the Cours Gambetta. It looked from a distance as though his beard was on fire, but as he came closer we saw the stub of a Gauloise among the whiskers. He lurched past in a cloud of Calvados fumes, attracting considerable attention from a group of small children. Their mothers would have some explaining to do.

The streets were strung with lights. Music came through the open doorways of bars and shops. Christmas trees were stacked in clumps on the pavement. A man with a throat microphone was selling bed linen from a stall in an alley. "Take a look at that, Madame. Pure Dralon! I'll give you five thousand francs if you can find a fault in it!" An old peasant woman began a millimeter-by-millimeter inspection, and the man snatched it away.

We turned the corner and nearly collided with the carcass of a deer, hanging outside the door of a butcher's shop, gazing blindly at the carcass of a *sanglier* hanging next to it. In the window, a line of tiny nude birds, their necks broken and their heads neatly arranged on their breastbones, were offered as a special pre-Christmas promotion, seven for the price of six. The butcher had closed their beaks and set them in a garnish of evergreen leaves and red ribbon. We shuddered, and moved on.

There was no doubt about the most important ingredient in a Provençal Christmas. Judging by the window displays, the queues, and the money changing hands, clothes and toys and stereo equipment and baubles were of incidental importance; the main event of Christmas was food. Oysters and crayfish and pheasant and hare, pâtés and cheeses, hams and capons, gâteaux and pink champagne—after a morning spent looking at it all we were suffering from visual indigestion. With our tree and our mistletoe and our dose of Christmas spirit, we came home.

Two uniformed men were waiting for us, parked outside the house in an unmarked car. The sight of them made me feel guilty, of what, I didn't know, but uniformed men have that effect on me. I tried to think what crimes I had committed recently against the Fifth Republic, and then the two men got out of the car and saluted. I relaxed. Even in France, where bureaucratic formality approaches the level of art, they don't salute before they arrest you.

In fact, they weren't policemen, but firemen, *pompiers* from Cavaillon. They asked if they could come into the house, and I wondered where we had put our chimney sweep's certificate. This was obviously a spot check designed to catch any householder with a soiled flue.

We sat around the dining room table. One of the men opened an attaché case. "We have brought the official calendar of the Pompiers de Vaucluse." He laid it on the table.

"As you will see, it shows all the saints' days."

And so it did, just like our post office calendar. But, instead of photographs of girls wearing coconut-shell brassieres, this calendar was illustrated with pictures of firemen scaling tall buildings, administering first aid to accident victims, rescuing mountaineers in distress, and manning loaded fire hoses. The *pompiers* in rural France provide an overall emergency service, and they will retrieve your dog from a pothole in the mountains or take you to a hospital, as well as fight your fires. They are in every way an admirable and deserving body of men.

I asked if a contribution would be acceptable.

"*Bien sûr.*"

We were given a receipt which also entitled us to call ourselves Friends of the Cavaillon Fire Department. After more salutes, the two *pompiers* left to try their luck farther up the valley, and we hoped that their training had prepared them for attacks by vicious dogs. Getting a contribution out of Massot would be only marginally less hazardous than putting out a fire. I could imagine him, squinting out from behind his curtains, shotgun at the ready, watching his Alsatians hurl themselves at the intruders. I had once seen the dogs attack the front wheel of a car for want of anything human, ripping away at the tire as though it were a hunk of raw beef, slavering and spitting out shreds of rubber while the terrified driver endeavored to reverse out of range, and Massot looked on, smoking and smiling.

We were now a two-calendar family, and as the days before Christmas slipped by we anticipated the delivery of a third, which would be worth a substantial contribution. Every Tuesday, Thursday, and Saturday for the past twelve months, the heroes of the sanitation department had stopped at the end of our drive to pick up shamefully large piles of empty bottles, the evil-smelling remains of *bouillabaisse* suppers, dog-food cans, broken glasses, sacks of rubble, chicken bones, and domestic fallout of every size and description. Nothing defeated them. No heap, however huge and ripe, was too much for the man who clung to the back of the truck, dropping off at each stop to toss the garbage into an open, greasy hold. In the summer, he must have come close to asphyxiation and, in the winter, close to tears with the cold.

He and his partner eventually turned up in a Peugeot which looked as if it was enjoying its final outing before going to the scrapyard—two cheerful, scruffy men with hard handshakes and pastis breath. On the backseat, I could see a brace of rabbits and some bottles of champagne, and I said that it was good to see them picking up some full bottles for a change.

"It's not the empty bottles we mind," said one of them. "But you should see what some people leave for us." He wrinkled his face and held his nose, little finger extended elegantly in the air. *"Dégeulasse."*

They were pleased with their tip. We hoped they would go out and have a glorious, messy meal, and let someone else clear up.

DIDIER WAS SQUATTING on his haunches with a dustpan and brush, sweeping crumbs of cement out of a corner. It was heartening to see this human machine of destruction engaged in such delicate chores; it meant that his work was over.

He stood up and emptied the dustpan into a paper bag and lit a cigarette. "That's it," he said. "*Normalement*, the painter will come tomorrow." We walked outside, where Eric was loading the shovels and buckets and toolboxes onto the back of the truck. Didier grinned. "It doesn't bother you if we take the cement mixer?"

I said I thought we could manage without it, and the two of them pushed it up a plank ramp and roped it tight against the back of the driver's cab. Didier's spaniel watched the progress of the cement mixer with her head cocked, and then jumped into the truck and lay along the dashboard.

"*Allez!*" Didier held out his hand. It felt like cracked leather. "See you on Sunday."

The painter came the next day, and painted, and left. Jean-Pierre the carpet layer arrived. The wives had obviously decided that everything should be ready for their state visit.

By Friday night, the carpet was laid except for the last couple of meters.

"I'll come in tomorrow morning," said Jean-Pierre, "and you'll be able to move the furniture in the afternoon."

By midday, all that remained to do was to fit the carpet under a wooden batten at the threshold of the room. It was while Jean-Pierre was drilling the holes to screw in the batten that he went through the hot-water pipe which ran under the floor, and a jet of water rose in a small and picturesque fountain, framed by the doorway.

We cut off the water supply, rolled back the sodden carpet,

and called Monsieur Menicucci. After a year of alarms and emergencies, I knew his number by heart, and I knew what his first words would be.

"*Oh là là.*" He meditated in silence for a moment. "The floor will have to be broken so that I can solder the pipe. You had better warn Madame. There will be a little dust."

Madame was out buying food. She was expecting to return to a bedroom, bathroom, and dressing room that were dry, clean, and carpeted. She would be surprised. I advised Jean-Pierre to go home for medical reasons. She would probably want to kill him.

"What's that noise?" she said when I met her as she was parking the car.

"It's Menicucci's jackhammer."

"Ah yes. Of course." She was unnaturally, dangerously calm. I was glad Jean-Pierre had left.

Menicucci, in his search for the leak, had drilled out a trench in the floor, and we were able to see the hot water pipe with its neat hole.

"*Bon,*" he said. "Now we must make sure there's no blockage in the pipe before I solder. You stay there and watch. I will blow through the tap in the bathroom."

I watched. Menicucci blew. I received a gout of dusty water in the face.

"What do you see?" he shouted from the bathroom.

"Water," I said.

"*Formidable.* The pipe must be clear."

He made his repairs, and went home to watch the rugby on television.

We started mopping up, telling each other that it really wasn't too bad. The carpet would dry out. There was barely enough rubble to fill a bucket. The scorch marks from the blowtorch could be painted over. All in all, as long as one disregarded the jagged, gaping trench, it was possible to look at the rooms and consider them finished. In any case, we had no choice. Sunday was only hours away.

We weren't expecting anyone before 11:30, but we had underestimated the magnetic appeal that champagne has for the French, and the first knock on the door came shortly after half past ten. Within an hour, everyone except Didier and his wife had arrived. They lined the walls of the living room, awkward with politeness and dressed in their best, darting away from the sanctuary of the walls from time to time to swoop on the food.

As the waiter in charge of keeping glasses filled, I became aware of yet another fundamental difference between the French and the English. When the English come for drinks, the glass is screwed firmly into the hand while talking, smoking or eating. It is set aside with reluctance to deal with calls of nature that require both hands—blowing the nose or visiting the lavatory— but it is never far away or out of sight.

It is different with the French. They are no sooner given a glass before they put it down, presumably because they find conversation difficult with only one hand free. So the glasses gather in groups, and after five minutes identification becomes impossible. The guests, unwilling to take another person's glass but unable to pick out their own, look with longing at the champagne bottle. Fresh glasses are distributed, and the process repeats itself.

I was wondering how long it would be before our supply of glasses ran out and we had to resort to teacups when there was the familiar sound of a diesel engine in labor, and Didier's truck pulled up behind the house, and he and his wife came in through the back door. It was strange. I knew that Didier had a car, and his wife was dressed from head to toe in fine brown suède which must have sat very uneasily on the gritty seat of the truck.

Christian came across the room and took me aside.

"I think we might have a little problem," he said. "You'd better come outside."

I followed him. Didier took my wife's arm and followed me. As we walked around the house, I looked back and saw that everyone was coming.

"*Voilà!*" said Christian, and pointed at Didier's truck.

On the back, in the space usually reserved for the cement mixer, was a bulbous shape, three feet high and four feet across. It was wrapped in brilliant green crêpe paper, and dotted with bows of white and red and blue.

"It's for you from all of us," said Christian. "*Allez*. Unwrap it."

Didier made a stirrup with his hands, and with effortless gallantry, his cigarette between his teeth, plucked my wife from the ground and lifted her to shoulder height so that she could step onto the back of the truck. I climbed up after her, and we peeled off the green wrapping.

The last strips of paper came away to applause and some piercing whistles from Ramon the plasterer, and we stood in the sunshine on the back of the truck, looking at the upturned faces that surrounded us, and our present.

It was an antique jardinière, a massive circular tub that had been cut by hand from a single block of stone long before the days of cutting machines. It was thick sided, slightly irregular, a pale, weathered gray. It had been filled with earth and planted with primulas.

We didn't know what to say or how to say it. Surprised, touched, and floundering in our inadequate French, we did the best we could. Mercifully, Ramon cut us short.

"*Merde!* I'm thirsty. That's enough speeches. Let's have a drink."

The formality of the first hour disappeared. Jackets came off and the champagne was attacked in earnest. The men took their wives around the house, showing off their work, pointing out the English bathroom taps marked "hot" and "cold," trying the drawers to check that the carpenter had finished the interiors smoothly, touching everything in the manner of curious children.

Christian organized a team to unload the great stone tub from the truck, and eight tipsy men in their Sunday clothes somehow managed to avoid being maimed as the lethal mass was maneuvered down two sagging planks and onto the ground. Madame Ramon supervised. "*Ah, les braves hommes,*" she said. "Mind you don't get your fingernails dirty."

The Menicuccis were the first to leave. Having acquitted themselves with honor among the pâtes and cheeses and flans and champagne, they were off to a late lunch, but not before observing the niceties. They made a ceremonial tour of the other guests, shaking hands, kissing cheeks, exchanging *bons appétits.* Their farewell lasted fifteen minutes.

The others looked as though they were settled for the remainder of the day, eating and drinking their way steadily through everything within reach. Ramon appointed himself the official comedian, and told a series of jokes which became progressively coarser and funnier. He stopped for a drink after explaining how to determine the sex of pigeons by putting them in the refrigerator.

"What made a nice woman like your wife ever marry a terrible old *mec* like you?" asked Didier.

With great deliberation, Ramon put down his champagne and held his hands out in front of him like a fisherman describing the one that got away. Fortunately, he was prevented from going into further revelations by a large piece of pizza which his wife delivered firmly into his mouth. She had heard the routine before.

As the sun moved across the courtyard and left it in afternoon shadow, the guests began to make their tours of departure, with more handshaking and kissing and pauses for one final glass.

"Come and have lunch," said Ramon. "Or dinner. What's the time?"

It was three o'clock. After four hours of eating and drinking, we were in no state for the *cous-cous* that Ramon was promoting.

"Ah well," he said, "if you're on a diet, *tant pis.*"

He gave his wife the car keys and leaned back in the passenger seat, hands clasped across his stomach, beaming at the thought of a solid meal. He had persuaded the other couples to join him. We waved them off and went back to the empty house, the empty plates, and the empty glasses. It had been a good party.

We looked through the window at the old stone tub, bright with flowers. It would take at least four men to move it away from the garage and into the garden, and organizing four men in Provence was, as we knew, not something that could be arranged overnight. There would be visits of inspection, drinks, heated arguments. Dates would be fixed, and then forgotten. Shoulders would be shrugged and time would pass by. Perhaps by next spring we would see the tub in its proper place. We were learning to think in seasons instead of days or weeks. Provence wasn't going to change its tempo for us.

Meanwhile, there was enough foie gras left over to have in warm, thin slices with salad, and one surviving bottle of champagne cooling in the shallow end of the swimming pool. We put some more logs on the fire and thought about the imminent prospect of our first Provençal Christmas.

It was ironic. Having had guests throughout the year, who often had to endure great inconvenience and primitive conditions because of the building work, we now had the house, clean and finished, to ourselves. The last guests had left the previous week, and the next were arriving to help us see in the New Year. But on Christmas Day we would be alone.

We woke up to sunshine and a quiet, empty valley, and a kitchen with no electricity. The gigot of lamb that was ready to go into the oven had a reprieve, and we faced the terrible possibility of bread and cheese for Christmas lunch. All the local restaurants would have been booked up for weeks.

It is at time like this, when crisis threatens the stomach, that the French display the most sympathetic side of their nature. Tell them stories of physical injury or financial ruin and they will either laugh or commiserate politely. But tell them you are facing gastronomic hardship, and they will move heaven and earth and even restaurant tables to help you.

We telephoned Maurice, the chef at the Auberge de la Loube in Buoux, and asked him if there had been any cancellations. No. Every seat was taken. We explained the problem. There was a horrified silence, and then: "You may have to eat in the kitchen, but come anyway. Something will be arranged."

He sat us at a tiny table between the kitchen door and the open fire, next to a large and festive family.

"I have gigot if you like it," he said. We told him we had thought of bringing our own and asking him to cook it, and he smiled. "It's not the day to be without an oven."

We ate long and well and talked about the months that had gone as quickly as weeks. There was so much we hadn't seen and done: our French was still an ungainly mixture of bad grammar and builders' slang; we had managed somehow to miss the entire Avignon festival, the donkey races at Goult, the accordion competition, Faustin's family outing to the Basses-Alpes in August, the wine festival in Gigondas, the Ménerbes dog show, and a good deal of what had been going on in the outside world. It had been a self-absorbed year, confined mostly to the house and the valley, fascinating to us in its daily detail, sometimes frustrating, often uncomfortable, but never dull or disappointing. And, above all, we felt at home.

Maurice brought glasses of *marc* and pulled up a chair.

"'Appy Christmas," he said, and then his English deserted him. *"Bonne Année."*

A NOTE ABOUT THE AUTHOR

Peter Mayle is the author of eleven books
on Provence. Recently he was awarded the
Légion d'Honneur by the French government.
He lives with his wife in Provence.

A NOTE ON THE TYPE

The text of this book was set in
Fairfield Medium, a type face designed by the
distinguished American artist and engraver
Rudolph Ruzicka (1883–1978). Both his original Fairfield
and this bolder version display the sober and sane
qualities of a master craftsman whose talent
was dedicated to clarity.
Rudolph Ruzicka was born in Bohemia and came to
America in 1894. He designed and illustrated
many books and was the creator of a
considerable list of individual
prints in a variety
of techniques.

Composed by Crane Typesetting Service, Inc.,
Barnstable, Massachusetts
Designed by Mia Vander Els